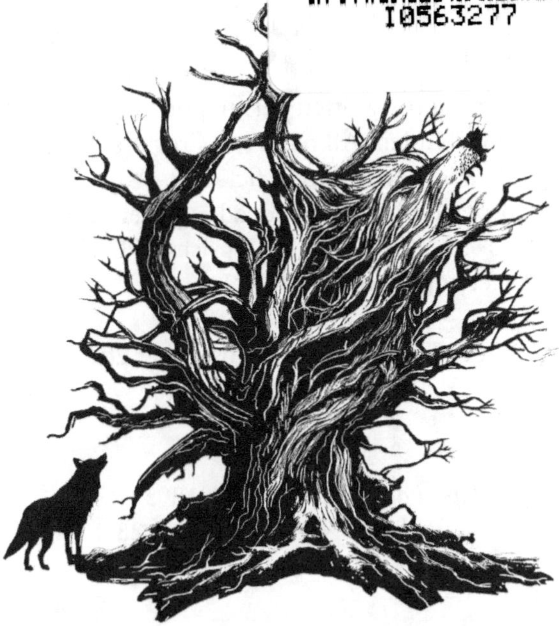

WHAT IT IS TO DO GOOD

THOMAS JOHN HOWARD BOGGIS

FIRST PRINTING, November 2025.
Harry Markos, Director.

Paperback: ISBN 978-1-918052-24-4
eBook: ISBN 978-1-918052-25-1

Book design by: Ian Sharman
Editor: Stephen Davis
Cover Art: Mark Gerrard

www.markosia.com

First Edition

CHAPTER 1
A Howl in the Night

A wolf howl, long and low, pierced the still night air and reverberated through the bedroom window of the young girl who had – until that moment – been deeply asleep. Clara Brown, her shoulder-length dark hair tousled and unkempt, sat up in bed and rubbed the sleep from her eyes as the sound was repeated – a wolf howling somewhere in the garden. She looked over towards the bedroom window, hidden by thin, torn curtains, and watched the shadows cast by the branches of the tree outside, playing across their surface, like skeletal hands reaching towards her.

Her face looked drawn and pale and there were dark rings around her eyes as she struggled towards the side of the bed and swung her legs over the edge, drawing in her breath sharply as her feet came in contact with the cold stone floor. She looked longingly towards the small fireplace at the centre of the far wall – the grate still full of the ashes of many a long dead fire – and wished that her father could afford enough fuel to keep her room warm through the twilight hours. It was so bitterly cold at the moment. Every night the wind whistled through the house, regardless of the amount of time her father spent patching it up with anything he could lay his hands on. Even now she felt the draft biting at her heels. It sent shivers up her spine that almost made her dive back beneath the covers where the cold could not quite reach her.

But another wolf howl held her where she was. Was she imagining this? Was it merely the wind playing tricks on her? Her mother had once told her that the voices of those who have passed on are alive in the air and the wind is their way of travelling the earth. Clara often fancied that she could hear these wind-people talking to each other in low, hushed voices. Was it a particularly mischievous wind-person playing a game with her, trying to lure her out of her nice warm bed?

Her curiosity got the better of her and she shifted her weight tentatively onto her feet and slowly got up, as though she had not done so for many days. A strange expression crossed her face as she stood unsteadily at her bedside, but it was gone in the blink of an eye as the wolf – or whatever it was – howled again.

She stepped falteringly across the room towards the window and looked out. The garden was veiled in darkness, the cold northern wind setting the trees at the far end swaying and making the shadows seem to come to life. Strange shapes and twisted figures danced eerily across the grass as the jet-black forms interwove hypnotically. Clara tore her eyes away and scanned the area for the wolf that had howled, but it was too dark to make out anything clearly.

The moon appeared suddenly from behind a cloud and chased the shadow creatures into distant corners, leaving the garden bathed in its subtle glow. There! In the tree line! A dim, hunched shape could be seen, its nose pointed upwards as it snuffed the air. Then its head turned slowly and looked right at her! Clara caught her breath in surprise. The wolf continued to gaze up at her as it sat down on its haunches, for all the world as though it was waiting for her…

She made up her mind in an instant.

The draft that blew through the house ruffled the hem of her nightdress as she crossed her bedroom quietly and pulled down her hand-knitted cardigan from behind the door. As she did so, the hook it hung on worked its way loose and clattered to the floor, rolling to a stop in one corner. Holding her breath, she listened intently to see if anyone had heard. When she was sure that no one had, she proceeded to cautiously open the door and creep out onto the icy landing.

From where she stood, she could see that the door to her parents' room was ajar, and so she tiptoed down the hallway to have a peek inside. The door creaked slightly as she poked her head through the gap and peered into the room. Her mother lay on her bed, wrapped up tightly in thick blankets and sheets. She was sweating and shivering and occasionally let out little anguished moans that sounded like words, although Clara could not make out what they were. Clara's father was asleep in his favourite armchair by her bedside, her right hand clasped limply in his own. He seemed to have aged so quickly. Grief and anxiety had begun to erode his features like waves breaking against a sandstone cliff. His breathing was light and even, yet his expression even in sleep was one of such suffering that Clara felt the prickle of tears behind her eyes. With the sleeve of her cardigan, she dashed them away as the first ones fell.

She looked sadly at her mother for several long moments, then pulled the door closed – to minimise the draft – and crept softly back along the passage where she began to descend the stairs. She let out a muffled yelp of pain as an exposed nail pierced her foot, the blood welling up dark crimson and spilling in little drops on the dusty, uneven steps. She clapped a hand to her mouth and hopped as fast and as carefully as she could all the way to the bottom.

She entered the kitchen and sat down on a chair, cradling her wounded foot in her lap. The blood continued to trickle slowly from the cut, ploughing a furrow through the dirt picked up on the walk through the house. As she sat there, she looked around the scantily furnished kitchen; at the peeling paint and grimy windows, at the piles of unwashed dishes, and at the spot where her mother used to stand when she was baking bread, pies and cakes. The long-gone smells of this kitchen reached her nostrils through the haze of memory, and she felt herself being transported back to a time when the word "depression" did not hold the same connotations as it now did. Indeed, she had not even heard the word until her father used it to describe why their family was now so poor. It seemed so strange that problems in a country as far away as America could have had such far reaching and devastating consequences for the rest of the world.

Clara stood up and hopped over to the sink, where she tore a strip from an old dishcloth to bandage around her foot. She did not want to waste too much time in case the wolf ran away, so she did not bother to find something cleaner.

How strange it is that a wolf could even be here, she thought, as she wrapped the bandage tightly around her foot. *This is the north of England; wolves aren't native to this area...*

She stood up gingerly and limped across to the back door where her wellington boots stood in a line next to her father's. She smiled at the disparity between their foot sizes. She often teased him about his big feet, asking him if he'd bought his boots from a troll, and in response he would tromp after her and try to catch her – which he always did – planting a kiss on her head every time.

She eased her wellies on then reached for the doorknob and carefully twisted it. The latch clicked as it opened and she slipped outside, shutting the door quietly behind her.

Standing on the back step, she felt the shadows press in around her. The wind whipped across the garden like a living thing and suddenly she regretted her choice to leave her cosy bed. But some impulse drove her to step forward and begin to cross towards the forest that bordered the back of the house. The grass had grown unchecked for many months – as Clara's father had spent nearly every waking moment working – and so the long stems reached above the tops of her boots as she strode quickly towards the trees.

Her pace slowed as she drew closer to the spot where she had seen the wolf sitting. It was only then that she realised how dangerous it was to approach a wild animal like this. It might be diseased, or – worse still – see her as a threat and become violent... Suddenly feeling very foolish indeed, and extremely nervous, Clara made to turn back towards the house, when a movement close by caught her eye.

As she slowly turned, it was not immediately clear what she had seen. However, by straining her eyes in the gloom, Clara could soon make out two gleaming orbs hanging a short distance off the ground by the base of a nearby tree. Puzzled now, she took a hesitant step closer, when the orbs blinked…

With a gasp, Clara tumbled backwards, her frightened gaze fixed on the eyes as they began to approach, revealing the ghostly outline of a wolf's head, but then – to her eternal shock and surprise – the eyes were suddenly rising, rising as they advanced, and the wolf's low muscular frame gave way to that of a tall, slim man, who somehow still appeared to have the visage of a wolf amidst the twisting shadows of the trees.

Scrabbling blindly away in the dry leaves and dirt, Clara held up her hands defensively against the dark figure.

'Stop! Please… don't come any closer!'

The figure held out his own hands in a placatory manner as he continued toward her, but slower now.

'I'm sorry I startled you,' the man said, his voice deep and rhythmic. 'But it was imperative that I speak with you, Clara Brown.'

Clara caught her breath.

'Who are you?' she whispered fearfully.

'My name is Vincent,' he said, taking a few steps closer. 'I have been sent here by my master, Lord Algernon, to offer you something that no other can.'

As he approached, Vincent entered a patch of moonlight and Clara was finally able to get a good look at him. Her surprise deepened as she saw that he was wearing an immaculate dark grey three-piece suit, looking for all the world like the Victorian gentlemen Clara had seen pictures of in her school textbooks. His gloved left hand rested on a long and beautiful cane, the head of which had been carved in the exquisite likeness of a wolf, and at his belt were a dizzying array of instruments and gadgets that Clara had never before seen, while tucked away almost out of sight, was that the handle of a revolver…?

But it was not these details that held her eye, no, it was the strange and frightening mask he wore over the upper half of his head, leaving only his piercing blue eyes and lower jaw with its greying stubble visible. Like the handle of his cane, it was carved in the lifelike image of a wolf's snarling face from a pale, silvery wood, and down the back of this mask hung a pelt of grey wolf fur that reached past his shoulders.

'What… what can you offer me…?' she asked falteringly as unvoiced questions rushed around inside her head:

This can't be real…?

Who is this man…?

How does he know my name…?

'A cure,' Vincent replied, cutting across her thoughts. 'My Lord has access to something that could save your mother's life.'

Clara's heart skipped a beat and she got unsteadily to her feet, her eyes wide, listening intently. 'Once every hundred years a flower blooms on the mountain slopes behind my Lord's manor, and this flower can cure any ailment,' Vincent continued. 'It is a great honour to be offered this, for usually the flower would be kept for one of my Lord's family, but… the situation calls for drastic measures and Lord Algernon believes that you will be able to help us… as do I.'

'Help you with what?' Clara asked, feeling the cold fingers of fear creeping up her spine.

'Time is of the essence, so I will be brief – our world is dying and my people are powerless to stop it,' he began earnestly. 'Regardless of what you think of yourself and your own capabilities, we *need* you. You are what we've been searching for all this time – I can feel it! You are the one to save us. You will not understand how yet, but I promise you, you *can* help. This may already sound dangerous and perhaps too high a price to pay, but the reward is just and fair. If you aid us, we can save your mother's life, so please… will you help?'

Although she could barely read his expression under the mask, Clara could feel the hope and anxiety radiating off Vincent like heat. She looked down at her feet and flexed her toes in her wellington boots as she struggled to process it all.

How can this be real…? she thought. *How can any of this be happening…?*

She looked back towards the house, her breathing quick and uneven, and pulled her cardigan tighter around her shoulders as she looked nervously up at Vincent.

Every instinct screamed at her to turn back, that her bed was where she should be right now, but even as the voices bellowed inside her head, she heard herself saying:

'All… alright…' Barely more than a whisper, a whisper buffeted by the wind. 'I… I will do what I can to help you.'

Vincent smiled in relief and his whole body seemed to relax, as though all his muscles had been tensed for flight if she had said no.

'Good! Good, I knew you wouldn't let us down. Some of the others… but never mind that now…'

Without another word, Vincent's shape slipped, his figure dropping towards the floor, his beautifully tailored suit giving way to soft, grey wolf fur until the man she had been speaking to was no more, and a lean, muscular wolf stood before her. Clara's eyes were wide with shock and disbelief as she watched Vincent raise his muzzle and snuff the chill night air, sensing for threats. When he was satisfied, his shape slipped again, rising once more until he had resumed his human form. He buttoned up his jacket casually as he looked down at her, apparently unaware just how unusual it was for her to witness such a thing.

'The coast is clear – follow me, if you will,' he said, as he turned and began to move deeper into the forest.

Clara tried to steady her breathing as she watched him move away, but her hands were shaking, and not just from the cold. She looked back at the house and saw her bedroom window like a dark eye looking out at her. For a moment she was torn once more – she knew what waited for her there; she knew that nothing would change if she went back now. If there was even the *slimmest* chance that Vincent was telling the truth – that he really could help her mother – then that was worth taking a shot at, right...?

Before she could change her mind, Clara had turned from her home and begun to follow Vincent off into the deep shadows amongst the trees.

They had been walking for around half an hour and Clara had not yet said anything to her guide. Vincent seemed too distracted as he led the way, changing now and then into a wolf to sniff the air, while she was still too shocked and overwhelmed to know what to say. But finally, after he next changed to and from his wolf shape, she could stay silent no longer.

'How...' she stammered. 'How do you do that...?'

He looked back at her, momentarily confused, then his face cleared.

'We call that the "Shift",' he began, as he swiped with his cane at some low hanging branches to clear the way. 'All the peoples of my world can Shift, even newborn babes, though they struggle to control it.'

He stopped for a moment and glanced left and right, as if uncertain of the way forward, then pressed on.

'Every Clan in my world honours a particular creature,' he continued, 'and it is into this creature – our Guardian – that they can Shift. It has been this way since... well... since ever... You have my Clan – Wolf – but there is also Bear, Hare and... others...'

He trailed off for a moment.

'Does it…' Clara began hesitantly. 'Does it… hurt…?'

Vincent chuckled at this.

'No, it does not hurt,' he replied. 'It is as painless and natural to us as putting on clothes.'

'Oh, I don't know,' Clara murmured back, with an effort at a smile. 'Have you ever tried to put on a jumper that's too tight?'

Vincent let out a bark of laughter at this.

'I must admit it is a strange sensation until you become accustomed,' he chuckled. 'But I cannot imagine a life without it.'

He stopped suddenly and Clara nearly walked into the back of him.

'We're here,' he said, as she looked up at him in surprise.

Clara moved to peer around him and could not see anything remarkable about the location they now found themselves in. They were standing in a small clearing surrounded by trees, at the centre of which was a small, shallow-looking pool that dimly reflected the pale moon above in its fractured, wind-ruffled surface.

'I… I don't see anything…' Clara replied quietly as she glanced about. Vincent pointed at the pool before them.

'It may not look like much,' he began, 'but that is a doorway – a doorway to my world.'

Clara's brow creased in confusion.

'But… how…?'

'You must have faith,' Vincent continued. 'To cross over you must have faith – I cannot say more than that. You must believe in it for it to work.'

Vincent laid a hand gently on her shoulder and guided her over to the edge of the pool, where they both looked down, side-by-side, into its surface and surveyed their distorted reflections staring back at them. Clara's face was pale and her hands twisted together nervously as the inky black water filled her vision.

'So… should I…?'

'This is your leap to take,' Vincent cut across her. 'I cannot tell you what to do, nor force you to do it against your will.'

Clara nodded nervously without taking her eyes off the pool. She had always been afraid of water, ever since a freak tidal wave had nearly carried her away while on a beach holiday with her parents several years ago. The awesome power that had gripped her that day had left her feeling frightfully small and weak, and she could now feel the self-same terror that had consumed her rising within once more.

She took a deep, steadying breath as she reminded herself why she was doing this. Images of her mother filled her mind – both from before the illness, and during – as she clamped her shaking hands at her sides and tried to fight the feeling of unreality that pervaded her.

I will do all I can to help you, mother… she thought fiercely. *I will do all I can…*

With that, and without a second thought, Clara fell forwards into the pool…

CHAPTER 2
The Poisoned World

…and stood up on the other side – completely dry – in another world…

Standing on the edge of the shallow pool, Clara felt a chill course throughout her body at the strange and disquieting sight that met her. She was still in the midst of a forest, but it bore no resemblance to the familiar place she had left behind. No, this was different; colder, darker, and dying…

Strangely, the only illumination seemed to come from the pool itself and by its dim, wavering light, her frightened eyes took in the scene. Everywhere she looked her gaze was met by a mass of twisted, skeletal trees, all colour and life drained out of them as if a fire has passed through, their gnarled branches twisting and grasping at their neighbours as though locked in a struggle for survival, so tightly-meshed together that she could not even see the sky.

The air around her felt thick and close, catching in her throat with every breath. Particles like ash drifted everywhere in the stillness and she could feel a cloying sense of pain and malice like an electric current running through her skin, setting the hairs on her neck and arms on end.

She shifted her weight and felt something crunch beneath her boot. Looking down, she saw a broken branch upon a bed of brittle, desiccated grass, the fractured wood leaking a thick sap that was a deep and disturbing shade of purple. But what stood out most of all was the smell – the smell of decay… The smell of death.

Clara had only encountered it once before at the funeral of her great aunt – and had hoped never to come across it again – but she knew it at once for what it was, and felt all of a sudden as though she was standing on the back of some huge, dying beast.

'Welcome to Comhlacht,' Vincent said, making her jump – she had almost forgotten who had brought her here. 'My world. It was once a beautiful place, or so I'm told… But now…'

He strode ahead of her and began to lead a path amidst the dying trees.

'I never saw our world before the change,' he continued, as Clara tentatively followed in his wake, placing her feet gingerly with every step. 'It happened decades before my time. But the stories passed down paint a picture of a land once lush and fertile – at one and in harmony with all those who lived upon it.'

Vincent used his cane to hack a path through some hanging vines blocking their way, the ground beneath them becoming spattered in purple sap as they broke.

'Until very recently – after the change – every Clan had always shown the utmost respect for our world, only taking what they needed and giving back as much, if not more, than they took, maintaining a healthy balance between our needs and Comhlacht's, and allowing both parties to thrive and flourish.'

Vincent stopped speaking briefly to hop over a fallen tree, which Clara was forced to slither under.

'For to do otherwise carried with it a grave warning,' he added, glancing back at Clara. 'It has always been said that Comhlacht is as alive and aware as we are, and must be treated with due respect and deference, or one day it may turn violent. And so the equilibrium was maintained, and peace reigned.'

Vincent stopped suddenly and his hand reached out to grasp a curtain of vines that obscured their view ahead.

'So, imagine our surprise when things changed,' he said quietly in a voice filled with sorrow, his head held low. 'Imagine our shock and confusion when – through no obvious fault of our own – our world began to turn against us. Imagine seeing your home – your perfect world – change from somewhere you knew and loved, into… into this…'

He took a breath, as if what he had to do next pained him, then he drew back the vines and Clara's hand rushed to her mouth to stifle a gasp of horror.

She was standing near the edge of a huge cliff band looking out over a vast plain, but it was like nothing she had ever seen. The land before her was barren and desolate, riven with huge cracks and tears like open wounds, the insides of which appeared to be encased in some substance the same purple as the sap that spilt from the vines. Nowhere she looked could Clara see anything that appeared to be living; not a hint of greenery, nor a tell-tale sign of fauna met her horrified eyes.

But, worst of all – and what made her heart race and her breathing quicken – was the sky that sat above this bleak landscape, a sky she could not have imagined in her worst nightmares. It was a deep and hellish shade of crimson, shrouded in banks of maroon cloud that pulsed with the frequency and intensity of a heartbeat, shifting and roiling in an almost hypnotic manner that made her feel unsteady on her feet.

Clara let out a startled little scream as a huge, indigo bolt of lightning crackled across the sky, branching off like veins in a multitude of directions and setting the surrounding clouds whirling worse than ever.

She looked up at Vincent in shock and disbelief as he beheld the scene beside her, his expression lost somewhere between anger and sadness.

'What…' Clara breathed, struggling for words. 'What happened here…?'

By way of an answer, Vincent unsheathed a lethal looking blade hidden within his cane and sliced at a nearby vine before drawing in the cold steel for her to inspect what was on it.

'It has gone by many names over the years, and some still refer to it in other ways, but to most of us it is simply "the Rot", Vincent said, as Clara looked in disgust at the purple sap glistening upon the blade. 'In our earliest recorded history, the Clans were like your Stone Age people, and they lived alongside their Guardian – their Clan animal – each taking strength from the other in a mutual and trusting bond. Over the centuries their societies and technologies evolved and advanced – much like yours – but peace and balance continued between the Clans and Comhlacht, and our link with our Guardians was maintained. And then it began…'

Vincent lowered his blade and wiped the sap onto the dry grass before sheathing it once more.

'It started with light earth tremors and fierce storms, and at first most people thought nothing of it and simply got on with their lives,' Vincent continued as he looked out across the plains. 'But soon these incidents began to grow in frequency and intensity until the earth began to split and the sky changed such that we could no longer tell day from night, and it became abundantly clear that something was terribly wrong…'

Here, Vincent looked down at Clara.

'The Rot had arrived…' he murmured, crouching down to pluck at some blackened, malformed weeds jutting from the dry earth. 'After this, things went from bad to worse. Our crops began to fail, water sources became poisoned, wildlife started to die off in droves and cataclysmic events became frighteningly commonplace.'

Clara was still staring transfixed at the crimson sky above, her eyes wide and fearful, but nonetheless listening intently.

'The Clans knew they had to do something and so they came together to study the problem and soon found the culprit,' Vincent continued, rubbing the weed between his fingers and watching it crumble to dust. 'They discovered the Rot, learned that it was eating away at the core of our world, and that it was spreading...'

Vincent wiped the dust from his hands and got back to his feet, moving to stand in front of Clara so she was forced to look up at him once more.

'Our world is in pain, Clara,' he said, staring into her eyes. 'It is suffering, and it will die if something is not done soon... I...'

But, before he could say any more, a sudden tremor rocked the ground beneath them and they both struggled to keep their feet as dead leaves and branches began to rain down. The rumbling intensified and Vincent tried to reach out for Clara's hand to steady her but missed her by a whisker as she tumbled backwards and hit the ground hard, the impact knocking the breath from her body.

A terrifying creaking rent the air as Clara fought to rise, failing to notice for a moment a wide crack shearing through the base of a tree to her right, but Vincent did not miss a trick…

As the crack ripped right through the tree's width and it began to fall, Vincent was already on the move, Shifting as he went into his wolf form and bearing down on Clara in the shadow of the toppling giant. He was at her side in a heartbeat. His jaws closed around the back of her cardigan and he flung her with such speed and ferocity that she almost popped out of it, instead tumbling to a stop several paces away just as the massive trunk slammed into the dirt behind them, sending dust and splinters flying in all directions.

Gradually the rumbling ceased, and the earth was still once more. They both looked back at the tree that had almost killed them, gasping for air.

'That… That nearly…' Clara managed to say between breaths. Vincent Shifted back to a man and offered a hand to help her up.

'This is what I was saying, Clara,' he said, as he heaved her to her feet. 'Comhlacht is in great pain, and it is lashing out at anyone and anything in its suffering. There was a time when it could tell friend from foe – distinguish between those who wanted to help it, and those who wanted to harm it – but not any more…'

As Clara dusted herself off, Vincent approached the fallen tree and looked down at the jagged stump it had left behind, at the Rot running through its core; watching as the purple sap-like substance slowly began to crystallize in the air.

'This world does not have long left,' he said, his gaze fixed squarely upon the Rot. 'It must be healed quickly, or soon there will be nothing left for us to save…'

He beckoned Clara over to him and she approached nervously, now eyeing the trees around her with apprehension. Vincent pointed out across the plains at a location she could not quite make out.

'Our destination is my home city, Croí, and we have not another moment to lose,' he said, squaring his shoulders. 'Come, we have a long journey ahead and allies to meet along the way. Let us go.' And, with that, he headed back into the forest, leaving a still stunned and trembling Clara standing in his wake, her gaze glassy and unfocused.

In her mind's eye she kept playing out the moment the tree had nearly crushed her; she felt again the rush of air as it landed, heard the boom of its impact, and each time she did her heart leapt within her as if trying to escape.

This was all too much. She had not been here more than a few minutes and had already almost lost her life to this place. Voices clamoured in her head once more.

What am I doing here?

Why does Vincent think I can help?

How can any of this – any of it – be real…?

As she stood there – feeling almost paralysed – the image in her mind's eye dimmed, the toppling tree being replaced by something she had not thought about in some time. A book was revealed:

a book resting upon a table in a darkened room, its pages gated behind a solid-looking padlock.

Clara wanted to look away from this book, wanted to forget all knowledge of its existence, but it held her gaze as tears began to slide down her cheeks. It was a book she had once written in, and could now barely recall its contents, but she feared it; feared what was last written in it, and she did not want to remember it, nor face it...

My deepest, darkest secret... a secret I can never let escape me – not now, not ev...

'Clara.'

Clara snapped out of her reverie at once at Vincent's concerned voice.

'Are you... are you alright?' he asked worriedly as he approached. Clara nodded back as her eyes refocused on him.

'I'm... I'm fine...' she replied shakily, while Vincent looked at her sideways.

'You weren't hurt by that tree, were you?' Vincent pressed. 'You'd tell me if...'

'I'm okay – honestly,' Clara cut across him.

When Vincent continued to look at her doubtfully, Clara set off along the path she had watched him take, glancing back over her shoulder.

'It was this way, wasn't it?'

Vincent nodded as he began to follow her, his expression still clouded with concern.

They had been walking for an hour or more – each wrapped up in their own thoughts – when

Clara noticed Vincent reach up to adjust his mask, and she felt compelled to ask what had been on the tip of her tongue since they'd met.

'Your mask...' she began tentatively. 'Is it... is it related to your Guardian in some way?' Vincent lowered his hand and looked down at her with a smile as Clara quickly added: 'If it's not a rude question, of course.'

Vincent's hand returned to his mask, his fingers lovingly tracing its intricate carving, then he shook his head slightly.

'It is not a rude question,' he replied. 'To be honest, I sometimes forget I'm wearing it – it is as much a part of me as my own head.'

His hand reached up to smooth down the pelt of grey wolf fur running from the back of the mask down his shoulders.

'This mask is the result of a rite of passage,' he continued. 'All children in Comhlacht must go through this ritual in order to transition to adulthood – it is known as the "Convergence". Once they reach thirteen, each Clan member is sent out on a hunt, to find and kill one of their Guardian animals.'

Clara looked shocked at this.

'But... but I thought you held your Guardian in high honour?' she asked in confusion.

'We do,' Vincent replied, 'and this is how we show that honour. Only those Guardians who are already nearing the end of their journeys are chosen for the hunt, and once their lives have been taken the energy, strength and spirit they garnered over a lifetime is absorbed into the new adult, helping them on the next stage of their journey, while enabling the Guardian to embark upon their own.'

'That is… that is beautiful,' Clara murmured.

'It is what has always been done,' Vincent remarked. 'Our bodies too will one day be returned to the earth, where they will provide strength to our Guardians so the cycle can continue.'

Vincent looked down at Clara and tapped the mask to draw her attention to it.

'Each mask is made to resemble the Guardian whose life was taken to enable the transition, and a part of their body becomes a permanent piece of it, while the rest is given in offering,' he continued, his hand reaching once more to the pelt at his back. 'This great creature was known as Kirath, and he was a renowned leader of his kind.'

Here Vincent sighed with long-held regret.

'But with the arrival of the Rot it has thrown the Convergence into turmoil,' he said bitterly. 'All wildlife in this land is struggling, just as we are, and their numbers are diminishing at a rate far beyond our worst projections, making completing this rite of passage significantly more troublesome. And without completing it our young struggle to control their Shifts, and always will…'

Vincent gripped his cane tighter as he walked.

'If we do not do something soon our Guardians will die out, and our bond along with them, and it seems clear we will not be far behind.'

Clara had been sadly nodding along with this, but now reached a hand up towards Vincent.

'May I… May I try it on?' she asked. Vincent chuckled.

'I would like to oblige,' he began, and Clara immediately withdrew her hand, 'but once placed upon our heads it is Clan law that our masks must never be removed.'

'I'm sorry,' Clara said, abashed. 'I didn't mean to…'

'It's alright,' Vincent reassured her. 'You weren't to know.'

At that moment, Clara heard a strange sound coming from above – a rhythmic drumming on the lofty branches that sounded like…

'Rain…' Vincent hissed in annoyance.

Clara looked up as the first drops began to punch through the tangle above and spatter the ground around them.

'That's just what we need,' he groaned, picking up his already fast pace. 'Come on, I know a place nearby we can shelter in – follow me.'

As the rain peppered Clara's upturned face, she held out her hands to catch the droplets, but was horrified to see that the water was a dirty, rusty brown in colour. She quickly lowered her head as she sped up after Vincent, but could not prevent a few drops trickling into her mouth, leaving a taste behind like iron, or blood…

It was not long before a shape appeared up ahead in the gloom; some kind of building nestled amidst the trees. As they hurried on towards it, Clara continued to feel the sense of unreality pervading her – soaking her though like this filthy rain – and a memory surfaced in her mind she had not thought about in a long time…

CHAPTER 3
Excess Energy

'For the last time, Clara – it's too wet for you to play football outside! Just look at it!' Emily Brown pointed through the kitchen window at the sheets of rain lashing the glass, then turned back to her daughter in exasperation. 'You'd catch your death if you went out there now!'

'But I'm bored!' Clara hurled back. 'And I want to play with my new ball – just a few minutes! Please!'

'No!' her mother replied sternly. 'Now give that to me.'

Emily approached Clara and took the football from her. For a moment it looked like Clara might resist, but instead she just scowled and folded her arms huffily.

'It's not fair!' she shouted.

'What's not fair is you catching a cold and then passing it on to your father when he needs to work,' Emily replied frostily as she placed the ball within the nearby dresser cupboard and closed the door. She then reached into a drawer and withdrew something that made Clara groan with annoyance.

'Ohh no!'

'Oh yes!' Emily countered. She knelt and began to fiddle with the latch on the cupboard, then stood back up to reveal that it had been padlocked shut.

'You can have it back tomorrow when it stops raining,' Emily said, slipping the key into her pocket. 'Now I want to hear no more about it, and I'll be telling your father how you've behaved when he gets home.'

With a low, animal growl, Clara stormed away upstairs and ducked into her room. She gripped the door in preparation to slam it, but then her attitude changed as she thought better of it. Stealthily, she threw her back against the wall by the door and peeked through the crack where she could just about see down the stairs and into the kitchen where her mother still stood. She was tapping her foot in agitation – clearly digesting what had just happened – then she turned and disappeared into the living room.

When Clara was sure she would not be returning any time soon, she looked away from the stairs, her brow knit in concentration. Finally, her face cleared and she dashed quietly over to her desk, where she rifled through the items upon it feverishly and quickly found what she was looking for – a paperclip…

Holding her treasure, Clara hurried back over to the door, checked that the coast was still clear, and made her way furtively downstairs…

Joseph Brown trudged slowly home from work through a light evening drizzle, his face and overalls blackened by coal dust and his hair filthy and bedraggled. In his left hand he held an empty lunch box and, in his right, his well-worn pickaxe, which he rested wearily against his shoulder. The sun sank steadily behind the hills in the west, casting long shadows across the ground and painting his silhouette over the cobbles. As he walked, Joseph watched this two-dimensional version of himself progress along the street, changing shape and orientation as he passed through pools of light spilling out of the windows on either side.

Tired as he was, Joseph still managed to feel cheerful, and a smile tugged at the corners of his mouth. He was finished for the day, work at the mine was plentiful and decently paid – as demand for coal was at an all-time high – and he had been given leave to finish a couple of hours early tomorrow. At last, he would be able to spend some quality time with Clara. Usually when he came home, she was already fast asleep in bed, and more often than not, he started work before she got up for school. But tomorrow would be different.

He would take her for a walk down to the pond in the afternoon sun and he would show her the frog spawn and the fish and teach her the names of the trees and flowers they passed on the way. She had – in an out-of-character moment – expressed a desire to try flower pressing, and he was pleased that she was showing an interest in something other than, well…

Joseph smiled as he thought of it. His daughter had always been rather hot-headed, and would never back down from a fight, to the point where it had practically become her hobby. He never worried too much about her – because she usually won – but, still… He knew that he had to quickly grab the opportunity flower pressing presented if he wanted to direct her exertions towards something a little safer.

He resolved to encourage her to pick some flowers the next day and set her on the road to her new activity right away.

Just then, the rain – which Joseph had been enjoying the cooling properties of – began to get much, much heavier. Soon, drops as big as penny pieces were falling in heavy sheets that beat against the cobbles, creating little rivulets between the stones and collecting in dips here and there. Within minutes Joseph was soaked to the skin and the coal dust that had clung to his face all day now ran into his eyes and mouth, forcing him to dash it away with a grubby hand. He picked up the pace and began to jog down the street, his boots splashing through the puddles, his pickaxe and sodden clothes weighing him down.

As he sloshed around a corner, Joseph looked up and saw the silhouette of his home in the distance, set against the darkening sky. It stood away from the other dwellings near the fringe of the forest, surrounded by its own little garden. His family had lived in that house for generations, and every one of them had made their living from the mine. The building itself had seen better days, but Joseph did what he could with the little spare time he had to keep it in good shape. The outer walls needed a fresh coat of paint, and the windows needed washing, but other than that he generally had just enough time and spare cash to make any necessary repairs.

He passed the village pond on his right and saw the dark grey storm clouds above reflected dully across its murky surface, broken by the raindrops striking it. His stomach rumbled loudly as he hurried on, the noise almost blotted out by the pounding raindrops and the thudding of his boots. He was looking forward to a good meal and a sit down in his favourite armchair when he got home.

The back door was unlocked as usual, so Joseph let himself into the house and closed it behind him. Wearily, he leaned his pick against the wall and awkwardly tugged his boots off, spattering mud across the floor. With a sheepish look at the mess, he hung his saturated coat on a hook, then turned and walked into the kitchen to find his wife standing by the sink and looking out of the window, her expression distant and thoughtful. He placed his lunch box upon the countertop, and she turned at the sound.

'Evening, dear,' he said, moving to her side to plant a kiss on her cheek.

'Oh, hello darling,' she replied, looking up into his face and studying his tired brown eyes. 'How was work today?'

'Oh, it was fine, fine,' he answered steadily. 'My arms feel like they're about to fall off, but that's nothing new,' he added with a smile. Emily, her mouth twitching as she tried to keep a straight face, indicated a heaped plate of food on the table nearby.

'So, I suppose you won't be able to lift a fork to feed yourself?' she said, her voice breaking as she tried not to laugh. 'Guess I'll just throw your dinner away then.'

'Wait... my arms, they suddenly feel much better!' Joseph said, picking up his wife and twirling her around the room.

'Yes, I thought they might once food was mentioned,' she replied, breaking into a fit of laughter. Joseph released his wife and placed her back upon the floor, but not before he had kissed her tenderly on the lips. Once back on solid ground, Emily picked up a dishcloth and clipped him around the head with it.

'Go and eat up, you big softy,' she said affectionately. Joseph sat down and dug hungrily into his plate.

'The foreman allowed me to finish a couple of hours early tomorrow,' he said around a mouthful of food.

'Don't speak with your mouth full – what kind of an example is that to set?' she asked, clipping him round the head once more.

'It's only you and I here right now,' he said, swallowing quickly and taking a swig from a pitcher of ale.

'That's not the point,' his wife reprimanded him.

'True, I'm sorry love,' he replied ruefully. 'Anyway, I thought maybe I could take Clara for a walk down to the pond after work tomorrow.'

At the mention of her daughter's name, Emily's face darkened.

'She and I had a bit of a run-in today…' she began.

'Oh aye…?' Joseph replied.

'Well, it's been raining on and off all day and I didn't want her going outside, so she's been practically bouncing off the walls up there,' she continued, indicating Clara's bedroom with a thumb. 'She wanted to take her new football out and wouldn't take "no" for an answer. So I locked it up in the dresser – and you know what she did…?'

'I'm guessing something that will make us question where on earth she learned it?' her husband replied with a smile he could not quite hide.

'She picked the lock!' Emily said in exasperation, her eyes narrowing as her husband tried and failed to contain his amusement. 'She picked the lock then went out to play and got soaking wet and muddy. She's in bed now and… this isn't funny!' she hissed, swatting him on the arm. Joseph almost choked on a mouthful of food as he struggled to stop laughing.

'You've got to admit… it's pretty impressive,' he finally managed to say.

Emily sat down at the kitchen table beside her husband and sighed resignedly, a smile now tugging at her own lips.

'She certainly takes after me…' she chuckled.

'I wasn't going to say that…' Joseph replied with a laugh.

'She's just… she's so full of energy at the moment,' Emily continued, watching her husband gulping down his food. 'She's got into scraps with boys twice her size, and won! She fought with that Jeremy Stephens last week, and I always hoped they'd be friends… Don't you know his father?'

'The doctor? Aye, I do,' Joseph replied between mouthfuls.

'I've been thinking about it, and we'll have to find an activity she can do a few times a week to try and expend some of the excess before she *really* gets herself into trouble.'

'What did you have in mind?' Joseph asked.

'Well, it might seem a tad… unusual for her, but I was thinking maybe we could try her at that new dancing school. You know, run by that woman, what's her name… Mrs Andrews. She used to be a history teacher somewhere down south.'

'I was just thinking that myself as I was walking home,' Joseph said, wiping his mouth on a handkerchief taken from his pocket. 'Well... not the bit about the dancing school, I'm not psychic,' he added, raising another smile on his wife's lips. 'But I was thinking about trying to direct her energies somewhere else. She said she wanted to try flower pressing and I was going to start her on that tomorrow, but if you think she'll go for the dancing school idea, then we could put it to her.'

'She can do both, you know,' Emily said with a smile, throwing an arm around her husband. 'She doesn't have to do one or the other.'

'What would I do without you?' Joseph said in a mock serious tone.

'I don't know, probably starve and make a string of foolish decisions,' his wife replied with a wink.

'More than likely,' he conceded. 'Anyway, we have enough money to send her to the dancing school, hmm... maybe once a week – twice at most? Why don't you go and ask her and see what she thinks?'

'She's meant to be asleep right now, but I bet she's secretly reading one of those adventure stories she loves so much. I'll catch her out and ask her about it. You should come up and kiss her goodnight in a few minutes.'

'Aye, I will do,' Joseph said, raising his pitcher to his lips and draining the contents. Emily kissed her husband on the cheek once again, hitched up her dress, and crept quietly up the stairs towards Clara's room.

CHAPTER 4
A Hopeless Case

'Stay behind me, and don't make a sound.'

Vincent drew his revolver as they approached the building through the pouring rain, their feet slipping and sliding in the mud. Clara was soaked through, and she clawed the wet hair nervously out of her eyes as the squat shape revealed itself out of the grim half-light to be a modest but rather dishevelled log cabin, its roof covered in dead leaves, branches and thick, black moss.

They reached the stairs leading to the front door and ascended the aging, creaking steps slowly up onto the covered veranda, where the sound of the rain pattering against it enveloped them. In front of her, Vincent threw his back against the wall by the door and Clara did the same, looking at it anxiously.

With his weapon held ready, Vincent reached out and gripped the handle. He glanced at Clara briefly, then – with practiced ease – burst through the door, his revolver sweeping the space for any sign of a threat.

Clara held her breath, waiting for shouts of alarm, but none came and instead she heard:

'You can come in, Clara – it's quite safe.'

With a sigh of relief, Clara entered the cabin to discover a large, single room that had clearly seen better days, but would be perfectly comfortable as a refuge from the rain. As she shut the door behind her, she took in the room's contents: a small bed in one corner, a writing desk in another, a table and chairs at the centre, a large wardrobe, a log burner stove, and finally the multiple bookshelves lining any free wall space.

'Whose house is this?' Clara asked as she continued to glance about, wrapping her arms around her chest to try to stay warm. Vincent holstered his revolver before replying.

'His name was Mikal, and he was of Panther Clan,' Vincent replied, his eyes still sweeping the cabin. 'A devastating tragedy all but wiped out his people, and he was driven to the brink of insanity. He retreated here to live a solitary, rage-fuelled existence, refusing to accept any help from the other Clans when offered. He died here alone…'

Clara dropped her gaze in pity and remorse and saw a faded stain on the floorboards that looked a lot like…

'Wolf Clan now maintain this cabin for times of need, such as this,' Vincent cut across her thoughts as he moved to check through a window. 'He may not have let the Clans help him in life, but they honour him now by looking after the last thing he ever built.'

Vincent turned back to Clara and saw that she was standing shivering at the centre of a rapidly growing puddle of rainwater from her sodden clothes. He smiled affectionately.

'I'm sorry, you must be chilled to the bone!' He pointed at the wardrobe across the room. 'There should be clean clothes in there, and I'll get a fire going.'

As Vincent opened the stove and began to fill it with sticks and paper, Clara approached the wardrobe – her teeth chattering – and tugged the big double doors open. Inside was a motley collection of clothes, some hung up, some stacked in neat piles, and all smelling rather musty, but otherwise looking perfectly clean.

Clara began to fish through the piles at random as she searched for something that would fit. Behind her, she heard Vincent strike a light and soon the homely crackle of flames reached her ears. He shut the grate and stood up as the glow from within lent an immediately warmer atmosphere to the cabin.

Clara had just tugged out a pair of trousers from the bottom of a pile and caused it to collapse across the floor, when Vincent appeared at her back and plucked a hooded cloak from a hook within the wardrobe. He stepped back and swung it over his shoulders as she looked up at him in confusion.

'Are we moving on already?' she asked in surprise.

'Not just yet,' he replied as he moved over to the door. 'I just want to do a quick check of the perimeter before we continue, and it will be easier alone. Please, take this time to dry off and warm up and I will be back as soon as I can.'

And, with that, he drew the hood of the cloak over his head and swept out of the cabin back into the rain. Clara stared at the door a little nonplussed, then returned to digging through the clothes where she soon discovered a shirt and jumper to go with the trousers she'd already found.

With her prizes in hand she made to undress, then – feeling embarrassed – quickly checked to make sure that there was absolutely no one who could see her. Once she was sure, she began to change out of her wet clothes and slip on her new ones. They were all a little too large for her, but she instantly felt better and could feel herself beginning to warm up.

Once dressed, she made her way over to the stove and held out her hands to catch the warmth, feeling it caress her fingers and spread throughout her body like sunshine. Unwilling to leave her cardigan behind – as it was one her mother had knitted her – Clara took the soggy article and placed it on the back of a chair beside the writing desk, and tugged this over to the stove where it could begin to dry.

With nothing else to do, she sat upon the chair and let the welcome heat sink into her bones, but – as was customary with her – she quickly became bored of this. Her eyes began to wander the room once more and they soon fell upon the writing desk, and the clutter of items upon it.

Clara got to her feet and moved towards it, where she began to rifle through the sundry artefacts she found: fountain pens, envelopes, a letter opener and a paperweight; she inspected them all and then placed them back neatly where she found them.

She was reaching for an oil lamp to inspect it when her elbow caught a stack of items on the edge of the desk and sent them tumbling to the floor.

'Oh, bother,' she muttered as she bent to retrieve them. It was as she lifted several loose scraps of paper that she noticed the book beneath them. Instantly intrigued, Clara reached for it and raised it up for a closer look. Its cover was leather and deep crimson in colour, its pages dog-eared and well-thumbed, as though it had been heavily used, or used hastily. There was no title upon it, but something about it caught Clara's attention, and she carried it over to the chair by the fire without picking up the rest of the items she'd disturbed.

As she sat down, she let her fingers trace the book's spine and the supple leather, then she flipped it open and her eyes took in the opening words on the first page: May 10th 1930 – Day One.

Clara instantly snapped the book shut with a guilty look on her face – this was someone's personal diary!

Clara glanced around her in embarrassment, aware that it was wrong to pry into other people's business, but Vincent had not yet returned and there was – after all – nothing else to do around here…

With one last look to check for watchful eyes, Clara flipped the diary open again, and began to read…

May 10th 1930 – Day One

I *hate* this place. I hate this miserable, dying world and those creatures – those wolves – who brought me to it. I hate the way they talk to me; like they're better than me – like they know something about me that no one else does, and they hold it over me with all the pleasure of a child keeping a toy from a younger sibling.

They brought me here on a promise, a promise I do not know if they can keep, but I am beginning to think it might have been better to have stayed back in London – the filthy smog and endless noise would be a welcome relief from this horrid place.

So, she is from my world too! Clara thought in surprise, before continuing to read.

My name is Melissa Carthage, and I am keeping this diary in the hope that – should the worst happen – maybe someone will discover my words and learn what happened to me, and bring the wrongdoers to justice.

As strange as it may sound, being brought to this dark, terrifying world and having to endure a torturous journey through a hellish landscape is not the worst thing that has happened to me. No, my life has gone inexorably downhill ever since *that day*. It was the worst day of my entire life, the worst thing I could *possibly* imagine – the worst thing any mother could imagine – and it all happened so quickly. One minute he was there – the apple of my eye, the centre of my world – and the next, he was gone, leaving behind only the shell of the being I cherished most on this earth.

He had always loved to watch the carriages go by on the cobbled street outside our house, loved to hail the drivers as they passed and ask if he could stroke their horses whenever they stopped nearby. He was a simple soul, and I adored that about him. He could always find joy in the smallest things, and that joy was overwhelmingly infectious. He would practically light up a room whenever he entered, and could shine a torch into even the darkest of hearts.

And that is why it is so hard to accept how suddenly that light was snatched away, how fragile it was, and how easily snuffed out.

Two steps… that was all it took. Two steps too far into the street, the echoing boom of a motorcar backfiring nearby, and one *stupid* woman who could not control her frightened horse, and he was gone.

In the moments that followed – as she rushed to my side to try to help, as the tears gushed down her horror-stricken face – I did not know how to feel towards her.

But now I do.

Anger. Fury. Rage.

These words do not cover it. These words do not describe the emotion that has gripped my heart knowing that she took him from me, that she can go on living her life while mine crumbles to pieces around me.

I have been consumed by it, this emotion. I have retreated into the darkness of its cave and do not know if I will ever emerge; do not know if I even *want* to. My marriage has ended as a result of it, I have lost my home because of it, and I exist now scratching a living on the streets fuelled only by this feeling, but it sustains me also.

These beasts – these wolves – promised me that they could "help me find what I had lost," if only I would help them save their world, but they declined to elaborate further on what they meant in either case. If there is even the slimmest hope of finding him once more then I will go to whatever ends necessary.

Clara looked up from the diary, her face white, as the bitter, angry words she had just read washed over her. For a moment she was not sure if she could continue to read, but she felt compelled to do so.

May 1930 – Day Unknown

I am already beginning to lose track of the days here, but it cannot have been more than a week or so – it is difficult to tell under this blood-red sky that makes my skin crawl every time I look at it. Something about this place makes me feel dirty all over, unclean; like there is a stain in my flesh that I cannot get out. I feel the sickness of this world pressing in upon me like a vice and I have found the journey harder going with every passing day. But the wolves show not the faintest signs of tiredness, or of slowing our relentless march.

They say we are heading for their home city – Craw or Croy or some such thing – and that I will be able to help them when we arrive, but they have still as yet declined to explain to me how on earth I can do that. I am no scientist; no botanist, geologist or great thinker – I am now only what that woman made me when she took my Charlie from me. Anything I was before that day is gone, and the person that remains can be of no help to these beasts.

They have gone to great lengths to explain to me their plight, to explain about this "Rot" and everything it has taken from them, everything they have lost, but if they are hoping for compassion from me after all that *I* have lost and all that they have put me through then they are sadly mistaken.

During this dreadful journey I have already come close to losing my life on multiple occasions to this violent, chaotic world. Sudden, angry lightning storms, flash floods, earthquakes; it feels like this world is doing all in its power to punish any fool stupid enough to be caught upon it.

I should never have come here. I should have listened to my first instinct on hearing the wolves' offer. I should have stayed back in London and continued my search…

Clara's eyes were wide as she stared at the dirty, ink-blotted page. She felt a strange mix of pity and distress as she read Melissa's words: pity at the tragedy she had been put through, and distress at her response to it. She glanced around – to see if there was any sign of Vincent – and when she saw none, she bent her head, and continued to read…

1930 – Month Unknown – Day Unknown

I have now lost all track of time and place as we continue our seemingly never-ending journey across this vile world. It is strange for once to be aware of some emotion other than the one that has gripped me since that day; strange to feel the fear scratching at the entrance to my cave – wanting to be let in, wanting to join me – but there is no room within, and although I acknowledge the fear is out there, I can barely feel it.

We have arrived at a cabin in the woods and I have – finally – been given the chance to sleep in a proper bed, although sleep is hard to come by in this place, even when your head is on a proper pillow.

Throughout my time in this world the beasts have been relentless in their questioning. Every day it is something new. They ask me about my past, before that day; who I was, what I did, how I felt towards my family and peers. They ask me about how I felt after that day, and they even ask me about the day itself. It seems obvious to me that they are angling towards something, but they are so frustratingly, *infuriatingly* vague and unable to just *get to the point*.

I get the impression – from their roundabout questioning – that they want me to confront, forgive or move past it, and they use their experiences as a simile for my own, but this only makes the rage within burn even brighter. They could *never* understand what it was like to have my Charlie taken from me, never know the depth of my suffering.

If they think forgiving or moving past this will somehow fix me, make me whole again, then they are sorely mistaken. I can *never*

forgive, and when this venture inevitably fails
and I return home to London, that bitch will
get what's coming to her…

Clara's hands were shaking as she looked up from
the diary, the words she had just read rattling her to
the core. Her eyes were unfocussed as she processed
the angry and hate-filled rhetoric; her limited world-
experience had not prepared her for the idea that
such wrathful people could exist.

Against her will, her eyes were drawn back to the
diary, and she was about to read on when the door to the
cabin burst open and Vincent – in wolf form – appeared,
soaked through and covered in mud and leaves.

In the blink of an eye, he had Shifted back to his
human form and – without a word – hurried over
to closest window to look out anxiously into the
darkened woods.

'What's the matter?' Clara asked worriedly.
'What's going on?'

But Vincent did not reply, and instead moved
over to another window to check outside. Clara held
up the diary in a shaking hand as she looked at him.

'I'm not the first person brought here from my
world, am I…?' she asked.

At this, Vincent looked at her for the first time
and saw the diary she held.

'No,' he replied quickly. 'Not by a long shot. But I
have faith that you will be the last.'

'What happened to her?' Clara whispered.

'We thought she could change, we thought she could forgive,' Vincent replied distractedly as he moved to another window. 'But she was too far gone…'

At that moment there was a loud snapping of branches from outside the cabin, but Clara had noticed another entry in the diary and had become fixated upon it.

'Wait, what's this…?' she murmured.

Her gaze had alighted upon the diary's last entry. This one bore no title or date – as vague as the last ones had been – and the handwriting was rough and almost illegible, the page covered by ink blots and what looked like tears… She began to read it aloud.

'It has finally happened. The wolves had told us we were being hunted, and that was why we had barely stopped moving, but I had begun to think they were telling tales to hurry me along. Now I know they were not. I hear them coming even now. They are surrounding us, encircling us; there must be dozens of them. Even those unflappable beasts seem frightened. The noise as they approach, it… it is not human… It sounds almost… mechanical… I see flames between the trees, like furnaces floating in the air… They are moving in… They are almost upon us… They…'

Clara turned to the next page to find it blank, and her terror-stricken eyes swept to Vincent's rigid and alert form by the window.

'What… What was it she saw…?' she asked, in barely more than a whisper.

Vincent looked at her regretfully as he drew the revolver from his belt once more and cocked it, the sounds of snapping branches outside growing in intensity.

'Unfortunately,' he breathed, 'you are about to find out...'

CHAPTER 5
Man or Machine?

'Can we not run?' Clara whispered as she tiptoed over to Vincent. 'Couldn't we…'

'No,' Vincent cut across her. 'No, if we ran now they would chase us down and kill us. Stay here, and keep out of sight.'

With his revolver held ready, Vincent headed for the door – still open after he had burst inside – and stepped out onto the covered veranda, while Clara stayed behind peeking out after him. The rain had finally stopped, and she watched as Vincent stepped off the veranda into a small clearing, hemmed in on all sides by trees with only impenetrable darkness beyond.

The sounds of cracking and crunching continued to build, and it was clear now that they were footsteps, but what was not clear was the low, growing sound beneath them. It was metallic and hissing – it reminded Clara of steam trains, but there could be no trains in these dense woods… *Mechanical*, that is what Melissa had called it.

As though an external force was pulling at her – and against Vincent's orders – Clara felt her curiosity dragging her inexorably through the doorway towards these strange noises, hugging the side of the cabin as she went. The sounds continued to escalate as Clara reached the building's corner, her gaze flicking from the shadowy trees to Vincent standing in the clearing, his revolver held tightly in one hand and his cane gripped in the other.

Pinpricks of light began to appear between the trees ahead of them, five in all, drifting closer and closer, wavering and flickering like…

'Flames…' Clara whispered, her heartbeat racing.

The light from these flames grew brighter and more intense, spread out in a semicircle meant to cut off their escape. At the centre of the clearing, Vincent unbuttoned his jacket and tucked it back, revealing the array of gadgets at his belt that Clara had spotted when she first met him.

She could not see much of his face from where she crouched, but his posture was that of a coiled spring, ready to leap into battle at a moment's notice. Clara's eyes flicked from Vincent back to the flames, and she saw now dim shapes behind each one, their movements odd and jerky, almost spasmodic.

All of a sudden, the five shapes stopped, as if at a command she had been unable to hear, and the woods fell silent.

Into this silence a hellish, twisted voice rang out from the shape at the centre of the semicircle, a sound unlike anything Clara had ever heard:

'I didn't think you Wolves would be stupid enough to come here again,' it rasped and grated, like rusty metal given voice.

A look of recognition swept across Vincent's face beneath his mask, and his grip tightened still further on his weapons.

'Ah, Darius,' Vincent replied with forced politeness. 'Good to see you again.'

The shape identified as Darius shifted as he peered more closely at his adversary.

'Is that you, Vincent?' Darius asked, his tone switching to match Vincent's. 'You know, we've been looking for you. Malone would very much like to speak with you in person, if you'd be so kind.'

'I'm sure he would,' Vincent returned. 'But I'm a little busy at the moment. Perhaps another time.'

'Oh, I'm afraid he won't like that answer much,' Darius replied regretfully, as if this news brought him great sorrow. 'He won't like that one bit… You and your comrades have caused us enough trouble of late, but Malone has instructed me that his offer to you still stands, should you wish to gratefully accept it.'

A snarl creased Vincent's lips, but he just about managed to maintain his manners.

'You can tell Malone my answer will never change,' he responded through gritted teeth. 'Now, I must bid you good day, and…'

'You *are* coming with us, Vincent,' Darius spat, all trace of false niceties gone in an instant. 'I *will* bring you before Malone, one way or another...' And with that he stepped forward into the clearing, and Clara only just stifled a gasp of utter horror from escaping her lips.

What Clara's petrified eyes bore witness to in that moment was almost too much for her twelve years of existence to process, for the creature that was Darius could not have occurred to her in her worst nightmares.

He had been a man once – that much was clear – for she could see patches of warped, necrotic flesh on what passed for his arms, legs and head, but most of his living tissue had been replaced with a horrifying array of mechanical parts that barely seemed to be holding him together as he clanked menacingly towards Vincent.

Clara's wide-eyed gaze took in the collection of pistons that had replaced his right leg and the lower half of his left, the triple-hinged contraption that had been swapped for his left arm, ending in a wickedly lethal-looking set of iron barbs, and the furnace at his core – powering it all – from which the hellish fire-glow emanated, up-lighting a twisted face set in a permanent sneer of decaying flesh, from which two eyes – switched for telescopic lenses – looked out, and surmounting it all was a mask, somewhat like Vincent's, but in the shape of a hissing snake.

All in all, he was the most hideous thing Clara could have possibly imagined, and she was hard pressed not to retch at the mere sight of him.

As Darius stopped a few paces in front of Vincent – steam hissing from vents on his back – his four comrades also advanced into the clearing, revealing their own horrifying range of mechanical alterations and weaponry that made Clara's already bloodless face blanch still further.

At the centre of the clearing, Darius stared at Vincent mockingly.

'Five to one, Vincent,' he jeered. 'Sure you don't want to just give up…?'

Vincent shook his head.

'Kind of you to ask,' he replied icily. 'But I'll take my chances, thank you.'

'Ha, you always…' Darius began, but as he raised his barbed weapon arm to point at Vincent, the sudden movement took Clara by surprise and this time she failed to stop the gasp escaping her lips, and in these silent, dying woods, she might as well have screamed.

Every head turned to her, and in that instant she felt frozen in place; paralysed by a mind-numbing terror like she had never before known. Darius' eyes telescoped out to get a better look at her, then he and Vincent turned back to each other for a moment, Darius' look of surprise being replaced by one of malicious delight, while Vincent's shock turned to steely determination.

'He's brought another one!' Darius yelled triumphantly to his group. 'Grab her!'

After this, everything happened very quickly, and Clara struggled to recall it all clearly, thanks to the shock and panic fogging her memory. But in truth she was glad of it, as she was sure the details would have haunted her sleep for years to come.

At Darius' words, one of his comrades, a female – or at least as far as Clara could tell from its features – lunged towards her, a metallic claw outstretched to grab her arm, but she never made it that far. Reading the situation in an instant, Vincent had already reacted, diving to one side to avoid Darius's swipe with his barbed weapon while simultaneously reaching to his belt and producing a small glass vial filled with a greenish liquid. With practiced precision, Vincent had hurled the vial at Clara's attacker before she had got more than two paces towards her. The vial hit the furnace at the creature's core and shattered, instantly engulfing her in a thick, cloying cloud of green smoke, and she shrieked in agony.

Thankfully, Clara had flinched away at this point or she would have seen what happened next, for the cloud acted with lethal efficiency, going to work on the metal in her body and forcing it to rapidly rust and contract, crumpling her in upon herself tighter and tighter until her screams were abruptly cut off and the cloud dissipated to reveal the remaining mass of twisted metal and flesh.

The second of Darius' comrades – who had also been advancing upon Clara – stopped in his tracks in shock, and this was all the time Vincent needed. Swiftly dodging another attack from an unperturbed Darius, Vincent raised his revolver and fired – once, twice, three times – each shot taking the creature full in the face and shattering the metal and glass lenses that served as his eyes.

With a howl of pain, he raised his arms to his face, revealing that – while his left arm was still human – his right had been switched out for a primitive Gatling gun, a belt of ammunition running from it to a metal container affixed to his back. Without breaking step, Vincent had swiftly holstered his revolver, Shifted to his wolf form, and already crossed the divide between them. Shifting back to human, he ducked down under the creature's flailing arms and caught hold of the Gatling gun in an iron grip, swinging it around to point at the third of Darius' comrades, who had been hurtling towards Vincent, but now skidded to a stop when he saw what was about to happen.

While the creature behind him still clutched at his ruined face, Vincent pulled the trigger and a deafening cacophony of gunfire echoed throughout the clearing. Darius and his fourth comrade had just enough time to dive for safety as a hail of gunfire eviscerated the unfortunate third combatant, sending shards of metal and bone flying in all directions.

As his remains slumped to the floor, Vincent was already moving again, spinning back to the creature behind him and turning its own weapon against it, holding down the trigger until the weapon clicked dry and little identifiable was left, its pain now over.

With Darius struggling to get back to his feet, his fourth comrade had already recovered and made strides towards Vincent, but on seeing it approach, the wily shapeshifter had reached to his belt once more and produced another curious gadget. With a snarl, the creature pounced at him and Vincent spun to one side like a bull fighter, hurling the gadget as it flashed past, but he was not quite quick enough and was caught on the shoulder by its machete-like appendage. But Vincent paid this injury no mind, watching the gadget as it burst in mid-air and propelled a large net that swiftly entangled his quarry and sent it tumbling back to earth.

Before it could even begin to struggle against its bonds, Vincent was upon it, reaching again to his belt and pulling out another vial, this one with a white-ish hue. Reaching down, Vincent gripped the grate handle to the furnace that powered the creature, wrenched it open, and tossed the vial inside. In the heat of the fire, it instantly burst, and a cloud of acrid white smoke billowed out, the carbon dioxide doing its work swiftly – killing the fire and instantly ceasing all activity from its host.

In one swift movement, Vincent got back to his feet and unsheathed the sword from his cane, then – in one sure slice – he severed the huge machete-like blade from the arm of the creature.

Darius, who by now had regained his feet and seen how the odds had shifted, was nevertheless not one to run from a fight, and charged at Vincent with an inhuman squeal of rage that sounded like steel grating on steel.

Reaching to the back of his belt now, Vincent produced one final gadget, and this he hurled at a low angle towards his approaching foe. The gadget split in flight to reveal two heavy weights attached together by a tough piece of rope – a bolas. The bolas wrapped around Darius' legs and tripped him, sending him spinning towards the dirt, but he had not even had chance to land before Vincent had picked up the huge machete and swung it low at the base of a nearby tree. The brittle, dead wood gave way immediately before the fearsome blade and the tree began to fall, landing upon Darius only a moment after he hit the ground.

The clearing suddenly fell still and quiet as Vincent – breathing a little heavily now – inspected the wound on his shoulder, then straightened his lapels and glanced back to ensure that Clara was alright.

This was one of the only things Clara remembered clearly from that terrifying ordeal – the look on Vincent's face. She had expected to see maybe anger, or shock, or perhaps pain from his injury, but it was none of those things. Instead, all she saw there was regret – a terrible, gut-wrenching remorse at what he had been forced to do, and she felt her heart clench with sorrow for him, but did not yet fully understand why she was seeing this.

A rasping cackle split the silence and Vincent turned from Clara and looked down at Darius, pinned beneath the tree.

'You were always good in a scrap, Vincent,' Darius chuckled before he was racked by a coughing fit.

'Maybe that's why Malone still likes you,' he added once he'd recovered. He tried feebly to shift the tree, but it was no use, and he slumped back again.

'You know you can't keep running from him... from us...' he continued, and as if on cue the growing sound of branches snapping – of approaching footsteps – began to ring out from amidst the trees. 'You can't fight progress! We are the future, Vincent, and your pathetic struggles against it mean nothing!'

As the sounds grew louder and louder, Vincent looked from his foe to their origin and back again, momentarily undecided. Then – his decision made – he turned to Clara and hurried over, taking her gently but firmly by the arm and leading her away from the sounds at a fast pace.

Before long they were once more deep within the woods, the sounds fading to nothing behind them. Clara – who was still trying to process everything that had just happened – looked up at Vincent in shock and confusion and asked the only question she could coherently form in her mind:

'Who... who on earth were they...?' she whispered.

Vincent glanced over his shoulder then set his gaze ahead once more, and Clara could still see the look of deep regret upon his face as he answered.

'They are Viper Clan,' he replied at last. 'And they do not want this world saved...'

CHAPTER 6
The Head of the Snake

Steam clouded the air, jetting from huge machines that clanked and whirred all around the cavernous factory floor at the heart of the Viper city; the sprawling, mighty, industrial Inchinn. The space was a hive of activity with Viper engineers and overseers – all sporting their own mechanical modifications – bustling to and fro with fierce and single-minded focus on their tasks.

To one side of the factory, carts filled with Rot crystals were being ferried to conveyer belts where they were whisked along into the path of large metal rollers that crushed them to a fine powder in moments. This powder was then channelled through chutes into a massive copper still, beneath which a fire burned at a constant high temperature, heating up the powder within until its gasses flowed through pipes into waiting canisters for collection, each marked with the label "C2".

To the other side, barrels of liquid Rot were being siphoned through tubes into their own – much smaller – copper still, beneath which another fire burned, sending the resulting gasses through pipes into separate canisters marked with the label "C1".

Talk was kept to a minimum – everyone knew their job, and no one wanted to be seen to be slacking off. They all knew what happened to those who didn't pull their weight, and they all knew the rewards for those who did.

A sudden, ear-splitting grinding and crunching cut through the ambient noise like a knife and the steel rollers – as well as the conveyer belt – ground to a shuddering halt. A high-pitched, tinny alarm bell began to ring and while it caused many heads to turn, no one slowed in their tasks for even a moment.

One overseer – whose job it was to keep the conveyer running – sprinted over to an engineer standing by the roller.

'What's happened?' the overseer hissed, glancing about in fearful agitation.

'Looks like a chunk of copper or iron got chucked in with the crystals…' the engineer replied nervously, as he stared at the frozen machinery.

'Well, get it out then!' the overseer barked at him.

'But I'll…'

'Just do it!' the overseer yelled, looking about him again.

The engineer – who had had both legs and arms replaced by mechanical equivalents – knew when to back down, and cautiously climbed up onto the conveyer and approached the rollers. His eyes beneath his Viper mask fell on the large hunk of iron that had somehow become mixed in with the crystals, and was now jamming the rollers, and he crouched down in front of it. Gingerly, he gripped it with the metal hooks he now called hands, and began to pull. The furnace at his core flared and steam gushed from the vents on his back as he heaved with all his might, but it would not budge…

'I can't shift it!' he called down to the overseer.

'You'll shift it or you'll…' his superior began to say, but he was cut off by a voice calling out from above.

'What's going on here?'

Both the overseer and the engineer's heads whipped around and stared up at the gangway above them, upon which stood a sight that turned their blood cold.

'I said, what's happening here?' Malone demanded of his two subordinates, staring over the rail at them from his lofty position.

'Nothing, Boss – we're handling it,' the overseer replied nervously.

'Nothing?' Malone returned icily.

Standing silhouetted against the huge window at the front of the factory, Malone cut a fearsome figure. Unlike most of the Vipers, Malone's flesh was largely unblemished and his alterations relatively few. Besides the furnace at his core and the vents at his back, only his right arm had been replaced, and this had been with an exquisitely crafted, fully articulated mechanical limb with a humanoid hand, driven by a dizzying array of pistons and pipes that he now vastly preferred to his original appendage. But, even without this, he would have been terrifying to look upon; his sheer size and muscle mass made him appear like a mountain given human form, and the viper-shaped mask upon his head was the stuff of nightmares – jet black, riven with scars and with teeth like knives.

At his shoulder was an air mask, leading via a tube to a tank attached to his back, labelled C1. Malone gripped the mask, thrust it over his mouth and inhaled deeply, his irises flashing purple for a moment as the Rot coursed through his veins. Then he gripped the rail and vaulted it.

He landed on the factory floor in a crouch – cracks shooting out from the concrete beneath him – and advanced upon the two men, who cowered away from him in terrified silence. Malone took in the situation in a moment, spotting the blockage and the engineer's failed attempts to clear it. He gestured at the floor beside him.

'If you would be so kind,' he said, with false courtesy. The engineer nodded soundlessly and hopped down from the conveyer belt, but his feet had barely touched the floor before Malone had gripped him by the throat with his mechanical arm and raised him into the air.

He stared at the unfortunate man like he was something nasty on the sole of his shoe and when he spoke, bile dripped from every word.

'What good are you to me if you can't even clear a simple blockage…?' he asked, as the engineer struggled and gasped.

Malone stared at him a moment longer, then – with a simple tightening of his hold – he had crushed the man's throat to a pulp. Instantly limp, Malone dropped him to the floor then stepped over him and reached into the roller, grasping the chunk of metal in his iron grip and ripping it free in a heartbeat.

The alarm that had been continuously ringing instantly fell quiet as the conveyer belt got back up to speed, and the machine resumed its work.

Malone turned back to the horrified overseer, but he did not seem to see him. Instead, he reached behind him and detached the canister from his back so that he could look at it. His human hand stroked the C1 label upon it and he sighed with pleasure.

'What a happy accident you were…' he whispered under his breath. 'What a stroke of unintentional genius… Who'd have thought fire could bring about such a miraculous transformation…'

As he said this, his hand reached up beneath his mask and traced the burn scars that covered the whole left side of his face – a reminder of a mistake made, and a new path discovered.

He reattached the canister to his back and looked up at the overseer, who was now fidgeting nervously.

'Th… thank you, Boss,' he stammered. 'It won't happen again…'

Malone stepped towards him and the man flinched away, but Malone simply took him gently by the shoulder and began to lead him along.

'I still marvel at what we've built, what we've achieved,' Malone said as they crossed the factory floor, his gaze taking in the complex machinery, the barrels of Rot, the stills and the canisters. His foot came into contact with something, and he picked it up without breaking stride.

'They call it "Rot", but we Vipers know better,' he continued, staring at the purple shard of crystal in his hand. 'It is a Cypher, and only we have the courage and fortitude to see its true potential.'

Malone began to lead the unwilling overseer up a flight of metal stairs toward a gangway above.

'It breaks my heart that none of the other Clans can see its real worth; that they cannot see the great benefit it could have for them all – how it could elevate us above what we were before, what we could *ever* have been without it.'

They reached the top of the stairs and began to continue along the gangway to a set of double doors ahead.

'It truly beggars belief that they would fight and struggle and die to rid the world of something that has only made us better, only made us smarter – that has given us so many *incredible* technological advancements… and that has so much more yet to give.'

They reached the door and Malone opened it, ushering the overseer through ahead of him. On the other side, they found themselves upon a platform high up in a cavernous warehouse, hemmed in by a sturdy railing. The overseer leant upon the railing and looked out, and – although he had seen all this before – he was still staggered by what he saw.

Malone gripped the railing beside him as he too looked out upon the marvel below with barely contained excitement and anticipation.

'So, it falls to me then to show them. If they will not choose to see its potential willingly, then there is always another way…' he whispered, and with that he hurled the overseer from the platform, where he landed on the concrete several stories below with a wet smack.

'Finish him,' Malone barked, watching as several heavily modified Viper soldiers fell upon the stricken man, his gaze drifting away from the melee to take in the rank upon rank of soldiers, vehicles and killing machines of all sorts – his army for the war to come…

CHAPTER 7
Friendly Faces

Clara had thought she would be happy to finally be free of that dreary, dying forest, but once out from beneath its canopy she fervently wished for it back, for there was now nothing to obstruct her view of the churning, blood-red sky above that made her weak at the knees with every step. As much as she tried not to look at it, her gaze was drawn magnetically back time and time again until she took to walking with a hand shaded over her eyes to block it out.

They had exited the forest some time ago and swiftly scrambled down into the base of a steep-sided and long since dried-up riverbed where they would – in Vincent's words – be 'Less visible to unfriendly eyes.'

He had briefly explained to her that this river had once been a huge source of life and prosperity to the area, serving many Clans and countless animals for miles around. Then the Rot had arrived and cut off the river at its source, forcing everything existing along its length to move on, or die… and the death it had caused was visible everywhere she looked. Not a single splash of greenery met her eyes, not one living being besides herself and Vincent did she see, but of one thing there was plenty of… bodies…

The bones of many a creature scattered the dry and dusty riverbed everywhere she looked. What exactly they had died of she would never know, but the scale of death that the loss of this river had brought was mind-boggling, and it tugged at her heart with every new discovery she made.

To take her mind off the horrible sights all around, she again made her plea to Vincent he had earlier refused: 'We must be far enough away by now – will you please let me look at your wound?'

Vincent, who still seemed tense and alert as he marched along several paces ahead, looked back at her briefly, then glanced down at the wound on his shoulder that was oozing blood over his meticulously tailored suit.

'There's no time – I'll deal with it when we meet the others,' he replied shortly.

Clara looked exasperated at this, but already knew better than to argue. Instead, she decided to ask the question he had been too distracted to answer during their initial flight from the battle.

'Then, tell me… who is Malone? And who are the Vipers? And… and why do they not want your world saved…?'

For a moment he did not respond, and she began to wonder if he had heard her, or if he was perhaps deliberately ignoring the question, but then he spoke, and when he did his voice seemed distant, his gaze vacant and unfocussed.

'The Viper, they... they were once an important ally of the Wolves – of all the Clans – and Malone, he... he was my closest friend...' Here Vincent fell silent for a moment before he gathered himself enough to continue. 'We had known each other since we were boys – we grew up together, mastered Shifting together, and both became fascinated with learning about the Rot. And for Malone, that... that was where it started... You see... when the Rot first arrived – long before my time – the Clans were united in a common goal of discovering what ailed Comhlacht, to help heal it and return it to its former glory. The best minds came together to solve this terrible puzzle and – not long after discovering the Rot at the core of our world – we discovered the cause... We found a link... a link to another place – a place this Rot was flowing in from, but we had no idea how to stop it...'

Clara listened to all this with wide-eyed curiosity and sadness as she trailed in Vincent's wake, glad for something to focus on other than the death all around her.

'Both Malone and myself were born into this period of searching for an answer,' Vincent continued, his voice hollow. 'Our respective parents had been engaged in the search themselves, and they passed their fervour down to us, and once we were old enough to begin researching it ourselves, it consumed us – for who would not want to be the saviour of their people? Of all peoples…?' A brief look of shame flitted across his face, but was gone in an instant.

'This search became our whole lives,' he resumed, 'from boy to man, and it must have been, hmm… maybe twenty years ago when Malone made his discovery…'

Clara, who by now had caught up to Vincent and walked squarely at his side, looked up at him.

'What discovery…?' she asked.

'I do not know the exact details,' Vincent began, 'only Malone himself knows what really happened – but what I do know is… there was a fire…'

'A fire…?' Clara echoed in little more than a whisper. Vincent nodded.

'We had already learned that there are two forms of the Rot,' he continued. 'It begins as a liquid, but it swiftly crystallizes on contact with our atmosphere into an impure form. Malone had managed to procure some of the liquid Rot and was performing experiments on it in his lab in the Viper city Inchinn, when – and no one but he truly knows how – a fire broke out and rapidly spread…'

As he said this, Vincent gripped his cane tightly in his fist and Clara could tell that it pained him to relate the story, but she had to know how it ended.

'The fire it… it almost killed him – it *should* have killed him – but he survived, and in so doing he made his discovery; he learned what is produced when the Rot is heated to extreme temperatures…'

'What was it…?' Clara asked in a hushed voice.

'Something diabolical,' Vincent replied quietly. 'A discovery that should never have been made – a transformative inhalant that soon spelled the end of our alliance with the Viper and… and the end of my friendship with my closest companion… For you see… the gas produced from heating either form of the Rot has the effect of boosting both the strength and intellect of any who inhale it, and for a short time Malone felt sure he had found the means to finally solve the question that had plagued the Clans for so long – that now he would, at long last, have the mental capacity to figure out a way to rid our world of this Rot. But then he… he began to change…'

Vincent let out a long, shuddering breath and Clara immediately felt guilty for asking him about any of this. She put a hand on his arm comfortingly.

'I'm sorry,' she said gently. 'You don't have to go on if…'

'I'm… I'm fine, thank you…' Vincent cut across her. He took another deep breath before continuing with his story. 'When Malone first came to me with his discovery, I could see at once that he was different – there was a light in his eyes that unnerved me, and when he asked me to try this gas he had created I flatly refused, and I ensured no other Wolves tried it either, for we had no idea what the side effects would be… But we soon did…' A barely contained shiver passed through Vincent then, which Clara could not fail to miss. 'With his newfound intellect, Malone rapidly rose through the ranks in the Viper society, and he swiftly made the use of the gas a part of his Clan's daily lives, whilst pioneering many unbelievable new inventions that catapulted them forwards technologically, leaving every other Clan to play catch-up via reverse-engineering what they could.' Here Vincent's hand slid unconsciously to the remaining gadgets at his belt. 'Before long he found himself at the head of the Viper Clan, but he was about to learn the price of his advancements – for the gas exacts a horrible toll… Yes, it increases strength and intellect, but it also causes the body to wear out far, far quicker than normal – necessitating those mechanical replacement parts you saw. But worse than this – worse than the fact that it also killed their ability to Shift – is that it warps and distorts the mind as much as it enhances it, and soon the reason he had been researching the Rot in the first place was forgotten. He no longer wanted to rid our world of it – he wanted to *spread its message*. He started referring to it as the "Cypher", like it was some code or puzzle only he could understand, and began trying to convert the other Clans to its use, and any who refused he… he annihilated…'

Here Clara gasped in shock.

'The first we heard about was Boar Clan,' Vincent whispered, forcing Clara to lean in to catch what he said. 'He offered them his Cypher, they refused, and

his killing machines wiped them from existence…
We have been at war with the Viper ever since…'

'I'm so, so sorry…' Clara murmured.

'I've seen Malone only once since the war
began,' Vincent continued dully, 'and I almost did
not recognise him – if there was any trace of the
person I grew up with left in there then I… I could
not see it. When he made his offer for me to join
him it broke my heart, for we had made a pact as
boys to always have each other's backs through
whatever came our way, but how could I hold true
to that after what he had done…? After what he
had become…?'

Here Vincent lapsed into silence once more, and
it was obvious that he had said all he would on the
subject. Clara had enough sensitivity not to press
him further at that time, so they continued on along
the desolate riverbed in silence, with Clara mulling
over everything she had been told.

Time slipped away as they walked, for it was
impossible to tell day from night beneath the
hellscape above, but soon Clara began to feel the
distance they had covered as an aching weariness
in her limbs, her once churning thoughts becoming
slow and dulled as tiredness eroded her. She was
reaching her limit and about to break the silence
and ask Vincent for a rest when he raised an arm
and pointed at something up ahead.

'We're here,' was all he said.

With an effort, Clara awkwardly raised her head from its stubborn downward slant and took in the sight that awaited them at the end of the extinct river. A sheer cliff blocked their path, disappearing into the distance to their left and right, while the riverbed itself appeared to continue along the plateau above. The cliff was of a jet-black stone, worn smooth above the river by the passage of water over many hundreds of years, and wherever Clara looked she saw dark, decaying vines hanging down from any crack or crevice they could cling to. It was an imposing sight, and appeared – to Clara at least – to be completely impassable...

'I am told a beautiful waterfall once existed here,' Vincent said as he took it all in sorrowfully. 'Namara's Falls it was known as. Many Clans used to come here to perform rites or receive blessings – it was considered a holy place... But now...' He trailed off as he came to a halt not far from the base of the cliff.

As Clara stopped by his side and looked up, she felt like she could almost see the waterfall as it once was; feel the cool, fresh spray on her face, see the diamonds of sunlight sparkling on its surface and hear it crashing down with all the power and earnestness of life. It reminded her again just how much this world had lost to the Rot – how much it had taken from them – and still it wanted more.

At that moment, a howl echoed out from somewhere nearby, and Clara froze in shock. At her side, Vincent had Shifted in an instant and was howling back a response of his own and right then Clara fervently wished she could understand their wolf tongue, for she had no idea if they were friend or foe.

She stared at the base of the cliff where the howl had come from and swiftly realised that what she was looking at was not in fact rock at all, it was a cave... and within this cave she could now discern two dark shapes striding slowly towards them, one small and low like Vincent in his wolf form, and the other big and hulking that moved with an odd, rolling gait.

Clara looked anxiously over at Vincent for reassurance, but his eyes were fixed only on the smaller of the two shapes, and he did not even glance at her. So, instead, she strained her eyes, staring into the gloom, and had to work hard to stifle her surprise when she realised what they were. It was another wolf, slightly smaller than Vincent and of a much fairer shade of grey, while walking alongside it was a great, towering mass of scarred muscle and fur – a bear...

Clara's eyes widened in fright as she stared at it – she had never seen a bear in real life before, but decided that they were much bigger in person than the pictures in her books had led her to believe.

As the wolf and bear exited the cave into the dry riverbed, Vincent suddenly bounded forward joyfully, and the other wolf did the same. They met a few paces away from Clara and interlocked their heads, each resting lovingly on the other's shoulder, and Clara was reminded forcefully of how her parents would greet each other after time spent apart.

When they had felt each other's closeness for a few moments longer, they drew apart and, as if on cue, they both Shifted, and Clara wondered if she would ever get used to seeing it, for where the other wolf had been there was suddenly a tall, beautiful woman standing before Vincent. Like him, she was wearing an immaculately tailored three-piece grey suit and on her head was a snarling, snow-white wolf mask with a pelt of white wolf fur at her shoulders, from beneath which a shock of fiery, bright red hair could be seen trailing down her back. At her belt, Clara could see many gadgets like Vincent's, as well as the bulge of a revolver at her right hip and some form of long-bladed weapon at her left.

Clara had barely had time to take this in when the bear at the woman's side reared up on its hind legs and Shifted, and Clara was amazed to see that the man who took its place was – if anything – bigger than the bear shape he had left behind. She had never seen a man so huge before and had to stop herself from gawping at him. He was wearing a dark brown suit – of a much poorer quality than Vincent or the woman's – with no tie, beneath a long, tan-coloured duster coat that trailed past his knees. On his head was a mask like Vincent's, but painted black and in the shape of a roaring bear, and down his back ran a pelt of black bear fur. On both hands he was wearing what appeared to be gauntlets with sharpened metal spikes like claws at each knuckle, and at his belt Clara could see the tell-tale sign of some form of firearm. All in all, the three of them made quite a sight, and it suddenly made Clara feel very small, and strangely alone.

There was a moment's silence before the man who had been the bear stepped forward and looked down at Vincent from his lofty viewpoint, his expression morose.

'You're late,' was all he said, as he continued to stare at him. Vincent cleared his throat.

'Yes, well... we ran into a spot of bother on the way,' he replied without looking at the other man, his eyes never leaving the woman opposite. The bear man spotted the wound on Vincent's shoulder at the same time the woman did.

'I can see that...' he said slowly. 'Darius?' Vincent nodded in response as the woman leant forward to look at the wound, trying valiantly to hide her concern.

'Must be slowing down if you let one of Darius' crew do this to you,' she said with a quick smile and a glance at him. 'Sit down and let me look at it.' For a moment it seemed like Vincent would resist, but then he relented and sat down on a rock, shrugging off his jacket and waistcoat as he went.

'And the shirt too,' she said, tapping her foot. This time Vincent didn't even think about fighting and obeyed instantly, unbuttoning his shirt and slipping it off his shoulder so she could get a proper look. Anxiously, Clara stepped forward and hissed through her teeth as she saw the injury he had sustained – it was several inches long and had torn open about half an inch wide, the flesh turning an angry red around it.

The woman, however, merely tutted and patted him on the back in mock consolation.

'Ah, it's barely a scratch, you big pansy,' she said. 'I've had worse than that clipping my toenails, but I'll patch you up. Hold still.' While she acted unfazed, Clara could tell at once that there was real tenderness behind the bravado as she reached into her belt and began to pull out various items to clean and stitch the wound.

'Something's brewing,' the bear man said. 'I can feel it. Darius' troops have been spotted all over the past few days. Where did you meet them?'

Vincent winced in pain as the woman dabbed at his wound with a cloth.

'Over by Mikal's cabin, I…' But the bear man cut across him angrily.

'You went back there? I thought we agreed never to…' But this time Vincent interrupted him.

'It was raining, Garret, and Clara was freezing! She…' Here Vincent stopped himself and suddenly looked over at Clara with a guilty expression. 'But where are my manners? Clara, please forgive me – I haven't yet made formal introductions.' He pointed up at the bear man.

'This morose, mountain of a man is Garret of the Bear Clan, son of their Chief.' Garret spared her a momentary glance – his expression grim – before his gaze slid away from her, and Clara had the funny feeling that she had offended him in some way.

'And this…' Vincent looked up at the woman who had begun stitching him up and locked eyes with her for a moment. 'This is my partner – Elizabeth.'

Elizabeth looked over at Clara and smiled warmly at her.

'It's El to my friends,' she said, and she held out a hand to Clara. Clara was about to shake it when she saw that it was covered in Vincent's blood, and she hesitated. Noticing this, El swiftly rubbed it off on her trousers then re-presented it for shaking. 'Oops, sorry about that. Husbands, eh? Always bleeding everywhere!' Clara smiled back and shook her hand.

'Nice to meet you, El,' she said shyly.

'Likewise,' El replied, returning to her stitching. 'I bet he's told you all about me and the kids, has he?' she added jokingly.

Clara looked over at Vincent in surprise.

'No, he… he never mentioned you…' she said quietly. El finished her stitching then bit off the remaining length of thread.

'Sorry – that was my natural sarcasm kicking in,' she said as she wrapped a bandage around the wound. 'Vincent's usually more of the "strong silent type" – if he's said more than a few words to you then you're honoured.' Here Vincent rolled his eyes as he tugged his shirt back on and began to button it up.

'So… you have children?' Clara asked.

'We have three,' El replied distractedly, as she put away her things in her belt. 'The oldest – Sisi – is fourteen and has already completed her Convergence, and then there's the twins – Bella and Ty – both eleven, so probably around your age? They all want to be warriors just like their…' But she never got to finish her sentence, for Garret had cut her off.

'We don't have time for this,' he said sternly, causing El to throw him a withering look. 'You can swap your stories on the road.' He turned to Vincent – who was now pulling on his waistcoat and jacket – and fixed him with a hard stare.

'What's your plan here, Vincent?' he continued, raising an arm to point at Clara. 'You're not seriously telling me you're still persisting with this fantasy?'

Under the weight of Garret's attention, Clara felt smaller and more insignificant than she had ever felt.

'What you're trying to do with her and the others, it… it's like trying to empty the ocean with a bucket,' Garret growled in anger and bewilderment. 'You must see that…?'

Vincent got suddenly to his feet and stepped towards Garret.

'Oh, I must, must I…?' he snarled back.

El sidled away and knelt beside Clara, leaning against her in a comradely way.

'Ooh, look, the men are getting fighty,' she murmured so only Clara could hear. 'What an incredibly unexpected turn of events.' Seeing that Clara looked anxious and upset, El put an arm around her and drew her close.

'Don't worry,' she continued, looking at her comfortingly. 'Garret's roar is worse than his bite. Anyway, this argument goes back way before any of our lifetimes and isn't going to get solved now.'

'Then… how…?' Clara asked. El looked at her and in her face Clara saw a strange mixture of hope and pity.

'Well – and not to put too fine a point on it – but hopefully… by you…'

Uncertain and afraid, Clara was about to reply when her thoughts were interrupted by Vincent and Garret.

'You don't need to believe in it,' Vincent was saying. 'You don't need to believe in her – you just need to help us get her to Croí.'

'So, that's where you're going,' Garret replied.

'Where else?' Vincent shot back. 'Why did you even agree to come here anyway?'

'Because he's never been one to pass up the chance for a fight,' El interjected, getting to her feet as Vincent and Garret turned to her. 'I think perhaps it's time we did as our illustrious Bear representative suggests and make a move, shall we…?'

'First sensible thing I've heard all day,' Garret agreed. 'But we can't go straight to Croí…'

'And why not…?' Vincent began angrily. Here Garret could not quite meet Vincent's eyes as he replied.

'The uh… the old man wants to see you,' he said slowly. Vincent growled in annoyance.

'We really don't have time for…'

'Neart isn't far out the way,' Garret butted in persistently.

'What's Neart?' Clara whispered to El.

'The Bear Clan's city,' she murmured back.

'It'll add no more than half a day – maybe a day at most,' Garret continued. 'Please, Vincent – he said it's important…'

They all turned to look at Vincent, and Clara could see that he was conflicted as he debated it internally. Finally, he relented.

'Fine, but we march all the faster once we leave,' he said.

'Wouldn't have it any other way,' Garret replied.

'Then let us quickly refresh ourselves and move on,' Vincent said.

As Garret and El unearthed a bag stashed nearby and opened it to reveal food and drink, Clara looked nervously up at the cliff that towered over them, blotting out the terrifying crimson sky above.

How on earth are we going to get past this…? she thought, a chill of apprehension rippling through her body.

CHAPTER 8
The Bears

'You're not… you're not serious… are you…?' Clara asked, trying and failing to keep the quaver out of her voice. 'I can't climb up that!' The mere thought of scaling the monstrous cliff made her feel lightheaded, but it was obvious that Vincent was not joking.

'You'll be perfectly safe,' Vincent reassured her. 'Garret will carry you on his back.'

'I'm not a mule,' Garret muttered, but Vincent ignored this.

'It's the only way forwards,' he continued. 'To go around it would add another day or more to our journey, and seeing as we're now detouring to Neart,' here he threw an annoyed look at Garret, 'every moment is precious to us.'

'Afraid of heights, are you?' El asked gently.

'I didn't think I was until I saw this…' Clara replied, swallowing nervously.

'Well, we're in the same boat then,' El said with a smile. 'And I can tell you that the way down here wasn't any more fun than the way up will be. But I'll be right with you the whole time – don't worry.'

'Then let's get to it,' Garret barked as he knelt with his back to Clara. 'Jump on up, girl.'

Even kneeling, Garret still dwarfed Clara standing, and it took her several attempts to climb onto the big man's back and wrap her arms and legs around him.

'Comfortable?' he asked her, once she was in place.

'Yes, thank you,' she said, not entirely truthfully.

'Well, that makes one of us,' he grumbled, bringing a blush to Clara's cheeks.

Before she had any chance to contemplate things further, Garret strode towards the cliff and looked up at the climb ahead, clashing his gauntlets together as he prepared himself. Glancing down for a moment, he tapped the heels of his boots on the floor and Clara could just about see as a metal spike shot out from beneath his toes on each. Looking to left and right, she saw Vincent and El do the same, then, before she knew it, they were climbing, and her stomach dropped away.

With her eyes squeezed shut, Clara clung on for grim life, her whole body shaking uncontrollably as the wind whipped them savagely and the ground receded below.

'Not so tight,' Garret growled. 'I still need to breathe, y'know.'

'Oops – sorry,' Clara stammered, fighting her instincts as she slackened her grip a little.

Dust and stones rained down on her as Garret heaved them slowly upwards, punching the claws of his gauntlets into any crack he spotted and stabbing the spikes on his boots in wherever he could. To Clara – as a passenger – the experience was nothing but pure, white-knuckle terror.

'We're about halfway now, Clara,' El called from a little way below them. 'You're doing great!'

And that was when things started to go wrong.

It began with a rumbling – like the earthquake Clara and Vincent had been through before – but this felt different, and Clara knew instinctively that it was bad.

'Oh, no… No, not now…' she heard Vincent hiss nearby. 'Climb faster – go!'

'I'm going!' Garret grunted back, putting on a burst of speed.

The rumbling intensified and Clara detected an odd, rushing, churning quality to it – like water passing through a pipe. Then it happened.

An arm's length away from where Garret and Clara were climbing, a crack began to form in the rock, swiftly growing and growing until – with the intensity of a cork popping out of a bottle – it burst open and a rush of liquid Rot spurted out, but it was only liquid for a moment and swiftly crystallised, leaving behind a huge and lethally sharp spur.

'Go! GO!' Vincent yelled from below as the three climbers pushed their bodies on harder than ever and more cracks began to form, shards of crystal Rot soon bursting out all around them.

'We're nearly at the top,' El yelled up. 'Just hold on tight, Clara!'

They were almost in reach of the plateau when disaster struck. A crack appeared right in front of Garret's face and on instinct he reacted, leaping to one side just as a spear of Rot burst through and narrowly missed him, but the sudden movement had dislodged Clara and she found herself – for a few horrifying, stomach-churning moments – freefalling through space.

She opened her mouth to scream, but all the air had been ripped from her lungs as the ground below filled her vision. Her arms reached up desperately but found nothing, then – miraculously – a hand gripped hers and she felt herself being swung upwards.

Somehow, El had caught her and she was now being hurled towards Vincent, who had stopped in his climb and was waiting, waiting to catch her, and he did so with a firm grip, immediately using her momentum to hurl her on up higher towards the plateau above – but it was not enough…

Clara could see that she was going to miss the edge by a whisker, and what was worse was that she was heading right for another crack forming in the rock ahead…

Time seemed to stand still as she watched the crack burst open and a lance of Rot hurtle out, and in the end, this was what saved her.

The Rot crystallised mere moments before she hit it and when she did she clung on like a limpet, then – with a strength born of terror – she hauled herself on top of it, reached up for the ledge, and tumbled over it in a heap.

Without wasting a moment, Clara was back up on her feet – if a little unsteadily – and had hurried back to the edge to check that the others were okay, petrified that they might have been shaken loose. She was relieved to see that all three of them were still struggling valiantly on and so she reached down and helped each of them up onto the plateau as the rumbling faded to nothing, and silence – other than their ragged breathing – fell over the land once more.

El was the last one up and she immediately folded Clara to her in a tight hug.

'Are you alright?' El asked, stroking her hair. 'You were so brave!'

'I'm… I'm fine…' Clara replied breathlessly. 'That was so scary! I'm never climbing anything again!'

'You and me both!' El smiled back. 'Climbing's for idiots – next time we take the long way round!' Clara giggled despite herself – despite the fact she was still trembling – as El released her from the hug and looked over at Vincent and Garret, who were both dusting themselves down.

'Where next, oh fearless navigator?' El asked her husband jokingly. 'Maybe we could try and wade through a field of lava? Or swim a river filled with piranhas?' Clara giggled again as Vincent threw a mock withering look at his spouse.

'If you want to pick the route the rest of the way then, please, be my guest,' he said, unable to keep a lopsided grin off his face.

'Challenge accepted!' El replied heartily. 'But mainly because I know it's a straight shot from here to Neart. If you two are done adjusting yourselves, shall we be on our way?'

Without waiting for a response, she took Clara gently by the shoulders and began to lead her off on the next stage of their journey, but, as she went, she glanced back at Vincent and the brave face she had put on for the young girl was replaced with a look that said: *That was too close.*

Trailing in their wake, Vincent – with Garret at his side – looked decidedly shaken at how close they had come to catastrophe.

'It's getting worse,' Garret muttered to him. 'Those breaches are becoming much more frequent…'

Vincent nodded grimly.

'Aye – we don't have long left…'

'Is that Neart?' Clara asked, squinting into the distance.

'You've got a good eye,' El praised her with a smile. 'It is indeed. We're almost there.'

They had been walking for many hours, the landscape around them a nondescript blur of arid plains and dying vegetation that – coupled with the never-changing sky above – had made Clara feel for a while like they were making no progress at all.

But now she could see the shape of what was clearly a city – surrounded by what appeared to be some kind of fortified wall – drawing closer and closer with every step they took.

'One word of warning,' El added, lowering her voice so only Clara could hear. 'Mind what you say to the Bears. They are a proud people – loyal and honest and brave – but they have been hit hard by the Rot, and it has brought them low. We offered them aid, but they… they refused it…'

Here El threw a swift glance at Garret, who was walking alongside Vincent.

'I have not visited Neart in some time,' she continued quietly, 'but whatever you may see… whatever you may hear… be respectful, and remember they were not always as they are now.'

Clara did not know how to respond, so instead simply nodded nervously.

They were walking down a long and poorly maintained dirt road, but now cut across a field that had clearly once borne crops – obvious from the long rigg and furrow pattern running its full length – but it was apparent that nothing had grown there in years. Tumbledown stone walls, barns and broken farming equipment were further testament to this as they drew up outside the main gate of Neart at last.

Garret stepped forward and cupped his hands around his mouth to yell up at the apparently unmanned wall top.

'Are you lot sleeping up there, or what? Get this gate open at once!'

A head appeared over the parapet as the wall guard peered down at them.

'Is that you, Garret?' the guard asked. 'No one told me you'd be back today.'

'Who the hell else would it be?' Garret barked up at him. 'Open this gate now before I kick it in and come give you something to complain about.'

With a morose grimace the guard disappeared, and a few moments later there came a series of muffled *clunks* from the other side of the gates, then they began to swing slowly open. Garret turned to Clara.

'Welcome to Neart,' he said with half-hearted courtesy and a feigned bow. 'The "great city of the Bears". I would say that I hope you enjoy your time here, but there has been little to enjoy in recent years.'

As the gate clattered fully open, he turned and began to walk inside, calling back over his shoulder: 'Follow me.'

El could see that Clara was nervous, and so she reached down and clasped her hand, giving it a gentle squeeze.

'I'll be at your side the whole time,' she whispered comfortingly. Clara smiled up at her and gave her hand a squeeze back, as she, El and Vincent followed Garret inside, the gates slamming shut behind them, pushed by the sour-faced wall guard.

Clara was not sure what she'd expected the Bear city to look like, but this was not it. A thrill of pity ran through her body as she looked about, taking in the drab and dismal surroundings.

The first thing that hit her was the abnormal quiet. Usually in a city there would be chatter – the hustle and bustle of everyday life – but here, and even with people almost everywhere she looked, she heard almost nothing.

As they walked down the uneven cobbled road from the gate, faces turned all around to look at them, and Clara was struck by just how desolate – how devoid of life and light – their expressions were behind their masks. Tired, grim, mistrustful eyes looked out at them from gaunt, dirty faces as the Bear people went about their jobs with little pleasure or enthusiasm. Most of them seemed to be working in the fields either side of the road leading from the gate to the city proper, and from the look of the harvest the only thing that would grow there was the hardiest of root vegetables.

In some places she spotted people in their bear forms, using their enhanced strength to tow ploughs or pull carts, and even in their animal shapes they looked weak and malnourished.

Shocked and saddened, Clara glanced up at El, who squeezed her hand reassuringly once again, but this did nothing to raise her spirits. A dark cloud hung over this community, and clearly had for some time…

Looking over her shoulder, Clara could see that the wall they had passed through appeared to have been thrown together hastily – to protect their city and their crops – and then patched and reinforced over time. She was about to ask El about it when she realised that she knew the answer: *It was constructed when the war with the Viper began...*

They left the fields behind and entered a narrow street on the outskirts of the city where tall, poorly constructed buildings oppressively hemmed them in on either side, many of them jutting out over the road or listing at crazy angles that made Clara fear to walk below them. It reminded her of a trip to York her family had once taken, where they had visited the famous street known as "The Shambles" and it had left an indelible mark on her memory.

As they made their way deeper into the city, Clara's nostrils were suddenly assailed by the stink of raw sewage, and she was hard pressed not to gag as she noticed rivers of the stuff running down the gutters either side of the road. She scrunched up her nose in disgust, but then realised that they were being watched from doorways and windows on either side, and quickly tried to hide her distaste, lest she appear rude in front of the Bears. She felt heat rising in her cheeks under the watchful eyes of so many, their expressions morose and listless to the last.

To take her mind off their staring she focussed on the city itself, noticing many more narrow streets branching off from theirs as well as various shops, including a grocer, a chemist and a blacksmith, where a tough-looking woman in a long leather apron was beating a piece of metal on an anvil with a disinterested monotony.

Clara found it hard to believe just how many buildings they had managed to cram into such a small area. Space was clearly at a premium here, which was why many of them were such odd shapes, having been built up and out to compensate for their tiny footprint.

Ahead, Garret took a sharp left and they followed him to find themselves in a much wider and busier street near the centre of the city, at the end of which stood a large structure that looked to Clara like some sort of town hall. The buildings here seemed to be of a higher quality than on the outskirts, and much better maintained, but they still showed little architectural flair or zeal.

Bear people bustled to and fro all around them, their outfits a drab array of ill-fitting Victorian-style suits, dresses and overalls that seemed to perfectly match the low moods of their wearers, their bear masks the only things that provided any real individuality. Here and there, Clara spotted a few people dressed like Garret, and realised that they must be their soldiers, for every one of them carried weapons.

Even here it was unnaturally quiet – there was the low hum of conversation, the odd monotonal yell from a merchant selling wares and the rumble of carts moving on the cobbles, but it spoke volumes as to the morale of this city's people.

They were nearing the large building at the end of the street when El leant down to whisper to Clara.

'This is the headquarters of the Bear's ruler, Chief Davin – Garret's father,' she said quietly. 'If you thought *he* was a bit of a grump then, well… You've seen nothing yet.'

Clara smiled nervously.

'Do you know why he wants to see Vincent?' Clara asked, glancing at him as he strode along beside Garret, the two of them deep in quiet conversation.

'Not for certain, but I have an inkling,' El replied. 'Now remember, be respectful, and it may be best not to speak unless spoken to – Davin is not a patient man.'

Clara nodded as they reached the steps outside the headquarters and began to ascend them to the main door.

Without knocking, Garret barged inside and held the doors open so Vincent, El and Clara could enter a large and echoing hallway. Like the rest of the city there was no trace of opulence here – no marble floor or pillars, no lush fabrics or vibrant colours – just a simple stone floor, whitewashed walls and plain wooden doors. It was obvious to Clara that they were a people who did not value such things – a people for whom extravagance meant very little, or nothing at all.

A pair of guards – dressed like Garret – stood either side of a set of double doors ahead, and it was to these that Garret marched.

'Is he in?' he barked at one of the guards.

'When is he not?' the man grunted back. To this, Garret merely nodded as he approached the doors and – this time – stopped to knock.

'Enter,' a voice boomed from within.

Before he did so, Garret gave Vincent a meaningful look. It was a look Clara did not understand, for it was almost apologetic, but then he had turned away and thrust open the doors, holding them wide to admit their entry.

Clara was ushered forth in front of El and found herself in a modest little office. The room had a few more creature comforts than the hall, including a small fireplace, some leather upholstered chairs, a couple of bookshelves and at the centre of the room was a large and – by Bear standards – ornately carved desk upon which writing implements, stacks of paper, letters and other administrative odds and ends were neatly arranged.

But it was not these items that held Clara's gaze; no, it was the large, heavy-set man standing with his back to them in front of the fireplace, within which a meagre blaze crackled. He was a man from whom strength and authority exuded like a physical force; the kind of person who could hold your attention without ever even saying a word.

As they came to a stop in front of his desk, Garret stepped forward to address his father.

'Chief, I've brought…' But Davin cut across his son with a quiet animosity before he'd had chance to finish speaking.

'I know who it is,' Davin said in a low voice. 'I can smell Wolves from a mile away.'

At this causal insult, El raised an elbow and sniffed her armpit.

'Was the walk here really that long?' she asked Clara in a stage whisper, and Clara had to fight hard not to giggle.

Davin spun around to face them, and Clara got her first proper look at him. He was a well-built man – not overweight exactly, but clearly not in his prime either. He was dressed in neat dark brown suit trousers and waistcoat over a spotless white shirt that was rolled up to the elbows and complimented by a black tie. His face was deep-set and craggy behind a fearsome bear mask like his son's, but this one was chocolate brown, and down his back ran a bear pelt of the same colour. A large but neatly trimmed beard – that was now much more white than grey – jutted out from beneath the mask and there was a tobacco pipe clamped between his lips that trailed thin smoke.

'What took you so long to find him?' he demanded of his son, ignoring El's quip. Garret glanced at his friend.

'Vincent had a run-in with some of Darius' crew,' he replied evenly. 'And there was another breach – this one over by Namara's Falls.'

'They're only going to get more frequent,' Davin replied darkly. 'Unless we do something…'

Here Davin turned to Vincent and fixed him with a silent, piercing stare. When the silence became too uncomfortable, Vincent finally spoke.

'You wanted to see me, Chief?' he prompted, his tone level but his eyes betraying a hint of anger – he already knew what this was about. For a moment Davin still said nothing, and Clara was beginning to wonder if he had even heard Vincent, when he finally responded.

'I did,' Davin replied at last. 'I wanted to ask if you'd finally come to your senses?' Here Vincent's expression darkened. 'If you and the other Wolves might finally see reason and agree with us on the course of action we should take – the course of action we *need* to take if we're to have any chance of saving our world!'

Here he looked over at Clara and she felt herself shrink before his intense glare.

'But I see now that you have not,' he said with a barely contained growl of rage. 'I see that you are still clinging to your old delusions – you are still blinded by good intentions while our world crumbles around you! You will be the death of us all!'

Vincent stepped forward now, his hands balled into fists and a snarl on his lips.

'Our course is the only real choice!' he fired back. 'It is – and always was – the *only* option we could pursue! If we do as you propose then nothing would ever change – nothing would ever get better, and our world would stay as it is now for the rest of time!'

'But at least we would still have a world!' Davin roared back. 'At least we would still have somewhere to raise our children!'

'What are they arguing about?'

Clara had meant to say this so that only El could hear, but in the sudden ringing silence after Davin finished speaking, everyone in the room heard. Mortified, Clara clapped a hand over her mouth, but it was too late to retract her words.

Vincent, softening a little, turned to look at her.

'I'm sorry, Clara,' he began. 'This must make little sense to you. This, uh… *discussion* has been going on between our Clans for many decades now. You remember how I told you that during the early research into the Rot we found a link to another a place – a place where the Rot is flowing in from?'

Clara nodded, still looking hugely embarrassed.

'Well…' he continued. 'Opinion differs over how to deal with this link… You see, we found a way to sever it entirely – to stop the flow of Rot into our world…'

'Then… why don't you?' Clara asked, mystified.

'Yes, why don't we…?' Davin hissed furiously.

'The Bear believe the link should be severed as soon as possible,' Garret explained to Clara, a little more evenly-toned than his father. 'We believe that we must cut off the Rot's ability to enter our world, and eradicate the Viper Clan before they can subjugate or destroy any more of its people.'

'And in so doing our world would never recover,' Vincent said, looking now at Davin once more. 'With the link gone there would be no way to remove the Rot and this cancer would forever remain at its heart.'

'But it would also never worsen,' Davin put in, a fire still behind every word.

'While that is believed to be true, the Wolves feel differently about it,' El cut in. 'We have always felt that our best hope is to find a way to remove the Rot first – to send it back where it came from – then sever the link so it can never again return, and our world can be given the chance to heal...'

'And every day we waste on your wild flights of fancy our world gets sicker and sicker!' Davin added hotly. 'We should sever the link and kill the Viper now!'

'But we cannot do it without the Wolves help,' Garret said, speaking to Clara but looking at Vincent. 'Our forces are strong and brave, but they are no match for Malone's technology.'

'But they can still be saved!' Vincent yelled fervently. 'The Viper are not past all hope! If we are able to remove the Rot I know that they will recover – just like our world will!'

'You only want to save your friend!' Garret snapped back, showing true anger for the first time in this exchange.

'Malone has nothing to do with this!' Vincent replied. 'I have always believed this is the best course for all – and I now know that we have found the key to it.'

Here he moved to stand beside Clara and placed a hand on her shoulder.

'Clara is different to all the others,' he continued, making Clara's stomach turn over. 'I know it! She is the one who will finally help loosen the Rot's hold on this world so that we can banish it forever! She is the one to save us!'

At this, Davin chuckled – a cold, mirthless sound – and all at once Clara felt as weak and small and useless as she had ever felt. Thoughts she had held at bay for a while lanced across her mind once more:

Why do they think I can help them?

How *am I supposed to help them?*

In that moment she retreated inside herself – retreated from the terrible unreality of her situation – and saw again through her mind's eye the book resting upon the table in the darkened room, its pages sealed by a heavy padlock, but this time it was closer... She knew her darkest secret resided within its pages, and knew too that it threw everything that was happening into question – for how could *any* of this be real…?

As Davin continued to chuckle, Vincent spun on his heel and marched out of the room without another word. Clara, looking shocked and scared, and El, looking unsurprised, followed them, while Garret glanced helplessly between the two groups.

Once back outside, Garret caught up to them and stepped in front of Vincent.

'I'm sorry,' he said quickly. 'That was not how I hoped that would go. It would be best not to leave things like that… Please, stay at my house tonight – my wife is out on patrol, so it's all yours. I'll speak to the Chief, and maybe we can all talk again in the morning…?' There was a note of real pleading in his voice that Clara had never heard there before. Vincent looked undecided for a moment, then nodded.

'Thank you for the hospitality – we will gladly accept for tonight,' he began. 'As for speaking to your father again… we shall see…'

Garret nodded in return, then hurried back into the headquarters while Vincent, El and Clara set off for Garret's house.

So many thoughts and questions were swirling inside Clara's mind that she barely remembered the journey there. Before she knew it, she had been led into a bedroom by El, tucked into a small but neatly made bed, and the instant her head hit the pillow she was asleep, and dreaming of times past…

CHAPTER 9
The Dancing School

Clara hopped from foot to foot as she stared eagerly up at her father, her ballet shoes clutched tightly against her chest, her eyes wide and excited.

'Is it time to go yet?' she asked for what must have been the hundredth time. Joseph Brown sighed in mock exasperation and looked down at his daughter, who had not stopped fidgeting for the past hour and a half. Leaping, twirling and throwing her arms into rather awkward postures – that she clearly believed were balletic – Clara had in fact barely sat still all week and had talked of nothing else.

'No, it's not quite time yet,' he replied wearily, giving the same answer he had used each and every time she asked. Clara continued to prance around the kitchen, but after a particularly energetic attempt at a pirouette almost resulted in her thumping her father in a tender area, he asked her to go and play in the other room. She turned on the spot and glided towards the living room. At least, her intention was to glide, but her movements were so graceless that she looked more like a foal trying to stand on ice. On several occasions she almost tripped as she attempted to dance and walk at the same time.

'I still can't believe she's so taken with the idea of ballet classes,' Joseph said to his wife, who had been watching the scene fondly from her seat at the kitchen table, whilst absent-mindedly darning some old socks. 'This is a girl who spends most of her afternoons playing football with the boys in her class. I've seen her. She once tackled a lad two years older than her, and made him cry! I never thought in a million years she would be even remotely interested in ballet.'

'Well, she's getting older, Joe,' Emily replied. 'Tastes change – the main thing is that she's happy.'

'Aye, she is that,' Joseph agreed, seating himself opposite his wife. He picked up a russet apple from a bowl and took a huge bite, spraying juice down his chin and across the table. He wiped it off with the back of his hand and looked guiltily at his wife, who was giving him a disapproving stare.

'Sorry, love,' he said sheepishly. He took another, smaller bite and swallowed it. 'Have you seen the way Clara's holding on to those ballet shoes?' he asked with a grin. 'You'd think they were made of gold or something.'

'I think anything you give her becomes precious to her,' his wife replied, laying a repaired sock on the table in front of her and starting on another. 'Where did you get them from anyway?' Joseph glanced around the room furtively before answering.

'A second hand shop a few streets away,' he said in an undertone. 'But please don't tell Clara. This is one of those occasions where I wish I could have bought her brand-new ones, but the foreman at the mine says there's trouble over in America that might affect us soon, and so – at least until it's passed – I just think we should be extra careful with our money. Anyway,' he continued, speaking more loudly now, 'I cleaned them up as best I could and they look alright, don't they?' Emily leaned in close to him and placed her hand over his.

'Joe, she would love them even if they had claws and smelt of dead cats. It's the fact that you gave them to her that she treasures them.'

'Thanks, dear,' he said, smiling at her.

At that moment, Clara bounded into the room and stopped in front of her father. She opened her mouth to speak, but he cut across her:

'No, it's not time to leave yet, but... we will anyway if you'll just give me a minute.' Her face lit up as her father leaned down towards her and placed his hands gently on her shoulders.

'Now, you do realise that we can only take you dancing once a week, right?' he asked his daughter, who nodded fervently.

'Yes, I know,' she replied with a smile.

'Your mother and I would like to take you more than that, but we just don't have the money at the moment. That might change in the future, but for now you'll just have to make do. Alright?'

'Yes,' she replied simply, and Joseph could tell that she was so excited she was barely listening.

'Go get your shoes on and we'll leave in a minute.'

Needing no further bidding, Clara hurried off to find her shoes which, as usual, she had misplaced somewhere.

'Are you ready to go too?' Joseph asked his wife. She had some pins in her mouth and did not answer straight away. She completed one final stitch and laid the sock on the table, pulling the pins from her mouth and putting them back into the small container she kept them in.

'Now I am,' she answered cheerily.

It was a fine day outside, and as they walked down the street to the dancing school, they passed many other people enjoying the weather. There were old folks out for a stroll, girls playing hopscotch, boys kicking a football around the green, and families having picnics by the river. Normally, Clara would have asked to join in with the football, but ballet seemed to have driven all else from her mind and she barely even registered the fact they were playing. So, when the ball suddenly flew across the road and rolled to a stop in front of them, it was up to her father to kick it back, as Clara's eyes were fixed straight ahead on the place where the dancing school lay, and she was oblivious to all else around her.

High above them the sky was as blue as a robin's egg, and clouds scudded serenely across it, driven by a light breeze. It was one of those days where they seemed to take on rough shapes, that are filled in with detail by the imagination of those who witness them.

'See that cloud, Clara?' her father asked, pointing up into the sky. 'It looks like one of those wolves from your picture book.'

Clara merely flicked her gaze up for a split second before fixing her eyes back on the spot where the dancing school lay. Joseph glanced across at his wife and shrugged, giving her a bemused look. He still could not comprehend his daughter's sudden and unshakeable urge to dance.

When they neared the dancing school, Clara began to tug harder on her father's hand, dragging him on and up the steps into the large and echoing building. They found themselves in a hall with a dusty, wood-panelled floor that squeaked plaintively as they walked across it. Looking around, Clara noticed that most of the walls were covered by tall mirrors that were split in two by polished wooden handrails. Several little girls were already there, dressed in leotards and ballet shoes, and they were using the railings to balance as they performed stretches. Clara continued to look around the hall and saw a massive window set into the furthest wall. Rays of sunlight passed through the panes of glass, daubing golden squares on the wooden floor and picking out the individual motes of dust that danced on the air, for all the world as though they wished to join in.

A jovial looking woman in her early forties, who – until a moment ago – had been standing speaking to another girl's parents, walked over to them and shook hands with Mr and Mrs Brown.

'Ah, you must be the Browns,' she said smiling at all of them, 'and you must be Clara. I'm very pleased to meet you. I'm Mrs Andrews.'

'Pleased to meet you too,' Clara said automatically, still staring excitedly around the hall. 'When do we start?' she added, her attention suddenly wholly upon Mrs Andrews.

'As soon as you're ready,' she replied with another smile. 'Go get changed and we can start. It's just through there,' she said, pointing at a door in one corner of the hall.

Holding her leotard and ballet shoes tightly, Clara scurried across the hall and disappeared into the changing room.

'She seems to be full of energy,' Mrs Andrews said pleasantly. Joseph and Emily gave each other a sideways look.

'You don't know the half of it,' Emily said with a laugh.

They chatted for a few minutes and discovered that Mrs Andrews had lived in London all her life, but after her husband was killed in the Great War, she had moved up north for – as she put it – "a fresh start". Mrs Brown was about to ask her what she thought of the area when Clara reappeared, dressed and ready to dance.

'Let's start, let's start!' she chanted, raising smiles on her parents' faces. Mrs Andrews clapped her hands together to get everyone's attention and was about to speak when the doors to the hall opened and a woman rushed in, dragging a very shamefaced and disgruntled looking boy behind her.

'I'm sorry, I'm so sorry, you haven't started yet, have you?' the woman asked.

'No...' Mrs Andrews replied, looking a little shocked.

'Oh, good,' the woman said, thrusting her son forward, 'because I want Jeremy here to join the class. It will be good for him to do something a little less rough for a change.'

Many of the girls in the hall tittered behind their hands and began to whisper to their friends as they watched Jeremy squirm embarrassedly on the spot. Clara glanced over at the newcomer and thought that he could not look more disgusted to be there if he tried. His face was set in a grimace the like of which she had never seen, as he gazed determinedly at the floor. Then she realised who he was and tugged on the sleeve of her father's coat.

'That's Jeremy Stephens – he's the boy I keep getting into fights with.'

'So that's the lad, is it?' he asked, looking over at him. 'No wonder you win every time.'

Joseph's statement was a justifiable one. Jeremy was by no means well built. He was of course still only young at twelve years old, but he was definitely small for his age. His hair was long and unkempt, and his face was smeared with grime, which his mother had clearly tried to clean off, but evidently given up on. His clothes were also dirty and torn at the knees and his mother looked as though she was at her wits' end.

Clara knew that Jeremy often got into trouble. He could be pleasant enough sometimes, but he was also extremely argumentative, and arguments with Jeremy usually ended in a fight, which Clara invariably won.

'Well, alright,' Mrs Andrews said. 'If you want him to join… he'll have to go and get changed before we can start.' Jeremy's mother handed him a bag and he slouched off to the changing room.

'And don't try and escape from this class or your father will hear about it!' his mother called after him. Jeremy did not say anything in response as he shuffled from the hall.

Over an hour later – at the end of the class – Clara was breathless and tired, but she was also exhilarated by the experience. Dancing made her feel free like she had never felt before. She did not delude herself into thinking she was very good yet, but in her imagination she kept seeing the same thing over and over.

She was dancing in front of a huge, rapturous crowd of people. Every single one of them was cheering her on and throwing flowers onto the stage in front of her. The music ebbed and swelled like the tide and her movements were so graceful and composed that they brought tears to the eyes of even the burliest men.

She knew she was a long way from achieving this, but after only one lesson her posture had significantly improved, and she had picked up enough pointers to be able to practice at home and progress further before next week's class.

She looked over at Jeremy – who had not spoken a word throughout the class and had only grudgingly done as Mrs Andrews told him to – and slowly sidled over. He was tugging on his shoes viciously as she moved to stand next to him.

'You know, you're a really terrible dancer,' she said, grinning cheekily at him.

'You can hardly talk,' he replied. 'I've seen hippos with more grace than you.'

They glared at each other for several seconds – neither wanting to back down first – then simultaneously cracked and began to laugh uproariously, tears of mirth spilling down their cheeks.

'Remember… remember when Mrs Andrews told you to do a pirouette?' Clara managed to splutter. 'And you span around and cracked your head off the mirror!' she added, dissolving once more into fits of laughter.

'Remember it?' he replied, wiping his eyes on his sleeve. 'I hit my head so hard I was seeing stars for the rest of the lesson. You don't forget something like that in a hurry!'

By now they were both laughing so hard that their faces hurt and their sides ached, and just like that a friendship that would last the rest of their lives was started.

CHAPTER 10
The Light of Understanding

'There it is – at last.'

Malone stood upon a low rise and looked out upon his prey, nestled in a shallow dip in the landscape in the near distance. He had thought about this moment for many years, hoping against hope that it would never arrive – that they would see sense and reason before then – but knowing in his heart that this was a fantasy; that they were far too stubborn, bull-headed and set in their ways to ever consider the possibility of something new.

It had always infuriated him – why the Clans felt the need to perpetually look backwards, to strive for what *had been* instead of what *could be*. Why could they not see things the way he did? Why could they not share his vision?

Malone was no fool. He knew he was no longer the man he had been before he discovered the Cypher – he could see that he was now something else entirely – but he also fervently believed that he had been made this way for a purpose, and what greater purpose was there than advancement? To further oneself and those around you for the betterment of all? Was there anything more pure or forward thinking than that? If there was, Malone could not imagine it.

He had not been here personally in some time, and as he looked upon it with eyes that had seen and changed so much in the two decades since his discovery, he felt a wave of memories wash over him that seemed to come from another life entirely, a life he barely even recognised any more. He pitied that person, pitied the fact that he had not been able to make his discovery sooner, for just think where they might be now if he had…

Malone thrust this thought away; he was never usually one for "what ifs" and he was not about to start now – he had important work to do…

'Boss!' The familiar voice cut across his thoughts, and he turned to see Darius advancing towards him.

'Where've you been?' Malone demanded of his second in command. 'You missed the first rendezvous.'

'We, uh… we hit some trouble, Boss…' Darius said guiltily as he came to a stop in front of Malone, unable to meet his eyes. 'We got into a scrap… with, uh… with Vincent…' His voice trailed off limply, his gaze still firmly on the ground, looking like a dog expecting to be beaten by its master.

Malone's expression stayed inert and unreadable as he glanced around Darius.

'And I take it by the fact you've returned alone that it didn't quite go your way…?' Malone said, an icy edge to his tone.

'Deek managed to slice him good, but I... I'm the only one who made it out...' Darius admitted weakly. At this, Malone took a threatening step closer to him, staring straight into his downcast eyes, and was just inhaling to launch into a tirade when Darius finally looked up at him with a faint sliver of hope.

'He... he had a girl with him!' Darius blurted out quickly. 'Vincent's brought over another one!'

This nugget of information stopped Malone dead. He closed his mouth, and his expression went from wrathful to thoughtful in a heartbeat. He stepped back from Darius, thinking quickly, a derisive smile now tugging at his lips as he looked out across the landscape unseeingly.

'I thought maybe they'd given up on that pathetic hope...' he murmured with a sneer. 'But it seems I gave them too much credit...'

He turned back to Darius and stared at him hard.

'You've always been a good second, Darius,' he began. 'But you know how I feel about failure... Did you at least do what I asked of you?'

'I did!' Darius yelped triumphantly. 'I burned Mikal's cabin to the ground – the Wolves will never be able to use it again!'

Malone nodded approvingly.

'Good, good, then maybe you can further redeem yourself,' he said benevolently, stepping up beside Darius and grasping him by the shoulder. 'Now, I don't believe for one second that this girl Vincent's found can help the Wolves' ridiculous plan in any way, but *I* might have a use for her...'

Malone bent closer to Darius, who could feel his hot breath on his gnarled face as he continued to speak in a low voice.

'I want you to bring her to me,' Malone hissed. 'Your one and only task from this moment on is to find her and transport her to Inchinn. I don't care what you do, I don't care how you do it, just get her there *alive*. Maybe – just maybe – she could help us further understand the Cypher, and if not, well... At least it'll piss off Vincent,' he finished with a smirk.

Darius nodded emphatically, trying to hide his relief at this outcome, for he had not expected to get off lightly.

'Will do, Boss!' he said. 'I'll join you for this, and if Vincent's moved on already, I'll get right back on his trail.'

Darius then turned towards their target and nodded at it meaningfully.

'So... you ready to do this, Boss?'

Malone looked up at it once more and his eyes narrowed.

'I tried so hard...' he said, more to himself that to Darius. 'I did all I could to bring them forward into the light of knowledge and understanding, but some people you just can't help... Some people only understand one thing...'

Malone turned and looked behind him, a cold smile spreading across his face at the sight. He raised his mechanical fist in the air and from above the wrist a large, wickedly sharp blade slid out in preparation.

'Are you ready, my warriors!?' Malone roared, feeling almost giddy as a cacophony of war cries rang out in response from the legions of assembled man and machine who were hanging on his every word, itching to slake their bloodlust.

'Then go!' Malone boomed, pointing his blade at their target. 'Take any who submit and kill all who don't! GO!'

With wild, guttural bellows of rage and excitement, Malone's army surged around him like a dark tide and flooded across the empty fields towards the quiet and oblivious city – Neart...

CHAPTER 11
Aggressive Expansion

'Clara! CLARA! Wake up!'

Clara struggled awake, her mind still foggy and addled, and looked up at the shape standing over her.

'The Viper are attacking!' Vincent yelled at her. 'We have to leave – now!'

Without another word, Vincent gripped her by the hand and dragged her from her bed where she stumbled after him on sleep-heavy limbs, rubbing at her eyes and desperately trying to process what on earth was going on. In a heartbeat they were back outside Garret's house, and she found herself engulfed by a wave of terrifying sound; gunfire, explosions, screams and crashes rent the air all around, seeming to rise and rise to a feverish intensity that made her struggle loose from Vincent's hold so she could clap her hands over her ears.

Even so, she could not fail to hear the tinny voices echoing from loudspeakers all over the city:

'Surrender to the Viper and join us, or be destroyed!'

As her blurred vision settled, she looked around her in a panic to see chaos everywhere – bullets and debris ripped through the air like hornets, fires raged in many of the once homely little buildings, and wherever she looked she saw life and death struggles being fought between the Bears and Malone's mechanically-enhanced fighters. Clara felt her senses being overwhelmed – it was all just too much to take in – when a pair of hands took hers and pulled them gently from her head, and she looked up to see El staring down at her gravely, but reassuringly.

'Stay by my side!' El shouted over the noise. 'I won't let anything happen to you!'

Clara nodded back – too frightened to speak – and looked up at Vincent, who was glancing about searchingly, his revolver in hand.

'We have to get Clara out of here!' El yelled at her husband. 'What's the plan?'

Vincent looked over at her, clearly thinking quickly, and was just about to respond when a small, round, metal object clattered to the floor at their feet and rolled to a stop. Vincent's eyes widened in shock, and he pointed away from it.

'Move!' he screamed, and El and Clara complied at once as he dived forwards, scooped up the grenade, and hurled it towards the closest Viper, who was engaged in kicking down the door of a nearby house. It had not even reached its target when it exploded in mid-air, scattering deadly fragments in every direction and blasting the unfortunate man through the door he had been attempting to breach.

With debris still flying around them, Vincent was back on his feet and beside El and Clara in a flash as he began to usher them deeper into the city.

'We must find Garret first!' he roared over the din. 'Then we get the hell out of here!'

El nodded back and, with Vincent in the lead, they raced on through the streets towards the Bear HQ.

Clara would never forget that frantic dash – seeing so much death was something no one her age should ever have to witness, and it changed her deeply. She had of course learned about war in history class and been told of the horrible loss of life in the Great War, but to experience it first hand was something else entirely. It was like nothing she had ever known, and as the adrenaline coursed through her veins, she saw things differently – colours appeared more contrasted, details seemed sharpened, and time felt like it moved slower, as if to give her the opportunity to absorb it all properly.

But even with all that she could only recall snapshots of it afterwards; little moments that had burned themselves into her memory, and she knew she would never be able to dislodge. One of these – the worst of them – was of a Shifted Bear grappling with one of the Viper outside the ruined front room of a little shop. The Bear had grabbed the Viper in a fierce death grip and buried its jaws into its victim's shoulder, but the Viper – unwilling to give in just yet – was using a blade attached to his mechanical arm to stab deeply into the Bear's flank over and over, and as the two of them wrestled for supremacy they fell backwards, crashing through the damaged wall of the shop and bringing the entire ceiling of the first floor down on top of them.

Clara did not have time to see if either had survived before she, El and Vincent had turned a corner and lost sight of them, their feet pounding on the cobbles and their lungs burning with fatigue.

They were just about to round another corner when a curtain of flames suddenly shot out in front of them, and they skidded to a stop. As the fire vanished, a fearsome figure stepped out into the smoke left behind. It was more machine than man – so many parts had been replaced that you could barely even call it human. Both legs and arms were now monstrous hinged pistons, its chest cavity bore the furnace that powered it, its back belched out smoke from vents alongside two large canisters, and on its right arm was a curious device that…

'Duck!' yelled El, as another jet of flame spewed from this weapon, missing them by inches. Looking left and right, Vincent saw their only way out and took it, diving through the low front window of a nearby pub, sending glass and splinters flying. As another gout of flame followed them, El and Clara leapt after him, tumbling through the opening and scrambling to make their way past the tables and chairs that sought to trip them.

Vincent reached the back door first and found it locked. As the Viper smashed its way through the brickwork below the window, Vincent tugged at the handle, but it wouldn't budge an inch. Pointing his revolver at the latch, he fired into it again and again but, looking behind them, he knew that they were out of time.

Before he could move a muscle, however, El had already started running. Fearlessly, she charged straight at the Viper, and as it raised its weapon and fired, she had already Shifted, her lower wolf shape allowing her to pass just below the flames where she Shifted again, sliding on her hip and picking up a piece of debris from the floor. Surprised, the Viper stopped firing and lowered its weapon, and this was both its first and last mistake.

In one smooth movement, El leapt back up to her feet and jammed the chunk of stone into the nozzle of the weapon. Enraged, and seemingly unaware of what had happened, the Viper raised its weapon again, but when it pulled the trigger the weapon exploded, sending shards of hot metal full into its face.

With a roar of agony, it spun around, clasping its hands to the injury, and El needed no second bidding. She kicked it hard in the rear, sending it flying towards the broken window, and had already Shifted to return to her comrades as Vincent – from across the room – raised his revolver and fired at the canisters on the Viper's back.

The explosion in the small space was deafening as the canisters erupted, engulfing the unlucky Viper and filling the room with a deadly wall of fire that surged towards them, but Vincent had already turned and bulled into the weakened door and he, Clara and El in her wolf shape cannoned through it together, chased by a cloud of flame that quickly dissipated behind them.

Clara, smarting from the closeness of the heat, did not have the chance to think before El had Shifted, gripped her hand again, and hauled her back to her feet to continue their punishing flight.

'Should we not just leave?' El shouted to Vincent as they ran. 'That was too close!'

'We need Garret for the rest of the journey!' Vincent shouted back. 'And besides... I must see if he's alright!'

They rounded another corner and Clara saw ahead the familiar shape of the Bear HQ at the end of the street – finally they were almost there... But they had not gone more than a few paces when they were jumped by two more of Malone's soldiers from alleys on either side, and they suddenly found themselves fighting for their lives.

Vincent had Shifted before Clara had even spotted the threat, and leapt with a snarl for the throat of the Viper on their right, while El was left to deal with the other. The huge brute tore from the shadows, wielding a chainsaw in place of its left arm that snarled and roared like a living beast as it swung wildly at El's head. She had let go of Clara's hand and unsheathed the blade at her side in an instant, using it to deflect the terrifying weapon as best she could, but she was quickly beaten back by the wildness of the attack.

Out of her mind with fear, Clara stumbled over something and fell backwards as El and the monster clashed viciously beside her. Looking around from her now prone position, Clara saw what had tripped her: it was a long, thin piece of metal – debris from one of the damaged houses nearby – and she had picked it up before she even knew what she was going to do with it.

By this point, El was in trouble. She had dropped to one knee under the punishing blows of the Viper's weapon and Clara could see that she was flagging, unable to find a window to counterattack.

As sparks flew above her, Clara looked over at the hideous mechanical limbs of the creature, and without another thought she had leant forwards and jammed the piece of metal between the pistons and gears of its right leg. The Viper – oblivious to this – tried to take another step closer to El, but as it did so the metal caught with an awful grinding sound and it stumbled, surprise blooming on its repulsive face. This was all the opening El needed.

With lethal, balletic grace she had leapt back to her feet in an instant and lopped off its chainsaw arm in one smooth swing, and before the severed limb had even hit the floor she had spun in closer and whisked off the creature's head as effortlessly as a dandelion.

As the monster crumpled to the ground behind her, El had already spun back to Clara and helped her to her feet – nodding her thanks – before turning to look over at Vincent, who had just finished tearing out the throat of the other Viper, who now lay still beneath him.

Vincent Shifted back to human and he and El locked eyes for a moment – each ensuring the other was okay – then they were back on the move again, flying towards the Bear HQ ahead.

They reached the entrance at last and barged inside to the echoing hallway, noticing immediately the lack of the two guards who had been protecting the entry to Davin's office.

As they approached the doors, they could hear raised voices coming from within, and with Vincent in the lead, they burst through them to find two sawn-off shotguns thrust into their faces by the suddenly silent figures of Garret and Chief Davin.

'Huh,' Davin grunted, as he slowly lowered his weapon. 'Might have known you lot would show up too. Have you come to tell me I should turn tail and run like my cur of a son here?'

Garret, his gun now lowered too, rounded on his father angrily.

'We are outnumbered!' he yelled in wrathful indignation. 'We are outmatched and have been caught on the back foot – you *must* see that!?'

'I see nothing of the sort!' Davin boomed back. 'The Bear are strong! We will send these Viper mongrels packing! If you would move aside and let me leave my damn office, I'd show you!'

As Davin made to move past him, Garret held up his arms to block him.

'Chief… Father… You know I want to destroy the Viper as much as you – more so even – but this is a fight we cannot win!' he began earnestly. 'Our one hope – our *only* hope now – is to flee! Flee and regroup so that we can strike back from a position of strength!'

'You truly believe we cannot win this?' Davin asked his son, a note of incredulity creeping into his voice. 'Has your faith shrunk that much? Do you believe so little in your own people…? The Bear are strong! They…'

'They *were* strong!' Garret cut across him fiercely. 'They were once… But against this foe, what strength we have left is as nothing! Have you not been outside in the last few years? Have you spent so much time shut away in here that you no longer know the people you rule? The Rot has broken them! Their spirits are in tatters and their bodies are following. If we are to stand any chance – *any* chance at all – of defeating this enemy, we need help… help and a plan…'

Davin – his face purple with rage – was almost too angry to speak as he stared at his son as though seeing him for the first time.

'You sound like them!' he bellowed at last, pointing past Garret at Vincent and El. 'You have always let yourself get too close to the Wolves, and look what it has turned you into! And you…' he continued, directing his fury now at Vincent.

'You have poisoned my son against his own! Your boyhood friendship with Malone has made you weak! You would risk us all for the chance to save the Viper instead of doing what is right – instead of doing what *must* be done!'

Davin tried to push past his son, but Garret would not let him by.

'Out of my way!' the Chief roared. 'I have had enough of your spineless naysaying! If we are as weak as you say, then this will be our final stand – but I will take down as many of those Viper bastards as I can!'

He tried to push past Garret once more, but again found himself gently but firmly repelled as Vincent stepped forward earnestly.

'Chief, I beg you to listen to me,' he began, locking eyes with the enraged Davin. 'You must see that it is as we always feared – this army Malone has built is for one purpose, and one purpose only… This is his *final* offensive – his last push to force the remaining Clans to bend to his will, or be destroyed… If we are to survive this, it can only be through unity – divided we will surely fall!'

Vincent took another step closer to Davin, who was breathing heavily and staring at him through hard, bloodshot eyes.

'I implore you,' Vincent continued. 'Help us rally the Clans… Help us rally the Clans and get Clara to Croí, and if we can hold off the Viper long enough, I believe – I *know* – that our faith in her will be rewarded.'

As all eyes turned to her, Clara felt the burden of her responsibility descend like a lead weight – a responsibility she still did not even remotely understand.

What power do I have against the Rot? she thought. *What can I do against such a thing…?*

Again, she saw in her mind's eye the book on the table in the darkened room, now almost close enough for her to reach out and touch it. She could see the padlock sealing its pages, knew its weight and its feel – for she had locked it herself – but knew that she never wished to open it again.

How… how is this real…? she thought.

'Faith, huh…' Davin spat, looking now at Vincent. 'You Wolves have been fuelled by faith and hope for far too long – and look where it has got you!'

Davin gesticulated through the window of his office at the chaos going on outside – at the smoke and the fires, the damage and the death.

'We should have taken the fight to the Viper long ago – before they had chance to build such an army – but you did not want to risk your friend!' Davin snarled. 'We should have…'

'Such talk is not useful!' Vincent cut in firmly. 'What we should or should not have done is irrelevant – we are where we are now, and must do what is best from here.'

Vincent took another step towards Davin and reached past Garret to place a hand on his shoulder.

'Chief, you must retreat,' Vincent said, as Davin shrugged away from his touch. 'You must send as many of your people as you can to Croí – for that is where the final confrontation will surely take place. You must…'

'No!' Davin fairly screamed, barging past Garret at last to stand before Vincent, every line of his body yelling defiance. 'We have put off this reckoning with the Viper long enough – it ends now!'

Garret stepped back between them quickly, holding out his hands beseechingly now.

'Father, you will be slaughtered!' he cried. 'This will be the end of the Bear! We must join with the other Clans! Please!'

'You may wish to run from battle, but I will not!' his father hissed at him.

'If you are to remain, then let me fight alongside you!' Garret said desperately, pleadingly.

At this, Davin turned and sneered at his son.

'No… No, I think not…' he said, quietly now. 'Go… Go with your Wolf friends and see where their madness takes them.' He turned away from Garret but continued to speak to him, unable to even look at him now. 'Though you are Bear by birth, you have always had a Wolf soul… Go with them…'

As Garret tried to protest, Davin cut across him.

'That's an order! Go!' he barked.

Garret, conflicted – torn asunder between loyalty and hope – turned away from his father and slunk slowly out of the room and Vincent, with a despairing look at Davin, followed him, trailed by El and Clara, who both looked pale and shell-shocked at what they had witnessed.

CHAPTER 12
Into the Tunnels

'Are you alright…?' Vincent murmured to Garret as they strode away from the Bear HQ.

'If we are to make it out of here, we must head for the tunnels,' Garret replied hollowly, avoiding the question. 'They will lead us under the walls and out of the city.'

'But what about your fa…' Vincent began.

'He has made his choice,' Garret replied quickly, 'and given me my orders. Come,' he continued, setting off through the ruins of the city. 'This is the fastest way.'

Vincent and El shared a look as they watched Garret turn and move off through the wreck and rubble of someone's home.

'This is wrong,' El said fervently. 'We cannot allow this to happen – we must do something!'

'There is little we can do,' Vincent replied quietly. 'We will rally who we can to head for the tunnels, but Clara must be our priority.'

El looked around her as screams and yells continued to fill the air, battling for supremacy over the constant rattle of gunfire and the dull, bass boom of explosions. She glanced down at Clara, then turned back to Vincent and nodded, her jaw tight with anger and frustration.

They quickly followed Garret, clambering over huge chunks of masonry that had once been a living room, and Clara's heart broke to see the mementos and knickknacks gathered over a family's lifetime strewn amidst the wreckage like fallen leaves. Under one piece of rubble she saw a child's china doll, its once blonde hair singed away, it's pretty face cracked, and spattered across its dress – in stark contrast to the white linen – was that…?

Vincent and El had just rounded a corner ahead of her when a crash from behind made Clara whirl around and she watched wide-eyed as Chief Davin – in his bear form – burst out through the front doors of the HQ. He reared up on his hind legs and roared his fury to the heavens before dropping back down and lumbering off towards the main gate, his mind set on vengeance.

Clara could not even begin to claim that she had any real concept of the forces at play here, but from what she had seen during this attack the battle seemed to be going one way, and one way only… It seemed likely – from what Vincent and Garret had said – that Davin was running straight to his death, and he seemed almost proud to do so. Clara realised that only then did she truly understand what Vincent had meant when he said that: *'soon there will be nothing left for us to save…'*

Our time is running out, Clara knew. *If I don't find out how I can help them soon, all this will end…*

A cry for help interrupted her thoughts, and she hurried to catch up with Vincent and El as they hastened after Garret who was making straight for the desperate pleas. They found the source of them in no time – a woman and her child were desperately trying to free a man from beneath a heavy wooden beam that had crashed down from the collapsed first floor of their small, cramped home.

The child was howling with distress and the woman's hands were cut and bleeding as she frantically tried to lift it, but to no avail. Garret was at her side in an instant. He shared no words with her but immediately Shifted to his bear form, ducked under the beam, and began to heave with all his might. Vincent and El hurried over to help and Clara joined them, doing what she could to heave it up just enough that the man could slide out – but it seemed that it would not budge… Garret, however, was not one to give up easily.

With a mighty effort, he stood on his hind legs, pushing with his back and shoulders, and as they all strained with him the beam moved just an inch, and it was enough. The woman gripped her husband under the arms and pulled, and with a cry of pain he was free, and she was kissing his face and hands with the desperate, uncontrollable relief of someone who thought she had lost him forever.

The man struggled back to his feet, limping badly, and nodded his thanks to Garret and the others.

'Will you join me at the gate, brother?' he asked of Garret, who had now Shifted back. 'We must repel these Viper scum!'

'Sam, no!' his wife cried. 'You can't…'

'You are in no state to fight, my friend,' Garret replied seriously. 'Look to your family now, for this is not a battle we can win.'

'Go to the tunnels,' El said, stepping forward. 'Take your family and head to Croí – tell as many as you can! Maybe together we can defeat them…'

Sam glanced from one to the other and for a moment it looked like he wouldn't listen. There was a faint trace of disgust in his expression as he looked at Garret – perhaps figuring him for a coward – but eventually he relented and nodded, but said nothing.

With his wife supporting him, the small family turned and headed off, soon disappearing from view behind another ruined house.

Clara turned her attention to Garret and saw that he was staring at the spot where Sam had vanished, his expression one of impotent fury – clearly he had seen the disgust on the other man's face, and did not like to be viewed as such.

'We must keep moving,' Vincent said to him in a low voice, gently placing a hand on Garret's arm to usher him forwards. 'There may be others we can help along the way…'

Without a word, Garret allowed himself to be steered forth and they continued their treacherous journey through the embattled city.

Several minutes later, they had travelled a decent distance and managed – by the skin of their teeth in some instances – to avoid any further trouble, but it seemed to be eating away at Garret's soul to do so; seeing his comrades in arms locked in mortal struggles all around him.

'I should be fighting,' Garret said, more to himself than to Vincent, who was walking alongside him. 'I should be doing as my father is and taking down as many of them as I can...'

Vincent looked at his friend and could see the fire burning there – the Bear in him wanting to slake its thirst for battle alongside his brothers and sisters.

'It would be death to do so,' Vincent replied levelly. 'And what would it ach...'

But he was not able to finish his sentence, as a Viper soldier had leapt down from a nearby roof with a howl of rage and gripped him savagely from behind, swiftly joined by another who had caught hold of El walking close by.

As Clara stumbled back with a gasp of shock and Vincent and El grappled with their opponents, Garret turned to them with murder in his eyes. An animal cry ripped from his human throat, morphing to the roar of his bear form as he Shifted and charged in the same moment.

The Viper did not know what hit them; one moment they had the upper hand with a couple of Wolves, the next they found themselves being torn away from their prey and smashed together over and over and over by the biggest Bear they had ever encountered, until their worlds suddenly went dark and they knew no more, their bodies rapidly reducing to nothing but piles of torn metal, flesh and bone by the whirlwind onslaught.

Clara watched all this transfixed with horror as the attack went on and on, the remains long since ceased any movement, but Garret continuing to pummel them with manic intensity, until she felt El's hand cover her eyes and turn her head away.

Vincent – who had until now kept his distance – finally stepped forward and placed a hand gingerly on Garret's bear shoulder. Garret whirled around and swiped at him with a claw, his eyes unseeing – clouded by rage – and Vincent reeled backwards.

Garret's ferocious snarl suddenly softened as he realised what he had almost done, and in a blink he had Shifted back to his human form.

'I'm… I'm sorry…' he murmured shamefully.

'Never mind that now,' Vincent replied, becoming very still. 'Do you hear that?'

All four of them stopped dead to listen, and at first Clara could not hear it – but she felt it… The ground had begun to tremble beneath them – rocks and other debris were skittering around as though they had a life of their own, and everywhere she looked she saw little avalanches of rubble were tumbling down. She sensed the power building through the soles of her feet, and realised it was similar to the earth tremor she had been caught in on first entering Comhlacht, but there was a different quality to it – something almost…

And *then* she heard it – a deep, mechanical rumble that set her teeth on edge and made her wish she was back in her nice, warm bed at home; wish that she was anywhere other than here. As one, they all turned towards the source of the sound as it crested a mound of rubble ahead, revealing a hellish silhouette straight out of a fever dream.

Vincent, El and Garret did not have words for what they were seeing – as this was another horrifying concoction of Malone's perverse technological revolution – but Clara did…

'It's a tank!' she screamed over the din.

And a tank it was. The body looked similar to the tanks Clara knew had been used in the Great War, but on each side it had two sets of hinged caterpillar tracks bearing large spikes for increased traction. At its top was a long-barrelled cannon on a pivot, behind which sat twin chimneys that belched smoke from the furnace powering it within. But what arrested the attention of them all was at the front of the terrifying machine – a pair of monstrous mandible-like jaws that clashed together as it drove, ready to crush anything that crossed its path.

As it crashed down off the pile of debris and righted itself, the beastly machine turned towards them, and the cannon began to slowly swing their way…

'Run!' Clara yelled. 'Run before it fires!'

Taking the lead for the first time, Clara dashed across the road and – with the others close behind her – dived inside the relatively undamaged interior of a large greengrocer. As they slid across the floor and ducked down behind the counter, the tank fired its cannon with a deafening *boom* and the front wall of the shop was obliterated in a hail of dust and shattered brickwork.

The whole structure rocked with the impact and a beam fell from the ceiling, falling across the only other door out of there.

'It'll need to reload!' Clara shouted over the still-echoing blast.

'Upstairs, now!' Vincent yelled, and together they scuttled across the room – past shelves and baskets of unappetising vegetables – and began to ascend the stairs to the first floor.

They soon found themselves in what appeared to be a storeroom and saw at once that their exit options were extremely limited. Glancing out of the window, Clara was horrified to see that the tank's cannon was raising slowly up to point right at her.

'Watch out!' she screamed. All four of them hit the dirt at once as the tank fired again, blasting a hole in the roof and showering them in yet more rubble and splinters.

Looking around frantically, El saw an opportunity through an open window across the room – a ladder leading up the outside of a tall tower opposite.

'This way! This way!' she cried, waving the others after her as she dashed for the window. As Clara made to follow, she could not help looking over her shoulder, and saw the tank powering towards their building, the mandible jaws open and ready to crush…

She knew at once that they would not make it, but they had to try, and so she ran after her friends as fast as she could as the tank crashed into the lower support column of the building, gripped it with its pincers, and tugged…

All at once their world went sideways as the whole first floor dropped to a forty-five-degree angle, and they began to slide…

Dust stung Clara's eyes as she and the others slid down towards the tank that awaited them at the bottom, its pincer jaws clashing together and its cannon lazily zeroing in on them for the final blow.

It had almost got a bead on them when Garret suddenly bounded forward out of his uncontrolled slide and jumped, Shifting mid-air to his bear form and landing with a snarl on the barrel of the cannon, the sudden impact causing it to swing away, and not a moment too soon, for the cannon fired a split-second later and the shot went wide, decimating a clock tower down the street.

The tank – aware of its new passenger – immediately attempted to shake him off by jerking the barrel up and down, but Garret clung on grimly as Vincent, Clara and El managed to arrest their slide, spin around, and scramble back up the ramped floor towards the window at the top.

They reached it at last and El thrust it open, ushering Clara ahead of her.

'You first, Clara,' El said, as Clara stepped forward and looked at the gap she would have to cross to reach the ladder.

'I can't jump that!' she wailed in horror.

'I'm sorry, but you have to!' El barked, nudging her forward.

Behind them, Garret was quickly losing his grip as the tank's efforts to remove him grew more violent. All of a sudden, its four caterpillar tracks began to pivot ninety degrees and before he knew what was happening the tank was crabbing sideways towards a nearby workshop, hoping to scrape him off.

'Hurry up!' Garret yelled, glancing back at his friends to see the minimal progress they had made.

'Clara, go!' Vincent yelled, and Clara – terrified witless and with no other options – steeled herself, and leapt…

She hit the ladder hard and all the wind was knocked out of her, her knees and elbows clattering painfully off the cold metal as she just about managed to keep hold. El leapt next and landed gracefully a few rungs above Clara, and Vincent was just about to follow when he glanced back and saw that they were in trouble.

As the tank's gun barrel swung towards the workshop – with Garret still clinging to it – he was forced to let go, dropping to the floor and Shifting back to human just as it collided, sending yet more debris flying.

He was up and off in a heartbeat, following after his friends, and Vincent – seeing that he was back with them – made the next jump across to the ladder, landing above El as she and Clara made their way down, but not quickly…

'Faster, Clara!' El called down, but Clara was too frightened – the drop to the ground still a sickening distance below – and thus her pace was glacial.

As Garret caught up to them and neared the window, he looked back to see that the tank's tracks had realigned and it was powering towards them, ramping up the fallen first floor with incredible speed as its gun barrel slowly swung round again.

'Go up!' Garret yelled, and they all turned back to see why he had said this.

'Up! Go up!' Vincent echoed, as he, El and Clara saw the danger, switched direction, and began to ascend.

As the tank swiftly caught up to Garret, he waited just long enough for Clara to climb past him – panic having leant her speed – then he jumped across, gripped the ladder and scooped her up in the same movement, tossing her onto his back as he began to climb with a rapidity that belied his size.

He avoided catastrophe by a hair's breadth as the tank – its mandible jaws open wide – ramped across the gap and careened into the side of the tower below them with an almighty crash. The four comrades were almost knocked loose by the initial impact, then the whole structure started to sway ominously – unsure yet which way it would go – before finally deciding and beginning to fall forwards, slowly levelling out beneath them as they continued to climb.

Time seemed to slow down as the tower toppled, swiftly reaching an angle that enabled them to let go of the ladder and begin running instead, Vincent and El now side by side and Garret just behind them with Clara clinging to his back with a vice-like grip.

As the tower continued to fall, the tank was able to back up a little on the rubble pile it had created, and, as it did so, twin launchers appeared from hatches on the front of the machine and pointed upwards. With a *thunk*, the launchers fired and two long grappling hooks on thick chains shot out, arching past the four small figures and latching onto the guttering of the collapsing structure.

With a mechanical whirr, the grappling hooks pulled taught as the tank reeled itself up onto the tower behind them and continued its pursuit, its cannon once more zeroing in on its prey.

'Down!' El yelled, as she glanced back and saw what was coming.

They all threw themselves down just in time as the shell whooshed over their heads, disappearing deep into the city where an echoing explosion resounded.

Finally – after what seemed like an age – the tower impacted with the street below and they were thrown off their feet in a cacophonous din and a vast, choking cloud of dust and smoke that swirled around them. As they tumbled head over heels, Clara was flung loose from Garret's back and she bounced and rolled painfully along the side of the tower, before toppling over the edge…

As Clara's world spun in a kaleidoscope of unintelligible information, she suddenly felt the lack of anything solid beneath her, and realised she was falling. But the sensation did not last long, for something had grabbed hold of her and she looked up – her sight still whirling – and saw that Garret had her by the arm.

Behind him, Vincent and El leapt back to their feet and looked at each other, nodding as an unspoken plan was agreed. As the tank continued to roll towards them – the cannon still spinning their way – El reached for her belt and produced a curious device, somewhere between a grenade and a stick of dynamite.

She held it, just long enough for the tank to reach a weakened section of the structure, then she twisted a dial and hurled it beneath the approaching machine. As the cannon came to rest with them in its sights, the device exploded and the tank dropped out of view, crashing through the side wall and landing within the fallen tower below.

As Garret hauled Clara up to safety behind him, Vincent was immediately on the move, reaching to his belt and producing his own strange gadget – a long, thin tube filled with two different coloured liquids.

Down inside the tower, the tank's tracks had already rotated, and it had begun crabbing its way towards the nearest wall in an attempt to break out and continue the chase.

Above it, Vincent reached the edge of the hole the tank had fallen through and leapt down without a moment's hesitation, landing lightly on top of it and moving swiftly for the chimneys at its rear. As he ran, he cracked the gadget at its centre and shook it, causing the two liquids to begin to merge. He had almost reached the chimney when the tank's cannon swung for him and he was forced to slide under it as it swished past.

He could hear voices clamouring within – they knew they were in trouble – but they had forced his hand, and he had to do what he had to do.

Arriving at the chimneys, he quickly knocked the cap off the closest one with his cane and dropped the gadget into its narrow funnel, then turned and began to run as it clattered its way down, and the voices within went quiet…

Looking up as he ran, Vincent saw El leaning down over the edge of the hole, her arm outstretched to catch him, and he leapt up onto the top of the cannon and jumped for her, holding out his hand. For a moment he thought he had misjudged – and indeed he had – but then El thrust herself dangerously over the lip and caught his hand in both of hers, then she too began to fall… but not far, for Garret was behind her and caught her by the legs, swiftly pulling her up with Clara's help.

As he was heaved over the edge, Vincent looked back to see the tank's upper hatch clang open and two Vipers struggle with each other to escape, but their struggle was short-lived as the tank exploded from within and gouts of blinding white flame erupted from the hatch, the chimneys and the cannon. Vincent had just rolled out of the way as a blast of superheated air swept past him, and the fire rapidly subsided.

For a moment they all lay on their backs on top of the fallen tower in the ringing aftermath, breathing heavily and thanking their lucky stars that they had survived.

'Is… Is everyone alright?' El gasped, still staring exhaustedly upwards.

'Yes,' Clara mumbled.

'Aye,' Garret grunted.

'Just about,' Vincent breathed, patting at some burning embers on his jacket.

'Then… we better get moving,' El panted, hauling herself to her feet. She moved over to Clara and helped her up gently, dusting down her clothes as she did so, then together they set off once again. With a groan, the others followed as they continued their journey to the tunnels.

A short time later they heard panicked voices ahead and soon joined up with several groups of Bear citizens, all fleeing as fast as they could for the tunnels. It was unclear if word had spread about pulling back to Croí, or if the battle was simply going that way, but whatever the reason the four comrades were pleased to see that not all the Bear were as suicidal as Davin.

As they finally neared the entrance, El produced something from her pocket and offered it to Vincent. He looked at it curiously and saw that it was some kind of root vegetable, and he shook his head.

'Did you take that from the greengrocer?' he asked.

'Waste not, want not,' El shrugged in response. She bit into it and her face crinkled in disgust.

'Yuck,' was her summation, swiftly spitting it out. 'No wonder the Bear are so miserable.'

The entrance to the tunnels was within an innocuous looking farm building via a hatch hidden beneath a false floor, and into this everyone streamed, and even with the fear that consumed them all they did so in an orderly manner, so the queue moved at pace.

As Clara began to descend the stairs into the tunnel alongside El, the sounds of battle swiftly receded to a dull roar behind her and soon vanished completely, to be replaced by the echo of tramping feet and hushed voices in the small space.

The tunnel was just tall enough for a grown man to stand and about three times as wide. Thankfully it had been well built, shored up here and there with columns and cross beams bearing gas lanterns for illumination, and with rope rails either side for those who needed them.

As they trudged on towards safety, Clara felt the adrenaline that had been fuelling her ever since Vincent woke her up begin to subside, and as it did so a crushing fatigue descended upon her, and she could not help but yawn mightily.

At her side, El looked down at her fondly.

'Don't worry, Clara,' she whispered. 'The exit's just up ahead, then we can take a break.'

Clara nodded sleepily without looking up and yawned again.

Behind them, Vincent and Garret walked side by side, the Bear with his head held low as he muttered fiercely under his breath. His fists were clenched at his sides as he strode rigidly along, glancing over his shoulder every now and then.

Finally, when they were not far from the exit, he stopped dead in the middle of the tunnel and, with annoyed murmurings, the people behind flowed around him like water. Vincent stopped and turned to face him, watching as Garret stared fixedly at the floor, his shoulders heaving and his hands now clenching and unclenching.

Vincent took a step towards him.

'Brother, what's…?' he started to say, but Garret cut in.

'I cannot go with you,' he said firmly, his gaze rising to meet Vincent's, his expression set. 'If this is to be the Bear's final battle, then I would be ashamed to run from it – even when ordered to…'

Vincent took another step towards him, looking into his eyes earnestly as scores of people continued to jostle past them.

'Garret... brother...' he began, searching his friend's face for a trace of hope. 'I know you never believed in our approach to the Rot – I know you may not believe in me. But I believe – as I always have – that our *only* way through this crisis is together. We need you – now more than ever – to help us get Clara safely to our city.'

As more aggrieved mutterings filled the air from the people passing by, Vincent placed a hand on Garret's shoulder.

'Whatever you may think, I have faith in your father – I know he will do the right thing. He will not let his people die here. He will not let the Bear Clan end like this. And if you cannot believe in that, then I beg you – believe in her...'

Here he turned and nodded at Clara, who had stopped not far away and was looking back at them alongside El, her expression tired but frightened, for she had heard all this and felt again the extreme pressure of her responsibility threaten to crush her.

As she stood there, Clara's mind's eye again revealed the book on the table in the darkened room, but now she was standing right in front of it; right where she could see the key for the padlock that bound it lying within easy reach, just waiting to be used...

This cannot be real...

Garret stared at Clara for a moment, then glanced back down the tunnel over the heads of the approaching crowds; back to the city where his father and comrades in arms still battled. He looked back at Clara, his gaze flicking to and fro as an internal war was fought, then, finally, he relented. He nodded at Vincent and began to shamble slowly onward to the exit, his shoulders slumped, and together he, Vincent, El and Clara left the tunnel at last.

Back in Neart, Chief Davin fought bravely on by the front gate, his fur stained red from a multitude of wounds. After hurling down another Viper soldier and savaging his face, Davin ducked away from the fray for a moment and returned to human to catch his breath, looking around him at his warriors fighting and dying for their home.

He turned to look at the ruin that was his city – at the fire and fury that were slowly levelling his birthplace – and his gaze swept to the spot where the escape tunnels lay.

For the first time his expression became conflicted as the suffering of his people filled his senses, and then his eyes squeezed shut with remorse…

CHAPTER 13
The Mountain of Malice

'Do you think they'll go?' Vincent asked in an undertone, glancing over his shoulder.

'Who can say,' Garret replied sombrely. 'But I hope so…'

After leaving the tunnel they had joined the Bear standing around the exit in loose groups, no one seeming to know what to do or where to go from there, the air crackling all around with fearful whispering. Garret had done what he could to rally them – to convince them that their best bet was to head for Croí – but other than a few small parties who set off in that direction, the rest of the congregation remained unmoving. Without the leadership of Davin, they seemed lost – broken and hopeless – and nothing Garret could say seemed to sway the majority.

Eventually – with time so short – they had been forced to move on with their own objective, and hope that the Bear would soon see sense, and so Clara's chance to rest had been curtailed as they set off walking once more.

They were now some distance from the tunnel exit crossing a dreary, rock-strewn plain that severely hampered their progress. Vincent and Garret took the lead, picking their way slowly through the razor-sharp protrusions, with Clara and El following as close behind as they could.

'So, we're going to Ana… Anu…' Clara fumbled hesitantly in her tiredness.

'Anam,' El finished for her. 'The Hare Clan's village.'

'But I thought we were going to Croí?' Clara asked sleepily, yawning again.

'The Viper attack changes everything,' Vincent said without turning to look at her as he concentrated on his footing. 'We must warn the Hare before what happens at Neart happens to them too – for all we know it may already be too late…'

Clara fell silent for a while as she thought about this. Finally, she looked up at El as she waited for her to complete a technical section of the climb around a huge boulder.

'What are the Hare Clan like?' she asked, trying to keep her mind occupied and forget her bone-deep weariness.

'They are…' El began, as she reached the top of the boulder and proffered a hand to help Clara. 'They are a… a very insular people…' she continued diplomatically, as she hauled Clara up alongside her.

'They're a bunch of cowards is what they are,' Garret grunted sourly from a little way ahead. El threw him an annoyed look.

'What they did, it was… it was less cowardice and more them reacting to what they thought was a sign,' El said to Clara, as the two of them picked their way forward after the others.

'What did they do?' Clara asked.

'Well…' El started awkwardly, 'when the Rot first hit they formed the belief that it was a message; a message from Comhlacht itself, telling us that we… that we have progressed too far – that our great leaps in technology are shameful and wrong and disrespect our ancestors. They took the Rot as a sign that we have strayed from our path, and must return to the way of life of our forebears – a simpler existence, a time when our bonds with our Guardians were far stronger than they are today.'

El jumped off another large rock and held out her arms to catch Clara as she hopped down.

'And so, when the Rot struck, they retreated,' El continued as they hurried on after Vincent and Garret. 'They retreated from all communication and alliance with the other Clans, and they regressed, shrugging off the technology that had once eased the burdens of their lives in favour of the rituals and practices of a bygone era, hoping against hope that in so doing it might quell Comhlacht's fury and stay the Rot. We have heard little of them since…'

'Every now and then we receive a message from them,' Vincent added as he squeezed through a narrow gap ahead. 'They try to convince us to follow in their footsteps; to destroy all our technology and revert to the old ways to appease Comhlacht – but these missals always lack any real conviction. I sometimes question whether they truly believe in their path, or whether it is just a convenient excuse…'

'We tried many times to explain to the Hare what we'd learned about the Rot,' El continued. 'We tried to prove to them that it came from elsewhere and is not Comhlacht's doing, and in no way the Clans' fault – but they will not hear of it.'

'Like the Viper, they can only see the situation in black and white,' Vincent put in.

'Yes, the Viper see the Rot as an edict to keep advancing at the expense of all else, while the Hare see it as a command to go backwards and shed themselves of the progress that made them stronger,' El said. 'Neither side can see it for what it is – a disease. And if – *when* – this disease is removed, our path forward is the same as it was before the Rot appeared: a path not of extremes but of balance; a balance between progress and environmental protection; a balance between looking ahead, but not forgetting where we came from.'

'In the end… what it comes down to is that the Hare only care about the Hare,' Vincent interjected, 'which is why they have shut themselves off and remain neutral – unwilling to be drawn into conflict with the Viper, or anyone else.'

'Soon they will not have a choice…' Garret said darkly. 'Malone does not care for neutrality.'

'Which is why we must get there quickly,' Vincent replied firmly. 'Regardless of whether they would help us or not, I do not wish to see what happened at Neart happen there.'

'Nor I,' Garret murmured.

For a time, the group fell silent again as they focussed on the task of scrambling through the seemingly endless field of boulders beneath the blood-red sky Clara had found herself oddly becoming used to. Before long, Clara's hands were cut and bleeding and her knees grazed and muddy and she found herself longing again for her cosy bed, which right now seemed about as far away as it could possibly be.

Even with all the activity, Clara felt herself beginning to nod, her head feeling as if she was trying to balance a planet on top of a pencil. To distract herself, she again looked up at El climbing alongside her.

'Will you tell me about your children?' she asked. 'What are they like?'

At this, the tiredness Clara had seen mirrored in El was instantly replaced with an expression of pride, and fierce love. The change in her was so quick and so transformative that she almost looked like a different person – her emotions shining out of her like the sun.

'They are everything to me,' she replied after a time, a faraway look in her eyes. 'Ever since they came into this world I have felt blessed; blessed and humbled. I know I'm biased, but I never thought anything so perfect could exist, let alone that I could create them. I mean this truly when I say that there is nothing I would not do for them – *nothing*. They are my whole world... My all... My everything...'

'And what about Vincent?' Clara asked teasingly. El glanced at him.

'Ehh, he's okay,' she replied with a shrug. For a moment they both tried to keep straight faces, while Vincent looked back at them and rolled his eyes, then they both fell about giggling until their ribs ached.

Finally, the laughter subsided, and El felt able to continue.

'I think I mentioned earlier, before certain grumpy individuals butted in,' El said, looking over at Garret, who ignored her, 'but only Sisi has completed her Convergence so far – Bella and Ty are both still a little young, but all three of them want to be warriors, like their foolish parents.'

Here El stared fondly at Vincent, who was still looking straight ahead, but Clara could tell that he was listening.

'They... they have had to grow up so fast... too fast...' El continued, and Clara was surprised to see the stoic woman's eyes glistening with tears behind her mask. 'Like Vincent and myself, they have known nothing except this world; this world tainted and torn apart by the Rot – this dying place that we call home. They have been born into a life of struggle, a desperate battle we have fought for years to try to cling on to our fading existence on this planet, and instead of feeling hopeless – instead of decrying "woe is me" – they have risen to the challenge. Every day they do what they can to help our cause; every day they do all in their power to aid those around them.'

'We do not deserve them,' Vincent said quietly.

'They are too good for this world,' El agreed. 'And that is why I would do anything, sacrifice *anything*, if only they could grow up and flourish in a better world than this; a better world than the one Vincent and I grew up in.'

El took a great, shuddering breath and fell silent at last, her eyes gazing unseeingly ahead and her mind in another place entirely. Clara stared at her and there were tears in her eyes too.

'I truly hope I get to meet them,' she whispered.

A few hours later they were still traversing the maze of twisted rocks and Clara was flagging badly. They dropped down into a shallow ravine and ahead was a narrow crevice they were forced to squeeze through sideways in order to progress, the rough stone walls further grazing Clara's dirty, sweaty skin.

With Vincent and Garret ahead of her, and El behind, all light was cut off except for the dull red glow above, and Clara had to trust to her sense of touch to feel her way forwards as she shuffled slowly along, accompanied by grunts of exertion from her comrades.

Finally, when claustrophobia had begun to set in and she felt like she could stand it no more, a light appeared ahead as Vincent and Garret exited the passage, and Clara emerged behind them to see an awe-inspiring sight.

A huge mountain reared out of the blasted landscape directly on their path, its jagged summit pricking the unearthly sky above through a vast swathe of steely grey clouds. Bolts of purple lightning emitted from these wispy forms at irregular intervals, streaking to earth like the veins of some giant creature and striking the slopes here and there in a hail of sparks and flame. The lower hills of the mountain – still monstrous in their own right – ran for miles and miles to their left and right, funnelling them directly towards this terrifying peak that crouched on the horizon like a coiled snake waiting to pounce.

'What is that…?' Clara asked breathlessly.

'It's in our way is what it is…' Garret muttered.

'It is a volcano known as "Comhlacht's Furnace",' El said, more helpfully. 'But it has more recently become known as…'

'The Mountain of Malice…' Vincent finished for her.

'It was once of great importance to the Clans,' El continued. 'In the old days it had been an integral part of the Convergence. All our young adults – after making their kill and absorbing the strength of their Guardian – would climb that mountain unaided and offer those remains not used for their mask to the Furnace within. They would then put on their mask, and officially – in the eyes of their Clan – come of age.'

'But since the Rot set in it has become too dangerous to ascend it,' Vincent murmured. 'That electrical storm never moves, and is always angry...'

'Nowadays, this ritual is instead held in the Clan's hometown,' Garret added, picking up the story. 'Huge fire pits are built and the remains are instead offered to their flames, which in some ways makes it a more shared experience, now everyone can easily attend, but it is no longer the true trial – the true rite of passage – it used to be...'

'Someday, I hope – with all my heart – to see this place as it once was,' El said quietly. 'I could die happy if Bella and Ty could complete their Convergence in the manner they were always meant to.'

'But, before that can happen, we need to get past this thing,' Garret intoned gravely. 'So... do we go around it, or over it?'

Here Vincent looked at El with a small smile.

'I believe I lost my route-picking privileges after the cliff debacle,' he said. 'What do you think?'

'I think the Hare are in for a very rough time if we don't get there ASAP,' El replied worriedly. 'We try to go around this thing and there's no chance we'll reach them before...' She trailed off, unable to finish the sentence.

'Then we go over it,' Garret said decisively, setting off for the mountain at once. 'Let's move.'

Vincent glanced at El and Clara and shrugged.

'You heard the man.'

Together they set off after Garret, with Vincent walking quicker to catch up to him.

'You're worried about your people,' he murmured as he drew alongside him. 'You feel you should have stayed behind to lead them from the tunnel.'

For a moment Garret was silent, his eyes not meeting Vincent's.

'Whatever I may feel it is too late to turn back,' he replied. 'All I can do now is hope that the choice I made was the right course…'

Vincent looked at him and nodded, before glancing back at Clara walking tiredly alongside El.

It all rests on you… he thought.

Crack!

A bolt of lightning tore from the swirling maelstrom above, striking a spindly, dying tree not far from their position, and Clara almost leapt out of her skin in fright.

They were skirting around the lower slopes of the Mountain of Malice, keeping as much distance as they could from the storm clouds that encircled the crater at the peak, but they were still far from being out of danger. In fact, their very presence seemed to have exacerbated things, for the lightning now seemed to be striking much more regularly than it had on their approach.

'How much further…?' Clara asked Garret fearfully, for she was now walking beside him while Vincent and El conversed ahead.

'Still a ways to go,' he replied gruffly, having already answered this question multiple times in the past few minutes. 'Ignore the storm and concentrate on your footing.'

Clara tried to do as bidden, but as the lightning continued to pound the slopes above her, she found her gaze straying towards it and kept stumbling over rocks as a result.

'Eyes forward, I said,' Garret growled irritably, 'If you're not careful you'll…' But, before he could finish speaking, another bolt of lightning struck a boulder a mere handful of paces up the slope from them and with a crash it was rocked loose and began to tumble their way.

'Move!' Garret bellowed, and he and Clara threw themselves forward just in time as the boulder rumbled past, inches away from crushing them.

As they watched it clatter off down the mountain, they had expected the rumbling of its passage to diminish, but it didn't… For in its place a new rumble was growing – a deep, bone shaking sound that set their teeth on edge and their hearts hammering within them. It was an awesome, primal noise – a noise rarely heard since the formation of their world. As one, they all turned and looked towards the peak, watching with growing horror as the lightning strikes intensified and the rumble grew and grew to a veritable fever pitch.

The ground began to shake then, softly at first, but building and building, its location gradually moving from below their feet towards the centre of the mountain itself. Then, all of a sudden, the rumbling stopped, and for a moment they thought that maybe it was over, but it was only just beginning…

An almighty *boom* like the impact of a comet tore from the crater above and a shockwave rippled outwards, blasting all four of them off their feet. As they staggered back upright – still staring at the summit – they felt a power rising within the mountain, growing and intensifying like a geyser about to blow, like a cork milliseconds from popping.

Their terrified eyes watched aghast as an immense pillar of black smoke abruptly burst forth from the peak, shrouding the sky in seconds and throwing the whole world below into stark shadow, then – with the force of a gunshot – a spray of volcanic rock cannoned heavenward, followed closely by a gout of magma that rapidly filled the crater and began its swift descent of the mountain in a deluge of fiery death.

The small group had but one option.

'RUN!' Vincent yelled, and all four of them took to their heels at once as chunks of flaming rock began to impact the slopes around them, sending sparks and ash in all directions.

Her mind blank with fear and her heart pumping adrenaline, Clara focussed only on keeping up with Garret who ran a few steps ahead of her, who in turn was sprinting to catch up with Vincent and El, now some distance in the lead. As blazing hot missiles continued to crash down everywhere and she desperately tried to mind her footing, Clara still found her attention drawn by a small outcropping of rocks on the slope ahead between Garret and El, who was hot on the heels of her husband. Lightning appeared to be striking the exact same spot over and over as though targeting it, the unearthly purple contrasting vividly with the blackened sky. The strikes became so frequent that, for a few moments, it formed an unbroken line between the heavens and the earth, and then, just as they were drawing level with it, it happened…

With another deafening *boom*, followed by a resounding *crack*, the mountain split asunder, as the pressure within the volcano became too much, and it blew one of its vents. Clara and Garret skidded to a stop just in time as a river of magma began to flow, cutting off their route to Vincent and El on the other side, who had turned at the sound to discover them trapped.

Frantically, Clara and Garret looked around for a way past it, and as they did so they saw – to their further horror – that there were shards of crystalline rot emerging from the wound in the mountainside, emitting clouds of purple smoke as they rapidly disintegrated.

'Cover your mouth!' Garret barked, doing so himself as Clara obeyed at once.

Through a swirling cocktail of heat haze, ash and smoke, Garret strained his eyes and spotted a possible way through – a series of stepping stones to the other side, but they were swiftly degrading…

'Follow me!' he bellowed over the din. 'This way!'

Without waiting for a response, Garret was off, making the first jump to an island of safety cleanly and proceeding to jump to the next, but, as Clara lined up for the first jump, her heart quailed within her.

'I can't make it!' she yelled. 'It's too far!' But Garret was already out of earshot.

Knowing she had only seconds left, Clara took a few steps back, then dashed forwards and leapt. For a moment she sailed through the air as the heat stung her face, then she crashed down onto the rock. Her feet immediately slipped from under her and for a heartbeat she was tipping backwards – her arms flailing – before she found her balance and stabilised.

But by this point Garret was out of sight, and, as she eyed up the jump to the next rock, she knew instinctively that there wasn't a hope in hell she could make it. She was stuck…

Some distance ahead, Garret was on the penultimate jump before reaching the other side, Vincent and El standing petrified on the fringe of the magma as helpless spectators.

'Where's Clara!' El screamed over the roar of the mountain.

'Why, she's…' Garret began, turning to check on her and realising only then that she was not right behind him. His face fell as he glanced between the relative safety ahead, and the path he had just taken…

As Clara stood upon her diminishing island, her hand still over her mouth, she could feel her skin beginning to sizzle as the fearsome heat drew in closer and closer around her. Several times she had steeled herself to make the jump, but she knew it would have been death to try. She had even considered going backwards, but that option was no longer open to her either.

She had tried calling out for Garret, but had been met by nothing but the volcano's growl and the trickery of the heat haze that surrounded her. Her breath began to catch in her throat around the mask of her hand and she started to feel lightheaded, the sudden wooziness soon bringing her to her knees. Her vision darkened, spots swirling before her eyes, as she watched an indistinct blob dance before her.

Another illusion… she thought. But she was wrong.

The shape grew larger, twisting and turning until it resolved itself into a being she recognised.

'Garret...' she gasped.

Garret, in his bear form, bounded across the gap and landed next to her, his great bulk barely fitting on the rock beside her. With surprising gentleness, he ducked his great head and scooped her up onto his back, where she gripped on tight to his fur as he lumbered around for the return journey.

With Clara on his back the going was tough, but Garret made the first few jumps with relative ease. Soon they were back in sight of Vincent and El, who cheered them on as he lined up for the last jump. It was as he bounded forward to leap that the rock gave way beneath one of his paws. The sudden loss of footing threw off his momentum and he found himself spinning awkwardly in mid-air. The unexpected jolt hurled Clara free of him and she flew head over heels straight into the waiting arms of El, who caught her before she even touched the ground. Garret, however, was not so lucky…

Although Vincent sprang forward to help him, it was not quick enough. While most of his body landed on the safety of the slope beside Vincent, Garret's back right paw half sank into the magma and he roared with pain, instantly Shifting back to a man as he drew his foot in close to inspect the damage.

As the magma continued to slide their way and volcanic rock incessantly hurtled to ground all around them, Vincent knelt by his friend.

'I'm sorry brother, but we must keep moving,' he said fervently, holding out a hand to help Garret up. The Bear nodded through gritted teeth as he allowed Vincent to support him, and together the four of them made their way quickly off the mountain.

'So… I guess now me and Garret have lost our route-picking privileges too, huh?' El asked as they went.

A short time later they were seated in the clearing of a small glade of dying trees some distance from the base of the Mountain of Malice, its dull amber glow diminishing as its fury slowly abated. El was bandaging Garret's foot beside a meagre fire, while Vincent was standing staring at the peak worriedly.

'Comhlacht's pain is getting worse,' he muttered, almost to himself. 'The Furnace has not blown in centuries...'

'And it's only going to get more desperate and violent if we don't do something soon...' El said, as she tied off the bandage. 'We should...'

'Why did you save me...?'

Vincent, Garret and El all turned as one to look at Clara. She was seated by the fire with her knees drawn up under her chin, staring blankly ahead.

'Why... Why save me...?' she said again. She was addressing Garret, but would not look at him. 'Why risk your life for me...? I thought you didn't like me... I thought you... you didn't believe in me...'

Garret glanced at her piercingly for a moment, then looked down at the bandage and flexed his foot while he thought.

'I'm... I'm not sure if I do...' he replied at last. 'Believe in you, I mean. But I... I have hope, and that will have to do for now.'

Here he shifted position to get a better look at her.

'But, besides that...' he continued. 'Hey, look at me...'

Clara awkwardly lifted her gaze to meet his eyes.

'Regardless of whether I believe or not, I would not let anything bad happen to someone in my care – that I promise you,' he finished earnestly.

Clara drew in a great, shuddering breath as tears filled her eyes, and she nodded her thanks to him. Garret nodded back, then returned to playing with his bandage.

'Right, you,' El said to Clara to fill the sudden silence. 'You've been dead on your feet for too long. Get some sleep now – we'll wake you when it's time to go.'

Clara nodded again and yawned tiredly. She rolled over onto her side with her back to the fire, and the last thing she remembered before falling asleep was El laying her jacket over her as a blanket.

CHAPTER 14
Depression

Jeremy sat despondently on the wooden floor in the centre of the hall, his legs crossed beneath him as he drew in the dust with a finger. The dust was so thick that every now and then he would break out in a sneezing fit, but still he did not get up and continued to aimlessly doodle. It was a while before he realised that each of the figures he had drawn resembled Clara, and once again he fell to wondering what had happened to her.

For the past few months they had been happily attending the dancing school together, and had become extremely close friends. While Jeremy was still a hopeless dancer, Clara had taken on a grace of poise and posture that he would not have thought possible after seeing her dance at their first lesson. It was as though she had transformed in the days following it, because by the second lesson she had already become the star pupil – surpassing even those who had been attending the class for weeks. When Jeremy had jokingly queried how she became so graceful so quickly – asking whether she was in fact the same Clara Brown and not some imposter – she had merely smiled and said: 'I don't know, I didn't practice much.'

But Jeremy had known that she was lying. Why she would lie about it he did not know, but it had been clear to him that she had spent every spare moment of the intervening week practicing. His only other thought had been that she might have signed a deal with the devil, but he didn't think that was too likely.

No, dancing had become an all-consuming passion for Clara, but what baffled him most was her obvious desire to hide this fact. Whenever people asked her what she was doing on the day of her dancing lesson, she would either make something up, or simply not answer them. He didn't know whether she was ashamed of her dancing, or worried she wasn't good enough, or what… But whatever it was that made her want to hide it saddened him, and so he took every opportunity to try to bolster her confidence.

'You shouldn't be ashamed of enjoying dancing, Clara,' he had told her during one lesson. 'I mean, look at me: I'm a boy doing dancing lessons – in fact, I'm the only boy here! If anyone should be ashamed it should be me, not you.' But she had merely smiled and given a derisive snort before continuing with her stretches, forcing him to take a different tack.

'You know you're the best dancer here, don't you?' he had asked, looking into her face. 'You've got a bright future ahead of you Clara, I can see it now – you could be in a show! You could have your *own* show!'

'Don't be silly!' she replied, giving him a playful shove before beginning to practice her pirouettes. He sighed at her dismissal of his compliments. There had to be some way to make her realise how good she was, to give her the confidence to tell anyone that asked that she loved to dance.

That had been several weeks ago, and he had not seen Clara at the dancing school since. In fact, he had not seen a lot of the usual pupils for a while. It was very strange, as though whole families had suddenly taken ill and had to be isolated. He had asked his father why Clara and the others weren't attending classes, and his father had mentioned something about a depression. When questioned further about this mysterious "depression", his father had told him that he would not understand the specifics, but put simply it stemmed from problems in America, and that it was now very difficult to find work over here, which was likely why Clara's father could not afford to send her dancing any more.

When he asked why their family had not been affected, Jeremy's father had told him that – because he was a doctor – his services would always be in demand, and even if they weren't, his own father had left him a substantial sum of money in his will. This, coupled with the money he had saved himself, meant that they should have enough to tide them over until things picked up again – as long as they were careful.

Jeremy had been, on the one hand, extremely relieved to hear that his family was going to be alright, but on the other, he was worried about Clara and her family, and he hated the thought of her being unhappy. He wanted to help her, but what could he do? He didn't have any money to give her, and he certainly couldn't ask his father for money; they would need it all to ride out the storm of this depression. He decided that if he could not help her in a monetary fashion, then he could at least try and cheer her up, and he had resolved to go and see her after this dancing lesson.

Mrs Andrews finally appeared in the hall and Jeremy glanced up from his doodling. She looked drawn and flustered and there were dark rings around her eyes, as though she had not slept in days.

This depression is affecting everyone, Jeremy thought.

He looked around at the two or three girls whose fathers could still afford the classes, and realised that there was now less than a quarter of the usual pupils in attendance. They had dropped out slowly but consistently over the past few weeks and months – as the depression claimed their families – and he knew it would not be long until the rest of them left too. He could tell by Mrs Andrew's expression that she knew this all too well.

'Right, class,' she said a little breathlessly, smoothing back the hair from her face. 'Are we ready to begin?'

With the lesson over, Jeremy strode briskly up the street in the direction of Clara's house. He had been there a couple of times to play, but he was still a little unsure of its location, because each of the previous times his father had accompanied him to make sure he arrived safely.

They had spent most of their time in the neat little garden when he had been there last, playing hide and seek and football on the freshly cut grass, so when he finally reached the house and saw the state the garden was in, he felt dismayed. The grass was long and wild, and the hedges had grown thick and unchecked, tangling up with the flowers in the beds before them and slowly strangling the life out of them. A spade stood in the earth nearby, looking forlorn and alone, and Jeremy was quite sure it had not been used in some time to remove weeds, dig holes or plant flowers.

He walked nervously towards the back door and climbed the few grimy steps before rapping loudly on the wood with his knuckles.

'Come in,' a voice called from the kitchen. Jeremy immediately detected a note of despair in those two small words, and he felt their emotions grip his heart. He opened the door and stepped through into the tiny kitchen, where he discovered a depressing scene. The Brown family were seated around the kitchen table eating a thin, bland-looking soup, and Jeremy immediately felt guilty about the toad-in-the-hole he had gobbled for lunch. Clara's face was wrinkled in distaste as she sipped the soup from her spoon, but when she saw Jeremy she dropped it into her bowl with a clatter and looked at her parents.

'May I leave the table?' Clara asked, turning to her father. He merely nodded in response, as though he could not muster the strength to speak. Indeed, he looked bone-weary. His trousers were covered in mud, his hands dirty and calloused, and even to Jeremy – who had only met him on a couple of occasions – he seemed like a different person. He was not his usual jovial self, and the spark of his strong spirit seemed to have left his eyes, as though snuffed out by an invisible hand.

Mrs Brown seemed different too. She was not laughing and joking with her husband, not questioning him about his day, not asking what Clara and Jeremy planned to do together. But it was the slump of her shoulders and her downcast eyes that gave away the change the most. Once so cheerful and proactive, she was now quiet and dejected, the uncertain future brought on by the depression weighing heavily upon her.

Clara jumped down from her chair and took Jeremy by the hand, leading him into the next room, as the image of the Brown family at their kitchen table was burned into his memory. They entered the living room and at once Jeremy saw in Clara the same change he had seen in her parents. It had only been a few weeks since he had last seen her, but the difference was immediately apparent. She had always been so full of life, so excitable, so restless that she always needed to be doing something. But the way she settled herself despondently into the dusty armchair and sat there, quite still, made him want to cry out in despair.

'Clara, I just wanted to say… I was hoping to… I wanted to tell you that…' he began, but he trailed off as he stared into her face and saw nothing but deepest anxiety and sadness there, emotions a child her age should never have to experience. 'I've missed you,' he finally whispered under his breath. 'I came here to try and cheer you up, but… I don't think anything I could say would do that.'

She did not look at him and instead gazed fixedly at a spot on the floor in front of his feet, where a hot ember from the fire had scorched the wood.

'What, er… what job is your father doing now?' he asked, hoping to evoke some form of response from her.

'He works as a caretaker and gravedigger down at the cemetery now,' she answered almost mechanically. 'The mine he used to work at had to shut down, and everyone there lost their jobs.'

'Is it… is it well paid?' he asked, instantly regretting the question, as the answer was obvious.

'No, he works even longer hours now for less pay, and I barely get to see him at all anymore,' she replied, still not looking at him. 'This is the first chance I've had to see him all week.'

Jeremy looked horrified and stood up immediately.

'Oh, I'm so sorry! I had no idea… I'll leave at once,' he said, making for the door.

'No,' Clara called after him. 'It's alright, please stay.'

He moved back to his chair and sat down slowly, wishing that he had something to say that would comfort her. When she said nothing, Jeremy reached for the first thing he could think of.

'Are… are you still dancing?' he asked, kicking himself again for not thinking about her feelings. 'Well, I mean… are you still practicing at home?'

She looked at him then for the first time and he saw real anguish rippling in her eyes. It was gone in the space of a second, but he knew he had caught a glimpse of the true root of her despair, and it made him hate himself even more for bringing it up.

'Mother has been trying to help me with my dancing, but… she is not a dancer herself and I… I do not feel like I am progressing with it anymore.' He saw tears well up in her eyes, but she was master of them and not a single drop fell. 'I know deep down that dancing is all I really want to do, but now… now that we can't afford…'

Her voice broke and she looked away from him, out of the window at the overgrown garden and the dark trees that stood beyond it.

By now Jeremy was feeling truly awful. His visit had swiftly become a train wreck and his well-intentioned efforts to cheer her up had severely backfired. He almost wished he hadn't come, but in a slightly selfish way he knew that *he* had wanted to see *her*, regardless of how the visit itself turned out, and whether or not she was cheered by it.

'I don't know if this will help at all, but even though you've missed a few weeks you're still a far better dancer than anyone else at the school,' he said, watching as she snapped her eyes away from the garden to look at him. 'Melinda has always thought she was better than you and last week she tried to do a quadruple pirouette – like you did during your last class – but she fell right on her backside.' A smile tugged at the corners of Clara's mouth, and he continued. 'Mrs Andrews tried to keep a straight face, but she couldn't hold it in. Melinda went off in a huff and the whole class couldn't stop laughing for the rest of the lesson!'

Clara giggled softly and her face lit up as she was transported back to her time at the dancing school, and for a moment Jeremy saw the old Clara shining through the despondent and anxious exterior. But then Mrs Brown called from the kitchen and Clara's face crumpled back to its previous downbeat expression.

'Clara, I think it's time for Jeremy to be going home now,' she said. 'It's getting late, and his family will be wondering where he is.'

'Alright, mother,' Clara called back, sliding out of the armchair. She led Jeremy back through the kitchen, but he stopped before reaching the door.

'Goodbye Mr and Mrs Brown, I… I hope everything turns out okay for you…' he trailed off lamely.

'Me too, dear,' Mrs Brown said wearily. 'Give my best to your parents.'

'I will,' he replied as Clara led him by the hand to the back door. She opened it for him and he stepped out into the pale, late afternoon sunlight. A cold breeze whipped around him and he dug his hands into his pockets as he turned to face Clara.

'Well, goodbye. I'll come round and see you as much as I can,' he promised.

'I'll be here,' she replied. 'Goodbye.'

He walked down the steps and strode out into the road. He looked back at the house and noticed that she was still at the door watching him. He felt her eyes upon him all the way down the street, until he turned a corner and broke her line of sight.

'That went well…' Jeremy whispered sarcastically under his breath, punching himself hard on the arm and feeling the pain mix with his pity and concern for the Browns.

CHAPTER 15
Hare-brained

'No sudden moves – we're being watched…'

Clara's body instantly tensed at these words as she tried to glance around without actually moving her head – a difficult task to pull off.

Since leaving their camp at the foot of the Mountain of Malice, they had been walking for what felt like weeks to Clara – the unchanging sky playing havoc with her sense of time – but in reality it could not have been more than a day's journey. They were now passing through a narrow, steep-sided ravine – almost like a corridor – as Vincent motioned them to show caution.

'Keep your hands away from your weapons…' he added, holding his out to the sides as he walked. 'We must not appear threatening…'

Clara – still flicking her gaze nervously around – thought she saw a shadow on the lip of the ravine wall above, but it vanished before she truly got a look at it. Another flash of movement on the other side snagged her attention, and again it was gone before she could focus on it, but this time a small shower of pebbles fell from the spot where the shape had been.

'The Hare have us in their sights...' Vincent murmured out of the corner of his mouth, and as if on cue an arrow zipped like a hornet from above and thudded neatly into the ground between his feet. Clara jumped in fright, but Vincent – who seemed to have been expecting this – did not even bat an eyelid. He casually stepped around it as he looked up at the spot the arrow had flown from.

'We mean you no harm,' he called up, his voice echoing back off the ravine walls. 'We come with a warning for your Chief, Maya.'

For a few moments there was no response, only the fading echoes of Vincent's own voice, and then they appeared. The Hare Clan archers were suddenly on either side above them, their bowstrings drawn tight and their arrows sighted on the intruders below. They were silent, intense, as numerous ropes were cast out and more Hare Clan warriors rappelled down to the ravine floor to confront them.

Clara noted at once the clothes they were wearing, which strongly reminded her of images she had seen of Stone Age people, for their garments – tunics and trousers mainly – were made from an odd assortment of animal skins and woven flax fibre. They each wore a unique, wooden, hare's-head-shaped mask covering the upper half of their heads, and around their necks, wrists and ankles they each bore some form of accessory, most appearing to be composed of animal bones or teeth.

The warriors now standing before them all gripped long spears made of wooden shafts surmounted by sharp, knapped stone blades tied on with lengths of sinew, and these weapons were pointed threateningly in their direction. All in all, they cut a strange sight, one both menacing but also – to Clara's eyes – a little comical. There was something about the way they held themselves that left her feeling unafraid of them. It was a nervous energy – a constant, buzzing jitter that made Clara believe that if she were to loudly stand on a twig right now, they would all turn tail and flee. It seemed clear to her that this display was largely all bluster, and had they been truly threatened, their paper-thin resolve would have quickly shattered.

'Chief Maya is busy, Wolf,' one of the Hare warriors finally called out from behind his spear, his voice wavering slightly. 'She does not have time for…'

'She will have time for this,' Vincent replied sternly. 'For it concerns you all.'

At this, the Hare warrior who had spoken shared a short, whispered conversation with his neighbour, their eyes never leaving Vincent and his companions. After nodding to each other, their elected leader spoke again.

'We'll be the judge of that,' he said, with as much confidence as he could muster, and with that he and his companions turned and began to head off along the ravine.

Vincent glanced back at the others and shrugged with an '*I guess that means we follow them,*' look on his face, so together they began to trail after them, the archers above still shadowing them closely with their arrows nocked.

It was not long after they exited the ravine that Clara finally laid eyes on the Hare Clan's village up ahead.

'There it is,' El murmured at her side. 'Anam. For the Wolves and Bear this is… this is like stepping back in time…'

And so it was for Clara too. Where Neart had felt familiar to towns and villages she had walked in her own world, this was something else entirely. Her gaze was first taken by the vast lake next to which the Hare had taken up residence, its immense surface reflecting back the blazing crimson sky above as if the setting sun had fallen flat to earth, or as if it was filled to the brim with blood.

As they drew closer, Clara was able to discern the myriad yurts that were their homes dotted around the encampment, all of which were made from interlaced sticks and straw, each with a small, triangular entrance and a smoke hole at their peak. They were arranged at irregular intervals, with no apparent thought given to layout or spacing, as if each of the families had simply happened upon a spot and started building at once, with no word to their neighbours.

Looking around, Vincent's comments about their neutrality were immediately apparent, for Clara saw no sign of any perimeter wall, no guard towers, no sentry posts – no indication of any defensive capabilities at all. Neutrality was one thing, but she had at least expected some basic forms of protection for their people, and the lack of any seemed naïve, even to Clara's limited understanding of Comhlacht.

As they entered the outskirts of the village, the intricacies of the Hares' lives were revealed to her. Everywhere she looked there were signs of activity and hard work; cooking fires, upon which meat or fish were being roasted, were closely attended, their thin plumes of smoke drifting lazily on the cool air. Drying racks, where animal skins or lines of fish were hung, stood by the threshold of most yurts, and stacks of wood for the fires were piled all over.

It took Clara a matter of seconds to sense a difference between the Hare and the Bear peoples; while the Bear had gone about their work in a morose, detached, unenthusiastic manner, it was immediately obvious that each and every one of the Hare took special care and attention over whatever task they were assigned, the focus and concentration clear on every single face.

Over by the lake she saw two women repairing the hull of a dugout canoe with resin, both whispering intently as they worked. Further up the bank she watched a man – with exacting care – knapping a piece of stone into a fearsome blade, to be attached to the wooden shaft in his lap. By the entrance to a yurt, she observed another man intricately sewing together two pieces of hide into some form of garment, his attention fixed on nothing but the needle and lengths of sinew in his hands.

But what really caught Clara's eye were the hares – they were *everywhere*. The normally skittish animals milled about the village as if they were pets, perfectly at ease alongside the people who honoured them as their Guardian. She watched a couple of children – a girl and a boy – playfully chasing a young hare around a bush, both giggling uproariously, and the hare itself clearly enjoying the game too. The children kept switching between their human and hare forms as they ran, still unable to fully control the Shift as they had not yet completed their Convergence. To Clara it was a beautiful sight – to see the respect and reverence with which the Hare treated the natural world, and her heart soared within her.

Overall, it was an entirely different atmosphere to that which Clara had felt in Neart and it begged the question, perhaps neutrality had been the right choice…?

She dragged her gaze from the joyous sight as she found that they were approaching a building near the centre of the village that was much larger than any of the others. It was long and low and constructed of a not particularly structurally-sound-looking combination of wood, straw, hide and hardened mud.

'Is that…?' Clara began to ask El beside her.

'Yes,' El replied at once. 'That is their Chief's longhouse.'

But, before they had even reached it, their progress was halted by a number of Hare warriors armed with spears, who stepped out in front of them and blocked the way to its entrance. Vincent, whose eyes had been locked on the longhouse's doorway, let out a low growl of frustration.

'What do we have here then?' one of the warriors asked, addressing their escorts while eyeing Clara and her friends suspiciously.

'Got a couple of Wolves, a Bear and a… I'm not sure what she is…' the escort replied, indicating Clara. 'They say they have a warning for Chief Maya and must speak with her at once – has she emerged yet?'

The warrior gave Vincent an unpleasant, disgruntled look, before returning his attention to the escort.

'No, the Chief is still deeply immersed in the ritual and cannot – *must not* – be disturbed, not by you,' he replied, throwing a look at Vincent, 'or anyone else,' he finished, looking back at the escort.

The escort nodded and turned to Vincent with a shrug.

'You see? I told you so, Wolf,' he began. 'She doesn't…'

But Vincent had already barged past him to speak to the warrior himself, who took a nervous step back at being approached in such a way.

'Chief Maya must hear my words,' Vincent said forcefully. 'We've travelled a very great distance, and I will not be turned away now.'

'If it's so important, you may wait for the ritual to complete and the Chief to emerge,' the warrior began pompously, trying to appear nonchalant in the shadow of the bigger man. 'But that could take…'

But Vincent had reached the limit of his patience.

'I don't have time for this!' he snapped, and without further ado he attempted to push his way past the guards. The effect was instantaneous. From out of nowhere, or so it seemed, a dozen Hare archers suddenly appeared in a loose semicircle around them, their weapons pointed straight at Vincent's head.

'Bad move, Wolf,' the warrior said dangerously. 'You can't just…'

'Look, you cretin,' Vincent snarled angrily. 'I have come here with a grave warning for your people. You are all in imminent danger and I must speak to Maya at once, or there could be dire consequences!'

'Is that a threat…?' the warrior asked darkly.

'I literally just told you it was a warning!' Vincent roared back.

'Great negotiator, isn't he…?' El whispered to Clara, who would have laughed if the situation hadn't been so serious.

Just as the warrior was inhaling to yell a retort, a young Hare huntress appeared from out of a nearby yurt and held up her hands as if to placate both sides.

'This is clearly getting you nowhere,' she began loudly, turning her attention to Vincent. 'As frustrating as it may be, it is Clan law that the Chief may not be disturbed during the ritual. So, I suggest you come take a seat by the fire,' and here she indicated a nearby fire not far from the longhouse, 'have a bite to eat, and we'll all hope that it ends quickly for once. Is that agreeable? Or would you rather beat the stuffing out of each other?'

For a moment it looked like Vincent would indeed prefer the latter option – his eyes remaining locked on the pugnacious warrior he had been speaking to – but finally he relented and bowed in acquiescence to her.

'Well spoken,' he replied politely. 'And I apologise for my tone, but I must speak to Maya as soon as she is done.'

The huntress pointed from the fire to the longhouse door, indicating the proximity and the clear line of sight.

'You'll be the first to know,' she replied. 'Now please, come, sit.'

With a swift nod at the others, Vincent, Garret, El and Clara moved to the fire and sat down around it, while the Hare warriors and archers all sidled off to return to their duties. After watching them go, the huntress moved to stand beside Vincent.

'My apologies again,' Vincent began. 'My frustration got the better of me. May I ask your name?'

'Tia,' she replied.

'I'm Vincent,' he returned, shaking her hand.

'El,' El piped up.

'Garret,' Garret grunted.

'And who might you be…?' Tia asked Clara curiously. Clara looked back at her with interest. She had never been good at guessing ages, but thought that she was perhaps around eighteen. She was tall and slim, but well-toned, and – although it was tough to tell behind the mask – appeared very pretty to Clara's eyes. The mask itself was striking; shaped like the upper half of a hare's head, it had long, beautifully-tapered ears and was made of a dark, chestnut-coloured wood, which matched the small pelt of hare fur that fell from the back of the mask over her shoulders.

'I'm Clara,' she quietly replied at last. 'Clara Brown.'

Clara saw that Tia was now looking at her with as much interest as she had shown her.

'I'm not sure what it is, but…' Tia began. 'I sense something about you…'

'I'm… I'm not from around here…' Clara answered, not intending to appear mysterious, but unsure how else to put it. Tia continued to stare at her intently.

'May I borrow her?' she asked the group at large. 'I'd like to chat with her, if that's alright…?'

Vincent looked to El.

'If she's okay with it,' El replied, glancing at Clara.

'I'd love to,' Clara said, getting to her feet and dusting herself down.

'Just don't go too far, got it?' El called after them, and Clara nodded back.

Together, she and Tia strode away from the fire and off through the village towards the lake.

'Now, Clara, who's "not from around here",' Tia said, still looking at her with that spark of genuine interest dancing in her eyes. 'I'd love to hear just where it is you *do* come from.'

'Well,' Clara started slowly. 'It's not exactly a quick story…'

Tia smiled back at her.

'Hare rituals always take an age – trust me, we have time.'

Clara took a deep breath as she tried to arrange her thoughts and recall everything that had happened since she was woken from her bed by Vincent's howl. Finally, when she felt ready, she launched into her narrative, relaying every detail as best she could. Tia listened – a rapt audience – as they reached the lake and began to slowly make their way around it. Every now and then, Tia would stop to check on a fishing line or net at the water's edge, showing Clara how to cast them out and carefully haul them back in again.

Time slipped away as Clara's tale unfolded, and she found herself just as intrigued by Tia's life as she was by hers. To save herself from talking non-stop, Clara would ask the odd question of her, and discovered more about their simple but fulfilling way of life. She learnt how they built their canoes – and even rode one briefly when they went out into the lake to check on a net – and, once back on land, got a crash course in filleting one of the fish Tia plucked from within it. Tia was an excellent tutor – progressive and patient – and for a short time Clara almost felt able to forget the weighty responsibility that faced her.

On the far side of the lake, they came across a couple of young Hare warriors practicing their archery on a range, who cheerily gave Clara an excellent beginner lesson in its subtle art. After a few wild early shots, she was able to land an arrow just shy of the target's centre, and all three of the watching Hare whooped in delight, bringing a flush to her cheeks.

Waving their farewells, Tia and Clara continued on and eventually, after what seemed like days, completed their circuit of the lake and Clara – her throat more than a little hoarse – at last caught Tia up to the present time in her story.

As Clara's voice trailed off, it was clear that Tia was deeply impacted by what she had heard.

'I knew things were bad,' she muttered. 'But I had no idea things had become *that* bad.'

They had stopped on a narrow, pebbled beach at the edge of the lake and Tia was absently hauling in another fishing line, upon which several slightly malformed fish flapped and fought. She looked over at Clara, her expression serious.

'I assume your friends have told you about the Hare,' she said, in a tone of voice that made it clear she believed her Clan would not have been spoken highly of. 'We have little dealings with other Clans, and so news like this about what's really going on is... well, it's rare...'

Without looking, she began to remove the fish from the line and skewer them on a thin, sharp stick, ready to be carried home.

'I know what they will have told you... I know how the Hare are seen by the other Clans, but I...'

Here she looked away for a moment before turning back to Clara intently. 'I want you to know that we are not all that way. We do not all believe the Rot is Comhlacht punishing us. We do not all believe our current course is the best for us, or the best for our world. Most of the younger generation here, we… we believe that societal isolation and devolution was not the right approach, as simple and carefree as our lives may seem. We believe – as the other Clans do – that the Rot came from elsewhere and is not Comhlacht's fault. We have tried to make the elders see sense, we…'

Tia's hands had balled into fists in her agitation, one of which was wrapped around a fish, and as the pressure mounted and her brows knit with fierce anger, it soon could take it no more and burst in her hand. Her expression relaxed a little as she realised this, and she glanced at Clara apologetically.

'We just wish we were doing more… doing *anything* really… just doing something to combat this Rot, and the Viper who spread it!' These last words came out in a rush, as if she knew she shouldn't be saying them, but did so anyway. 'We have had our heads in the sand too long – hidden ourselves from the truth – and our world is only getting worse. We are being held back by the chains of ignorance, ritual and tradition – handy excuses to avoid confronting what's really going on. I… I am proud of my heritage, but I will not be a slave to it, and I will not let it blind me.'

Tia looked up and there was fiery pride in her eyes – pride and determination.

'And now you say that the Viper are coming to Anam…' she added fiercely. 'But our rituals of the past deafen us to the warnings of friends….'

She began to stride away from the lake, her fish forgotten, and Clara hurried to catch up to her. 'I will not stand by and let death come to my people because we were too set in our ways to listen…' she said defiantly. She had not gone more than a few paces when she stopped suddenly, and Clara almost ran into the back of her.

'But first,' Tia said, turning back to Clara. 'I want to thank you for lighting a fire in me with your story. It is a fire that has always burned, but it burns the brighter now. Please, take this,' she added, holding out a beautifully made knife with a stone blade, a handle of polished wood and a grip of tightly bound sinew. 'You have been through so much already, and shown such bravery – you should have the means to defend yourself.'

Clara accepted it gratefully, unsure what to say, but Tia was not finished yet. She reached behind her neck and unclasped the necklace she wore there.

'These necklaces are normally worn only by Hare hunters,' she said, as she gently fitted it around Clara's neck. 'They are said to bring good luck to those who wear them. You hunt something different to our usual prey – an end to the Rot – but I hope it may bring you good fortune on your journey.'

As they drew apart, Clara stared at the pendants upon the necklace, all made from bones or teeth – that should have made it grisly to her – but that were so exquisitely crafted she found herself lost for words.

'Th… thank you,' she finally murmured when she found her voice.

'It's nothing,' Tia replied. 'Come, let's go see the Chief…'

Minutes later, they were approaching the longhouse with Tia striding determinedly ahead, her eyes locked on the curtain of hide that served as its door. They were just passing the fire where Vincent, Garret and El still sat, and El was just about to ask where they were going, when a horn call rang out from somewhere within the longhouse – a high, quavering note that echoed across the village and caused all those in range to turn towards it.

'What… what does that mean…?' Clara asked Tia uncertainly. Tia, who had stopped abruptly – a little thrown off by this sudden development – turned to her.

'The ritual is over,' she replied quietly. 'The Chief will now address the village.'

In a matter of moments, a huge crowd of Hare had gathered by the fire in front of the longhouse, around which Vincent, Garret, El, Clara and Tia all now stood expectantly.

Another horn call blared, this one shorter and lower and followed by two quick blasts, then silence fell again, a tense excitement now buzzing amongst the massed Hare.

Finally, there was movement in the longhouse; a shadow fell behind the curtain across the door, which was at last drawn aside to reveal Chief Maya. She stepped forward into the light and Clara was afforded her first look at her, and she had to admit that she cut a rather impressive figure. Dressed head to toe in flowing robes of deepest black, and bearing a tall staff surmounted by a hare's skull that rattled as she moved due to the myriad bones that adorned it, it was immediately obvious why she commanded such respect. On her head was her own hare mask, made from a rough wood painted black as tar, her bright green eyes flashing intently from within its eye sockets. One of the mask's ears was missing – whether this was due to an accident or a tribute to the Guardian whose life she had taken, Clara would never know – but it only made her appear more mysterious.

She strode forward slowly and stopped once she was in full view of the breathless crowd watching her. Her gaze swept the gathering, taking in every face there, before at last falling on the group of visitors she had not been expecting. She regarded them coolly for a while, silently reading them, then she raised her hands to speak... but, before she could do so, Vincent had stepped forth.

'Oh, here we go...' El muttered grimly.

He came to a halt a few paces in front of Maya and addressed her.

'Chief Maya, forgive my rudeness,' he began, 'but I have been waiting to speak with you. We have come here with a warning: Malone and his Viper Clan are on the warpath – they have already decimated Neart, and are likely on their way here right now.'

Several Hare warriors – too flabbergasted by this brazen move to act – had found their composure and were now barging through the crowd towards Vincent, but with a wave of her hand, Maya warded them off.

'This is their last offensive,' Vincent continued, heedless of this. 'They will visit each and every Clan that remains and bend them to their cause, or wipe them from existence. As I told the Bear, our one remaining hope now is to *work together*. I have already seen what happens when these words are ignored, so I beg you – for the sake of your people – head to Croí. Join us in our defence against the Viper, and help us deliver Clara safely to my people.'

Here he pointed at Clara, and Maya stared at her searchingly.

'And who is this "Clara",' she asked, speaking for the first time, her voice rich and thick, like honey.

'We believe she is our means of defeating the Rot,' Vincent replied confidently. 'We believe she has it in her to help us remove it from our world, once and for all. That is why she must reach Croí as fast as possible.'

For a moment Vincent fell silent, staring at Maya intently, waiting for her response – but none came…

'What say you?' he prompted, but Maya continued to regard Clara silently for some time, before she finally turned back to him.

'No,' she said simply.

'No…?' Vincent replied, unsure if he had heard that.

'No,' she confirmed.

'But… you cannot…'

'I can, and I will…' she cut across him. 'I have been communing with our ancestors for the past day – imploring them for their help and wisdom in these dark times – and do you know what they said?' she asked, but Vincent's face had crumpled into helpless anger, and he did not deign to respond.

'They confirmed that our path forward – as always – is in following the footsteps of the past,' Maya continued, answering her own question. 'We must continue to live with the grace and dignity of our forefathers; we must continue to honour tradition above all else – it is only through this that we will stay Comhlacht's fury. At least for the Hare.'

'And how's that been working out for you?' Vincent snapped furiously.

Maya spread her arms effusively.

'We are still here,' she replied.

'Still here, while the rest of our world – that's right, *our* world – crumbles around your ears,' Vincent snarled back. 'Your traditions are a blindfold you donned yourselves. I do not believe you truly think this Rot is Comhlacht's own doing – it is just an excuse to divest yourselves of responsibility.'

He took a step towards Maya, staring at her imploringly.

'If our world is to survive you must see reason,' he continued, his voice softening. 'This Rot is an outside force and the "punishment" you think you are seeing is just Comhlacht lashing out in its pain. If we are to defeat this Rot and cure our world we must do so together! Please… come to Croí – help us hold off the Viper!'

'We. Cannot. Get. Involved.' Maya spoke each word slowly and loudly, as if speaking to a child. 'We are neutral in all of this. We have never had any problems with the Viper, and anyway… if they were to attack, we would simply do as the hare does…' She held Vincent's hopeless gaze for a moment. '… and run,' she finished.

'No!'

The crowd all turned as one at the voice that suddenly echoed from amongst them as Tia strode forward to stand before her leader.

'We Hare have stood on the side-lines for far too long!' she continued, her voice rising powerfully. 'Choosing to live like our ancestors has done nothing to rid the world of this Rot – if we have largely avoided its effects thus far it can be nothing but dumb luck. We can no longer sit idly by and let our world go to ruin around us – we must stand up and do whatever we can to help it!' She turned to address the crowd now. 'If we are to forge any change in this world we must not look to the rituals of the past but the reality of the present! The Hare *must fight!*'

A tangled roar of voices from the crowd greeted this statement. While most of the elderly Hare seemed to be shouting her down, the younger Hare were all bellowing their agreement, both side's words lost in the cacophonous din. Maya was now glaring at Tia with mounting rage, and she was about to retort when Tia got there first.

'It seems we have a disagreement,' she said loudly, the voices of the crowd gradually diminishing as they listened. 'I say – we call a vote!'

A hubbub of voices broke out again; arguments between Clan members popping up everywhere, in some cases escalating as far as shoving and threats.

Maya had to scream at the top of her voice to be heard.

'We do not question the ancestors!' she screeched, bringing silence once more. 'They have told us the path we must take, and that is…' But she got no further, as a sudden, earth-shaking rumble split the air, and – in a deluge of dirt and rock and a deafening mechanical whirring – a huge, terrifying machine burst from the ground not twenty paces behind Maya, and crashed down through the walls of her longhouse.

CHAPTER 16
Death from Below

The village was thrown into chaos as the monstrous burrowing machine – its nose surmounted by a massive drill – spun around to face them in the wreckage of the longhouse, pivoting on its twin set of caterpillar tracks. All over its riveted metal shell pistons hissed and thumped, cogs whirled and clanked, and steam rushed from vents, but thankfully it did not appear to bear any weapons.

The last wall of the longhouse still standing crashed to earth as the diabolical contraption came to a stop, facing the onlookers who stood frozen in horror. Before any of them could gather themselves enough to react, another drilling machine erupted from the ground through a yurt to their right, then another in the midst of some drying racks to their left, then another and another – they were surrounded…

From loudspeakers mounted on the dreadful machines, a tinny voice echoed across the village:

'Surrender to the Viper and join us, or be destroyed!'

Then, as if on cue, hatches on the sides of each machine were suddenly flung open and, with guttural roars, dozens of Viper soldiers began to pour forth into the village and lay waste to all around them in a barrage of gunfire and explosions, fires swiftly springing up everywhere they went.

For most of the Hare this was their first sighting of the Viper in many years – if at all – and seeing their hideous, ungodly mechanical alterations was all too much for them. In the shadow of these hellish monstrosities most of the Hare quailed, and their bravery snapped like a twig.

'Defend yourselves!' Vincent roared over the high-pitched whine of the machines' drills and the grating voice from the loudspeakers, but his command went unheeded by many.

With cries of terror, much of the group Shifted and ran for their lives – doing as their Guardian would do – but not all of them… The younger Hare were not so easily shaken and took up arms at once to fight for their home, while all around them their elders – including Maya – backed away or out-and-out fled.

'You must stand together!' Vincent boomed. 'We must repel them!'

As the younger Hare leapt into battle – their arrows and spears seeming like child's toys against the Viper weaponry – their elders continued to turn tail, turning their backs on their friends, their families and their home in the process.

Tia, who was loosing arrow after arrow into the approaching Viper, glanced back to see her people fleeing and was filled with righteous indignation.

'Enough running!' she screamed over the din, her voice carrying across the carnage. 'The legacy of the Hare is not in flight, but in speed – speed and intellect! We know this place better than these Viper bastards ever will – let's show 'em what we've got!'

At her words, several of the elders still in earshot felt the pang of shame, but with it the glow of pride in their people, and they found themselves turning back to the fray.

'Hit 'em hard, hit 'em fast, then move!' Tia yelled. 'Let's go hunting!'

With that, the Hare that remained – young and old alike – let out a strange, ululating war cry that stopped many of the Viper dead in their tracks; then they scattered, Shifting and spreading out around the village in their less-visible Hare forms to engage in guerrilla warfare, the Viper suddenly finding themselves fighting on multiple fronts at once. Arrows began zipping from every conceivable angle and the Viper – caught in unfamiliar terrain – began to take heavy losses, and their fury knew no bounds.

Still standing at the centre of the village, Vincent, Garret and El fired their weapons into the approaching Viper until they clicked dry, then ducked out of sight behind a yurt with Clara to reload and regroup.

'What do we do?' El shouted over the noise. 'Do we stay and fight…? Or do we get Clara to safety…?'

Vincent did not answer for a moment as he reloaded, his mind racing, then he looked over at her.

'We cannot risk Clara by staying too long,' he said at last. 'But we can help even the odds a little before we go…'

He cocked his pistol, then looked at Garret.

'Follow me, brother,' he said, then he turned to El. 'Keep Clara safe – we'll be back in a jiffy.'

With that, he nodded at Garret and the two of them hurried off with their weapons held ready.

'Where are they going?' Clara asked anxiously.

'To do something brave and stupid, no doubt,' El replied with a worried fondness.

Vincent and Garret darted through the village, dodging skirmishes left, right and centre and engaging only when they had to.

'What's the plan?' Garret asked breathlessly as he ran at his friend's side. Vincent merely nodded at one of the burrowing machines ahead, and Garret instantly got his meaning.

A Viper soldier with a viciously sharp sickle-like weapon lunged at Vincent, but he dodged the haphazard swing and kicked his attacker fiercely in the back, sending him headfirst into a large fire pit. Another emerged from behind a burning yurt and hurled himself at Garret, who swiftly Shifted to his bear form and tore into him, shredding flesh and dismantling metal alike.

Barely breaking stride, the two of them continued on towards the machine that crouched in the wreckage of a stack of canoes ahead, its drill still spinning in a lethal blur. Two more Viper soldiers – after dispatching a young Hare warrior – turned and pounced at them; one Vincent shot down with his revolver, while the other Garret dispatched with the metal claws on his gauntlets, separating the unfortunate soldier from his weapon arm, and then his head.

They raced on, watching Hare warriors and hunters popping up from all over to harangue and harry the Viper as best they could – their speedy hare forms and superior knowledge of the environment helping to make up their deficit in the weapon department.

They soon reached the drill and threw their backs against it, Vincent instantly searching for the way in. He spotted the hatch the Viper had exited from and pointed it out to Garret.

'If you would do the honours,' he asked politely.

With a slight nod, Garret gripped the handle and heaved with all his might, but it would not budge. His hand balled into a fist and with one strike he punched the claws of his gauntlet through the locking mechanism and twisted, then gripped the handle again and wrenched the hatch open, letting Vincent slide in ahead of him.

The interior of the machine was much more spacious than Vincent would have thought, its rear quarters housing a couple of small rooms, while its front end…

Vincent did not have time to take in any more before a knife was zipping through the air towards him. He Shifted to his lower wolf shape to dodge it, the blade passing within millimetres of him and instead clanging into the wall not far from where Garret was just entering.

The driver – who had thrown it – scrambled out of the cockpit towards them and Vincent wasted no time in bounding towards him and savaging his throat to ribbons. Unbeknownst to him, a second Viper driver began to emerge from the cockpit and was just raising his hammer-like left appendage to crash down on Vincent's head when two shots rang out and he fell back dead. Vincent turned from the dead driver beneath him, his muzzle stained red, to see Garret lowering his sawn-off shotgun, the barrel still smoking.

Vincent Shifted back to human – wiping his mouth and nodding his thanks to his friend – before he turned and climbed into the cockpit. Taking a seat in one of the two drivers' chairs, Vincent found himself confronted by a dizzying array of controls that he didn't have the faintest idea what to do with. Garret appeared behind him and whistled quietly at the sight.

'Just start pushing things, I guess,' he suggested.

To get his bearings, Vincent peered out of the small slit windows positioned above the still-spinning drill, then gripped one of a pair of levers and pushed it forward. The machine began to rotate clockwise immediately, and Vincent let go of the lever before pushing the other one forward, to discover that this spun the machine counterclockwise.

After a bit more fiddling he had got the basic idea, and quickly pivoted around until they were facing another of the terrible machines standing side-on to them, not more than fifty paces away.

'Get ready to run...' Vincent murmured to his friend, then he thrust both levers forward at once and the machine surged forth, directly at its target.

Outside, a group of Viper soldiers had cornered a trio of Hare warriors up against the blazing remains of their home and were closing in, looking scornfully at the primitive spears their adversaries held while licking the blades and barrels of their own horrific array of weapons in anticipation of the slaughter to come.

At the sound of the drilling machine behind them powering forward under Vincent's control, they all turned and their faces fell in dismay as they took in the situation in an instant.

'What are they doing!?' one of them yelled. 'They'll destroy them both!'

'Get it moved!' another yelled. 'That's our ticket out of here!'

Forgetting their cornered prey, the Viper soldiers raced toward the machine Vincent had targeted, frantic in their efforts to save it.

Back inside the machine, Vincent watched them rushing to its aid, but knew they would never make it.

'Time to leave,' he called out over the roar of the drill. With one final adjustment to its course, Vincent jammed the two levers forward once more, then turned and leapt out of the cockpit, following close behind Garret.

The machine was not more than ten paces from its target when the two friends tumbled out of its hatch, Shifting as they did so and making a beeline for safety as fast as their legs would carry them.

Over by the targeted machine, one of the Viper soldiers had managed to race inside and hurry towards the cockpit.

'Get this thing moving!' he screamed at the two shocked drivers. 'We're about to be…'

But what they were about to be became immediately apparent to them all as Vincent's machine impacted with theirs, its massive drill puncturing the metal shell like an egg and ripping straight through its furnace and piping in a hail of lethal debris.

As the intricate machinery was shredded, various gases began to mix within the two tangled hulls, and everywhere sparks continued to fly…

Vincent and Garret had barely got more than a hundred paces from the two machines when they were blasted off their feet by a shockwave as the machinery ignited behind them in an explosion the like of which Comhlacht had never seen, the detonation sending a towering mushroom cloud into the sky and launching white-hot shards of metal and rubble in all directions. Many Viper in close proximity were instantly incinerated, while the Hare watched it all from their guerrilla positions around the village.

Briefly cowed, but far from beaten, the rest of the Viper turned from the vast column of choking black smoke and leapt back into the fray.

Shaking themselves vigorously, Vincent and Garret got straight to their feet where they spotted Tia battling with a couple of Viper nearby. Arrow after arrow flew from her bow and finally one of her opponents fell, but then the other was upon her and she was forced to switch to her spear. With a quick glance at each other, Vincent and Garret hurtled over to help, but just as they arrived Tia dodged under a vicious swing from her attacker and clambered up his back like a monkey, evading his lumbering swipes at her and bringing her spear straight down through the top of his head. With a grunt of pain, the great, mechanically-altered monster collapsed to the ground and Tia leapt aside.

Impressed, Vincent and Garret Shifted back to human to address her.

'I'm afraid we cannot stay any longer…' Vincent began, but Tia was already nodding her understanding.

'I know – you must get Clara to safety,' she said. Vincent nodded back.

'I do not know if this is a fight you can win,' he continued honestly. 'But – if you are able – *please…* fall back to Croí. Convince as many as you can to join you and head for Croí, for that is where the final battle will be fought… and we will need all the help we can get if any of us are to survive this…'

'I will do all I can,' Tia assured him. 'I will not let the Hare end here – that I promise you.'

Vincent looked at her and there was no doubt in his mind.

'I'm certain of it,' he replied. 'Y'know – you'd make a great Chief one day.'

And with that, he and Garret set off running back towards El and Clara, while Tia Shifted and raced off to find her next opponent.

Thus far, El and Clara had largely avoided being drawn into combat, but after the explosion the Viper seemed to have redoubled their efforts and were now searching every nook and cranny for Hare to capture or kill.

Huddled behind a yurt, they watched breathless as the shadow of a Viper soldier slowly approached their position, one of its arms – shaped like an executioner-style axe – raised high in preparation to strike. El had one hand clamped on Clara's shoulder to keep her in place, while the other held her blade in readiness to attack.

As the Viper slid into view around the structure, El – thinking quickly – let go of Clara, picked up a piece of debris and hurled it past him, the sudden movement making him look away. It was a fatal mistake.

Before he knew what had happened, El had leapt up, lunged forward, and driven her blade straight through his throat, dropping him without a sound, but it made no difference…

'There's one over there!' a nearby Viper yelled to his comrades. 'Get her!'

El dived back down behind the yurt and glanced at Clara.

'That could have gone better…' she muttered. 'Time to…'

But, before she could finish speaking, a small metal object landed between them and rolled to a stop, a mechanism within ticking steadily.

'Oh damn… MOVE!' El yelled and the two of them scattered in opposite directions, barely making it to cover before the grenade exploded, sending dirt and debris flying everywhere and blasting a crater where they had stood.

Clara had dived forward and now tumbled end over end, finally coming to a stop some distance away with her ears ringing, her head pounding, and spots dancing before her eyes like fireworks.

Groggily, she staggered to her feet and turned to look back through the haze of smoke to see if El was alright.

'El!' she called out hoarsely. 'El, are you okay?' But she could not see her anywhere.

Shifting her gaze, Clara looked out through the decimated village and spotted someone she would rather not have seen – Darius…

He and his cronies were standing by one of the drilling machines not far from where she was, and they were pointing right at her…

Clara knew she was in trouble and turned to run, but she was still so dazed that she stumbled over a pile of fallen logs and crashed to the ground, and within seconds the Viper were upon her. She swiftly found herself being hauled to her feet by two sets of arms, and felt her world close in around her. For just a second, she thought about giving up – as it would be so easy to do – but found that she could not…

As the two Viper began to manhandle her towards their machine, she felt a furious rage bubble up inside her, as all the confusion, fear, sadness and anger she had experienced since arriving in this world threatened to swallow her whole, but instead transformed itself into affirmative action.

With a wrathful snarl that would have done Vincent proud, Clara tore her arm out of the grip of one of her captors, reached to her belt where the stone blade Tia had given her was stored, gripped it tight in one hand, then leapt up at her other captor and rammed it into his neck up to the hilt. The stunned Viper let go of her at once as he clasped the wound, then he crumpled to the ground and within moments lay still, while Clara had already spun away to slash at the other Viper, who was swiftly getting over his surprise.

'What are you playing at?' Darius called from nearby, advancing towards them. 'Grab her!'

As Clara swiped viciously at her target, just about holding him at bay, she failed to mind her surroundings and was grabbed from behind by Darius himself.

'Let me go!' she screamed, kicking and biting at any part of him she could. 'Let me go!'

But he was too strong from her. The blade was knocked from her hand, and she found herself being dragged once more towards the machine. She thrashed like a landed fish – looking around desperately for help – when her eyes fell on a welcome sight.

'Vincent! El!' she yelled. 'Help!'

Her two friends, with Garret behind them, were heading her way – their eyes locked on hers, desperate to reach her – but their path was blocked by at least a dozen Viper. As she reached the hatch leading into the machine, she bucked and fought, grabbing at anything to stop herself from being hauled inside, watching helpless as Vincent battled with a Viper armed with a wicked-looking blade, his own cane sword ringing off its steel as they clashed.

As she was finally prised loose and pulled into the machine, the last thing she saw was Vincent taking his opponent's blade in the side and toppling to earth and she cried out in anguish as if it had been her flesh pierced.

'NO!'

The hatch slammed shut behind her and for a moment she could not see, but she continued to fight tooth and nail – frantic in her efforts to reach Vincent – the explosive effort quickly sapping her remaining strength as she was lugged towards a cell at the rear. In the dim light she could make out the shapes of several small people inside and realised they were Hare children, and this only made her fight harder.

'Do something about her!' Darius yelled at a nearby figure.

The next thing Clara knew, she was cracked over the head with the butt of a blunt weapon, and everything went dark…

CHAPTER 17
Into the Viper's Nest

Lancing pain. Strobing lights. Dim voices.

As Clara struggled slowly back to consciousness – like wading through deep mud – a kaleidoscope of images pressed in behind her closed eyes. She saw the terrible machines breaching the earth in Anam. Tia handing her the necklace and stone blade. Vincent clashing swords with that Viper. And again, the book on the table in the darkened room of her subconscious, the key now in her hand, poised over the padlock, ready to reveal what awaited within…

'Stop!'

Clara jerked awake with a gasp and a cry, desperate not to open the book – frantic to avoid facing the words written upon its pages.

She sat bolt upright, clasping at her chest as her breath came in short, sharp bursts, her clothes drenched in sweat and her sight blurred and unsteady. Her head pounded with the incessant rhythm of a marching band's drum, and she clapped a hand to the affected area, feeling a wetness there and drawing away to see the dull glisten of blood on her palm.

She winced in pain as it all came flooding back to her at once.

'Vincent!' she breathed in dismay.

She tried to get to her feet – her vision still foggy – but at that moment she felt the ground jolt beneath her and she fell back onto the bench she'd awoken on. It was then that she detected the little tremors and vibrations all around – heard the tell-tale sounds – and realised what was happening.

We're moving...

She turned on the spot and saw the vague outline of a window just above her – light streaming through the bars that covered it – and so she climbed up onto the bench to peer out. At first, all this bright light did was make her head hurt worse and for a time she had to shield her eyes and wait for them to adjust. Gradually, the ache in her head lessened, her vision slowly clearing until she was at last able to get a good look at where she was, and when she did her stomach dropped away in fear.

'Inchinn...' she whispered in horror. 'They've brought me to Inchinn...'

And indeed they had.

To Clara, the Viper city skyline was at once familiar, and terrifying – reminding her of places she knew, but also of the terrible lengths man will go to in order to get what he wants. Wherever her frightened eyes looked she saw nothing of comfort

– nothing green or good or pure, nothing that spoke of home or hearth; nothing but immense, awe-inspiring factories and warehouses built of dull, soot-blackened brick everywhere. The harsh, jagged lines of their construction gave them a dangerous, almost weaponised look, and their minimal windows made them appear secretive and closed off, denying those within the opportunity to be distracted by goings-on outside. These fearsome structures seemed to press in around Clara, towering into the sky like silent sentinels and making her feel no bigger than a mouse.

Rising above this drab, regimented arrangement of buildings were the silhouettes of massive cranes lifting crates and girders to and fro, and here and there she saw huge chimneys thrusting into the sky like lances and belching out thick, oily smoke into the atmosphere. Her wide-eyed gaze followed these pillars skyward to the colossal black cloud that hung over the whole city, completely blotting out the hellish sky above.

Shoving her head through the bars to see better, Clara immediately choked on the acrid air as she craned her neck awkwardly to look ahead and discovered that they were rumbling down a cobbled street in some kind of steam-powered prison bus. Glancing around, she was able to peer through the doors of some of the buildings they passed and catch glimpses of what was going on within, and it chilled her to the bone. In every single one there were instruments of death being designed and developed by legions of Malone's people, each working with a fierce and obsessive intensity.

In one building she saw racks of weapons being tested and stacked, ranging from blades and axes to machine guns and flamethrowers. In another she witnessed the dim shapes of vehicles – like the tank they had faced in Neart, and some even more monstrous than that – rolling down a production line as the finishing touches were added by engineers. And in another she saw mechanical replacement parts – legs, arms and eyes mainly – being fitted to Viper soldiers and tested by their new owners, to varying degrees of success.

The fanatical order, drive and *coldness* of it all was what affected Clara the most – seeing these people going about their warmongering as if they were simply churning out nothing more alarming than clothes made her spine tingle. Here they were preparing for war, while the other Clans worked to save their world, and the Viper along with it. Anger rose within her like bile at the thought of it, and she felt her hands ball into fists as she watched more of the Viper military industrial complex pass her by. A helpless, furious scream began to work its way up her throat, but before it could find its way out, a small voice stopped her cold.

'What Clan do you think she is…?'

With an effort, Clara tugged her head back through the bars as another voice replied.

'Dunno – but not Bear, for sure.'

'Nor Hare,' another added.

Clara spun around on the bench and peered warily into the darkness of the prison bus's interior, her eyes struggling to adjust after the brightness outside.

'Who's there…?' she said nervously. There was a moment's silence, then a shape leant forward into the shaft of light coming from the barred window, then another and another and another until there were ten children in all staring up at her, five on either side of the bus.

Clara was taken aback, as she had had no idea there was anyone else in there with her, and so at first was at a loss for words. Into this stunned silence a boy of about eleven with a grimy face and a slightly pugnacious aspect spoke, looking her up and down as he did so.

'We're prisoners, like you,' he said, rather matter-of-factly. 'Got grabbed when the Viper attacked Neart.'

Her eyes now accustomed to the light, Clara was at last able to see that both he and the four other children on his bench were all dressed like the Bear citizens she had seen in Neart, and each one of them looked dirty and malnourished, with a strange kind of grim acceptance on their faces, rather than fear.

Looking over to the other bench, she could see that all five children seated upon it were of the Hare Clan – their clothing and hairstyles an instant giveaway – and she noted that on their faces was real terror, their eyes round and glassy as they looked at her. Not one of the children there wore a mask, so she knew at once that they were all younger than thirteen and had not yet completed their Convergence.

Why no adults…? she thought. *Why have they only captured children…?*

'So – what Clan are you from then…?' the Bear boy asked, interrupting her thoughts.

'I'm…' Clara began, before she knew what she was going to say. 'I'm not from any Clan… I'm from… somewhere else…' she finished lamely.

'Oh,' the Bear boy responded, accepting this explanation at face value. 'What are you doing here then?' he asked.

'I'm… I'm still figuring that out…' Clara replied vaguely.

'Do you know where we are?' a small Hare girl asked her fearfully.

'We already told you,' the Bear boy replied scathingly. 'This is Inchinn – the Viper Clan's city. Don't you Hare know anything?'

'But what do they want with us…?' another Hare child asked breathlessly.

'I heard they kidnap children to experiment on 'em,' a Bear girl said, leaning further forward. 'The Viper lost their ability to Shift from all the Rot they've used, and they want to recapture it by studying kids coming up to their Convergence.'

'They say the tests are agonising,' another Bear child added grimly. 'Most of the kids don't make it through 'em alive…'

'And those that don't they burn in their furnaces to fuel their machines,' the Bear girl added. 'They think it makes 'em stronger.'

All five of the Hare children recoiled fearfully at this, several of them covering their heads with their hands in anguish. Clara listened to all this with mounting anger, for it was only serving to terrify the Hare children even more.

'Well, I heard they indoc... indoctri...' the Bear boy began.

'Indoctrinate,' the Bear girl finished for him.

'Yeah indoctrinate,' he continued, 'the kids they capture to join their cause, and any who won't join 'em they put to work 'til they can't work no more and drop dead where they stand.'

'They just... drop dead...?' the small Hare girl asked, in barely more than a whisper.

'Yeah, stone dead,' the Bear boy replied. 'Thems that don't get crushed crawling inside their machines to fix 'em.'

The small Hare girl's eyes were wide as saucers as she listened – her face as white as a sheet – and Clara could see that she was trembling.

'Nah, they don't make 'em work,' the Bear girl said derisively. 'It's experiments – my nan told me so.' The Bear boy scoffed at this.

'How could they learn how to Shift again by studying kids?' he said scornfully. 'They just put 'em to work building their machines 'til they die – that's all. They...'

'Enough!'

Every one of the children present jumped at Clara's sudden outburst, and all turned to look at her in surprise.

'Enough of this!' Clara continued sternly, addressing the Bear kids. 'This kind of speculation isn't helping – all you're doing is frightening everyone!'

Looking abashed, the Bear children dropped their gaze to the floor, the Bear boy mumbling mutinously under his breath.

Getting to her feet, Clara moved to sit beside the petrified little Hare girl and put her arm around her. She desperately wanted to say something reassuring – to tell her that it was going to be alright – but the words would not come, so instead she just held her close as her body shook and tears ran down her face.

As she sat there, Clara began to hear muffled voices emanating from outside and so – after gently extricating herself from the Hare girl – she immediately got up and returned to the barred window to peek out. From where they were, Clara could see that they were passing across a stone bridge over a deep, wide river littered with docks, where innumerable boats stood tightly moored as crates and barrels were unloaded from them by hand or by crane.

As they continued along, the source of the voices came into a view – a kind of checkpoint at the end of the bridge where several Viper guards stood waiting, speaking together loudly.

At that moment, the prison bus braked suddenly to a stop and they were all nearly thrown from their seats, Clara just managing to avoid a nasty fall by clinging to the bars. A cackle of laughter from the front of the vehicle reached them through a small grate in the metalwork as they heard a fist pounding upon the divide, followed by a raspy voice calling out:

'You all awake back there? 'Cos we've nearly arrived!'

Sticking her head through the bars once more, Clara was just about able to see the driver of the vehicle now speaking to the guards at the checkpoint, who raised the barrier blocking his path and waved him through.

The vehicle started moving once more and Clara climbed down from the bench and turned to survey the area around her. The back of the bus consisted of large double doors, but when she approached to inspect them she could see no obvious locking mechanism on this side. She turned back around and instead studied the bench she had been standing on and saw that one of its metal legs was loose.

Getting down on her hands and knees, she approached, gripping the leg tightly and pulling with all her might. It shifted, but did not come loose.

'Help me with this!' she called to the Bear boy, and she was surprised to see that he immediately complied, joining her on the floor and gripping the leg alongside her.

'One, two, three – heave!' Clara said, and they both strained against the weakened metal and felt it budge.

'Again – heave!'

They pulled as hard as they could and with a *crack* the short length of metal came free in their grip and Clara picked it up, hefting it in one hand.

Right then the vehicle slowed to a halt, and they all heard the murmured voices coming from just outside. Clara glanced up to see that every one of the scared children was staring at her with a quiet intensity – they didn't know what she was planning, but all looked to her now as their only possible hope.

'Stay… stay behind me…' she said, struggling to fight the tremble in her voice. 'And I'll… I'll do what I can…'

She turned to face the doors behind her, gripping her improvised weapon tightly as footsteps approached the rear of the vehicle and a hand was placed on the latch. With a *clank,* the lock was drawn back and, before the doors were even fully open, Clara had exploded into action.

With a furious cry, she leapt from within and bore the first Viper she spotted to the ground, beating at his chest and face with the bench leg and scoring many deep cuts on his awful, ravaged, mechanically-altered body.

'Get her off me!' the Viper roared at his comrades as the blows continued to rain down.

Clara felt herself gripped from behind and thrown aside, but the instant she landed she was moving again – racing at the next Viper and thrashing him as hard as she could with her weapon, while the

Hare and Bear children in the bus watched with open mouths.

This time she was kicked aside, but again recovered at once and bounded back to the offence with all the speed and ferocity of a wildcat.

'Grab her before Malone sees!' another voice hissed, and this one she recognised – Darius.

She soon found herself backed up against a stack of crates with nowhere left to run, and before she knew it, they had grabbed her and wrenched the weapon from her grip. She continued to kick and scratch with all her strength until she felt a metal hand slap her hard across the face and her vision went white, all the fight knocked out of her in a second. Held tightly between two Vipers, her head hung limply, blood dripping from a badly split lip and a huge bruise already discolouring her cheek.

'That's better,' Darius hissed. 'Cuff her – I don't want this happening again.'

Too groggy to resist, Clara felt her wrists being bound by handcuffs and soon they were dragging her roughly across the cobbles. Out of the corner of her eye, she saw the other children being meekly unloaded and led along behind her, so she turned to look where they were heading, and her breath caught in fear.

A titanic factory – the biggest she had yet seen – loomed above her, the vast entrance large enough to admit her entire house through, and her mind boggled that anyone could build something so huge.

As they passed across the threshold, Clara's fuzzy vision picked out bursts of light and colour where sparks flew and molten metal was poured, while all else seemed like a dull blur.

With Darius in the lead, she was hauled up a steep flight of stairs and soon she and the other children found themselves standing outside of a large, innocuous-looking office. Darius rapped smartly upon the door, and waited for a response.

'Enter,' a deep, sonorous voice intoned from within.

Darius nodded meaningfully at the two Viper holding Clara, his icy stare threatening repercussions if they allowed any more nonsense from her, then he gripped the handle and thrust the door open, the group trailing in after him.

Seated behind his desk in a high-backed chair, Malone cut a chilling figure as he watched them filter in over a clipboard held in one hand, his gaze fierce and unblinking and his face lit by the flickering glow of the furnace at his core. To Clara's still-bleary eyes he was little more than an indistinct shape in the pale light from the window, but she knew at once who she had been brought before – it could be no one else…

'Got you a fresh batch, Boss,' Darius began. 'And a little extra too…'

He strode over to Clara and gripped her by the arm, presenting her to Malone.

'I found her, Boss!' he continued proudly. 'I found you the one Vincent brought over from Gaia!'

Gaia...? Clara thought. *Is that what they call my world...?*

At this, Malone's aspect changed. He dropped the clipboard and got to his feet, moving around the desk and sitting upon its front edge so he could get a better look at her, a wide, mirthless smile on his face. For a minute he said nothing as he studied her, then at last he spoke.

'You've done well, Darius,' Malone said with quiet glee. 'If only I could see Vincent's face right now.'

'You might never see it again, Boss,' Darius replied. 'Pretty sure I saw Tam stick him.'

On hearing this, Clara let out a little gasp of distress that Malone could not fail to miss, and it only made him smile all the wider. After savouring her pain a moment longer, Malone stood and faced the assembled children, none of whom would meet his eyes.

'Forget the lives you knew,' he began slowly, enjoying every word. 'Forget the places you lived and the friends and family you had. You are now my *property*. You belong to *me*. But I am not completely heartless...' Here he looked at the furnace at his core and spread his hands wide. 'Metaphorically, of course,' he added. 'I will give you a choice.'

He began to pace up and down before them, his steps heavy on the wooden floor.

'The choice is this,' he continued. 'You can choose to join us; join the Viper and become one with the Cypher, helping us to reshape this world and drag it kicking and screaming into the future – a future it deserves, no... *needs* to reach... Or...'

He stopped pacing and stared at them, his mechanical right hand curling into a fist as steam hissed from the vents on his back.

'Or… you can be put to work until your backs break, your hearts give out, or you change your minds…' Malone left the sentence hanging in the air.

'Or, there is the third option…' Darius added with a snigger.

A flush of fresh terror rippled across the faces of the children as their future was laid out for them, every one of them trembling violently.

'I will give you until tomorrow to think about it and make your choice,' Malone said magnanimously. 'Let us hope you all choose wisely…'

He turned his attention back to Clara for a moment, then glanced over at Darius.

'Put her with the others for now,' he murmured. 'I'll take the night to ponder how we can use her…'

'Sure thing, Boss,' Darius replied, then he turned and began to usher everyone out of the office. As she left, hauled along by her guards, Clara could feel Malone's eyes boring into the back of her head, until the door was closed carefully behind her.

The next few minutes were a blur as she was led down corridors and walkways that took her deeper and deeper into the factory, until finally they came to a stop in a large room lined with holding cells.

'I've got her,' Darius said, taking Clara by the arm. Her guards nodded and moved off with the rest of the children, who stared after Clara fearfully, frightened at being separated.

'Where are you taking me?' Clara asked fiercely, as Darius dragged her away.

'To your kind,' he spat back.

They reached a darkened cell, and he nodded at a nearby guard who quickly removed the complicated array of locks sealing the door and thrust it open. Darius bent to the cuffs on her wrists, a key in his hand, then stopped himself.

'Are you going to behave?' he asked her.

'No,' Clara threw back. Darius simply sneered and undid the cuffs anyway, the sneer soon vanishing as she kicked him hard on the closest bit of exposed flesh she could reach.

With a snarl of rage, Darius hurled her into the cell before turning and striding away, as the guard locked the door behind her and trailed after him.

Left in a ringing silence, Clara glanced nervously around the shadowy confines of the cell, and immediately detected movement in the darkness.

'Hello…?' she whispered nervously.

She stumbled backwards as two shapes materialised from the gloom and approached her slowly. One of them – a girl – cocked her head to one side.

'Not from round here either – are you…?' she said.

CHAPTER 18
New Allies

'Yeah, you ain't from the Clans,' the girl said, nodding emphatically. 'You're from our world, ain't ya? Got a Northern look about ya – that right?'

Clara – too stunned to know what to say – nodded.

'Yes, I… I am, yes…' she mumbled.

'Thought so,' the girl said, pleased with her assessment. 'If I hadn't got it from your face, your accent woulda given it away, for sure. I'm from the South meself – Essex.'

The girl took a step closer, craning her neck to get a better look at Clara.

'Cor, they really did a number on your face!' she said, taking another step into a shaft of weak light and affording Clara a decent look at her. She was a tall, scrawny girl of thirteen with a thin face and small, mistrustful eyes – one blue and one brown – that darted about as they sized Clara up. Her hair was a dull, dirty red and was long and unkempt, trailing down past her hips in a matted tangle and her clothes – dark blue dungarees over a multicoloured striped jumper – were ragged and filthy. Her long-fingered hands – thumbs hooked in her pockets – drummed incessantly on her thighs as she continued to scrutinise the younger girl.

'What you do to make 'em beat you up?' she asked.

'I attacked a group of them,' Clara replied, her confidence slowly returning.

'Pull the other one!' the girl scoffed. 'A skinny little thing like you?'

Clara was annoyed at this response, but decided not to be drawn on it and remain as pleasant as possible.

'I'm Clara – Clara Brown,' she said, changing direction. 'What's your name?'

'Why you want to know…?' the girl replied suspiciously, and when Clara simply stared back at her with a bewildered, questioning look she soon relented.

'It's Darcy Granger – okay?' she replied brusquely. 'And I'm…' But Clara's attention had been caught by the other figure in the room, who had taken a step nearer. Darcy saw where Clara was looking and rolled her eyes.

'Ah, ignore 'im,' she said dismissively. 'Dull as dishwater – barely says a word.'

The figure moved closer still, taking quick, nervous strides, until he too was illuminated by the shaft of light, revealing a short and rather portly boy of about eleven years dressed in a dark grey school uniform. Anxious green eyes looked out at her from a round, flushed face, every facet of his being exuding a tense, nervy energy, his left hand constantly moving as he fiddled with what appeared to be a well-worn coin.

'Hello,' Clara said to him, a little uncertainly. 'And who are you…?'

'H… Hi…' the boy replied timidly. 'I'm… I'm… I'm…'

'He's Marcus,' Darcy put in impatiently. 'Marcus Kent – not that it matters… And yeah – he's from our world too.'

Clara ignored Darcy and kept her attention on Marcus.

'And how long have you been in Comhlacht?' Clara asked him. She noticed that he seemed unable to meet her eyes, his gaze occasionally grazing hers before moving swiftly on.

'Three… three months…' he stammered eventually. 'I was only…'

'Been 'ere for about six months meself,' Darcy interjected unprompted. 'Six months since those bloody Wolves brought me over. I was only with 'em a week before the Viper attacked us and snatched me – spent the rest o' me time 'ere.'

'The Wolves brought you over too?' Clara asked, turning her attention back to Darcy.

'Yeah – Wolves brought us both over,' Darcy replied, picking at her teeth with a fingernail. 'They seemed to think we could help 'em in some way – help do something about the Rot – but they never explained what…'

'They said the same thing to me,' Clara replied thoughtfully. 'My whole time here I've been terrified because I have no idea what I can do to help…'

'Well, it doesn't matter now,' Darcy said, inspecting something picked from her teeth before flicking it away. 'We're stuck in 'ere for good 'cos o' them, so the whole bloody place can go to hell for all I care.'

'And did they promise you anything in return for helping them…?' Clara asked, her gaze flicking between the two of them. Darcy stiffened a little at this.

'And what's it to you?' she replied warily.

'They… they promised…' Marcus began haltingly. 'They promised to help "find what I had lost" – that… that was what they said,' he finished.

'Yeah,' Darcy grunted in agreement. 'Same.'

'And did you know what they meant by that?' Clara asked Marcus.

'No… I had no idea…' he replied, still playing with the coin in his hand, rolling it skilfully over his knuckles. 'But I…'

'I didn't know either,' Darcy cut in again, and Clara had to work hard to control her temper at the interruptions. 'But if I've lost something then I bloody well want to find it again before someone else makes off with it!'

'So… so you were kidnapped from the Wolves too?' Clara asked Marcus, wanting to give him chance to speak.

'Yes… I was only with them three days before we were…' he faltered for a moment. 'We were ambushed by a Viper patrol… I don't think any of the Wolves made it…'

'And good riddance too,' Darcy spat nastily. 'They're the reason we're all in this mess! They *promised* they'd look after us! They promised we'd be safe! And where are they, huh?' She spread her arms expansively. 'Where the hell are they? They've made no attempt to save us – not one! If we were so important to help save this ugly, dying world, then where are they…?'

To this, Clara did not know what to say, and so instead she changed tack a little.

'Why have they even kept you here?' she asked. 'What have they been doing with you?'

The result of this simple question was instant, for Marcus immediately recoiled with a little moan of distress and backed off into the corner of the room.

'Don't…' he whined. 'I don't want to think about it!'

'I'm sorry…' Clara stammered in surprise. 'I didn't mean to…'

'Don't… Don't want to…' Marcus repeated fearfully. 'Don't want to think…'

'They experiment on us – okay?' Darcy said bluntly. 'They run tests on us *every single day*… and they never tell us why…' Darcy was trying to appear cool – unfazed by it all – but she could not prevent the shudder that ran through her body.

'The tests, they're… they're *horrible… awful…*' Marcus murmured from the corner where he was now crouched, hugging his knees.

'And they never seem to get 'em anywhere,' Darcy added. 'But they keep doing 'em anyway…'

'They experiment on the Clan kids too...' Marcus whispered.

'But they do that separate, someplace else,' Darcy muttered. 'I think those're for different reasons.'

'I'd rather be in the mine...' Marcus said, now rocking back and forth on his heels, his eyes wide and staring.

Clara's face had drained of all colour as she listened to this.

'The mine...?' she asked nervously.

'You really are new here,' Darcy said, with as much self-importance as she could muster. 'Most kids that won't join the Viper get sent to the mine.'

'And none of them have ever returned...' Marcus added in a sibilant whisper.

'What's... what's this mine for?' Clara asked.

'I reckon it's gotta be where they gather the Rot for processing in their factories,' Darcy said, now pacing up and down. 'Where else would they be getting it all from?'

Clara had never thought about it before, but she guessed it made sense.

'They work kids there 'til they die...' Marcus said, his voice now a dull monotone as he continued to play with his coin. 'But it's got to be better than this...'

Darcy, who had now stopped by the cell door, let out a growl of helpless rage and kicked the bars hard with her boot.

'This is all those damn Wolves' fault!' she snarled. 'Why did I trust 'em? How could I have been so bloody stupid!?' She thumped her fist against the bars. 'Well, I'm never making that mistake again! Ma always said, she said: "Family's the only one you can trust", and she was right – she was bloody right! You let your guard down for one minute – *one minute* – and this is what happens! This is the thanks I get! Well, never again!'

She strode away from the door and Clara moved to take her place, poking her head through the bars to inspect the locks for any weakness.

'I shoulda just stayed at home,' Darcy continued to mutter. 'I shoulda told that Wolf: "No, thank you – you can keep whatever it is I lost" – but no, I decided to trust 'im. Idiot!'

She stopped speaking and cocked her head as Clara reached through the bars and jiggled the locks.

'Won't work,' she said dully. 'Don't you think we tried that?'

'We've tried everything,' Marcus said from his corner. 'It can… can only be opened from outside by the guard.' But Clara continued to fiddle with the locks in the vain hope that maybe she could figure out a way to escape.

'Don't you get it?' Darcy said, anger creeping into her voice. 'There's no way out of 'ere! We're finished, over! We'll be 'ere 'til the Viper are done with us, then we'll be nothing but fuel for their fires! Get it?' But still Clara continued to poke and prod at the locks, straining through the bars to reach for the top bolt.

'Just pack it in, will ya!?' Darcy yelled. 'You can't…'

'No!'

Clara turned to face Darcy sternly.

'I will not give in!' she continued firmly. 'You may have, but I will not! Things are bleak now, but I know my friends – El, Garret and… and…' Her voice trailed off for a moment, for she had no idea if Vincent was alive or dead – if any of them were alive – but she had to keep up hope. 'They will come for me – they are the strongest, bravest people I have ever met, and they will not leave me in here to die! They will come – and together we will figure out a way to defeat this Rot!'

Darcy snorted in derision.

'If you truly believe all that – if you still trust 'em after all this – then you're a bigger fool than I took you for,' she said viciously.

'I guess I'll just have to trust for both of us then,' Clara said defiantly. 'Because they will come – you'll see.' The girls locked eyes for a moment, then Darcy scoffed again and turned away. Clara could see that she had done nothing to sway Darcy's thinking, but she turned to see that Marcus had arisen from his corner and was now standing close by, looking at her hopefully.

'You really think your friends will come save us?' he asked. Clara nodded emphatically.

'I do,' she replied, without a shadow of a doubt. A shuddering gasp of relief escaped Marcus' lips, and he was just about to speak when something clattered against the bars behind them, and they all whirled around to see the Viper guard looking in at them. Unlike most of the other Viper they had seen, this one looked far more human, only his mechanical left hand and his furnace heart having been swapped out. He banged the bars again with his metal fist.

'Quiet down in there! It's time you all went to sleep!' he barked. Clara was just about to fire back an angry retort when the guard glanced quickly over his shoulder – watching a patrol of soldiers move away – then leant in conspiratorially.

'Hey, keep your chins up,' he whispered. 'Help is on the way, so get some rest – you'll need it…'

And with that he turned and vanished into the shadows, leaving the children surprised, but cheered. Even Darcy looked taken aback, the faintest glimmer of hope now dancing in her eyes.

With nothing else to do but wait, Clara lay down in a quiet corner and – after much tossing and turning – fell into a fitful slumber.

CHAPTER 19
The Recital

It was a glorious Saturday afternoon, and Jeremy was on his way over to Clara's house. He had been visiting at least once a week since his horrible attempt to cheer her up and had been doing a much better job of it since. Although he was still a hopeless dancer, he had made it his mission in life to pass on everything he learned from Mrs Andrews as best he could so that Clara could continue to grow and improve in her craft.

In fact, they had been – in secret – working on a little dance recital of their own, stringing together various tricks they had learned from the classes into an original routine that Clara had largely masterminded and dubbed: "The Ballad of the Swan Princess."

Jeremy had to admit that he was a little mortified by his role in it as "The Swan Prince", and still did not actually enjoy dancing himself, but seeing how it so delighted and elevated Clara made it worth the embarrassment – *every single moment* of it. His mother had, in point of fact, actually asked him if he still wanted to continue the classes – offering him an easy way out – and he would have taken it if it had not been for Clara.

Losing her access to the classes had all but destroyed her. It still pained Jeremy to see Clara as she was now, limping along through life without them, with only the crutch of his meagre tutelage to help her. In the wake of the Depression, Clara had become another person entirely, and the Brown household was a very different place from the one he had first visited before it had struck.

After his first failed attempt to cheer her up he had become much more careful about scheduling his visits to ensure they never clashed with time with her father, for he knew how rare and precious these moments now were to her. However, today's visit had been specifically planned at a time when her father would be home – because today was the day of the recital.

Jeremy found that he was nervous, for he had never done a performance in front of an audience before, always choosing to hide behind other members of the class when Mrs Andrews asked someone to step forward and demonstrate something. The knowledge that he still wasn't any good did nothing for his confidence, but this did not matter – for he knew her parents' eyes would be fixed on Clara, and Clara alone, throughout.

Up ahead, he saw the Browns' house appear around the corner and he quickened his pace, his heart thumping a little faster, as it always did just before seeing her. It made him smile to recall how they had once been – the arguments and fist fights that had defined their relationship before they had got to know each other properly at the dancing class.

How could I not see in her what I do now? he often asked himself, but he did not know the answer.

At last, he reached their house and was unsurprised to see it still in a state of disrepair, the garden more wild and unruly than it had ever been. But he did not have eyes for this as he hurried up the stairs to the door and knocked on it loudly.

Within seconds he heard quick footsteps approach and the door was wrenched open by Clara, already dressed in her leotard and ballet shoes.

'What took you so long?' she asked, with a friendly scowl and a light punch on his arm.

'Would you believe that I was practicing for the recital?' he replied hopefully.

'More likely you were stuffing your face with lunch!' she fired back with a laugh.

'Ah, you got me!' he chortled. 'But I needed my strength if I'm going to perform!'

Clara prodded him playfully in the belly.

'Any more "strength" and I think you'd burst!' she giggled.

'Any more comments like that and when I do burst I'll aim it at you!' he retorted, and they both collapsed laughing.

Wiping tears from his eyes, Jeremy looked over at the still-giggling Clara and it made his spirit soar to see her happy again, even if it was just for a moment.

If only I could do more than make her laugh, he thought, as he always did.

Finally, Clara's laughter subsided and she looked over at him.

'Come on,' she said. 'Let's go and do one last practice run.'

He nodded back at her.

'I've got something new I can show you too,' he remembered. 'Mrs Andrews just taught us it last lesson, she…'

But, as Clara was moving to stand up, she suddenly winced in pain and clutched at her side.

'Are you alright?' Jeremy asked in concern, hurrying to take her arm and help her up.

'Yeah… yeah, I'm fine,' she replied, waving him away. 'Just been having some odd pains – that's all… C'mon – this way.'

Clara turned and walked away – still holding her side – and Jeremy watched her go nervously.

What was that…? he wondered.

Half an hour later, they had done not one but two "final" practice runs in the living room, and Jeremy still had a few notes for her.

'Your last arabesque was great, but you were a little wobbly,' he said. 'Show me it again.'

Clara tutted and rolled her eyes, but assumed the pose anyway, balancing on one leg while the other stuck out gracefully behind her.

'That's it – much better!' Jeremy smiled appreciatively. 'You...' But at that moment Clara hissed in pain again and swayed, but somehow held the position.

'Are you sure you're alright?' he asked for the umpteenth time this had happened.

'Yes, I'm fine – stop nagging,' she replied tightly. 'Is this okay?'

'Yeah... it's... it's much better,' he murmured, still looking at her uncertainly. 'Y'know, we could postpone this to another time if you're not feeling up to it?'

Clara stared at him wide-eyed, as if he was an idiot.

'This is the only chance I have in the next two weeks to perform this for my father,' she said curtly. 'You know how much he...'

'Yes, I know you two don't get much time together,' Jeremy replied worriedly. 'But maybe you should be having a lie down or something...?'

'I'm not wasting any time in bed,' she retorted, dropping out of the arabesque. 'Now, what was that move you wanted to show me? Maybe we can fit it in somewhere.'

Jeremy sighed in defeat, knowing how impossible it was to get Clara to change her mind once she'd fixed on something.

'It was a lift,' he said. 'You run at me and jump, I catch you and lift you above my head, then we twirl together.'

Clara looked at him askance, one eyebrow raised.

'And you actually did this in class…?' she asked in disbelief. 'Successfully…?'

'Yeah… I…' Jeremy began, a little hurt. 'Well, I got it on the third try anyway…'

'And what happened the first two times…?' Clara queried doubtfully.

'Melinda got very mad at me – that's what,' Jeremy replied, a little shamefaced. 'But I got it in the end. Look, can we just try it? I was thinking it would be a nice way to end it – the Swan Prince raising the Princess above him to show how she's ascended.'

'Hmm,' Clara responded thoughtfully. 'Yeah, that would tie it all up nicely, *if* you can pull it off…'

'I've got this,' Jeremy said, with as much confidence as he could summon. 'Assuming you're feeling well enough to try it?'

'Don't you worry about how I'm feeling now,' Clara fired back tartly. 'Worry about how I *will* be feeling if you drop me, and how I will make *you* feel if you do!'

'I'm very scared of you right now,' Jeremy replied with a wan smile.

'You should be!' Clara retorted, breaking into laughter before backing off a few paces. 'Now, lift me, Swan Prince!'

'It would be my honour,' Jeremy grinned back, as Clara began to run at him. But she had not gone more than two paces when she stumbled again with a gasp of pain and fell to her knees.

'Clara!' Jeremy exclaimed, running to her side. 'I really think we should tell your parents! There's clearly...'

'No!' Clara's pained shout cut through Jeremy to his core. 'No. We are doing this performance, and nothing is going to stop it.'

She got to her feet once more and backed away from him.

'Okay, let's try again...' she said.

'I'm so excited!' Emily Brown whispered to her husband. 'The two of them have been so secretive about this whole performance – you'd think they were spies or something! Has she given you any hints about it?'

Joseph Brown glanced at his wife and smiled, shaking his head slightly.

'She accidentally let slip something about a swan last week,' he replied, 'but then immediately clammed up and I've heard nothing else since.'

The two proud parents sat in comfy armchairs in the living room facing a pair of bedsheets hung haphazardly across the space as makeshift curtains, numerous lamps littering the carpet before them in place of stage lights. Behind the illuminated fabric they could see two small shadows moving about and hear their excited whispering.

'I can't tell you how good it feels to see her like this,' Emily sighed happily. 'Just like she used to be.'

At this, Joseph put an arm around her and hugged her close.

'This Depression will pass, love – given time,' he said, kissing her on the forehead. 'You'll see – and once it does and things pick up, she'll be right back at that dancing school, making all the progress her heart desires.' Emily rested her head on his shoulder.

'I'm just so grateful to Jeremy for passing on what he's learned – for keeping her motivated. Lord knows I'm no dancer!' she chuckled. 'He's a good friend to her.'

'That he is,' Joseph agreed. 'Though I think he wants to be more than that…'

Emily broke apart from him and looked at her husband in disbelief.

'Go on with you!' she exclaimed. 'Kids their age aren't thinking like that yet!'

Now it was Joseph's turn to chuckle.

'Oh, really?' he said with a smile. 'I seem to remember receiving a love note from a certain young girl of about their age when we…' Emily cut him off with a loud tut.

'That was a different time!' she replied.

'Times don't change as much as you think,' he laughed. 'I know love when I see it…' At that moment the curtain began to be drawn awkwardly aside revealing Jeremy standing there pulling on his half. '…and that boy is smitten,' Joseph finished.

After a particularly hard yank on his side of the curtain – resulting in the whole thing collapsing to the ground – both Emily and Joseph Brown were afforded their first look at the stage, and the hand-painted backdrop of a lake and a bridge the two children had made. Emily gasped with delight at the sight of it and looked at her husband proudly, but he had eyes only for his daughter as the recital began.

Twenty minutes later, "The Ballad of the Swan Princess" was drawing to its conclusion, and while Emily had tears on her cheeks, Joseph's face was afire with pride and love. They had known Clara had a passion for dancing – of course they did – and it had torn them apart to have to deprive her of the classes she loved so much, but seeing what she had been able to achieve without them – the narrative she had been able to tell with her body alone – transcended mere passion and elevated it to another level entirely.

'I have to get her back in those classes,' Joseph whispered to his wife, his eyes never leaving Clara as she floated about the stage. 'She has to have the opportunity to follow this through properly.'

'But how will you afford it…?' Emily asked, as mesmerised as her husband.

'You let me worry about that,' he replied quietly.

The show was approaching its climax and Clara had just bounded to stage right, now facing Jeremy on the opposite side. With a graceful twirl she set off moving, gliding serenely towards him, then she leapt forward, and Emily gasped in fear as Jeremy caught her and lifted her high above him, spinning slowly on the spot as she held a magnificent pose.

Sunlight lanced through the windowpane behind her and for a few moments Emily and Joseph saw their daughter's head surrounded by a halo of light, and they knew that neither of them had ever seen anything so good or pure in their entire lives, but it did not last…

As she rotated through the air above Jeremy, Clara suddenly gasped in agony and bucked like a startled horse, the unexpected movement wrenching her from his grasp and bringing her tumbling down on top of him. Both Emily and Joseph were immediately on their feet and hurrying over to her side at once.

'Clara! Clara! Are you alright?' Emily asked anxiously, smoothing the hair from her daughter's face as she lay on her back, but Clara did not respond. She was shivering violently, beads of sweat running down her face, her eyes glassy and unfocussed. She winced again and gasped, pain seeming to stab at random parts of her as the shivering intensified.

'I'm… I'm cold…' she gasped at last.

'I didn't mean to drop her!' Jeremy said in shock. 'She's been having pains all day, but told me not to say anything!'

'Clara!' Joseph said, leaning over her, trying to keep his voice steady. 'Clara! Where does it hurt?'

As Clara continued to flinch in pain, tears began to fall from her eyes.

'Every… everywhere…' she managed to whisper.

Joseph turned to Jeremy.

'Run – get your father. Hurry!'

Jeremy nodded in fear – his face a ghostly white – then he spun on his heel and ran for the door. He stopped before he reached it and glanced back. He had one last fleeting glimpse of Clara, lying trembling on the floor, before he turned and raced from the house with tears streaking from his eyes.

CHAPTER 20
All Aboard!

'Wakey wakey!'

Clara's eyes snapped open as these words were swiftly followed by the clatter of something running along the bars of their cell. She got quickly to her feet and turned to face the door, barely stifling a gasp of shock to see none other than Malone himself staring in at her.

'Sleep well?' he asked, the coldness of his gaze belying the meagre pleasantry. 'Any bad dreams? Perhaps about an ex-best friend of mine who should have made better choices?'

Clara did not dignify this with a response, instead fixing him with an icy glare. Malone tutted with disappointment.

'I expected a bit more fire from you,' he said with a sad little shake of his head. 'You who put two of my men in the hospital yesterday.'

'And I'd do it again!' Clara hurled back. Malone smiled.

'That's a bit more like it!' he laughed. 'They tried to hide it, but I *always* find out – nothing stays hidden from me. And trust me – they'll never leave that hospital again… Would've been kinder if you'd killed them.'

Clara stared at him in disgust.

'You're vile!' she whispered. Malone shrugged in response.

'Hey, you put them there,' he replied. 'If you want to blame anyone, blame yourself.'

He turned and leant back against the door, not even bothering to look at her anymore.

'I guess the other two have told you what's been happening to them?' he asked. 'How are you both doing by the way?' he called loudly over his shoulder.

Darcy had now got to her feet and was standing a few paces behind Clara, while Marcus had not left his corner, but neither of them said anything.

'That good, eh?' Malone continued unperturbed. 'Anyway, so you'll know that I've had my best scientists working on this – on them – for months now, but…' He sighed in exasperation. 'We have tried everything – *everything* – we can think of to examine on you kids to help us better understand the Cypher, and it has got us nowhere – absolutely *nowhere*. I hadn't expected to find much, if I'm honest, but to find nothing whatsoever, well – you can imagine how angry that made me.'

To her intense annoyance, Clara found her curiosity overriding her anger and hatred of this man, and she felt compelled to ask the question that had sprung to her lips.

'Why…?' she whispered. 'Why do you think that *we* would be able to help you understand the Rot?'

On hearing this, Malone went very still for a moment, then slowly turned to face her.

'Ohh,' he said, as realisation dawned. 'So, they… they never told you – did they…?'

'Tell me… what…?' Clara replied, nervous now. But Malone was shaking his head.

'I always knew Vincent liked to play his cards close to his chest,' he muttered, 'but to keep you in the dark like that, well…'

'Keep me in the dark about what?' Clara asked.

'About where the "Rot" – as you call it – comes from,' Malone replied, enjoying every second of this. 'About the fact that the place we Viper call Gaia – the place where the "Rot" is pouring in from – is well known to you; *very* well known – for it is *your* world…'

Clara suddenly felt like she was falling from a great height as it finally hit her. She had never thought about it until now – never thought to question Vincent on it – but she realised it had been staring her in the face all along. Vincent had told her the Rot came from "another place", but she had never made the connection between that and the link to her world, the link Vincent had used to bring her over when they first met. It seemed so obvious now, but it still did not explain what the Rot actually was, and she wasn't about to give Malone the satisfaction of asking him, and so instead she said nothing.

Malone chuckled to himself at her shocked expression – an expression she fought desperately to hide, but was unsuccessful.

'Vincent was always cunning,' Malone drawled. 'Always so good at controlling the flow of information – it's probably why I was first drawn to him. Don't be upset that he fooled you – he's done it to so many others before…'

Why…? Clara thought, doing her best to keep her expression blank. *Why did he keep it from me? Why did he not just tell me the truth from the start…?*

'I guess you'll never find out now, huh?' Malone continued, reading her like a book. 'You may not believe this, but it truly pains me to know that I'll never see my old friend again. Never hear another of his self-righteous tirades… You see, the problem with Vincent was that he… he always lacked… vision…'

As he said this, it looked like Malone was having a vision of his own, as he was struck by a sudden thought.

'Ohh… Ohh, yes – I've got it!' Malone said gleefully. 'Because the thing about me is, vision has never been a problem…'

He began to stride up and down as he thought the idea through.

'Yes… Yes, it's perfect!' he murmured to himself. 'The one thing we haven't tried yet: we take you kids to the source – right to where we mine it, and then… then we see what happens… And if nothing does, well… you can just stay there until something does happen, or you drop dead…' He turned on the spot and yelled. 'Guard!'

A Viper guard appeared at double time – the same one who had told them help was on the way last night – and he stopped before Malone.

'Boss?' he enquired.

'Put them on the next train to the mine,' he commanded. 'And send me Kal, he'll be going with them.'

'Your chief scientist?' the guard asked. 'You, uh… you had him executed last week…'

Malone rubbed his jaw thoughtfully, then shrugged.

'Well, send me whoever replaced him then – and hurry up about it!'

'Yes, Boss!' the guard replied, hurrying over to the cell and fumbling with his keys.

As Malone moved off, the guard unlocked the door and let them out.

'Follow me,' he said quietly. 'I wasn't expecting this and it changes things, but it might actually be easier… I'll get a message to the Wolves to tell them where you're headed. Don't worry – they won't let you rot in that mine…'

Clara tried to say something, but he gently shushed her.

'Best if you don't speak,' he said. 'Just follow quick and quiet. This way.'

As the guard moved off, Clara, Darcy and Marcus shared a look and silently agreed that this was indeed their best option, so they began to hurry after him.

They were whisked through the streets by the friendly guard – their progress seemingly monitored at every turn by armed soldiers – and before long Clara heard the whistle of a steam train, and they found themselves outside the station.

'This is where I leave you,' the guard murmured to them. 'I'll send a message to the Wolves now – with any luck you'll never even reach the mine. Stay strong!'

With that, and after a short conversation with the soldiers blocking access to the station, he handed the children over and they were swiftly led inside, their hearts hammering with fear – regardless of the assurances of their ally. They were bustled through the cavernous foyer onto a platform shrouded in steam, and as the steam cleared Clara was forced to stop dead and rub her eyes in disbelief at what she saw.

At first glance she thought it looked like a fairly average steam train, much like the ones she knew back home: it was painted in a matte black and had a large and powerful-looking engine with a trio of chimney stacks spewing smoke and a cabin where the driver stood, shovelling coal onto its fire, and behind this was linked an array of carriages, ranging from cargo bearers to more passenger-oriented cabins.

It took several long moments for the true strangeness of it to sink in – for the incongruent details to become patently obvious to her. Because this train was far from ordinary, for where its wheels should have been there was instead row upon row of huge, insectoid, mechanical legs sticking out – powered by a dizzying array of gears and pistons – that made the machine look like some mad-scientist's blend of steam train and centipede. Clara had to shake herself to be assured that she wasn't dreaming, for she had never seen anything quite like it in her entire life.

'You… you're seeing this too… right…?' Marcus asked breathlessly. But Clara could only nod in response as she stared at it.

'Stop gawping,' the soldier leading them barked. 'Train's leaving any minute now – move!'

With no other choice, they allowed themselves to be jostled towards the remarkable machine, glancing around them as they went and watching other Vipers boarding it or loading it with supplies. As they approached the door to one of the passenger carriages, it suddenly hissed open with a jet of steam and folded vertically downward to create a bridge from the platform to the interior.

'Go on!' the soldier yelled. 'Hurry up!'

One at a time, they filtered inside where they discovered row upon row of seating on either side of the aisle, but these seats bore complex harnesses that went over the shoulders and between the legs.

'What do you think those are for…?' Clara whispered to Marcus.

'No talking!' the soldier growled. 'Straight to the end – the cage!'

At the back of the carriage – past the rows of seats – stood a large cage with more of the same seating within, and so they proceeded towards it as commanded and were bundled unceremoniously inside.

'Now, I want to hear no gossip!' the soldier snarled, locking them in and pocketing the key. 'Oh, and you might want to buckle up,' he added, with a nasty sneer. He turned then and marched quickly to the far end of the carriage, buckling himself securely in a seat facing their cage. At that moment, the train whistled twice and began to move out of the station.

Clara, keen to see where they were going, scrambled over to the open window by the cage, and – by climbing onto the seat and sticking her head through the bars – was able to peek outside and look ahead.

'That's a great way to get decapitated,' the soldier remarked idly.

As she watched, Clara could see the station interior whipping past as the mechanical legs skittered along beneath them, powering them speedily on towards the outskirts of the city, and she quickly realised that this train did not need tracks of any kind. She also noticed that they appeared to be heading straight toward an enormous cliff face that completely blocked their path ahead.

'Get in your seats!' she yelled to her friends.

'You don't tell me what to do!' Darcy replied belligerently. 'I...'

'Suit yourself,' Clara interrupted, already in her seat and doing up her harness. 'But we're about to crash!'

With a little gasp of shock, Marcus followed suit, while Darcy just looked at them askance.

'We're not going to...' she began to say, but right then they all felt a ripple through the soles of their feet – a sudden change in the movement and power of the train as something shifted up ahead. A shadow passed over and they all looked up through the skylights to see the cliff face rearing above them, but what they had not expected to see was the train ahead climbing vertically up this impediment as smoothly and effortlessly as it had navigated the flat.

On seeing this, Darcy immediately threw herself into the first available seat, snapping in her buckle as fast as her trembling fingers would allow, and she was only just in time...

A split second later their carriage was tilting backwards, tilting and tilting until they were lying flat on their backs in their seats, flying straight up the cliff at a breakneck speed. Their hearts in their mouths, the children clung on tightly, and would have enjoyed the experience if not for where their ride was taking them.

Moments later, they reached the top of the cliff and felt the train level out around them, and all three of them let out a collective gasp of relief.

'Well, never done that before...' Clara said breathlessly.

A short while later they were racing across a vast, empty expanse of arid plain, the crimson sky above blanketing everything in its oppressive embrace. The soldier who had brought them there was now slumped against the window and appeared dead to the world.

Sensing an opportunity, Clara undid her harness and got to her feet, moving furtively towards the cage door to check the lock. As she did so the soldier grunted and looked up.

'What are you doing?' he asked suspiciously.

'Nothing!' Clara replied quickly, jumping back into her seat and belting back in. The soldier growled and leant back, appearing to fall asleep once more.

With that option gone and nothing else to do but wait, Clara turned to Darcy.

'So… whereabouts in Essex do you live?' she asked pleasantly. Darcy immediately shot back a look of outright mistrust.

'Why are you asking?' she replied warily. 'What's it to ya?' Clara held up her hands.

'I'm just making conversation,' she replied in aggrieved bewilderment. 'Why are you so defensive? You seemed happy enough to talk and talk last night.'

Darcy looked away from her.

'Yeah, well… I'm just not used to bein' asked personal questions without some other intent behind 'em, alright?' she said, now picking at her fingernails. 'But, if you must know… I don't live anywhere specific… not for very long anyway…'

She sighed and glanced out of the window – past Marcus as he continued to play with his coin – at the dreary landscape flashing past.

'My family, we… we stay as long as we can in one place, before the landowners or the rozzers arrive, then we move on sharpish,' she continued, now biting at her fingernails. 'Keeps us on our toes, I can tell ya. Home for me, it's… it's wherever we can park the caravan.'

'So, you're…' Clara began slowly.

'Yeah – it's not an easy life,' she added, before throwing an acid glare at Clara. 'But I don't want no sympathy – alright?' Clara held up her hands again to indicate that she submitted, and Darcy turned away once more. Her gaze this time fell on Marcus and her hand flashed out, pinching the coin from him.

'H-hey!' he yelled, lunging for it. 'G-give that back!' But Darcy easily avoided his feeble attempts and inspected the coin closely.

'Why you always playin' with this thing?' she asked. 'It's just an old coin – nowt special about it.'

As quick as a whip, Clara pounced, snatching the coin away from her and immediately handing it back to Marcus, his face flooding with relief.

'Oi!' Darcy said, annoyed. 'I was just wondering why it's so important to 'im! It's not so sp…'

'I-it is… special!' Marcus stammered angrily. 'This is a… a special coin.' He gently stroked the surface of the cold metal, staring at fondly. 'M-my father gave it to me. It has a defect – the date on it is ten… ten years in the future. Father told me that as long as I have this coin it'll… it'll help me to feel brave… brave and confident…'

'And how's that been workin' out for ya…?' Darcy asked scathingly.

She was about to say more when a tinny hiss blared over the loudspeakers along the walls of the carriage, and a voice rang out shrilly.

'We're under attack! Everyone to battle stations!'

The soldier who had been guarding them jerked awake as though stung and glanced over at their cage – reassuring himself they were still there – then he unstrapped and darted to the window to look outside. Clara, Darcy and Marcus unbelted themselves and did likewise, all three of them pressing together to peer out, where they saw an incredible sight.

Hurtling towards them across the plains were two trails of dust, kicked up by a pair of machines travelling at tremendous speed. As they drew closer their shapes became clearer, and the three children gasped at what they saw, for it was even stranger still than the centipede train they were riding. The machines were formed of riveted metal in a perfect ring shape, as tall as the train but less than half its width, within which they could see a compact steam engine at the rear powering it all and a line of seats with the driver at the front, controlling it with various levers and buttons and something akin to bicycle handles.

But it was underneath the ring that was strangest, for rows of mechanical insectoid legs – like those on the train, but smaller – worked feverishly to power it forwards, seemingly able to cope with any incline in the terrain by simply sliding around the outside of the ring, while keeping the occupants within perfectly level.

It was a miraculous sight, but Clara did not have eyes for the engineering wonder she was witnessing – not when she saw who was piloting the machine…

'Vincent!' she gasped in wide-eyed relief and jubilation.

And Vincent it was. Both he and El were at the helm of one of the machines, while Garret raced along beside them at the controls of the other.

At the window, the soldier scowled with fury and turned away.

'No funny business!' he yelled at them, before disappearing into the next carriage.

He was only gone a few moments before they detected movement through the skylights and watched helpless as a Gatling gun turret rose into view from the roof, the soldier at the trigger. His face was grim and focussed as he opened fire, bullets ripping from the barrels and peppering the ground around the two machines, instantly forcing them to swerve apart. More guns joined in from other carriages and the machines soon found themselves dodging a deadly hail of bullets from all sides.

At a signal from Vincent, Garret broke away fully and raced off towards the front of the train to run interference, while Vincent and El manoeuvred closer to it – starting some way back from Clara's carriage – and began to work their way slowly towards them, scanning each one they passed.

Wasting no time, Clara stuck her head and right arm through the bars and out of the open window, and began to wave and holler to get their attention.

'Vincent! El!' she bellowed over the mechanical whirring of the train's legs and the constant *rat-a-tat* of the Gatling guns. 'Over here!'

Even from this distance, Clara could see both of their faces light up as they spotted her, and it made her heart sing to see them adjust course and surge towards her.

From within the machine, El had her revolver drawn and was firing on one of the Gatling guns, its barrels suddenly going quiet as her shots struck home, enabling them to pull up alongside Clara.

Keeping pace with them, both Vincent and El looked in at her fondly.

'Fancy seeing you here,' El said with a wolfish grin. 'Need a ride?'

'You're okay!' Clara said joyously. 'How…?'

'Time for explanations later!' Vincent cut in. 'Can you get out to us?'

Clara gripped the bars that penned them in and shook them futilely.

'We're locked in!' she yelled back. Vincent and El turned to each other and shared a quick, whispered conversation.

'I'm coming over!' Vincent called, switching places with El so she could take the controls.

As El pulled them in even closer and Vincent prepared to jump across, Clara turned away – she needed to help! Her gaze fell on the locked cage door and her hand went immediately to the Hare necklace Tia had given her back in Anam. Maybe there was a way…

Clara quickly unclasped the necklace and selected one of its bone pendants that was thin and dagger-like, then she hurried to the lock and jammed it in, immediately setting to work fiddling with it.

'Go on,' Darcy scoffed, trying to play it cool but unable to hide her fear. 'You can't pick that lock!'

'Oh, I can!' Clara replied. 'Had to rescue my football several times…'

Behind her, she heard a thump as Vincent made it across to their carriage and swiftly climbed to the roof. As her fingers continued to work away, she glanced up through the skylight to see him – with his revolver drawn – moving atop the carriage. The Gatling gun operated by the soldier who had been guarding them swung towards him, but it was too late, as three retorts from Vincent's gun took him through the chest, sending him tumbling from the train.

As Vincent disappeared from sight, Clara returned her full attention to the lock and continued.

'Nearly got it…' she whispered to herself.

'C-come on, Clara!' Marcus cheered beside her. 'You can do it!'

At that moment there was a commotion ahead, and the door at the far end of the carriage burst open as Vincent – in his wolf form – bore a Viper soldier to the ground and tore out his throat with one snap.

'Vincent!' Clara yelled happily.

On seeing her, Vincent Shifted back to human and hurried towards her, but at that moment they all felt a change in the train's momentum, and they knew something was up.

'Hold on!' Vincent yelled, grabbing the nearest seat. While both Marcus and Darcy did likewise – strapping themselves back in – Clara continued to fiddle with the lock.

'Nearly there…' she hissed through her teeth.

It was at the same instant the lock clicked and the cage door swung open that the train suddenly dived headfirst down a steep cliff to a near-vertical angle, and Clara found herself plunging forward through the now open door, her hands reaching back desperately and just about finding a grip on a bar to arrest her descent.

Hanging there with the full length of the carriage to fall through, Clara screamed in fright.

'Vincent, help!'

Below her, and barely holding onto the seat beneath him, Vincent stared up at her in horror.

'I'm coming!' he yelled back as he began to scramble awkwardly up the seats towards her. But Clara's grip on the bar was weakening, her sweat-slicked hands beginning to slide. Above her, belted into his seat, Marcus tried to reach for her, but was nowhere near.

Vincent had made some progress, but was still far from in-range, as Clara's grip finally gave out and she fell.

A howl of terror ripped from her lungs as she dropped like a stone through the now vertical carriage, the wall at the opposite end rushing up to meet her. She closed her eyes and waited for the impact, but it never came…

A hand gripped hers tightly and she swung inwards, clattering painfully against the seats, but she did not fall.

'I've got you!' Vincent gasped, and at that moment the train levelled out beneath them and they tumbled back to the floor.

With no time to spare, Vincent was back on his feet in a heartbeat.

'Are you alright?' he asked Clara, helping her up.

'I'm… I'm fine…' she replied, trembling but otherwise unscathed. They both looked up as Darcy and Marcus approached them nervously.

'Follow me,' Vincent said. 'This way!'

He led them out through the door he had burst in by, and they found themselves in the gap between the carriages looking out at the plains flashing past, and El's machine nipping about, dodging gunfire.

Darcy nudged Clara and nodded at Vincent as he beckoned El over.

'How do you know we can trust 'im?' she asked doubtfully.

'If you can't trust him after that, then nothing will sway you,' she replied in disbelief. 'He's the most loyal, courageous man I've ever known.'

El pulled in as close as she dared with her machine, firing off a few rounds from her revolver whenever she could.

'Hop on!' she yelled to the children. Darcy glanced again at Clara, still unconvinced, but knew she had few other options. She eyed the jump nervously as El held out a hand to her.

Steeling herself, she leapt across and El caught her expertly, helping her to one of the seats, then she turned to Marcus.

'You next!' she called.

Marcus stared at the gap he would have to leap, and his heart quailed.

'It's too far!' he shrieked. 'I'll never make that!'

Clara leant in close, and her hand closed over his – the one that still clutched his coin.

'You've got your coin,' she told him reassuringly. 'With it you can do anything – you can be brave! Just like you father said.'

Marcus took a shuddering breath and nodded. He faced the jump – faced El in the machine and her waiting hand – and he leapt.

His jump was short and would have been catastrophic if El hadn't caught him and swung him up – almost losing control of the machine at the same time – but he had made it.

'Now you, Clara,' Vincent said. Clara nodded and barely paused for breath as she took two steps back then ran and sprang, clearing the gap easily and landing inside the machine. She turned around at once to see that Vincent was not following them, instead climbing to the roof of the train once more and making his way towards the engine.

'Where's he going?' Clara asked El over the roar of the machine.

'Most likely to make a big mess,' she replied, powering forward to catch up with Garret.

On the roof of the train, Vincent pushed forward against the strong wind that assailed him, dodging gunfire from more turrets and shooting down their operators at every opportunity. He was a few cars from the locomotive and approaching another turret that had not yet seen him – focused as it was on Garret – when a pair of Viper hauled themselves up on to the roof between them.

One of the brutes had a belt of knives at its waist and began to hurl these at him as they closed in, but Vincent expertly batted them away with his sword, sending them zinging in all directions. Vincent had just deflected the last of these missiles when the other Viper reached for its own weapon – a small hatchet – and, after drawing its arm back, lobbed this at him with lethal accuracy. But Vincent had already clocked this weapon, and was ready for it.

As it cartwheeled towards his head, Vincent reached up and plucked it from the air with all the speed of a striking snake, and before its owner could blink, he had returned it to sender. The axe crunched into the man's chest and with a bark of agony he collapsed to his knees and slipped from the train, crashing to earth like a ragdoll and disappearing in a cloud of dust.

At his cry, the operator of the nearby turret disengaged from Garret and began to swing the gun barrel their way. Following Vincent's gaze, the remaining Viper noticed this and – knowing what was coming – turned to his comrade and held up his hands defensively.

'No, wait…!' he yelled, but it did no good.

The turret operator opened fire, and in the same instant Vincent made his move, gripping the unfortunate Viper by the shoulder and thrusting him before him as a living shield. As bullets thudded into the unlucky creature's body, Vincent continued to push forward, his revolver held ready. As the Viper breathed his last and the gap between them and the turret narrowed, Vincent held on just a little longer, then peeked out from his improvised cover and fired off two well-aimed rounds, and the turret finally went quiet.

Releasing the eviscerated Viper, Vincent pressed on, and before long he had made it to the locomotive itself.

Glancing to the side, he noticed Garret keeping pace with him in his machine, nimbly evading gunshots and returning fire when he could. They locked eyes for a moment and Vincent nodded to him, his friend nodding back in response.

Without further preamble, Vincent leapt down and burst into the engine, where he was confronted by a Viper driver and his engineer. Shifting to his wolf form, he made quick work of them, their carcasses soon ejected from the cabin and out under the pounding legs below.

Shifting back to human, Vincent reached for his belt and produced a vial filled with a blue powder. With the toe of his boot, he heaved open the grate of the engine's furnace, then he shook the bottle, hurled it inside, and immediately spun on his heel and ran.

Once outside, he signalled to Garret who pulled in close, enabling him to jump smoothly across in one flowing movement. The second he was on board, Garret veered away on the double, and only just in time.

As the two machines re-joined each other, their occupants all turned to watch as – with a hissing and a cracking like fireworks – the engine's chimneys began to billow dark blue smoke and spray sparks, then – with a thunderous *boom* that tore across the empty expanse for miles – the engine exploded in a plume of shredded metal and the entire array of carriages behind impacted with it, toppling over one another in a whirlwind of carnage and a cacophonous din, spreading themselves in a huge, chaotic vortex of churning debris that took many minutes to settle entirely. But the two machines were already well out of sight of this as their passengers sought a place to catch their breath and regroup.

'How are you still alive!?'

The two vehicles had not stopped moving for some time, only coming to a halt when Vincent felt sure they were not being followed. Hidden as they were, Clara could not contain her excitement any longer and did not wait for a response as she hurled herself at Vincent and hugged him tight.

'I… I thought he'd killed you!' she added in a muffled voice.

'He very nearly did,' Vincent replied with a wan smile as they broke apart. He lifted his shirt to show her the ragged wound in his side that El had stitched for him. 'Couple of inches the other way and I wouldn't be here.'

'So, you got the message then?' Clara asked, eagerly changing the topic.

'We did,' Vincent replied. 'We have a new spy in their midst – recently turned. We didn't know if he'd come through for us, but…' Here he simply smiled down at Clara.

'We're all happy to be back together again,' Garret cut in abruptly. 'But we need to get back on the road to Croí, now.'

'We can't!' Clara said resolutely. 'There's somewhere we need to go first – a mine… Kids are sent there by the Viper to work until they die – we have to save them!'

At this, Vincent looked suddenly abashed.

'We… we knew about this…' he began awkwardly. 'Not all the details, and I never saw it myself, but… it was decided by our Lord that attacking it was too risky…'

'But they're just kids!' Clara implored him. 'Many of them even younger than me! They don't deserve this – none of them do! This is not how their stories should end! We can't just leave them there!'

Clara turned to look at El pleadingly, who in turn looked at her husband, determination in her eyes.

'You already know my thoughts on the mine,' El said quietly.

Garret looked between them all and sighed in resignation.

'If we do this, we may not reach Croí before the battle is joined,' he murmured to Vincent.

A war of emotions played out over Vincent's face beneath his mask as he contemplated this – shame and anger battled with the knowledge that time was not on their side, and in the end his conscience won out.

'Alright,' he said at last. 'Let's go take a look at this mine...'

CHAPTER 21
A Change of Plan

'Say that again…'

Seated in the high-backed chair behind his large, ornate desk, Malone surveyed the nervous overseer standing before him, a clipboard clutched in his trembling hands. As he watched the unfortunate man fumble for words, he reached for the breathing mask hanging at his shoulder, drew it over his mouth, and inhaled deeply from the C1 tank on his back, his irises glinting purple in the flickering light of the furnace at his core.

'I'm sorry, Boss, but… reserve stocks of the C1 variant are almost exhausted,' the overseer repeated, his voice dry with fear. 'We have enough for a few more days at best… but its extraction and refinement is extremely labour intensive, and right now we don't have enough manpower to produce it fast enough… I'm afraid that – for a while at least – you and your chosen may need to resort to… to using the C2 variant…'

Malone withdrew the mask from his mouth and let it settle back on his shoulder, his eyes never leaving the lowered gaze of the overseer. For several minutes he said nothing and simply regarded the other man, watching as the tension built inside him until he was as tightly wound as a spring. Then he spoke.

'Do you know why we have two variants of the refined Cypher?' he asked, his voice mild and almost encouraging, but his eyes as hard as flint.

'Y-yes...' the overseer replied shakily. 'The C2 variant is made from the crystallised Cypher, and as such is riddled with impurities, but... but still results in significantly enhanced strength and intellect in its users, with rapid bodily deterioration as a side effect, while the C1 variant is made from the pure, liquid Cypher and... and consequently is a higher overall quality, producing far greater enhancements in strength and intellect, and a slower rate of decomposition in the user. The C2 is in general use, while the C1 is only for yourself and... select others...'

Malone clapped slowly, a smile on his lips that did not reach his eyes.

'A textbook answer,' he said. 'Couldn't have put it better myself. Except... that is the "what" and not the "why" of the different variants.'

He got up from his chair and moved over to the large window that looked out over the factory below.

'The why of the variants is quite simple, really,' he began, staring down at his workers as they raced to and fro about their tasks. 'It's a reason as old as time – something people like us have sought since the beginning...'

Here he turned from the window to face the pale, quivering overseer.

'*Control…*' he whispered. 'So hard to attain and so easily lost – it is a slippery prize indeed…'

He turned back to the window and the overseer visibly relaxed a little to be free of his gaze.

'When I uncovered the different properties of the Cypher's two forms, my first instinct was altruism,' Malone continued. 'I wanted to share my great discovery with all – I wanted each and every one of us with enough vision to be given the opportunity to partake of the miraculous benefits of C1. I even offered it to the other Clans… early on… but they had not the wit to see…'

He leant his head against the cool glass, staring into the reflection of his own eyes behind his mask.

'And what did I get for my great generosity?' he asked, knowing the other man would not respond. 'Betrayal…'

As he gazed into his eyes, he could see the capillaries pumping purple as the recently-imbibed Cypher continued to course through his body.

'My rapid rise through the Viper society was unwelcome to some, and they used the guile *my discovery* gave them to try to get rid of me,' he spat viciously. 'They failed – of course – but I knew then that if I was to successfully bring my whole culture along into the future, I could not do it as equals with them…'

Malone reached behind his back and disconnected the C1 tank, turning it gently in his hands and staring at it lovingly.

'And so I began the production of the C2 variant in secret,' he continued. 'None of my remaining competitors – no one at all – knew they were using an inferior version until months later, once my continued use of C1 had ensured my position at the top of the pile.'

With one last fond stroke of the tank, Malone reconnected it to his back.

'And once that divide was created, it has been surprisingly easy to maintain,' he added, turning back to the overseer, who blanched again. 'Everyone accepted the new normal for what it was – for the C2 still made them far stronger and smarter than members of almost any other Clan, which was exactly what I needed if I was going to change the world...'

Malone began to approach the other man slowly.

'As I said, it all comes back to control...' he murmured, laying a hand on the shoulder of the overseer, who could not help but flinch away. 'You all believe that there are others who use C1 – right? My chosen few who I deem worthy? The prize for those who manage to impress me? The goal you all toil and struggle to achieve? Right...?'

'R-right...' the terrified overseer replied in a whimper.

'Wrong!' Malone shot back in a fierce hiss. '*I am the only one who uses it*, and that... *that* is the essence of control! And I will not lose it because you cannot compel your workforce to do their jobs fast enough!'

Malone gripped the overseer by the throat with his mechanical arm and lifted him high in the air before driving him backwards and slamming him into the wall.

'Got it!?' Malone demanded again.

'G-got…' the gasping man tried to respond.

At that moment, two figures burst through the door of his office unannounced – a Viper soldier, and Darius.

'I'm busy!' Malone growled, still holding the struggling man aloft.

'Boss!' Darius began. 'The train, it's… it's been attacked!'

'What!' Malone barked in shock, his grip on the overseer never loosening. 'What happened!?'

'Reports are still coming in, but… it was Vincent,' the Viper soldier interjected.

'Vincent!?' Malone roared in bewilderment, staring at Darius. 'You told me he was dead!?'

'I… Well, I…' Darius stammered in fear. 'I never said I saw him die, I just said that I…'

'You – shut up!' Malone spat, pointing at Darius. 'You – continue!' he added, now indicating the Viper soldier.

'He… he had help from some friends, Boss,' the soldier went on fearfully. 'They attacked the train en route to the mine, rescued the Gaia kids on board, then took out the driver and destroyed it. We lost sight of them after that…'

With a howl of rage, Malone swung his free fist wildly at the overseer in his grasp, his neck snapping like a twig with an audible *crack*.

Malone released the suddenly-still body and it slumped to the floor. He turned back to the Viper soldier and pointed at him again.

'Get a message to the mine – you tell them to step up security, now!'

The soldier dithered for a moment, paralysed with fear.

'Do it!' Malone screeched. 'Do it now or you end up like him!' he finished, now pointing at the body of the overseer. The Viper soldier nodded frantically and scurried away, tripping over himself in his haste.

Breathing heavily, Malone turned his furious gaze on Darius.

'We're bringing forward the timeline…' he said darkly. Darius looked at him in shock.

'But, Boss, we're not…'

'Croí must fall!' Malone bawled, cutting across him. 'And it must fall soon! There's only one thing I need to do first…'

He reached for his mask and took a huge breath of the C1, feeling it surge through his veins like fire.

'If I know my old friend like I think I do, his next stop will be the mine,' he breathed, releasing the mask. 'Come with me…'

And with that, Malone turned and stalked from his office with Darius hot on his heels, looking nervously at his commander.

CHAPTER 22
The Rot Goes Deep

'So… are we all clear on the plan?' Vincent asked.

It had not taken them long to find the mine, for clouds of smoke billowed from it like a beacon, darkening the skies above, the silhouettes of its ghastly machinery stark against the horizon. The group crouched now on a small plateau looking out on the intricate workings below them, the whole area a hive of feverish activity.

The mine sat within a hollow in a gargantuan cliff band, at the centre of which stood machinery that looked – to Clara at least – like that used for drilling oil, but here the prize they sought was far more dangerous and insidious; the liquid Rot. The apparatus was inactive now – still and silent – but engineers buzzed around it like flies, oiling here, tightening there, prepping for its next operation.

Encircling the machine throughout the many-tiered hollow were loops of mine cart tracks, with branches leading off into innumerable tunnels in the rock, as well as to a large station platform where the recovered material was loaded onto trains to be returned to Inchinn. Even from this distance they could see young Clan children here and there pushing the carts – some piled with Rot crystals ready for the train, others empty and returning for filling. Viper soldiers stood guard at regular intervals, several of them using the lash on those they felt weren't working hard enough. It made Clara's blood boil to see them treated this way.

'I said – are we clear on the plan?' Vincent repeated, glancing at the faces before him, their eyes locked on the scene below.

'I deal with the guards,' Garret replied in a low growl, his gaze fixed on a small Bear child pushing a cart below him, a Viper guard roughly chivvying him on. By his side, Marcus tried to catch Vincent's attention, his coin still flashing between his fingers.

'H-hey, um… excuse me…' he began timidly, but Vincent seemed not to hear him.

'I rescue the kids,' El replied next, fiercely determined.

'Excuse me – I need to say…' Marcus tried again.

'If we're going with shorthand answers,' Vincent continued, unaware Marcus had even spoken, 'then, I guess: I get the explosives to take down the machine.' He glanced at the huge drill at the centre of the mine, then turned to Clara and added: 'And you kids are…?'

'Staying out of sight so as not to get caught,' she intoned mutinously, repeating back the words she had been told. 'But I want to help! I…'

'You have helped,' Vincent gently reassured her. 'And if you want to continue to help you need to stay here and you need to stay safe – alright?' Clara nodded sullenly as Marcus raised a hand.

'I just need to say…' he began again meekly, but Vincent had already switched his gaze to Garret.

'Brother, would you check if the coast is clear?' he asked his friend. Garret nodded and disappeared without a word.

Silence fell for a few moments, and in that brief pause Marcus swallowed nervously and took a step towards Vincent, but Clara – unaware of this – had already moved to stand beside him and spoke without making eye contact.

'I know we don't have long,' she began slowly, 'but I need to ask you something… I've been trying to figure out the best way to do this after Malone told us, but nothing's coming, so I'll… I'll just be direct…' She took a breath then looked up at him, meeting his gaze levelly. 'Why didn't you tell us the Rot was from our world…?'

Whatever he had been expecting to be asked, it was clearly not this. For a moment Vincent was at a loss for words, looking both ashamed and saddened as he grappled with how best to respond. After a time, he sighed and crouched down to Clara's eye level.

'I'm… I'm sorry you found out that way…' he began sorrowfully. 'That was not how I wanted you to learn the truth of our plight… I hope you can believe me when I say that I did not withhold this information from you with any malicious intent, it is just… It was best that this realisation came to you gradually – if I had laid it all out for you upfront, I fear… I fear it would have been too much for you to take in; it would have been too much weight to drop on you in one go and I did not want to see you crushed by it. I…'

Here Vincent looked away as he once more struggled with how best to ease the vulnerable young girl into their truth. He spotted a lump of Rot crystal nearby and picked it up with a gloved hand. He stared at it for a moment, watching his distorted reflection in its surface.

'I had planned to wait a little longer,' he continued. 'But now is as good a time as any for you to know, I guess… You have shown you can handle it.' He held the Rot crystal up between them, both now gazing into it. 'So, you know that the Rot comes from your world. You know that it is poisoning Comhlacht, and you know that the Viper are using it to enhance their strength and intellect – but you do not yet know what it actually *is*…'

Vincent began to twist the crystal in his hand, watching the light play off its hard surface.

'There is no easy way to say this…' he went on slowly. 'But the Rot is a product of the people of your world…' He sighed again, looking at her sadly as she stared back, shocked and mystified. 'Wherever you go in life, Clara, you will find both good and bad people, both light and darkness, for we have the two in all of us – each of us feeding one side or the other through the choices we make each and every day of our lives.' He shook the crystal gently before her, his voice earnest. 'The Rot is a physical manifestation of all the evil, all the hatred and all the darkness perpetrated by the people of your world: it is every life taken, every dark thought, every wasted opportunity and every cruel word ever spoken…'

Clara's breathing quickened as she listened – her chest constricting with emotion.

'The poison of these acts has filled your world to bursting,' he continued, 'and when it could take no more, when there was nowhere left for it to go, the dam burst and – for some reason none of us can fathom – it broke through to our world and unleashed the Rot upon us, and it has continued to pour in ever since.'

Clara – her eyes damp with tears – struggled to speak, but finally found her voice.

'I… I still don't understand how I…' she began, her voice breaking with emotion. 'How I can help…'

'This poison is from your people,' Vincent reiterated gently. 'It is the result of their darkness, and it is only through them that it can be removed – that is why the Bear's plan to sever the link to your world and stop the Rot entering would have left Comhlacht in this crippled state. If we no longer had the ability to bring people over from your side to help, we would not be able to remove the Rot already present and Comhlacht would forever remain diseased and in pain, and we... we would never see it return to its former glory...'

Seeing the tears streaking down her face, Vincent pulled a handkerchief from his breast pocket and handed it to her to dry her eyes.

'Please, don't cry,' he said reassuringly. 'We bear your kind no ill will – we have only sympathy that your world has got to such a state, but we must do what we can to protect our people and our home from extinction.'

Clara dabbed at her eyes with the handkerchief, then handed it back as she let out a long, slow breath, trying to compose herself.

'I... I will do everything in my power to help you,' she began resolutely, her eyes now dry. 'But... But I'm still not sure how I actually...'

Heavy footsteps cut across her as Garret reappeared, looking harassed, and hurried over to Vincent.

'Vincent, we've got a...' he began, as a siren began to wail throughout the mine. 'Problem...' he finished. 'I think they heard about the train...'

They all glanced over the edge of the plateau to see alerted Viper soldiers now rushing hither and thither, while the Clan children had stopped their work and begun to cluster together at one side of the mine.

'This changes nothing,' Vincent said confidently. 'The plan is exactly the same, I...'

'No!'

As the siren continued to blare, they all turned in surprise to look at Marcus who was standing before them determinedly, staring at Vincent with as much confidence as he could muster, his coin clasped in one hand.

'You… you need to listen to me!' he continued, his voice only quavering a little. 'The plan is… is wrong! If you place the explosives where you said, you'll b-barely do any damage to the drill! You need to place them th-there!' He moved to the edge of the plateau and pointed. Vincent, looking a little bemused, stepped up beside him and looked down at the spot Marcus was indicating.

'If you place them where you said, they'll just fix it again in no time,' he added, his voice gathering strength. 'But, place them there under the derrick and it'll be totally destroyed.'

Vincent stared at the spot thoughtfully for a few moments, then turned to Marcus with a newfound respect in his eyes.

'Yes, that… that makes sense…' he began. 'Very clever – how do you know this?'

'My father is an engineer,' Marcus said importantly. 'And I've always loved learning how things f-fit together – we talk about his work all the time.'

Vincent clapped a hand on his shoulder.

'Well, I'm impressed,' he smiled. 'Your father must be very proud.'

He turned away from Marcus who was now positively glowing with pride.

'Okay, you heard the boy,' he continued. 'We do what he said. Everybody ready?'

They all nodded determinedly, ready to perform their parts of the plan. Vincent nodded back.

'If everything goes well, we meet in the compound below the station as soon as we can, then get back on the road to Croí,' he said, glancing around the group. 'Best of luck.'

And, with that, he set off down one passageway, while Garret and El disappeared down another, leaving the three children suddenly alone on the plateau as the siren continued to sound and raised voices echoed throughout the mine.

'So… we just wait 'ere do we?' Darcy said in frustration. 'We just stand around and hope they return?'

'I'm not happy about it either,' Clara said, sympathising but also stern. 'But it's what Vincent asked us to do, so I'll do it.'

'So, you just do anything he says, like a good little puppy?' Darcy said nastily, making Clara bristle. 'How do we know they'll come back? How do we know they won't just turn us over to the first guard they come across?'

Clara stared at her like she was a lunatic.

'They just rescued us from the train, and you think they're going to hand us off to the Viper now…?' she asked in bewilderment. 'They're on our side – it's in their interest as much as ours to keep us safe.'

By her side, Marcus was once again fiddling nervously with his coin, upset by the confrontation between the two, but unsure what to say. Darcy pointed angrily at Clara.

'You may have bought into their lies, but not me!' she said fiercely. 'I know who I can trust around 'ere and it ain't any o' them lot, nor either o' you!' She turned and glanced around her at the passageways leading off from the plateau. 'I'm getting out of 'ere. Come along if ya like – but I ain't slowing down for ya!'

Without another word, she turned and hurried off down one of the passageways.

'Darcy – wait!' Clara called after her, but she had already disappeared around a corner.

'We have to bring her back!' Clara said to Marcus. 'She's going to get herself killed!' She began to move after Darcy, but Marcus gripped her by the arm.

'We c-can't go!' he whispered nervously. 'Vincent said to wait here!'

'I know,' Clara replied. 'But I can't just let her go off and get hurt – Vincent would understand.'

Pulling herself gently from his grasp, she spun away and raced after Darcy, and – after a few moments of nervous fidgeting – Marcus stumbled after her, his coin darting between his fingers.

It did not take more than a few minutes for Darcy to find herself hopelessly lost amidst the maze-like mine, wandering blindly down passageways as she searched for a way out, all the while muttering rebelliously to herself.

'Can't believe she'd get so suckered in by those Wolves – why can't she see they're trouble?'

She was still murmuring to herself when she rounded a corner and ran right into the burly figure of a Viper guard, the impact knocking her flat on her backside.

'What the hell's this!' the Viper said in shock as Darcy scrambled away from him. 'What you doing up here?' Darcy had almost got back to her feet when the guard grabbed her by the arm and hauled her up. 'I said – what you doing up here?' he barked again.

'Let me go!' Darcy yelled, struggling to break free.

'Not until you tell me who you are,' the Viper spat back. 'You don't look like you're from a Clan.'

Swiftly realising that escape was now impossible, Darcy instantly and smoothly changed tack.

'There are other kids!' she began excitedly. 'There are two other kids like me wandering round 'ere: you let me go and I'll show you where they are – deal?' The guard looked her up and down and grunted.

'Take me to 'em,' he growled. Darcy nodded mutely and began to lead the guard back the way she'd come.

Clara moved cautiously down a passageway – hoping against hope that she was still on Darcy's trail – but in this confusing mine she had no way of knowing. At the sound of footsteps behind her, she whipped around and was relieved to see that it was only Marcus catching up to her.

'There you are,' he began breathlessly. 'I thought I'd...'

But he trailed off looking suddenly perplexed and began to pat his pockets frantically, glancing all around him.

'No…' he breathed. 'No, no, no… I've lost it!'

'Lost what?' Clara asked, confused.

'My coin!' he wailed. 'The special coin my dad gave me! I can't be brave without it!'

He turned and began to hurry back along the passage, away from Clara, who called after him anxiously.

'Hey! Come back! We need to find…' But he had already vanished from sight as he scoured the area for his treasure. Clara glanced one way then the other, torn with indecision – should she go after Darcy, or Marcus?

At that moment she heard Darcy's voice approaching from ahead.

'It was this way… I think…'

Clara breathed a sigh of relief and began to move towards the voice, when Darcy spoke again.

'Ow! You're hurting my arm! I'm taking you to them – you don't have to squeeze so hard!'

Clara froze, instantly realising that Darcy was not alone. She had barely had chance to turn to flee when the two figures rounded the corner and the guard spotted her.

'Oi!' he yelled. 'Stop right there!'

Moving faster than she would have thought possible, the guard was suddenly upon her, holding the two girls by their arms.

'And what do we have here then?' he said triumphantly, as Clara struggled against his vicelike grip.

'There's another one,' Darcy piped up. 'A boy called Marcus; I help you find him too and you let me go – that was the deal, right?'

'I didn't agree to no deal,' he sneered. 'You're both going in a cell until this alert is sorted and we can figure out what to do with you…'

Darcy tried to protest, but the guard shook her into silence and began to lead them away, Clara staring at the other girl in furious disbelief.

Minutes later, they found themselves locked in adjacent cells, barely bigger than a cupboard, the guard leering in at them with the ring of keys at his belt.

'Get comfortable,' he jeered. 'You might be in there a while…'

A soldier was just passing by the cells, and the guard threw out a hand to stop him.

'Be on the lookout for a kid,' he instructed. 'There's been a couple of them wandering about up top.' The soldier nodded and hurried away. Watching him go, the guard gave the girls one last taunting look, then moved back to his lookout post down an adjoining corridor from the cells.

Clara waited just long enough for him to be out of sight before she darted to the door, took off her Hare necklace, and began to fiddle with the lock, using the same pendant with which she had picked the lock on the train cage.

'I can't believe you sold us out…' she said tightly, her brows knit in concentration. Then she thought better of this. 'Actually… yeah… yeah, I can believe you did…'

'Oh, come on,' Darcy retorted. 'Like you wouldn't have done the same!'

'Unlike you…' Clara began to say, as she struggled with the lock. 'I'm not a…' But at that moment the pendant snapped, the pieces bouncing away across the floor.

'No!' Clara yelled in frustration. She inspected the remaining pendants on the necklace, but none of them were suitable to pick a lock. 'Now what do I do…?'

But right then a small voice whispered nearby.

'Hey! Clara!'

Clara looked up and sighed with relief – it was Marcus. He approached slowly, glancing nervously about, tears in his eyes.

'Marcus – thank goodness!' Clara breathed, as he stopped outside her cell. 'You have to get us out of here!' But Marcus seemed not to have heard her.

'I can't find it!' he moaned. 'My coin is lost for good!'

'No! No, it's not!' Clara replied, reaching into her pocket in the same breath and pulling something out. 'I found it after we were grabbed.'

She handed it to him through the bars and Marcus hugged it tightly to his chest, shuddering with relief.

'Now, you have to free us!' she said forcefully. 'The guard is just down there,' she added, pointing down the corridor he had disappeared along. 'You have to get the keys on his belt and bring them back to us!'

Marcus blanched at this.

'I can't do that!' he gasped.

'You'll be alright,' Clara said reassuringly. 'You have your coin again now – you can be brave!'

'But… But what if he sees me!?' Marcus protested.

'You can do this!' Clara said, gripping his shoulder through the bars. 'I believe in you.'

Marcus swallowed nervously and glanced down the passage Clara had indicated. He gave his coin another firm squeeze and nodded, then – slowly, falteringly – he began to move off down the corridor.

Shortly after, Marcus found himself at the end of the passage where a lookout post was stationed that provided overwatch of the whole mine. The guard was standing at alert with his back to him, his gaze flicking around like a hawk for any sign of a threat.

From the shadows, Marcus took in the layout of the room, and he soon spotted the ring of keys hanging at the guard's belt. He swallowed fearfully again, rubbing his coin between his fingers, and was just about to make his move when a figure appeared from another corridor, and he shrank back out of sight.

'No sign of that kid you mentioned,' the soldier the guard had spoken to earlier reported. 'What makes you think there's a kid anyway?'

'The red-headed girl I caught told me,' the guard replied. 'Led me to one of her other little friends too. Just keep an eye out, will ya? What a day…'

The soldier nodded in response and left the room as Marcus's face screwed up in disbelief – *so Darcy betrayed us…?*

Angry now, Marcus steadied himself and began to advance towards the guard, quiet as a mouse. He was within touching distance of his prey – his hand reaching for the keys – when the guard suddenly yelled out.

'Hey!' He leaned precariously over the ledge – the keys going with him – and pointed at something across the mine. 'I saw someone over there – go check it out!' he barked at a soldier just below his position. The man nodded and raced away.

The guard watched him for a few moments then leant back and returned to scouring the area, Marcus crouching frozen in terror behind him.

As soon as his breathing had calmed a little, Marcus steeled himself once more and reached out for the keys – his hand trembling like a leaf…

'I got them!'

Marcus stumbled into view outside Clara's cell, his breathing ragged, the ring of keys clutched in one hand and his coin in the other.

'I knew you could do it!' Clara beamed at him as he rapidly ran through the keys until he found the right one and the lock to her door clicked open. Clara bounded out and hugged him tight, then they both turned to look at Darcy, who stared out at them sullenly from her cell.

'Go on then,' she said morosely. 'Bugger off and leave me here.'

Clara did not give it a second thought. She took the keys from Marcus and moved towards her.

'What are you doing!?' Marcus asked in bewilderment. 'She tried to sell us out! We should just leave her here and go find the others.'

At these words, Clara hesitated – but only for a moment – then slid the key into the lock.

'No,' she said firmly, her eyes meeting Darcy's. 'I will not give up on her.'

Clara turned the key and opened the door, her eyes never leaving Darcy's, whose own were now flooding with confusion. Clara held out her hand to Darcy.

'Everyone deserves a second chance,' she added.

Darcy – lost for words – quietly took Clara's hand and left the cell.

'Damn it!'

Vincent threw his back against the wall, hissing through his teeth at how close he had come to being caught, watching as the soldier moved on with his patrol. He gripped the explosives in his hand, checked that the coast was indeed now clear, then slunk away, finally reaching the spot Marcus had indicated at the base of the drilling machine's derrick.

With utmost caution, Vincent placed the explosives into position as directed, then inserted a long fuse – knowing he needed all the time he could get. He took a deep breath – *this was it* – then grabbed a match from his pocket, struck it, and lit the fuse.

The instant it caught, Vincent was up and speeding along the nearest gantry that hung a dizzying height above the mine floor below. He had not got far when a gunshot rang out and he felt a searing pain as the bullet grazed his shoulder, sending him spinning to the cold, latticed metal. A second shot ricocheted off the railing next to him in a shower of sparks.

With a hand clapped to his wound, he peeked out and spotted the shooter, who was just lining up a shot that would have taken him through the chest, but before he could fire again Garret lunged into view in his Bear form and knocked the man to the ground, shouts of alarm now echoing all around as more soldiers spotted this and raced to engage.

Vincent said a silent thanks and was just getting to his feet when an all too familiar voice spoke from behind him.

'My old friend… So good to see you here…'

Turning slowly on the spot, Vincent faced the speaker, his eyes clouding with pain and disbelief at what he saw.

'Malone…' he breathed, horror-struck. 'What have you done to yourself…?'

'Done?' Malone replied defiantly. 'I have only done what was necessary. I have only done what *needed* to be done.' He spread his arms wide, inviting Vincent to marvel at him. 'You are looking at progress, Vincent. You are looking at the next stage in our evolution – at the future of our species.'

Vincent stared at the creature standing before him, struggling to see through the twisted exterior to the childhood friend he once knew, distraught at the changes he had gone through since they last met.

'Are you so far gone that you truly believe that?' Vincent said at last, unable to hide the anguish in his voice. 'You must know that we have no future if the Rot continues unchecked…? Comhlacht will wither and die – and us along with it!'

'Comhlacht is but a vessel upon which we voyage down our new path,' Malone replied. 'And it is a path I would prefer to travel with my old friend.'

He held out a hand to Vincent; the hand that was now nought but metal and gears and pistons – cold and lifeless.

'Will you join me, brother?' he asked, fixing Vincent with a piercing stare.

Vincent looked at the outstretched hand and saw it for what it was – the epitome of the gap that had come between them since the day Malone discovered his Cypher. No matter what they had gone through as boys, no matter how close they had once been, Vincent knew that he could never side with him after the choices he had made – after seeing the man he had become. There was only one hope for him now, and it grieved Vincent to know that he would never take it.

'You know that I can't,' Vincent replied. 'And I believe that you know – buried deep down inside – why that is, and why you must stop this.'

He took a step nearer to Malone, whose hand was still held out towards him.

'It is not too late!' Vincent said fervently. 'There is still time for you to end all this! Help us remove the Rot from our world and I have faith that you will be saved too!'

At this, Malone began to chuckle, and Vincent knew that he had lost him.

'Saved?' Malone snorted with mirth. 'The fact that you still think I need saving after all this time shows just how small-minded you truly ARE!'

Malone roared the last word as the concealed blade just above his outstretched mechanical wrist flicked out and swung viciously at Vincent, who only just drew his cane sword in time to parry it, steel ringing on steel as Malone surged towards him like a hurricane.

'*I* am trying to save *you*!' Malone bellowed like thunder as he rained blow after punishing blow down on Vincent, who was hard-pressed to deflect them. 'All I have ever wanted is to show you the light – to show you the opportunity – yet you prefer to remain blind!'

Vincent found that he was slowly being forced back along the gantry under the hammer-like impacts that sent sparks flying and his bones ringing and knew that – even now – he did not want to hurt his friend.

'Fight back!' Malone bawled. 'Or are you blind to this too!?'

With his arms aching, Vincent continued to endure the impacts on his blade, chancing a glance to his left, where he saw Garret engaged in mortal combat with at least a dozen enemies, and then to his right, where he spotted El leading a group of Clan children to safety along a passage. He then looked back the way he had come and could just about see the lit fuse on the explosives, and it was almost spent...

'Fight me!' Malone screamed, swinging his blade with all his might. 'FIGHT ME!'

Knowing he was out of time, Vincent took a momentary lull in Malone's attack to kick him hard in the chest and send him reeling backwards, and at that second the explosives detonated. A gigantic fireball erupted from the base of the derrick, spitting shards of metal and rock flying in a lethal hail, and both Vincent and Malone ducked in the same instant. The whole structure buckled with an ear-splitting creaking as clouds of smoke billowed out around it, and it slowly began to fall.

By the time Vincent and Malone realised where it was falling, it was too late. They turned to run, but had not got more than a few paces when the top of the derrick impacted with the furthest end of the gantry and it sheared in two, one side dropping away while the side they were on swung in towards the wall of the mine.

Malone was instantly shaken loose and landed hard on the dirt floor below, tumbling to a stop and narrowly avoiding being crushed by falling debris, while Vincent was able to cling on as the gantry hit the wall and rebounded, somehow staying attached to the remaining section above. Vincent looked over his shoulder to see what had become of Malone, before he hauled himself up the now vertical gantry and rolled onto the plateau in a sweating, trembling heap.

He stayed on his back just long enough to catch a few shuddering breaths, then hauled himself to his feet and looked over to where he had last seen Garret, but now saw that he was gone.

Time for me to go too, he thought.

'Is everybody okay?'

Vincent had only just appeared in the compound below the station and already he was checking up on everyone, glad to see that Clara, Marcus, Darcy, El, Garret and the Clan children had all apparently made it there safely.

'We're fine, but we need to get moving!' El said as she ushered several of the Clan kids into one of the strange ring-shaped vehicles, lines of which stood waiting throughout the compound. 'I've already sent a few groups on to Croí.'

As she bent to instruct one of the older kids in its usage, Garret turned to Vincent.

'You caused quite a stir,' he said grimly. 'Used it to slip away, but they'll be here in no time. We have to leave…' Vincent glanced over his shoulder and nodded as the vehicle filled with Clan children slowly pulled away and soon shot off across the plains.

'Alright – last one!' El said, as she began to load up another vehicle with the remaining kids.

'The rest of you – with me!' Vincent barked, and Garret, Clara, Marcus and Darcy followed him to another vehicle as angry shouts began to echo down the passage behind them.

Taking a seat at the controls, Vincent made ready to leave, while Garret took up position and drew his shotgun and Clara, Marcus and Darcy sat down and held on tight.

'Okay – go! Go!' El yelled as she sent the last vehicle of Clan children on its way and watched it veer drunkenly but quickly out of sight. She drew her revolver and raced to Vincent's waiting ride, just as Viper soldiers began to pour into the compound, yelling the alert at the sight of them.

As Vincent pulled away, Garret and El opened fire, their foe diving for cover as they rapidly powered away from the mine and off across the plains.

Behind them, Malone emerged from the passage and watched them recede into the distance. Darius appeared at his side and glanced nervously at his superior.

'What do you want me to do, Boss?' he asked. Malone was silent for a moment as he contemplated this. Then at last he spoke.

'Hunt them down…' he hissed, his eyes never leaving his quarry.

CHAPTER 23
Hunted

'They're gaining on us!' Clara yelled over the din of the vehicle's pounding legs as she looked fearfully over her shoulder at the rapidly-approaching shapes in the distance.

'Damn it!' Garret growled, reloading his shotgun while keeping his gaze fixed on the enemy. 'Can't this thing go any faster?'

'There's less of them per vehicle,' El said, squinting with a hand shading her eyes. 'They're going to catch us unless we do something…'

'Well, we're all going to have to slow down soon,' Vincent declared, pointing at a strange shape that was rapidly growing on the horizon. 'Look.'

They all turned to stare ahead and could see at once what he was referring to, but – to Clara at least – exactly what it was remained a mystery.

'What is it?' she asked nervously, struggling to make sense of what she was seeing. El glanced down at her sorrowfully.

'The Crystal Forest…' she whispered, and Clara could hear the anguish in every word.

As they drew closer, Clara could see what looked like tightly-meshed trees sprouting out of the ground, blocking their path, but they were like no trees she had ever seen before – something was wrong with them…

El placed a hand gently on her shoulder.

'Back in the early days of the Rot, Panther Clan used to live there,' she said quietly, her eyes staring unseeingly ahead. 'They were once one of the largest and most respected Clans in all of Comhlacht, until the day of the breach…'

El's grip on Clara's shoulder tightened momentarily as she thought about the horror they must have endured.

'We did not yet know enough about the Rot – did not fully understand what it was doing to our world,' she continued. 'This was the first occurrence of its kind, and still – to this day – the worst we have yet seen…'

They were now closer still to the forest and Clara could see that they were not trees at all, for they glinted in the dim light like glass.

'It started as a tremor that grew to a crescendo in seconds and tore the earth apart,' Garret said sombrely, picking up the story. 'And where it tore, great gouts of Rot burst forth like lances, puncturing Comhlacht's face with a multitude of wounds and crystallising into the shapes you now see…'

The hideous purple colouring of the "trees" was now all too evident, and it sickened Clara to see them – this hideous mockery of nature.

'Panther Clan did not know what hit them,' El continued, her voice barely more than a whisper. 'Their homes, their people, their community were ripped asunder by this sickness – wiped off the map in a matter of moments… Almost none survived…'

'Mikal was one of the very few who did,' Vincent put in, glancing back at Clara for a moment. 'You stayed in his cabin shortly after you arrived here.'

'He was driven to madness by his loss,' El added. 'Even with all the help offered by the other Clans soon he – and the rest of his remaining people – faded from existence, but not from memory…'

'No – never from memory…' Vincent agreed.

Clara listened to all this sadly, but did not know what to say to her friends, and so instead lowered her gaze and offered up a silent prayer to those lost to the evils of the Rot.

They were now not far from the fringe of the forest, and their pursuers were rapidly closing the distance between them. But, the nearer they got to the trees, the more obvious it became to Clara that their vehicle would never fit through the narrow gaps between the imposing structures thrusting out of the ground everywhere she looked.

'How are we going to get through?' she asked fearfully.

'Yeah – no way we're gettin' this thing through there!' Darcy chipped in apprehensively.

'We're going to have to go on foot,' Vincent said firmly, bringing the vehicle to a stop by the edge of the forest as their enemies continued to hurtle towards them. 'We have no other option – let's move!'

'B-but they'll catch us!' Marcus squeaked, gaining him nothing but a firm shove from his seat by Garret.

'Not if you get moving!' he growled.

And so, they hastily disembarked and entered the Crystal Forest at a run, just as their pursuers drew up behind them and leapt down to give chase…

They had not gone far into the forest before they came across the first signs of the people who had once lived there. The fragmented remains of a cobbled road traced a path ahead of them and as they followed it deeper, weaving their way between the mighty crystals surrounding them, they began to come across the shattered remnants of beautiful homes built of stone and wood that had been obliterated by the fingers of Rot punching through the earth beneath them.

Tumbledown debris, reclaimed by vines and weeds, littered the area, threatening to trip the unwary at every turn, and wherever Clara now looked she saw evidence of lives ripped apart in a heartbeat by this cruel twist of fate. Her headlong dash behind El abruptly stopped when her eyes fell on the unmistakeable ruins of a schoolhouse near what must have been the centre of the city, a towering branch of crystal Rot protruding from the bell tower that had once called its students to their daily studies.

As Clara stared mournfully at the collapsed roof, she could almost hear the final cries of the children within as tons of slate rained down upon them, and then the sudden silence that followed…

'Clara…' El had reappeared at her side and was shaking her gently. 'We cannot stop here…'

Clara swallowed and nodded, picking up the pace once more and racing after the others, past more reminders of the lives lived and lost here.

Together, the group continued on, but even at their fastest, it was not enough to outrun the enhanced strength and stamina of the Viper, and they could soon hear their malicious, gleeful shouts echoing off the glass-like structures all around them.

'What do we do?' Garret murmured to Vincent at the head of the group. 'There's no way we can outpace them with the kids here…'

Vincent thought about this for a moment, then glanced at his friend.

'Keep leading the group – I'll do what I can,' he said, and with that he reduced his pace, dropping back to the rear of the party and motioning for El to follow him, both reaching for the dwindling supply of gadgets at their belts.

They had each drawn vials with a reddish hue from their holders when the first of the Viper soldiers appeared, no more than twenty paces away.

'There they are!' he screeched, pointing their way. 'Get 'em!'

Vincent made a polite gesture for El to go first, and she obliged with a slight bow. Gripping her vial tightly, she drew back her arm and hurled it with all her might. It sailed through the air, past the group of soldiers now hurtling towards them, and impacted with the base of a crystal tree behind them. The vial smashed and, with a roar like a banshee, crimson flames bloomed in a devastating, fiery flower that sent cracks shooting up the tree's mighty structure, swiftly covering every inch of it until it could no longer hold itself up, and it shattered.

Lethal shards of the crystal Rot began to lance down and several of the Viper were instantly crushed or impaled, while several more were merely wounded. Unperturbed, the rest shook the dust off and made their way past the debris to advance with renewed vigour.

As Vincent and El continued to retreat after their group, an ominous rumble shook the ground beneath them, but they had no time to pay it any heed. El now motioned for Vincent to take his turn and he complied, gripping his vial and targeting the base of another crystal tree beside the soldiers still thundering towards them. It hit home and burst in a mesmerising spray of flames, and soon a deluge of lethal rain was falling upon their embattled enemy – many of whom would never leave that spot – but there were many more still who simply climbed past the blockage and continued the pursuit.

Vincent and El were reaching for more vials at their belts just as another tremor rippled through the earth below like a frightened shudder, the crystals all around them rattling and swaying threateningly.

'Stop!' Garret yelled from the head of the fleeing group, pausing for just a moment. 'You're going to bring the whole bloody place down on us! Just run!'

With the rumble continuing unabated, Vincent and El had to agree he was right, and so turned and raced after their comrades with the Viper hot on their heels, fragments of crystal beginning to shower down all around them from the teetering trees.

By the time they reached the other edge of the forest their legs were burning and their chests constricting, and their only reward was a yawning expanse of open plain ahead, with not a single island of safety in sight.

'Where do we g-go?' Marcus asked frantically as they stopped within the boundary of the forest. But, with the tremors intensifying and lethal shards falling everywhere, the answer was obvious.

'We… keep running,' Vincent said as he struggled to catch his breath. 'We can't stay here – so we just… keep running…'

He set off once more and the group wearily followed him, going against their instincts and leaving a location with many hiding places for one with none.

As they stumbled tiredly on, they glanced back to see that the Viper – led by Darius himself – had already made it through the forest, and there were dozens of them remaining. They all knew they were being run into the ground, and they did not have long left…

With the gap between the two groups narrowing, Vincent, El and Garret tried to chivvy the younger members on, but Clara, Darcy and Marcus were all flagging badly, and could not continue much longer. Gunshots suddenly rang out from behind, clear against the deep, sonorous rumble below, bullets impacting the earth all around them as their enemy sought to bring them down.

'There's nothing else for it,' Vincent murmured to El and Garret as they continued to urge the kids along. 'We'll have to stand and fight them – do what we can to protect the children. We…'

But at that moment the rumbling changed, the ground shifting beneath them as if some vast beast had rolled over just below the surface and both they and their pursuers were bucked to the dirt, tumbling to a stop in a cloud of dust.

Bruised and shaken, they all got unsteadily to their feet, only for another sudden quake to sweep the legs from under them again as the rumbling shifted up a gear – growing and building like an approaching storm. The blood red sky above began to darken, throwing the land below into deeper shadow, as the tremors rapidly approached their climax.

As though of one mind, the gaze of everyone present – including the Viper – was suddenly drawn to the Crystal Forest behind them where the trees continued to shake forebodingly, many of the smaller structures shattering under the stress and collapsing.

Then, quite suddenly, the rumbling ceased – but only for a moment… A sound like a million bones snapping at once suddenly rent the air as the ground beneath the forest split apart, sending the remains of the Panther city and the crystal trees tumbling down into the abyss, never to be seen again. But the crack did not stop there…

As if driven by some malevolent sentience it began to spread, spidering out from the initial opening and ripping through the earth, leaving a long gaping wound in its wake – and it was heading right for them…

'Oh hell – run!' yelled El, and she and the rest of the group forgot their weariness in a surge of adrenaline as they began to sprint away from the devastation pursuing them, the Viper hot on their trail, but thinking now only about saving their own skin.

The crack raced closer, offshoots branching away in all directions, the sky above roiling like the sea. Driven by self-preservation, the Viper began to gain on the group, but, as the tear rapidly caught up to them, many of the stragglers at the rear attempted to veer to one side, only for a fork to chase them down and send them freefalling to their doom.

Oblivious to this, Darius too began to swerve to one side, off the path Vincent and the others had taken, and his men went with him, but this time the tear wholly banked to follow them.

At the rear of their group, Darcy struggled onwards as fast as she was able, but as the crack veered away towards Darius and his men she was caught at the corner where the ground gave way and she tumbled out of sight, a scream tearing from her lungs as she went.

Ahead, Clara heard this and whipped around to see that Darcy was no longer behind them.

'Darcy!' she yelled in horror, instantly skidding to a halt and sprinting back to where she had last seen her. Clara threw herself down on her belly at the edge of the tear and slid forward to peer into the void.

'Please be alright…' she breathed. 'Please be alright…'

At first, Clara could see nothing, and a hand of ice clutched at her heart, but then she saw – hanging by nothing but a thin root jutting out of the wall – Darcy staring up at her with wide, terrified eyes, her mouth open in a soundless shriek.

'Darcy!' Clara gasped in shock, reaching out towards her in same breath. 'Grab my hand!'

Hanging there – rigid with fear – Darcy looked up at the hand reaching out to her, desperate to take it, but too scared to move.

'I… I… can't…' she whispered, afraid to even raise her voice.

'Yes, you can!' Clara said firmly. 'Yes, you bloody well can! You grab my hand!'

Darcy took a deep breath and shifted her grip a little, one hand raising a fraction of an inch towards her, but then the root shifted and she immediately grabbed it again with both hands.

'I'm going to fall…!' she sobbed. 'I'm going to fall!'

'No!' Clara yelled. 'No, you're not! Not if you grab my hand right now!'

As she said this, the ground began to crumble beneath Clara, raining dirt and pebbles down on Darcy, who coughed and spluttered in response.

'You're going to fall too!' Darcy said, staring up into Clara's eyes hopelessly. 'Just go!'

'I'm not going anywhere!' Clara said resolutely, as cracks blossomed around her. 'Not without you!'

Darcy stared up at her in confusion.

'Why…?' she asked, unable to comprehend her motivations.

'Because you're my friend,' Clara said simply. 'Now take my hand and let's get out of here!'

For a few more seconds Darcy continued to gaze up at her in bewilderment – this girl she had shown nothing but contempt for – and then she slowly released her hold with one hand, reached out towards Clara, and gripped her palm.

As Clara began to haul Darcy upwards, the root she was holding in her other hand gave way and tore from the wall, but Clara had her in a vice-like grip, and she did not fall. At that moment, Darcy felt other hands take her arms as Vincent, El and Garret arrived to help, and she was pulled roughly to safety out of the grip of the void below, the edge they had been standing on disintegrating to nothing behind them as they stumbled backwards.

Crouched in the dirt side by side – breathless and sweating – they all looked up to see the crack still pursuing the Viper across the plains until the last of their fleeing shapes was swallowed into the abyss, vanishing from sight. As the last one fell, they all felt a change in the earth beneath them – like muscles unclenching – and the rumbling slowly receded, then died completely, leaving a strange taut silence in its wake.

Vincent got slowly to his feet and stared at the ruin left behind, tracing the ragged wound in the earth from its end point to its origin, noting its change in direction along the way. From where he stood, he could see that its walls were coated in crystallised Rot, and it laid bare just how deep the Rot went – how ravaged the core of their world truly was. It tore at his heart to see the extent of the corruption so clearly, but this only made the realisation he had come to all the more miraculous, and worthy of hope.

'I had thought that Comhlacht had lost itself in its pain…' he began slowly, his eyes fixed on the Rot-covered walls. 'I had thought that it no longer knew us… But now, after seeing this… I feel that perhaps Comhlacht *can* still tell friend from foe…'

El got to her feet and stood beside him, following his gaze.

'Then there is hope yet,' she said. 'And all the more reason for us to hurry on to Croí.'

'Which path will get us there quickest?' Garret asked, stepping over to them.

'We could cut through the Wolf burial grounds,' El suggested, glancing at Vincent. 'It's the shortest route, and we can pay our respects on the way.'

Vincent nodded in response.

'Aye, we'll do that,' he agreed. 'Let's make a move. Everybody ready?'

Everyone barring Darcy nodded in response and began to move off after Vincent, but Darcy stayed behind, staring at Clara, her expression still lost in confusion. She opened her mouth to speak, but closed it again. She rallied herself and tried once more.

'Clara!' she called after her, and Clara turned to face her. Darcy struggled for a moment, grappling with the words, and finally spoke. 'Thank you,' was all she said.

Clara looked at her with a small smile on her face, then simply nodded and turned to resume following the others. Watching her go, Darcy let a smile cross her face too – just for a moment – then it was gone, and she was hurrying to catch up as they continued on their journey.

Not far away – unseen by any of them – a strange sound echoed from within the tear, growing closer and closer, then a mechanical arm appeared over the edge, scrabbling for purchase, and a grizzled head lurched into view...

CHAPTER 24
The Burial Grounds

Valiantly dragging their bone-weary bodies onward, the group wove their way through a narrow mountain pass and soon rounded a corner where they were afforded the first view of their destination.

'There it is,' El murmured to Clara. 'The Wolf burial grounds.'

From this distance it did not look like much. The rough stone path they were following led up some coarsely hewn steps to a wide plateau near the summit of the mountain where there stood nothing but rocks, shrubs and one lone tree – a strange, gnarled growth that twisted and contorted into the oddest shape Clara had ever seen, its bark a pale, wolf-grey and its branches cold and bare – devoid of any growth.

Clara's eyes remained fixed on it as they continued their approach, fascinated by its mesmerising loops and swirls and the odd patterns covering it that seemed to dance and shift the closer she got to them. She barely even noticed as she ascended the steps to the plateau; was oblivious to all else as she approached the tree and laid a hand upon it, savouring the coarseness beneath her fingers and – somehow, impossibly – feeling it shift under her palm as if it was breathing.

'That is the Wolf Tree,' El said quietly from behind her. 'It is said to have been born from the First Wolf – the precursor to our Clan.'

El stepped up beside her and placed a hand alongside Clara's, her eyes closing as she felt the tree's energy flowing through her.

'His name was Amarl, and it was through him and his mate Mala that our entire bloodline began,' she continued. 'They passed their strength down through the ages and we all still feel it – even to this day.'

El stepped back from the tree and looked up at it respectfully.

'He lived for many decades and at the end – when his great strength finally failed him – he died, right here, on this spot,' she whispered, pointing at the base of the tree. 'His body was reclaimed by the earth and from his remains this tree grew, to stand guard over all those who will follow him on to the next life.'

El indicated the plateau around her, and Clara became aware of the innumerable mounds and rock piles that were the unmistakeable signs of graves, each one denoted by the decaying remains of Wolf masks.

'This is the final resting place for us Wolves,' she went on. 'We take from our Guardians to help transition us during our Convergence, and, when it is our time, we come here and return our bodies to the earth, so that we can feed our Guardians in turn through the circle of life.'

Clara looked around her sorrowfully and El – seeing this – smiled.

'I understand if being here makes you sad,' El said. 'For there are so many good souls laid to rest all around us. But for me, it… it just reminds me that we're all connected, even in death… and I find that very comforting… If you would excuse me a moment.'

El turned away and moved off towards one of the mounds, and in the void that she left behind Clara saw Vincent standing by the edge of the plateau looking off into the distance. She walked quietly up to him and stopped by his side, feeling suddenly awkward about disturbing him in this place. She was about to move away again when he spoke.

'We are nearing the end of our journey, Clara,' he murmured, without looking at her.

Clara glanced at him then followed his gaze, past the sheer drop beneath him and off towards the horizon, where she saw a strange shape huddled at the foot of a vast mountain range.

'Is that…?' she whispered breathlessly.

'Yes,' Vincent replied. 'That is Croí – my home.'

Squinting as best she could, Clara could just about make out the city. It was nestled in a crescent-shaped hollow at the mountain's base that provided protection on all sides except the front, which was bordered by a wall and a wide moat – formed from a diverted river – making the city only accessible via a huge drawbridge.

As he stared at it, Vincent's eyes shone with pleasure behind his mask, knowing that he would soon be home.

'It doesn't matter how long I am away,' he began slowly. 'Every single moment feels like an eternity. It will be good to return.'

He looked down at her in a fatherly manner.

'You must be missing your home too?' he murmured. At the mention of home, Clara felt her eyes mist up, for she had barely given it a thought in some time, and in that moment it all came rushing back to her: why she was doing this – why she was here at all.

'I do not miss my bed,' she began, stifling a sob. 'But I miss my mother… and my father… so, so much…'

Vincent smiled at her.

'You will see them again soon,' he promised. Clara nodded and wiped her nose with her hand.

'You must be missing your children?' she asked him.

'More than anything,' he replied, looking past Clara. 'And I know their mother does too.'

El appeared at Clara's side once more, gazing out at Croí alongside them.

'They are as vital to me as breathing,' El said lovingly. 'As necessary as food and water. I can no longer imagine life without them – do not even want to think about it – but every day I dream of a better world than this for them.'

'That world is coming,' Vincent assured her, no trace of doubt in his voice. 'I know it.'

El looked over at him affectionately.

'My love,' she began. 'You always…' But she got no further, her words cut off by a grunt of pain, her body jolting from a sudden impact, her eyes wide with shock. Both Vincent and Clara stared at her in horror as – with a rending of flesh and a spray of viscera – a barbed weapon suddenly burst from her chest. El stared down at it in disbelief and reached numbly for it, weakly trying to pull it out, when it was suddenly withdrawn and she crumpled to the floor, and in her place stood a hellish creature they had thought was dead – a monstrosity that had no right to be alive – Darius…

'Hello, Vincent!' he hissed.

Paralysed by mind-numbing, heart-rending shock, Vincent remained frozen for a few moments, staring at the limp form of his partner – his soulmate – lying in the dirt. His heart jack-hammered in his chest and he struggled to breathe, his vision blurring in disbelief at what he was seeing, his fracturing psyche unable to process the image before it. But it did not last long…

With a wild roar that turned into a guttural snarl he pounced, Shifting as he did so and lunging at Darius as a wolf with murder gleaming in his eyes. As the two combatants clashed, Garret arrived on the scene like a tornado, unleashing a deafening bellow of grief and fury. Shifting to his bear form, he hurled himself into battle alongside his friend, the two of them snapping and swiping with ferocious energy as Darius dodged and slashed with his barbed weapon.

Standing immobile, Clara, Darcy and Marcus stared at El's body, and she seemed smaller than they had ever seen her, her bright red hair fanning out around her as her life's blood did the same. Clara felt herself swaying giddily – *this could not be happening* – but she knew her eyes were not lying to her, though she wished dearly that they were.

Like a switch being flicked she snapped back to herself and surged forward with an animal scream, picking up the closest thing she could find – a large rock – and bounding with it onto Darius' back, where she proceeded to batter him over the head with it until she drew blood.

Behind her, Marcus was still staring at El's body, his face streaked with tears, his coin flashing between his fingers. Finally, he gripped it tight in one fist, grabbed a nearby branch fallen from the Wolf Tree, and hurled himself into the fight, swinging with all his might at any part of Darius he could reach.

This left only Darcy, standing scared and alone on the fringes, her frightened eyes darting from El's body to the furious melee going on by the edge of the plateau. She knew what she should do, but was afraid to do it, held back by years of conditioning that had led her to believe that only her family mattered.

They are nothing to me... she thought. *Their people brought me to this terrible place and left me to die!*

But these *people saved you...* another voice in her mind whispered. *And you know they would do it again in an instant...*

And Darcy knew that it was right. Casting around her, she picked up an armful of rocks, dashed in close, and began hurling them with surprising accuracy at Darius, the missiles striking home and distracting him enough for Vincent to dart in and tear a patch of flesh from his arm, and Garret to slash at his chest with a paw, sending him spinning to the ground and hurling Clara off his back.

But Darius was not down long. He was up again in a heartbeat, a monstrous backhand sending Garret reeling away, while a thrust from his barbed weapon caught Vincent on the shoulder and sent the wolf tumbling to the ground. A kick from Darius sent Marcus skidding backwards, clutching his chest, while a well thrown rock sent Darcy diving for cover, leaving him alone with Clara, who struggled to rise after the breath was knocked out of her by the fall.

Darius towered over her, breathing raggedly, the necrotic flesh on his body peeling away from a multitude of wounds, the furnace in his chest glowing weakly.

'You should've stayed at the mine,' Darius said harshly. 'It would have been a hard life, but a life nonetheless. Now I've gotta do what I've gotta do...

Boss wouldn't want you making it to Croí – that I'm certain of…'

He raised his barbed weapon and prepared to take her life.

'Sorry, kid,' he muttered, and Clara threw up her arms to shield herself.

He had just begun to lunge towards her when something dived onto his back and gripped him tight around the throat, staying his weapon arm at the same time. Realising that the blow hadn't come, Clara looked up and saw – to her amazement – that it was El clinging onto her adversary. Blood poured from her mouth and chest, her skin deathly pale, but in her hand was the blade she always kept at her side, and she drove this now straight down into Darius' neck, causing him to screech in agony.

Not far away, Vincent had Shifted back to human and was getting to his feet, staring stricken at his love as she grappled with the hideous creature, thrusting the blade in deeper and deeper. Driven half mad with pain, Darius began to flail around, trying to throw her off, but El clung on like a limpet, her eyes fixed on those of her husband, and he could feel the love radiating from her like heat.

'My love, you must do one thing for me,' she said over the grunts and snorts of Darius. 'You must protect our children at all costs, and…' She fought to maintain control, knowing she did not have long left. 'And make sure they one day reach that better world…'

Vincent took a step towards her, his hand reaching out, but she was already pulling away. By gripping the handle of the deeply embedded blade and twisting, she managed to drag Darius backwards, back towards the edge of the plateau, his great bulk already weakening from blood-loss, unable to fight the inevitable.

They neared the edge and teetered upon the brink, Darius' arms now flailing wildly, while El stared at Vincent and soundlessly mouthed: *I love you.*

Then, they fell.

And with that, she was gone.

Slowly, brokenly, Vincent dragged his numb body towards the edge, and he stared down at the base of the cliff where the two small forms now lay upon the rocks below. Tears fell from his eyes, plunging the way of his love, but they were not enough to speak the loss in his heart.

His legs gave way beneath him and as he dropped to the floor he Shifted to his wolf form and gave vent to his feelings, howling his torturous pain to the sky; the long, low, mournful note running on and on until his breath was all but spent.

With faltering steps, Clara appeared beside him, feeling at first unable to look over the cliff, but eventually forcing herself to do so, the tears falling like rain. As Vincent lay down, his muzzle in the dirt, Clara placed a hand upon his shoulder, her whole body shuddering with grief.

'Vincent, my dear,' she whispered. 'I'm... I'm so sorry...'

In that moment – as she stared down at her friend – Clara realised then that she had never felt worse in her whole life, except for one time…

CHAPTER 25
My Bed Is My Prison

Clara lay on her bed in silence, staring up at the ceiling, the cracks that criss-crossed it appearing to her like the veins of some weather-beaten creature's skin. Through the bedroom window, which was only open a crack to let the air circulate, she could hear the sounds of children playing in the street. The familiar thud and bounce of a football, the slap of a skipping rope hitting the pavement, the happy laughter of many active, able-bodied children enjoying a free afternoon.

The sounds infuriated her and at times, when she was sure she was alone, she wept in frustration. It was maddening to listen to them having the time of their lives when she was stuck up here in bed, instructed not to move. But the worst thing of it all was that she was no longer able to dance. Not even at home. Losing her access to the dancing school had been heart-rending, but now she couldn't even practice alone. Sometimes, she felt as though unseen forces were working against her, conspiring to prevent her from enacting her passion, and she wanted to cry just thinking about it. Other than her family and friends, dancing had become the one thing she truly cared about. It had blotted out her love of football and adventure books, and as swiftly as she had made its discovery it had been snatched away from her.

Polio, the doctor called it, and while she was not told the implications of this illness, what she did know was that it left her in a lot of pain. Her body ached all over, and several times now she had tried getting out of bed to dance, when her mother was downstairs, but every time she did, the pain was so bad that she was forced to climb back under the covers and lie down once more.

Clara wondered how long this illness would last, because she didn't think she could go many more days without exercising her need to dance. She had asked her mother on numerous occasions how long she would be bed-bound for, but each time she received only vague answers, and she was sure that once she had heard her mother stifle a cry as she left the room.

Because of this lack of information, she was left to judge her time in bed by her previous brushes with illness. She had had colds on occasion and had once contracted flu, and each time she had only been stuck in bed for a few days – perhaps a week at the most. But, so far, she had already been in bed for three weeks, and the doctor had been in at least every other day.

Clara often pondered how her father was able to pay for all these visits. She saw him less and less these days, and her mother had told her that he was working very hard and doing extra hours, so she supposed that was how he was paying for it. The fact that the doctor was Jeremy's father might also have been beneficial – maybe he wasn't charging so much for the visits?

Thinking about Jeremy only sank her deeper into depression. She missed him fiercely; missed seeing him whenever she wanted; missed his awkward attempts to pass on tips he gained from the dancing school. Sure, he had been over to see her a few times since the fateful day of the recital, but these visits were now limited by her condition, and when she did see him, they could not play or dance together anymore. She could see the pain and grief deepen in his face with each meeting, and although he tried his best to cheer her up, all she could feel was despair. She pretended to laugh at his jokes and his amusing anecdotes, but each time she saw him it just made her wish even more that she could walk and run and jump by his side, as she used to do. But those days were fast slipping into memory, and it did not look like she would be seeing them again any time soon.

Her father came in to visit that evening and brought with him a book that Jeremy had left for her the last time he visited. She had not even glanced at it and in fact had not opened a single book since becoming ill. She just could not bring herself to read about excited young children having adventures; searching for buried treasure, climbing trees, solving mysteries – all these things were closed off to her now.

Her father put on a brave face, told her that she was going to be fine and that he would find some way to pay for her dancing lessons once she was well again, but in her present mood she even found it difficult to believe *him*, her hero.

He opened the book and began reading. At first, she found that she barely listened to the story, lulled instead by the sound of her father's voice, but, as it progressed, she began to sit up and take notice.

A long time ago, in a faraway land, there was a village. The families of this village had lived there for generations – they worked and farmed the land in the same manner as their forebears, passing down practices and traditions from father to son, mother to daughter. The village had had its ups and downs over the years – as do all people in all settlements – but recently had fallen on hard times.

First their crops began to fail, blighted by disease or eaten by pests. For a time, their people went hungry, but they tended their crops lovingly and slowly they returned to health and recovered, and everyone could eat their fill again.

Then came terrible storms that battered their village and livestock with wind and rain and hail. But they simply repaired and reinforced

*any damage done, sheltered their animals in
their homes to keep them safe, and harvested
their crops early to avoid loss, and together they
weathered the fury of the storms.*

Joseph glanced over at Clara and smiled wanly.

'Hmm, perhaps they should just leave,' he
chuckled. 'What do you think?'

'Keep reading,' Clara replied with a yawn. 'Please.'

Joseph nodded fondly and hugged her close to
him as he continued to read.

*Next, a terrible sickness began to take their
livestock, covering their hides in hideous boils that
caused great pain and made their products – their
meat and their milk – inedible. But the villagers
were not perturbed – they healed the ones they
could, culled those they couldn't, and bred more.*

*After this came the bandits. They arrived
in the night, pillaging and killing with wanton
disregard. They stole whatever they could carry
and spoiled anything they couldn't, slaking the
thirst of their blades in the flesh of the villagers,
spilling their blood over the ground they farmed
with such great care…*

At this point, Joseph lowered the book and
looked down at Clara with concern.

'I'm not sure this is really the best thing for you in your
current state, Clara,' he said worriedly. 'What about if I…'

'But I'm enjoying it,' Clara said weakly. 'Please, read more…'

Joseph stared into her eyes a moment longer, then – against his better judgement – relented and read on.

The bandits came night after night, but the villagers fought them off every time, rebuilding and re-growing what they lost until their enemy lost interest and moved on.

It was then that war arrived. Most of the men were summoned to fight – and very few returned – leaving the village struggling to continue with those that remained. But they fought bravely on, and gradually their sons and daughters took over and ensured its continuance.

At this time in history, dragons still roamed the land, and it was around this point that a great Dragon Lord heard about this village and its indomitable inhabitants, and he decided to put them to the test – to show them the true meaning of hardship.

He arrived at the village in a blaze of fire and fury. With his lethal breath and his claws like axe blades he made short work of the settlement, decimating everything he touched and ensuring that many who lived there would never rise again. Leaving nought but ruins in his wake, he flew away once more, cruel laughter on his lips.

A year or so later, the Dragon Lord was flying south to his winter home when he saw what looked like a village up ahead, and – driven by curiosity – he flew over to investigate. To his disbelief, the Dragon Lord discovered that the village had been rebuilt – exactly as it was – and its people were once again hard at work in its fields.

The Dragon Lord was amazed at their strength of will – at their refusal to give up – and so he landed, slowly and respectfully, by the village entrance, and called to their chieftain. The Chief arrived – with no shred of fear – and explained that his people would never leave this place. This was their ancestral home: they had grown their crops there, raised their children there, and buried their dead there, and they would not give up on this land for anything.

The Dragon Lord was stunned by their enduring spirit – by their will to fight on, no matter the cost and no matter the enemy – and he knew this could not go unrewarded. He heaped upon them everything he could conceive of: gold from his private stores, seeds from distant lands, and promised that – as long as he lived – they would never be preyed upon again.

Her father closed the book and placed it upon the bed, his eyes serious.

'I'm not sure that was wholly appropriate for you, Clara,' he said. 'And I will not be reading it to you again.' He flipped the book over and looked at the cover solemnly. 'I wonder where Jeremy got this from?' he murmured, more to himself than to her.

'But I liked it,' Clara said, rolling painfully onto her side. He looked at her tenderly and bent to kiss her forehead.

'I'll read you a different book tomorrow night; a nicer book, I promise.'

He stood up then, gripping the book in one hand, and moved to the window, shutting it gently against the draft. Then he backed out of the room, as though he did not want to take his eyes off her, and finally shut the door.

She rolled onto her other side and stared out of the darkened window, the reflection of the room around her blending strangely with the faint outlines of the trees at the far end of the garden. Her last thought before she fell into a disturbed sleep was:

How much longer will I have to stay in this bed?

The next day, the doctor – Jeremy's father – came to visit again. She did not like it when he came to see her. She didn't like the way they all crowded around her bed: her mother, the doctor and his assistant, all staring at her with expressions she could never quite fathom. She felt so disconnected from them all, as though she was viewing them from behind a pane of glass. The way the assistant sometimes looked at her made her feel different, other, and it only made her question her protracted time in bed even more.

How much longer could she *possibly* be confined here for? Surely the illness would leave her body sooner or later? But the doctor never spoke to her about her condition, he only ever spoke to her mother. He would offer Clara general reassurance, empty words that she always found difficult to believe because – although she could not fully read his expression – she could see the doubt in his eyes. She never said this out loud, but it terrified her.

He finished his examination and gave her a hollow smile, telling her that she was going to be fine and he would check up on her again in a few days. She nodded and turned over, pretending to fall asleep. Quietly, the doctor left the room with her mother and began a whispered conversation in the corridor. Clara shuffled across the bed so that she was as close to the door as possible and listened hard, trying to catch what they were saying.

'…is very far advanced,' was the first thing she heard. 'She is a strong-willed little girl, but I fear the Polio is getting the best of her. I… I worry that…' His voice broke off and Clara could hear her mother's sharp, distressed breathing. 'I fear that she may never leave that bed again…'

Clara's mother burst into muffled tears and asked the doctor something, but Clara no longer heard them. A ringing had started in her ears and all other sounds faded away, as though they were no longer of any importance. She did not cry, did not break down and beseech the heavens for aid, but a feeling of numb hopelessness washed over her, pervading every inch of her fragile body. The room and the world around her seemed to recede into the distance until all she could see was her bed and her own pain-riddled body stretched out beneath her quilt.

I may never get out of this bed again... Clara thought. *Let alone dance, or skip or play with Jeremy. This bed is my prison...*

CHAPTER 26
Late to the Battle

As Clara crouched by Vincent's side with her hand upon the rough fur of his shoulder, the total unreality of her situation collapsed in on her again, like cliffs crumbling into a stormy sea.

How...? she thought in disbelief. *How is any of this possible...? I was told I would never leave my bed again... So how... how can I be here...? How can this be real...?*

Once again, she saw in her mind's eye the book on the table in the darkened room, but this time the key to the padlock was not only in her hand, it was in the lock... One turn and it would open, and reveal what it hid from her – the secret she had hoped never to openly face again...

The muscles in her hand clenched, ready to turn the key, but she stopped herself... As unreal and unbelievable as this all was, there was one thing she knew in her heart was real. Love. The love El felt for her children, the love Vincent still felt for them – and felt for her – was real. Clara knew with an iron-clad certainty that this love was real, and it was the beacon to which she clung as all else seemed to disintegrate to dust around her.

If this love was real, then who knew what else was possible. Maybe she truly could help the people of Comhlacht. Maybe she would indeed be rewarded with the means to save her mother's life. Right then she had no way of knowing, so while she did not know if she could believe that everything that was happening was real, as Garret had once said: she had hope – and that would have to do for now.

Clara gently took Vincent's muzzle in her hands and stared straight into his amber eyes; eyes that were hollow and vacant with grief.

'My dear, my Vincent,' she began, mastering a sob. 'The pain you feel right now is yours and I share in it, but I will not tell you how to feel it. I will not tell you that I understand it or that it will pass in time – for some wounds never heal, and that is simply the way of things. Loss is the keenest of blades, and it always cuts the deepest, and some pierced by it never recover.'

Clara wiped a tear from her cheek, determined not to let another fall while she faced him.

'But what I will tell you is this,' she continued, gripping his muzzle tighter, gazing strongly into his face. 'You cannot give up now. You *must* not. You have lost so much already – given so much of yourself – but your world still needs you, your people still need you, your children still need you…'

She placed her forehead tenderly against his. 'And *I* still need you…'

She drew away from him then and got resolutely to her feet, staring down at him as he looked up from his prone position.

'So, what will you do?' she asked firmly. 'Will you stay here and mourn…?' She held out her hand to him. 'Or will you keep going, for all those who need you…?'

For a few moments Vincent stared up at her with an expression she could not read, then he glanced away and struggled to his feet.

The mound looked small and cold by the time they had finished, and they had no flowers to decorate it, but they had been able to place it right in the shadow of the Wolf Tree, which Vincent knew she had wanted. Her mask lay at its head, partially buried in the disturbed earth, the only time it had ever been removed since her Convergence.

Vincent stared at it now – human again – and Clara knew it would take every ounce of his strength to tear himself away, but he finally managed it as he turned to face Croí.

'We must move,' he said at last, his voice dim and distant. 'I fear the battle has been joined – we may already be out of time…'

Like one sleepwalking, he drifted away from the grave and Clara, Garret, Darcy and Marcus followed after him for the last stage of their journey.

Clara barely remembered that final stretch to Croí. After everything that had happened, the five of them strode along in silence, lost in the darkness of their own thoughts – processing events as best they could. What route they had taken or what they had passed along the way she could not tell you, her thoughts filled with memories of El, and while her loss tore at Clara's heart, she was able to force herself onwards with hope – hope that El had not died in vain; hope that their world could still be saved.

It was the clash and clamour of combat that brought them all back to themselves as they finally exited a stretch of forest and approached Croí. It seemed that Vincent had been right, and the battle had already begun in their absence. After their silent, disconnected journey, Clara felt as if she was waking from a dream, but what she beheld made her fear she had slipped into a nightmare.

For a time, her brain could not even begin to comprehend what it was seeing before it – the turmoil of the melee was too fast and too wild and the sights so strange and unnatural that her mind revolted at the mere sight of it. But Vincent suffered no such problems.

'I don't believe it…' he breathed. 'They're… they're here…'

'Who's here?' Clara asked, still struggling to make sense of it all.

'Bear…' he whispered back. 'Bear… and Hare…'

Slowly, the chaotic images that danced before her began to untangle in her mind and she soon saw things as Vincent did. Ahead of them stood Croí, crouched in its hollow at the foot of the mountains, its tall, beautiful buildings and spires visible behind the vast stone wall that protected its front entrance – the only side not bordered by sheer cliffs. Its drawbridge was raised, blocking access across the moat, but this was not stopping the Viper... Hordes of them swarmed around the front of the city, firing off weapons and launching projectiles, and, in many places, Clara could see that the wall was already broken and crumbling.

Strange machines driven by large steam-powered engines moved into position, unfurling bridges that spanned the moat and offered access to the holes they had punctured, and, roaring, screaming Viper soldiers snarled and jostled to be the first ones across.

In amongst these, Clara saw more of the frightening drill-like contraptions beginning to dig into the ground to attack the city from below, the Viper plan hinging on spreading the Wolf forces thin via multiple entry points. And here and there she saw more of the terrible tanks they had encountered in Neart rolling into position to bring devastation to the wall and the buildings beyond. All in all, it was an awesome and terrifying sight to see so many instruments of death and destruction in one place, driven by the ferocious and unrelenting will of their master, Malone.

But the Wolves were not alone in their battle against the Viper, and this was what Vincent had seen in a heartbeat, for – upon the walls, fighting alongside their Wolf comrades – were the unmistakeable forms of Bear Clan soldiers, unloading their weapons into the enemy below. And – at the rear of the conflict, hitting them from behind – Clara was overjoyed to see Hare Clan warriors; delighted both that they had survived the surprise attack on Anam, and had chosen to help out after all.

Vincent – his brow furrowed as his mind ran through a thousand possibilities – turned to face them, focussing on Clara, Darcy and Marcus.

'We need to get you kids to the Lord's manor,' he said quickly. 'It is where your journey has been leading all this time, and it is the only way to end this…'

At these words, Clara's heart thudded painfully fast – *I still don't know how I can help!* – but her hope got her through.

'So, stay close behind Garret and I – we will find a way in,' he said, drawing his revolver and cocking it, nodding at Garret as he hefted his shotgun. 'Follow me.'

Going against all their instincts, the three children hurried after their protectors, racing towards the gunshots, explosions and screams of pain that fought for supremacy in the cacophonous tumult of battle. Bullets and debris zipped all around them as they ran bent double, using cover where they could, desperate not to fall behind – for to fall behind would be to fall forever.

A group of Viper soldiers spotted them and leapt into their path, but Vincent and Garret emptied their weapons into them, a well-thrown vial from Vincent's belt taking out the remainder in a plume of flame, and the way was clear again.

The next group they tackled in their Shifted forms, ripping flesh and tearing off limbs with the ferocity of loss and the tenacity of hope, bulling their way through with the impact of a hurricane and sending their enemy tumbling like skittles.

Heedless of the whirling, roaring shapes around her, Clara focussed intently on following Vincent, doing what she could to help Marcus and Darcy keep up. At one point, Marcus stumbled on a fallen Viper and felt his ankle gripped in its metal grasp as it struggled to rise once more, but she and Darcy beat and kicked at it until it let go, and they were able to struggle on.

Through the maelstrom they spotted a Viper to their right wielding a grenade, his arm drawn back ready to throw, but a shot rang out and he was struck between the eyes, dropping him limply to the floor, the grenade rolling into their path. Clara saw the danger in an instant and – disregarding her own safety – dashed in and kicked it, sending it hurtling into a group of Viper nearby where it detonated, spraying shrapnel in all directions.

With their ears ringing they hurtled onwards, and it was then – after Vincent and Garret broke through another line of Viper – that they found themselves in the midst of the Hare, who were engaged in attacking the Viper's rear, and they spotted a friendly face near the forefront of the charge.

'Tia!' Clara called over the roar of battle. Her friend looked up at once and smiled with no apparent surprise to see her there.

'Clara!' she replied delightedly, extricating herself from the fight to speak to them. 'I was wondering when you'd show up.'

'I'm so glad you came!' Clara beamed as she pulled her into a hug, while Vincent scanned for threats beside them, firing off shots as he listened in. 'But how are you here?'

'It was tough, but we were just about able to beat back the Viper in Anam,' Tia replied as they drew apart. 'We didn't know when their next attack would come, but we knew it would... It still took some time to convince the whole Clan – you know what we Hare are like – but, after having it hit home like that, it became obvious what we should do.'

A Viper soldier lurched towards them and Tia bounded forward, slashing his throat with her stone blade and sending him tumbling to the ground.

'Everyone just seemed to look to me after the decision was made,' she continued, as if nothing had happened. 'By the time we arrived here the battle had already been joined – now we're just trying to break through so we can fight alongside our brothers and sisters of the Wolf and Bear.'

Sensing a lull in the conversation, Vincent stepped in.

'Sorry to interrupt, but do you think you can get us to that?' he asked, pointing at one of the ring-shaped machines they had ridden in previously standing empty ahead of them. Tia sized up the huddle of Viper surrounding it, and nodded.

'Aye, we can get you there,' she replied.

Tia was as good as her word. Calling a group of her best warriors, she explained the goal and they were on the move in a matter of moments, battering their way through the Viper with the help of Vincent and Garret. Fed up with feeling useless, and motivated by the grit and determination in the faces of their comrades, Clara, Marcus and Darcy looked at each other and nodded. Picking up stone blades dropped by fallen Hare, they joined in the fight too, following in their friends' wake, slashing and swiping at any Viper foolish enough to come close.

Their arms were tiring by the time they made it to the vehicle, the Hare warriors spreading out around it to protect them while they boarded. Vincent turned to Tia and nodded at her.

'My thanks,' he said with a bow. 'I'm sure I'll see you in there. And I meant what I said before – you really would make a great Chief…'

Tia smiled modestly.

'If we make it through this and my Clan continue to look to me, then, well…' she shrugged. 'Who knows what might happen…'

Vincent bowed again, then he turned and ushered the others into the vehicle before taking his seat at the controls. The steam engine at the rear belched smoke as Vincent flipped switches and tapped buttons, and soon they bounded forwards, the mechanical legs below skittering frantically and making short work of the bodies, rubble and craters they encountered.

Many Viper soldiers – who did not spot the danger quick enough – were trampled beneath the vehicle as Vincent wove his way through the melee, racing towards one of the bridging machines outside the wall. As they flew along, Garret hung off one side and unloaded his shotgun into any Viper that tried to board, while Clara, Marcus and Darcy swung their blades at anything in reach.

They were approaching the bridging machine when a terrifying sight rolled into view through the swirling dust of combat – a tank. Its cannon fired, the shot missing them by a whisker and sailing off deep into the city. But Vincent forged on unperturbed, heading directly for the bridge. Another shot rang out, the shell impacting the ground beside them, spraying dirt and stones everywhere and almost tipping them over – each of them barely clinging on – but Vincent was able to right them again as they surged onto the bridge.

Garret – looking suddenly nervous – pointed ahead.

'Uh, there's no way through, Vincent,' he yelled above the noise.

As the dust ahead cleared, Vincent saw that the wall stood undamaged before them, blocking their path.

'I see it,' his friend replied grimly.

As they powered towards the solid stone another retort echoed from the tank, and the shell hurtled their way. With milliseconds to spare, Vincent veered to one side and the shot went wide, impacting the wall and blasting a hole directly in their path. As dust and debris rained down, they swiftly darted through this unexpected entrance and found themselves – at last – inside the city.

Their vehicle passed easily over the rubble and down onto a wide, cobbled street surrounded by tall, statuesque buildings – a mixture of homes, stores, workshops and what appeared to be places of worship – looking for all the world like Victorian London. The detailing and the architecture were astonishing, and this only made the devastation of the conflict all the more painful, for this once-beautiful city was already battered and scarred. The streets were pockmarked with craters, holes had been blasted in the facade of many buildings – exposing their floors like a doll's house - and fires burned everywhere, smoke rising like beacons wherever they looked.

As Clara gazed around her, she found she could see past the wreck and ruin to what it had so recently been – she could almost see the Wolf people walking the streets, perusing the shops, eating in the cafés and working at their jobs. She could feel the history here – the life and the love – and she knew she could not let it come to an end. The imagined images faded

from her view and she saw it again as it was now –
saw the battles being fought with the Viper who had
made it past the wall; the mortal struggles going on
in these once lively streets.

With the buildings flashing past on either side,
Vincent glanced back at them.

'That's where we're headed,' he called, pointing at
a large manor house that sat on a raised plateau at
the rear of the city. 'I just need to make a quick stop
along the way…'

He turned hard, taking them off the main road
and down a narrower side street where the buildings
were lower, more residential. Finally, they pulled up
outside a small, homely looking residence that stood
apart from the others, fronted by a tidy little garden
that somehow still bore flowers in the face of the Rot.

Vincent leapt down, his expression fraught with
concern, and Clara wondered where they were, but,
as they followed him inside, the photographs on the
mantel above the fire gave it away at once – it was his
family home.

'Kids!' he yelled. 'Sisi! Are you here?'

Receiving no response, he hurried on through
the back entrance with Clara, Marcus and Darcy
trailing after him, while Garret waited at the front.
Moving straight to a trap door set below the kitchen
window, Vincent hurled the double doors open and
ducked inside.

'Hello?' he called into the darkness as he
descended the stairs. 'Hello!'

He reached the bottom and quickly lit a nearby gas lamp as Clara appeared behind him. Holding it aloft, Vincent shone the light into every corner.

'Kids?' he called again. 'Kids!?'

'Father?' a small voice whispered.

'Sisi?' Vincent replied. 'Is that you?'

From the shadows, a figure appeared with a knife in its trembling hand, two smaller forms close behind it. As they came forth into the light, Clara had to choke back a cry, believing for a moment that El was standing before her once more, for fourteen-year-old Sisi was the spitting image of her mother, from the flaming red hair to the bright white wolf mask. Her two siblings – the eleven-year-old twins Bella and Ty – also bore their mother's hair, but had not yet completed their Convergence and so had no masks, but Clara could see El in them both.

'What took you so long!' Sisi cried, displaying her mother's fire as she lowered her knife and rushed forward to envelop her father in a hug, Bella and Ty swiftly following suit.

'I'm so sorry, my darlings,' Vincent said as he hugged them fiercely. 'The journey took far longer than expected, but I'm glad to see you did as we'd always agreed.'

They broke apart then, anger and frustration on Sisi's face behind her mask.

'I did not want to disobey you,' she began irately. 'But hiding down here while the others fight is almost more than I can bear! I…'

'You did what was best for your brother and sister,' Vincent said gently, cupping her cheek in a hand. 'They needed you to protect them.'

'We do not need protecting!' Ty yelled stoutly.

'No – we want to fight too!' Bella piped up. Vincent sighed.

'Your mother would not…'

'Where *is* mother…?' Sisi cut in. 'Is she with you?'

A dagger of ice pierced Vincent's heart at these words. He crouched down in front of his children and gathered them close.

'My dears,' he began, and Clara could feel the struggle going on within – his desperate need to master his emotions and stay strong for his young. 'There is something I must tell you…'

Many tears were shed as Vincent relayed his story, each word he spoke a hammer-blow to his heart, but somehow both his and Sisi's eyes remained dry as they comforted the twins throughout. Clara could see so much of El in Sisi, knew that she was a warrior through and through, as she listened silently to her father's tale, and when it was finished all she said was:

'Father, I want to fight… I *need* to…'

'Me… me too…' Bella sniffed.

'And me…' Ty agreed.

'Your mother told me to protect you…' Vincent replied sorrowfully. 'I must not let any harm come to you…'

'And she also told you to make sure we reach that better world…' Sisi said, placing a hand on her father's shoulder. 'And the only way we do that – as you always say – is by all of us pulling together...' She stared earnestly into her father's eyes. 'This is a turning point for our world... You *must* let us help... You must let us do all we can... Please...'

Vincent gazed proudly at his three children, all staring at him with the unquenchable fire and determination their mother had forever exhibited. His eyes flicked back and forth between them – searching their faces – and finally he relented.

'Alright...' he whispered, pulling them all into another hug. 'I don't know what I ever did to deserve you three...'

He got to his feet and moved over to a corner where several packing cases were stacked. Separating them out and flipping them open, he revealed a stash of weaponry and invited the children to take what they needed. When they had armed themselves, Vincent reached inside one and replenished the gadgets and ammunition at his belt, then turned back to them. He took a breath.

'Are we ready?' he asked.

They all nodded back fervently.

'Do you know where you're headed?' he asked once they were back out front with Garret.

'The kids were sent to defend the west side of the wall,' Sisi replied determinedly. Vincent nodded.

'Okay, you be careful,' he said, still torn at his decision. 'You look after your brother and sister at all costs – you hear me?'

Sisi nodded as each of the three children hugged him in turn and began to move off towards the wall.

'If anything happens you come find me at the Lord's manor!' Vincent yelled, and Sisi waved in response. They disappeared around a corner and for a time Vincent simply stared after them, lost in self-doubt and wondering, *have I made the right choice? What would you have done, El…?*

'We must keep moving,' Garret murmured at his side and Vincent nodded, climbing back into the vehicle with his eyes still locked on the corner where he had lost sight of the kids. Finally, he snapped his gaze away and they drove off, back on the road to their final destination.

As they powered along, Clara clambered over to sit behind Vincent at the controls and asked the question she had been hesitant to voice for so long.

'Vincent, now that it comes to it – now that we are almost there – I must ask…' she began. 'I feel like you have been keeping something from me… You know how I can help your world – you have known from the start – but you seem unwilling to say it… I know the Rot comes from my world, I know that it is only through my people that it can be removed… But, how…? How do I help you…? Please… Tell me…'

Vincent glanced back at her and there was a look on his face that he had never shown her before – it was pity…

'Clara…' he started to say. 'I…' But he got no further, for something suddenly struck the side of their vehicle with a bone-shaking impact and they were roughly flipped over. Sparks flew as the ring ground against the cobbles and all five of them were flung off, tumbling end over end and skidding to a slow, painful stop in a battered and bruised heap. The furnace of the vehicle's steam engine spluttered and died, and the mechanical legs were stilled.

'Something hit us!' Vincent gasped, and, as he glanced around in confusion, he spotted what looked like the remains of a broken chimney top lying next to the machine. 'Is everyone alright?' he added, and Garret, Clara and Darcy all replied yes, but there was one voice that did not speak.

'Marcus!' Clara wailed, spotting his small unconscious figure pinned beneath the ring. She rushed to his side and threw her head against his chest and was relieved to hear a heartbeat. 'We must get him out!' she yelled to Vincent, but then they all froze as a sudden pounding like monstrous footsteps filled the air, and the crown jewel of Malone's army stomped into view around a building and entered the town square.

While the tank in Neart had borne some resemblance to machinery she knew from her world, this was something completely other, and Clara's mind boggled at the sight of it. Striding towards them was what could only be described as an immense metal man – many times taller than the tallest adult she knew – its mechanical legs and arms driven by huge gears and pistons and powered by an immense furnace in its chest cavity, vents on its back ejecting steam in a cloying cloud that made its image flicker like heat haze. Above the furnace and near the head – which was shaped like a Viper mask – she could see what appeared to be a pilot sitting at the controls and sneering down at them.

'Get Marcus to safety,' Vincent called to Clara and Darcy, his eyes not leaving the machine. 'We will do what we can with this…'

Leaving the children to help Marcus, Vincent and Garret moved towards the centre of the square to face it. Glancing at each other worriedly, they raised their weapons and fired, emptying their chambers, but their rounds clanged harmlessly off the machine's casing without a scratch. The gigantic contraption took a step towards them and one of its massive hands reached out, snapping the chimney off a nearby building and hurling it directly at them. Vincent and Garret only just dived aside in time as it impacted the street, spraying fragments of brick and stone everywhere.

'What do we do against this!?' Garret roared.

'How the hell should I know!' Vincent yelled back. 'Duck!' They both threw themselves flat as a mobile stall whistled overhead and was dashed to splinters on the cobbles.

The machine took another few paces towards them, its arms reaching out to grip the spire of a tall, ornate building beside it. With all its might it tugged, the stonework crumbling under the strain, dust raining down, and finally it gave way and plummeted toward them. Vincent and Garret hurled themselves aside again as it crashed to earth, smashing a huge hollow in the street and spreading rubble far and wide.

'I'm getting tired of this,' Vincent growled. He reached for his belt and drew out a number of different coloured vials. He threw two to Garret – one yellow and one red – and began to race towards the machine with a yell of: 'Follow my lead!'

With a weary shake of his head, Garret hurried after his friend, ducking to the left when indicated while Vincent darted right.

The pilot of the machine, sensing a coordinated attack, began to lash out at them, its great fists pummelling the street as it sought to smash them to a pulp, its wild swings missing them by inches. Narrowly dodging another punch, Vincent drew back his fist holding a yellow vial and lobbed it directly at the machine. Though it tried to avoid this it was too slow, the vial breaking on impact right within the gears of its articulated left foot. A blinding white flame began to burn, its intensity building and building as sparks flew, the heat rapidly rising until the metal began to melt and fuse together.

The pilot instantly knew that something was up, for when it next tried to move it staggered and almost fell, having lost full mobility. Furious now, it kicked out at Vincent with its malfunctioning leg, and though he spun aside he was not quick enough and it caught him a glancing blow, sending him tumbling to the ground.

With his focus on Vincent, the pilot did not see Garret until it was too late, and another yellow vial exploded on its right foot, the complex mechanisms within quickly heating up and melting together. Its range of motion now dramatically limited, the machine lumbered around, its movements jerky and erratic as the molten metal ran from its feet and stuck to the cobbles.

Vincent, back on his feet but clutching his side, regrouped with Garret in the shadow of a colossal, obelisk-like monument at the centre of the square. As the machine staggered awkwardly towards them, he glanced up at it apologetically.

'Sorry about this, Atherton,' he said. 'You were a damn good architect.'

With a nod to Garret, they waited just long enough for the machine to get in range – its hands clawing for them – then they turned and hurled their red vials at the base of the monument and dived for cover. The vials exploded in a burst of flame and a shower of masonry and the whole structure shifted. The pilot of the machine saw what was coming and tried to avoid disaster, but the liquid metal still running from its feet had now fused it to the ground, and it wasn't going anywhere.

Slowly, inevitably, the monument began to topple, its shadow falling over the machine as it sank lower and lower and finally impacted with it in a deafening screech of grinding metal and a whirlwind of debris. Pinned beneath the rubble, the machine was still not done. As sparks flew from its joints and its gears ground together, it reached for the remains of the edifice and tried to pry it loose.

Vincent and Garret glanced at each other hopelessly, and were just wondering what to do when they heard a wild, animal roar from the rooftop of a nearby building and looked up. A huge bear bellowed its fury to the sky as it launched itself into the air, hurtling towards the prone machine and Shifting in mid-flight to land upon it in a roll.

'It cannot be…' Garret breathed in disbelief.

'It is,' Vincent replied with a small smile.

Chief Davin raced across the machine's chest and reached the cockpit, where the pilot struggled with the damaged controls. Pulling forth his shotgun, he emptied it into the unfortunate man's face, then turned and hailed Vincent below him.

'Here!' he yelled. Catching his meaning, Vincent grabbed a blue vial from his belt and hurled it up to the Bear Chief. Deftly plucking it from the air, Davin flung it into the waning flames of the machine's furnace then leapt down beside them, just as blue smoke began to belch forth and its entire chest cavity exploded in a vast plume of flame.

Heedless of the shrapnel raining around them, Garret stared at Davin in shock and relief.

'Fath… Chief…' he corrected himself. 'You're… You're alive…?'

For a moment, Davin's face wore the same grim seriousness it always did as he looked upon his son, then his expression crumbled into relief and regret as he drew Garret to him in a hug.

'I'm… I'm sorry, son…' he said quietly. 'It took time for your words to hit home – too long, really – but hit home they did.' They drew apart and he held his son at arm's length, staring into his face. 'As I watched our people fighting and dying in Neart, I thought it was what I wanted – to die in combat with our enemy. But it would have been a wasted death…'

Davin turned and surveyed the battle around them, taking in the distant booms and yells from the front gate.

'So, we beat back the Viper as best we could, then retreated into the tunnels and blew the entrance so they couldn't follow,' he continued. 'Never retreated in my life – and it didn't feel great – but I realised it was the only choice to make.'

He turned back from the battle.

'You two were right all along,' he went on, now glancing between Garret and Vincent. 'Our only chance in this fight is to stand together, and I hope we've bought you the time you need.' He focussed his attention now on Vincent. 'I may not truly believe in what you're attempting, but a slim hope is better than none at all,' he added. 'Now… how can I help…?'

At that moment, Clara and Darcy appeared supporting Marcus – who was limping, but

THOMAS JOHN HOWARD BOGGIS

otherwise unhurt – and they stopped beside them, Clara looking at Davin in surprise.

Vincent was just about to reply to the Chief when a shadow passed over them, and they all looked up in horror. A shape was winging its way towards them, growing larger and clearer against the blood red sky, diving closer and closer until finally they saw it for what it was: a monstrous metal bird – a harbinger of doom – and, at its helm… none other than Malone himself, his fierce gaze locked on Vincent as he careened straight for them…

CHAPTER 27
Never Giving Up

'VINCENT!' Malone screamed as he dove his flying machine directly at his old friend and now mortal enemy.

Vincent hurriedly turned to Clara, Darcy and Marcus.

'Go!' he urged them, pointing up the street. 'Head for the Lord's manor now – he is expecting you!'

Clara hesitated, looking back at him fearfully.

'I still don't know how I…' she began, but Vincent cut across her.

'You will know soon enough!' he replied. 'Go! Please go before he gets here!'

For a moment Clara dithered as Malone swept closer, then she knew what she must do: she must trust Vincent – as she had done all this time – and trust to the hope she held in her heart.

Clara nodded determinedly and turned away, she and Darcy helping Marcus to hobble quickly up the road and out of sight. She had just disappeared around a corner when Malone grazed the roof of a building at the far end of the square and surged towards Vincent with murder in his heart, diving recklessly at the ground.

The flying machine rapidly narrowed the gap but, rather than moving, Vincent closed his eyes, taking a long, slow breath as Garret and Davin sprinted out of its path to either side of him. He could hear the roar of its steam engine approaching, the whistle of its great bulk cutting the air. It was nearly upon him…

His eyes snapped open and he dove to the side, the machine missing him by a hair's breadth as it impacted with the street in a whirl of shredded metal, ploughing a deep furrow through the cobbles, its huge wings breaking apart and its tail shearing under the pressure. The machine ground on and on until it collided with a building and finally shuddered to a stop, flames springing up around it.

Vincent struggled to his feet and looked over to it – knowing what he would see – and, sure enough, through the clouds of smoke now rising from it a figure appeared…

'VINCENT!' Malone bellowed again.

As Vincent watched him approach, Garret and Davin arrived at his side once more, their weapons drawn and ready. But at that moment they heard the thrum of a multitude of footsteps from the other end of the square and turned to see a veritable horde of Viper approaching, wreaking havoc as they went.

'We'll deal with them,' Garret said before clapping Vincent on the shoulder. 'Good luck.'

'To you also,' Vincent replied. 'And you have my sincerest thanks – we would not have got this far without your help.'

Garret nodded.

'My hope goes with you,' he murmured as he and his father raced away side by side to head off the Viper. Vincent turned back to Malone who was now only a few paces from him.

'Just you and me then, is it?' he snarled. 'Well let us finish what we STARTED!'

The blade above his mechanical wrist sprang out and he lunged, stabbing and slashing with wild rage, Vincent only just managing to dodge or parry the ferocious swings with his cane sword. Steel clashed on steel, sparks flew, and Vincent found – once again – that he was being driven back, back towards a building behind him.

'Still pulling your punches, eh, Vincent?' Malone sneered as he continued to rain blows down upon him. 'Still think you can save me? Can't you see? I DON'T NEED SAVING!'

Vincent's back was against a door and Malone kicked him viciously in the chest, sending him rocketing through it, smashing it from its hinges as he tumbled to a stop at the foot of a set of stairs within, his opponent rushing after him.

'That must be it.'

Clara, Marcus and Darcy had arrived outside the Lord's manor and Clara now pointed at it, her hand only shaking a little.

'Yeah, but… what do we do once we get inside…?' Darcy asked apprehensively.

'They always said w-we could help, but… never how…' Marcus said, wincing a little.

'There's only one way to find out now…' Clara replied. 'C'mon – let's head in.'

Together – with Clara and Darcy still supporting Marcus – they pushed through the wide front gates and began to crunch along the gravel, past stone benches, exquisitely wrought fountains and withered hedges, towards the huge double doors at the front. While Clara had thought the city was stunning, it was as nothing compared to the Lord's manor. Spread across four floors and comprised of east and west wings with huge bay windows set around a central hall, the building towered above them, every square inch of it masterfully carved from soft grey stone – the likenesses of howling wolves present on the lintels and columns supporting the covered porch. The dark-slated roof rose in twin gables at each wing, surmounted by myriad chimneys from which pale white smoke drifted. Mullioned windows stared down at them like dark eyes as they ascended a low flight of stairs – flanked by stone wolves – and entered the covered porch to approach the front entrance.

With apprehensive looks at one another, Clara raised a hand and knocked upon the door, the sound echoing loudly off the walls around them. When there was no response, she knocked again, but still nothing…

'Try the handle,' Darcy said.

Clara took a breath, then reached for it and turned, but the door was stiff and would not budge. She threw a shoulder against it and pushed with all her might, and it slowly began to swing open with an ear-splitting *creak* that set their teeth on edge. It finally came to a stop and their eyes widened in awe of the beautiful full-height entrance hall it revealed, their gaze gliding over the polished marble floors, lifelike statues, intricately detailed paintings and the magnificent central staircase leading to the upper floors, carpeted in lush crimson tones.

They stepped nervously across the threshold and headed for the stairs, their footsteps sounding infinitely magnified in the cavernous space.

'Where do we go…?' Marcus asked uncertainly.

Clara was about to reply when they all heard sounds from upstairs – were those voices?

They shared another worried look, then came to a silent agreement. Carefully supporting Marcus, they made their way upwards, fighting back the aching weariness that pervaded their bodies after their long and gruelling journey.

As they neared the top, they looked to their right to see a regal set of double doors at the far end of the corridor, and it was from within that the muffled voices seemed to be emanating. They approached them slowly and came to a halt outside. Without pausing, Clara immediately reached for the handle but swiftly stopped herself, her breathing ragged with anxiety.

'We've come too far to quit now,' Darcy said encouragingly. 'Open it.'

With sweating, trembling hands, Clara reached again for the handle, and thrust the door open...

Garret and Davin – father and son – stood alone in the street as the horde of roaring, rioting Viper stampeded towards them like a vast tidal wave. Their filthy, guttural screams went unheeded by either of the Bear as they turned to look at each other.

'Together?' Davin asked, holding his son's gaze.

'Together,' his son agreed, ignoring the rabble of voices drawing ever nearer. 'But... what about the Bear? Who will lead them after?'

Davin placed a hand on his son's shoulder and gripped it tight.

'The Bear will be fine,' he replied, staring proudly at him. 'Because they learned from you...'

With one last, long look at each other, they turned to face their enemy, Shifted to their mighty bear forms, and hurled themselves into their midst with roars that quailed even the sturdiest Viper heart.

Battling valiantly, the two brave warriors took the lives of many Viper soldiers that day as their flesh was cut to ribbons and their life's blood leaked into the good earth they fought to protect.

'FIGHT ME!'

Vincent cannoned backwards, bursting through another door and cartwheeling across the roof into a low brick wall, his momentum almost carrying him over the edge into the dizzying drop to the street below. From the stairway, Malone stalked after him, grinding his blade against the stone in a trail of sparks. As Vincent pushed away from the wall and got painfully to his feet, Malone was on him again, battering him backwards until he was hanging over the edge once more, barely holding Malone's blade back with his own as his childhood friend glared down at him.

'Don't you understand?' Malone said, staring at him in despair. 'I did this for you! I did this for all of us! We can solve the problems the Cypher has caused by using the gifts it has given us! It is both the problem and the solution – I just need more time!'

As Vincent's own blade began to be forced closer and closer to his throat, he looked back at his old friend with pity.

'Comhlacht is out of time,' Vincent gasped. 'And even if it wasn't, the price you've paid for its "gifts" is too high, but you are too far gone to see it!'

A desolate, hopeless snarl tore from Malone's lips as he pressed down with all his might, and Vincent began to slide over the edge…

'Ahh, welcome! I see you have finally made it here safely.'

The warm, comforting voice seemed to come from nowhere as Clara, Darcy and Marcus nervously entered the upstairs room to find an enormous, extravagant office. Looking around in search of the voice, they saw that the wall to their left was taken up by a huge set of double doors, while the wall to their right held a trio of windows, framed by luxurious crimson and gold curtains. The remaining wall space was taken up with floor to ceiling bookshelves – the uppermost levels reachable only via ladders strung on metal rails – and, opposite them, a large and expertly carved desk stood, behind which was a chair, wreathed in shadows.

As the three youngsters hovered uncertainly in the doorway, the voice called out again.

'Come, come, now, don't be shy! We have lots to discuss!'

Behind the desk, a figure could be seen standing up from its chair.

With a quick glance at each other, the children approached the desk warily and stopped a respectful distance from it. Ensuring that Darcy was supporting Marcus, Clara let go of him and took a step forward.

'Lord… Lord Algernon, I presume…?'

The shape behind the desk chuckled.

'I never liked that title, but my people will continue to refer to me in that way,' he laughed. 'But yes – yes, I am he.'

Clara took a deep, steadying breath – everything, *everything* she had done had led her to this moment…

'My Lord,' she began, her eyes now filled with a steely determination, her gaze level and her hands no longer trembling. 'I have travelled a very long way and fought through hell to be here right now. I have seen death – so much death – and lost a very dear friend along the road. I have witnessed things I never imagined in my wildest dreams and made friendships I hope will last a lifetime. I have done all this not knowing how *any* of this can be true – not necessarily believing in what had been promised, but instead merely hoping it to be true. I was told that somehow I could help heal your world, and that in return I would be given a flower that would save my mother's life. After everything I have been through – all the things I have seen – I still do not know how I can help you, but I stand here now ready and willing to do anything, *anything* I can to help – and I will not give up until I do!'

As she stood there, her fists clenched, a fire of resolve behind her eyes, she felt a tingling throughout her whole body, a rising force that grew and grew with the intensity of a universe exploding into being, and all of a sudden a pulse of light and sound rippled out of her and began to spread, passing through the walls of the manor and out into the city. Clara was taken aback as more pulses followed, but Lord Algernon simply laughed good-naturedly and stepped forward into the light.

His wolf mask was a pale white, the pelt of fur down his back and the shoulder length hair beneath of the same colour. He wore an immaculate grey three-piece suit – much like Vincent's – beneath long, flowing robes of deepest mauve. Stopping in front of Clara, he looked down at her determined expression with fondness.

'I think you will find that our world may already be saved…' he said simply.

Outside – as the pulses continued to emanate from Lord Algernon's office – the Viper soldiers caught by it began to fall to their knees, clutching at their heads, the Wolf, Bear and Hare soldiers who witnessed this looking at each other in surprise.

Up on the rooftop, the pulses reached the struggling forms of Vincent and Malone. As the first one struck them Malone reeled back, gripping his temples in pain and dropping to his knees. With nothing left to hold onto, Vincent found himself slipping backwards. His cane sword slid from his grip and clattered off the wall before crashing to the street below as he grasped wildly at anything to stay his fall. His fingertips found a window ledge and he clung on desperately, but he could already feel his hold giving way. He cast about frantically for something – *anything* – but there was nothing that would save him.

Muscles aching, heart pounding, he held on as long as he could, then his grip gave, and he fell…

For a moment he was tumbling, and he knew that he would not survive this. His arms reached up to the heavens for aid, then suddenly – against all the odds – a hand gripped his own. He jerked to a stop, feeling as though his shoulder had been wrenched from its socket, and he looked up in shock and confusion.

Malone stared down at him from the roof, the look of shock on his face mirroring his own. One hand still clasped his head and from his skin a purple ooze slid like tar and sank into the ground.

'What's… What's happening…?' Malone asked dazedly.

With pulses still emanating from her, Clara hurried uncertainly to the window in Algernon's office and looked out to see that every Viper soldier throughout the city was writhing on the floor, purple fluid leaking from them. Then, from across the room behind her, a voice suddenly rang out triumphantly.

'It's charging! It's charging!'

Clara whirled around just as the huge double doors on the opposite wall were thrown open to reveal an awe-inspiring sight. A vast cave within the mountain met their eyes, at the centre of which – crouched over a great, jagged tear in the earth that seemed to go on infinitely downward through an eternity of Rot – was a marvel of a machine, all oversized coils and wires and lights set within burnished metal plating.

A Wolf engineer stood before it, watching elatedly as the pulses continued to strike it and a series of lights on one panel gradually illuminated in sequence.

Tearing her eyes away from this, Clara looked at Algernon, her expression once more worried and confused.

'My Lord...' she stammered. 'If your world is already saved, then... then may I have the flower anyway? My mother, she... she is in desperate need of it...'

Algernon looked back at her and for a moment she found that she could not read his expression, but it unnerved her.

'I am afraid to say, my child,' he began, no trace of malice or anger in his voice – nothing but calm reasoning. 'Such a flower has never existed.' At this, Clara gasped in shock. 'It never existed, but you also never needed it... All you ever needed to save your mother was... you...'

Clara stared back at him in total bewilderment.

'I... I'm not sure what you mean...?' she replied in little more than a whisper, fingers of ice clutching her breast. Algernon looked at her and there was both sorrow and sympathy in his eyes.

'Did you never wonder why your mother fell ill?' he asked her.

CHAPTER 28
Grief Is A Cancer

Joseph Brown sat quietly at the kitchen table, his shoulders slumped and his head bowed. His left hand loosely clutched a cup of weak tea and with his free hand he massaged his temple gently. He glanced at the door as though expecting someone, then drew a great, shuddering breath. His hand shook as he conveyed the cup to his mouth and took a sip. By the time he lowered it his hand was shaking so badly that tea slopped all over the table. It became so severe that the cup slipped from his grasp and shattered on the floor. He looked down at the mess as though he could not see it, then sank onto the table and buried his face in his arms.

For the first time in a long time, he wept. His shoulders rose and fell as his body was wracked with emotion; a mixture of furious confusion and sorrow at the injustice of it all. When Clara had fallen ill, he had taken it extremely badly, but he had not wept. He had put his faith in the Lord; *surely* He would not let his daughter die? No, she would be fine, she would pull through – this was just some kind of test for all of them. Yes, that was all. By the end of this terrible period they would all come out of this as stronger and better people for having endured it.

Those thoughts had been the only thing keeping him going each day, the shining light at the end of the tunnel. It was all part of some plan, it had to be, at the end of which its true meaning and purpose would jump out at them, *hello!* and they would realise that He had been right all along.

Joseph had believed that all through Clara's illness, but now? How could he still believe it? How could it possibly be part of the same plan? How could this in any way make them stronger or better people?

When Emily had fallen ill it had not been sudden, but a gradual decline that at first had been difficult to notice for what it was. During the first few months of Clara's illness, Emily had become prone to headaches and was perpetually tired, but Joseph just assumed that this was a side effect of looking after Clara and worrying over her. But then she began to faint.

She hid these from her husband at first until one day, when they were making dinner together, she fell and hit her head off the sideboard and Joseph was forced to call the doctor. But Jeremy's father was out of town – as was the only other doctor – and it was several days before this other doctor returned and was able to visit, and by that time she had taken on a fever.

The symptoms were strange and misleading, but the one thing that was sure was that Emily was getting weaker by the day. She was fading fast, and the doctor was hard pressed to explain what was happening to her. So, Joseph called Doctor Matthew Stephens – Jeremy's father – the moment he returned home to get his opinion, and had been awaiting his arrival.

'I've seen this before,' Matthew told him later in hushed, consoling tones. They were sitting in the kitchen just after visiting Clara and her mother. Matthew was drinking a cup of tea, but at that time Joseph did not think he could stomach another. 'You often see this in cases where children fall ill. It hits the mother very hard and she feels guilty, impotent, unable to help in any way, and her grief and her worry begin to weaken her, opening her up to all kinds of illnesses and infections. Heartache, some would call it, but basically her immune system is not functioning as well as it should and so she will be unable to fight off sickness. She will just keep getting worse until…' His voice died away as he saw the despairing look on Joseph's face.

'Is there…' Joseph cleared his throat and tried again. 'Is there anything you can do for her, Matthew?' Matthew sighed and his eyes glistened as he looked on the helpless man. Their families had been friends ever since Jeremy and Clara had become companions and it pained him to see Joseph like this. He thought too of how badly Clara's illness was affecting his son. Jeremy ate very little these days, slept badly, and seemed to have lost the vitality of youth. His natural exuberance and irrepressible nature had been quelled, and while he had not fallen ill like Clara's mother, he was certainly not the same person. He was quiet and docile, and their family home no longer felt as it once did. It seemed that Clara's illness was having far reaching consequences, yet he could see no way to help her and put an end to all this.

'The only way your wife will recover is if your daughter fights through her illness,' he said, in a hoarse voice. 'But I have done all I can to help her. It is up to Clara now to pull herself out of this, but even with all my medicines the pain must still be so great… no child should have to endure what she…' He was breathing heavily as he fought to contain his emotions. 'I'm sorry,' he said, 'I have seen so many of these child cases, yet it… it never gets any easier.'

'So… so there's nothing to do but wait and see?' Joseph asked, a plaintive note edging into his voice.

'And pray,' Matthew added.

'I am done with prayer,' Joseph replied shortly, but even as he said this his hand unconsciously went to the crucifix at his throat, and his fingers ran over the surface of the dull wood.

'Do not give up on your faith, Joseph,' Matthew said in a stern tone. 'Your daughter is up there fighting against a crippling disease and you, *you* are thinking of giving up already? Your daughter looks up to you. You are *everything* to her. You *need* to set an example. You need to be strong for her, or she has no hope at all. So pray for Clara, and do not give up on the hope that God will restore her to you. I have faith that Clara will pull through this, and I need you – *she* needs you – to believe that too.' Joseph looked up at him and there were tears in his eyes.

'I do believe it,' he said, 'I never stopped believing it. But these past few weeks I… it has just been so hard to continue blindly on, not knowing what the next day will bring, not knowing if my family will even make it to tomorrow.'

'That's what faith is,' Matthew answered in gentler tones. 'You must trust that, however bad things may look now, they will resolve themselves. You must take strength in that knowledge and by having that strength within you, your daughter may just find the strength in her to fight on too.' Joseph wiped his eyes on his sleeve and sniffed.

'Thank you, Matthew,' he said thickly. 'Thank you for your kind words and for making my wife and daughter as comfortable as you are able. I… I cannot pay you right now, but I am working extra hours at the cemetery and I assure you…' Matthew held up a hand to stop him.

'Please, think nothing of it – I have not taken money from you yet and would not take it from you now, even if you had it to hand,' he replied.

'But, I cannot… surely I must…' But Matthew stopped him again.

'No, no,' he cut across him. 'The best thing you can do for me is to be strong for your daughter and hope and pray that she gets well again. That would make me happier than all the money you could ever muster.'

'Thank you,' Joseph repeated humbly. 'You are too kind to us.' Matthew nodded, then stood up and headed for the porch. He took his hat off the nail by the door and placed it on his head, then said his farewells and departed.

Joseph shut and locked the door behind him, then stumped slowly up the stairs to the landing. He went first to the room he shared with his wife to check up on her. She was lying on the bed, bundled up with sheets and quilts. A dim fire illuminated the grate in the corner of the room. By its weak light he saw that she was pale as milk and her eyelids twitched in her disturbed sleep. Using his handkerchief, he mopped the sweat from her brow and her body quivered at his touch. He tucked the blankets in tighter around her then bent and kissed her on the cheek.

'Don't worry, my dear,' he said tenderly. 'Our Clara is a tough one, she won't give up. She'll fight through this and return to us, you wait and see. We'll be together again soon.' He moved to the fireplace and threw a few more sticks on the embers, then left the room quietly and crossed the hall to Clara's bedroom.

Clara looked no better than her mother, worse even, and it tore at his heart to see her this way. The fire in her room had all but gone out and Joseph could see that she was shivering under her blankets.

He hurried over to the fireplace and rekindled the blaze, blowing on the glowing embers to bring them back to life and soon, after feeding it plenty of wood and paper, the room was lit by the flickering glow

Joseph returned to the side of Clara's bed and fell to his knees, clasping his hands together in prayer.

'Heavenly Father, I beseech you,' he began, his eyes squeezed shut. 'Please help my daughter. Please look after her and give her the strength and tenacity to win the battle against this illness. She has always been a fighter, but I fear this sickness, this polio, has taken its toll on her and I can see that she is getting weaker.' Tears fell silently down his cheeks as he looked upwards imploringly. 'Lord, if my daughter were to pass then my whole family would be snatched away from me, for I know my wife would follow soon after, and I... I would not be able to go on without them. I ask you... I beg you, please, help us, please... *please*...' Tears splashed onto Clara's bedspread as he made the sign of the cross and bent over his daughter. He smoothed the hair from her face and kissed her forehead.

'It's all down to you now, my darling,' he said brokenly. 'I have faith in you. Do not give up. You *must* endure... Fight... *Fight*...'

CHAPTER 29
What It Is To Do Good

'I know, Clara.'

Clara turned at these words to see Vincent – battered and bleeding – approaching her from the doorway to the hall.

'I know what you have been struggling to face all this time,' he said quietly, wincing with pain as he knelt at her feet to look into her eyes. 'I know what you have buried down so deep you have almost forgotten it's there... But I know... I know that you had given up on life...'

A shiver ran through her at these words and in her mind's eye, Clara saw again the book on the table in the darkened room. Against her will, her fingers finally turned the key in the padlock and the cover snapped open. As though a strong wind was blowing, the pages began to turn themselves, faster and faster and faster. Clara caught glimpses of memories she recalled from her early days – her days before the illness – days of light, love, hope and happiness, but, as the pages continued to turn, the entries began to dwindle, the memories becoming darker – fragile and hopeless – until only four words remained on the pages that followed, repeating over and over in an endless loop: *I cannot go on…*

With tears in her eyes, Clara stared back at Vincent.

'I know that you want an end to the suffering,' he continued softly. 'I know that you spent those long days lying in bed wondering why you and why not someone else, but you cannot give up. You must *never* give up. A warrior in ancient times once said, "If one were to say what it is to do good, in a single word, it would be to endure suffering. Not enduring is bad without exception." You could not have known, and it was not your intention, *of course* it wasn't, but when you became ill and began to slip away, your mother could not bear to see you that way, and she too gradually fell ill. And when you could stand it no more and finally gave up on your life, it affected us too…' Vincent took her shaking hand gently in his. 'A child giving up, it… it gives the Rot the greatest foothold it could ever ask for,' he went on. 'By not fighting this illness, by not enduring and instead allowing it to worsen in the hope of ending it quickly, your mother's condition worsened too, and the Rot only grew stronger.'

Clara rubbed her eyes with the back of her hand, but the tears kept falling.

'I never told anyone,' she whispered. 'I never once told any of them that all I wanted was for it to be over, one way or another. Every day I had people coming into my room, telling me not to give up, to fight on against this disease. I remember a prayer my father said at my bedside now, but I could think of nothing other than my own pain. I did not think about how it must be affecting others, all I could think was, "I'm the one that's sick, not you". At the peak of suffering a… a selfishness creeps in and it is difficult to see the situation from other perspectives. I tried to, but it… it sharpens your focus and draws it in squarely upon yourself.'

'Each and every one of us has an impact, Clara Brown,' Vincent said earnestly. 'For good or bad, for better or worse, we are all a part of a rich tapestry. We cannot always see the impact we are having on our world and those within it, or understand the impact our presence may someday have, but in most cases the world would be a much darker place without us – for the people we leave behind, or the deeds we leave undone. We are all born as a spark of potential to have a positive influence, to do good things for our fellows and our environment. Some feed this spark and let it grow into a roaring flame for change, others feed it enough to warm themselves and their family, while others still cannot see or even deny this spark, and let it dwindle to nothing. Not everyone in this world will do great things; we are not all born to be leaders or icons, but if your presence alone is enough to brighten the lives of those around you, then it is a life worth living – a potential fulfilled – and you should never give up on it.'

Vincent stood then, still lightly holding Clara's hand.

'When I came to you, I knew that the only way to get you to fight was to offer you a means to help your mother,' he continued. 'Something physical, something you could hold in the palm of your hand – like a flower – and it drove you to fight on. The Wolf's plan all this time has been to bring people over from your world and help them to work through their darkness – to conquer it if they can – and in so doing the hope was that we could destabilise the Rot long enough to banish it from Comhlacht once and for all.'

Turning, Vincent faced the grand machine in the cave as the pulses continued to emanate from Clara, and the lights continued to fill.

'Until now, all our attempts have failed,' he breathed. 'But I *knew* you were different…'

He turned back from the machine to face her.

'Through all these trials you have shown your true grit and courage – you have shown that you can endure, Clara Brown,' Vincent smiled proudly. 'You have fought and triumphed and now it is time for you to get out of your bed! You have your whole life ahead of you, a life full of potential. You will have both happiness and hardship, wins and losses, but it is your life – your spark of potential – and it is worth fighting for to the end.'

As Vincent's words washed over her, Clara saw scenes from her life play out before her eyes as vividly as a dream; laughing with her mother and father at the breakfast table, dancing at the school in front of her proud teacher, the happiness in Jeremy's face as they played in the garden, and she felt the emotions of those memories rise up in her like a tide and was filled with determination – a determination not to be beaten, to not let those memories fade from existence and to create new ones like them – many more – a life full of them, bursting to the brim with them.

She turned back to Vincent and he saw a wildfire burning there, clear as day – the fire of renewed life.

'I will not let it beat me,' she said, determination ringing in her voice like the sonorous call of a thousand bells. 'If this disease is to take me then it will not do so lightly. I see now that giving up was just the easy way out, but nothing worth its salt is ever come by easily. I do not know what my future holds – what impacts I may have – but I am willing to fight to find out.'

As she stood there – her fists clenched with resolve – a voice cut across the room like a knife.

'It's not enough!'

From his position beside the machine, the Wolf engineer yelled out, pointing at the lights that were no longer filling. 'The energy she's generating is *huge*, but it's not quite enough!'

Filled with a vitality and life-force she had not known in a long time, Clara was struck by a realisation, and knew what she must do…

With purposeful steps she turned from Vincent and approached Marcus, who was looking around nervously, still flipping his coin between his fingers. Marcus looked up at her uncertainly, gasping at the light behind her eyes.

'I know that you have lost all confidence in yourself,' Clara said to him, her voice filled with an infectious power. 'I know that you feel you can only be brave with the help of your coin – the special coin your father gave to you.' She pointed at the coin and he stopped playing with it, holding it still between his fingers. 'Would you take a look at it, please?'

Looking confused, Marcus obeyed, raising the coin to glance at it, then shrugged.

'I… I don't understand…' he stammered.

'Look closer,' Clara urged. Bewildered, Marcus raised the coin once more and squinted at it closely, flipping it from one side to the other, then his eyes widened in shock – the date…

'This… This isn't my coin…' he whispered in shock.

'No,' Clara smiled at him. 'It was just a coin I had in my pocket when you lost yours.'

She gripped both his hands in hers and stared intently into his eyes.

'I gave you that to prove something,' she said. 'I wanted to prove that you don't need it – that you *never* needed it. It was *you* who stole the key from the Viper guard and rescued us, *you* who helped fight Darius at the burial grounds and *you* who fought alongside us outside Croí. You did it all without your coin, and I feel – I *know* – that you can do so much more.'

On hearing these words Marcus lit up as if kissed by the rays of the morning sun and he too began to pulse, ripples spreading out from him, blending and melding with Clara's as they went, his face alight with pride and confidence.

Over by the machine, the lights began to fill once more…

Clara next moved to Darcy and looked up at the older girl, who still struggled to meet her eyes after everything that had happened.

'Darcy,' Clara said kindly. 'I know that you have lost your faith in mankind – I know you feel that you can no longer trust anyone but your family, but you must not give up on them.'

Clara took a step closer to Darcy.

'Even in the short time I've known you I have seen you change,' Clara continued. 'And after all our time together I can confidently say now – I trust you…'

Clara held out a hand to Darcy.

'Can you trust me too?' Clara asked.

As Darcy looked at Clara's outstretched arm, she saw again Clara offering her the same hand when she freed her from the cell in the mine; the same hand when she saved her from the earthquake. With a shuddering breath she finally raised her eyes and looked into Clara's – saw the fire there reflected back in her own – and she took Clara's hand in hers.

'I… I trust you…' she whispered back.

Darcy gasped as a thrill of energy flickered to life inside her, as if a star had taken up residence in her breast, and she too began to pulse, adding hers to those of Clara and Marcus.

Over at the machine the final lights on the panel rapidly blinked on as the pulses hit it over and over like waves against rocks – it was fully charged…

The Wolf engineer whooped in delight and immediately flicked a switch on one of the consoles. At once a beam of white light shot out of the machine, straight down into the pitch-black void below, and as they watched they could see the Rot already beginning to recede, to retreat as if in pain, sliding deeper and deeper down until it vanished from sight at last.

The engineer – leaning precariously over the edge to stare down into the pit – cheered again and turned to face them all triumphantly.

'It's working! It's actually bloody working!' he yelled. He turned his attention to Clara, Darcy and Marcus as they stood side by side, still emitting their pulses. 'But you do not have long – the link must be severed soon, or the Rot will simply flow back in like water! If you want to return to your own world you must go, *now*!'

CHAPTER 30
Homeward Bound

Clara, Darcy and Marcus – led by Vincent and followed by Lord Algernon – hurried back outside, down the steps of the manor, across the grounds, and out through the front gate where they were taken aback to hear loud cheering erupt from all around them. Seated or standing everywhere they looked, the remaining Wolf, Bear and Hare fighters – who stood guard over the defeated Viper – clapped their hands or waved them in the air, exulting in the defeat of the Rot, their eyes fixed gratefully on the three young children.

Feeling embarrassed and self-conscious, Clara, Darcy and Marcus followed in Vincent's wake, nodding at those they passed and receiving handshakes and pats on the back from many more. Their eyes slid over the happy smiles of the Wolf, Bear and Hare to the confused and battle-weary faces of the Viper soldiers, who sat with vacant, lost expressions – the sudden removal of the Rot coming as a huge shock to their systems.

As they neared the large square at the centre of town, Clara spotted Malone sitting amongst a group of Viper. He was quiet and shivering, his gaze distant and unfocused like an addict in withdrawal. Clara tugged on Vincent's sleeve and pointed at him, but he had already seen something that had arrested his attention.

'My darlings!' he gasped, opening his arms wide as his three children – looking tired but unscathed – sprinted towards him to be enveloped in a hug. 'I'm so glad you're alright!'

'Father!' Sisi choked. 'I cannot believe this day has finally come!'

'It has, my dears,' Vincent replied, hugging them with a fierce intensity. 'Our faith has finally been rewarded – but it is not quite over yet…'

Standing awkwardly nearby, Clara looked up to see another friendly face approaching from a group of Hare fighters.

'I knew there was something about you,' Tia smiled as she stepped up and embraced Clara. 'I could sense something special the second we met.' She drew away and looked at Clara proudly. 'You are one in a million, Clara Brown.'

Clara smiled embarrassedly, unsure how to respond.

'So, what will become of the Hare?' she asked, to deflect attention from herself. 'Do you know where you will go from here?'

'There will be many discussions to come – days and days if I know the Hare,' Tia replied with a chuckle. 'But there are rumours that... maybe... I could become the next Chief...'

Clara beamed with pleasure at this.

'They could not make a finer choice,' she said. 'You are exactly what the Hare need right now.'

Tia shrugged.

'If it happens then there will be big changes ahead,' she said emphatically. 'Under my leadership the Hare will no longer bury their heads in the sand. No longer be ruled only by tradition, nor hide themselves from the world, but instead push for its betterment – push for a balance that works for all of us, and do it in collaboration with others, instead of trying to go it alone.'

'I have no doubt in my mind that you will succeed,' Clara replied with utter certainty.

She was about to say more when an approaching Bear soldier caught her eye, his heavy gait and downcast eyes speaking of ill omens as he neared Vincent and his children. As he drew close, Clara recognised him as Sam – the man they had rescued from the collapsed building during their flight from Neart. He was limping badly, and Vincent's expression fell as he spotted him. Sam stopped before Vincent and looked at him gravely.

'I... I thank you for all you have done...' he began in a sombre voice. 'And I wish I could bring you something other than this news, but I felt you had a right to know...' He fumbled for a moment, unsure how to say what needed to be said. 'I am sorry to say that… both Chief Davin and his son Garret, they… they perished in battle…'

Vincent caught his breath at these words, and his children gripped him in support.

'I did not see it myself…' Sam went on. 'But they died as bears, they died as warriors – fighting to their last breath – and if I know my leaders like… like I think I did… then they would not have had it any other way… They were Bear through and through…'

Vincent's breathing was ragged as he struggled to fight back his grief, the comforting touch of his children only just keeping him strong. After a few failed attempts to speak, he finally replied.

'Thank… thank you for telling me,' he said shakily. 'They were true Bear indeed – loyal and valiant to the core… What…' He trailed off and for a moment he could not speak, but with some hushed words from Sisi he went on. 'What happens next for Bear Clan…?'

'The Bear are resilient,' Sam replied, his previously downbeat voice rising powerfully. 'It would be a lie to say that the Rot has not laid us low, but now we will start anew: we will rebuild our homes, refocus on our community, and together pick up the broken pieces of our lives and mend them, returning stronger than ever. We will do all this, and we will hope for an even greater relationship with the Wolves than we ever had before.'

At this, Vincent bowed to him nobly.

'I shall look forward to it with great anticipation,' he declared. 'Now, if you would excuse me, I have something I must attend to, but… please… do not… do not bury them until I return…'

'We will do nothing without you,' Sam nodded.

Vincent shook his hand and as he was turning to face Clara another figure stepped into view – Malone… As he approached Vincent, so too did Lord Algernon, and Malone stopped before them, glancing ashamedly between the two men. Free of the Rot, Malone looked different – like a puppet without a hand. While his skin and body were nowhere near as necrotic and decaying as his followers, he was far from the man he had once been. Looking on him now, Vincent wondered if he would ever be the same again – if his body would even be able to survive much longer without the Rot that had held it together.

For a time no one spoke, then Lord Algernon broke the silence.

'You made some very unwise choices,' was all he said, his expression soft yet disappointed.

Though delivered gently, those words struck Malone like a fist. He fought to meet the eyes of two people he had once called friends, and managed it at last.

'I know this will mean little now – next to nothing,' he whispered hoarsely. 'But… I am sorry… I let this… this poison consume me – body and soul… I truly thought I was doing what was best for our people – for all of us – but I… I was viewing the world through a veil I no longer had the power to remove…'

He glanced around him then at all the destruction he had wrought – at the lives he had reduced to ashes.

'These are not deeds you come back from,' he murmured, once more unable to meet their eyes. 'I know that... I know there is no forgiveness for this, and would not insult you by asking for it... But I want you to know – I *need* you to know – that if I could take it all back, I would do so in a heartbeat... I...'

He was abruptly cut off by a sudden echoing roar that made every person present stop what they were doing and look up into the sky – whose hue was already beginning to lighten from its hellish shade. In the distance – rocketing towards them and leaving a trail of black smoke and flame – was a large, dark, aerodynamic object.

'No...' Malone breathed in horrified realisation. 'Oh no, no, no... I'd forgotten...'

'What is that thing...?' Vincent demanded, pointing at it.

'Something I should never have had made...' Malone responded in a voice that was barely audible. 'A prototype unmanned aerial explosive... It was set to target Croí unless I called it off with a flare when the battle was won.'

'Then call it off!' Vincent yelled. 'Call it off now!'

'I... I can't...' Malone replied frantically. 'I lost it somewhere during our fight...'

'Then we go search for it!' Vincent barked back, already setting off, but Malone stopped him.

'We'll never find it in time!' he said, shaking his head, the fearful expression on his face gradually being replaced by one of resolve. 'There is only one thing to do…'

Malone took to his heels and raced off towards a damaged flying machine lying atop a pile of rubble at one edge of the square. Alarmed, Vincent called after him.

'What are you doing?'

'This is my mess!' Malone shouted back over his shoulder. ''And I will fix it…'

He reached the flying machine and clambered inside. By flicking switches and tapping buttons, the waning embers in its steam engine suddenly glowed white hot and it spluttered to life. Within moments Malone was airborne and flying recklessly towards the approaching machine.

Glancing around desperately, Vincent's gaze fell on Clara, Darcy and Marcus.

'I do not know if he will succeed – we need to get you out of here,' he said, turning his attention to a nearby Wolf soldier. 'Albert, would you take Marcus and Darcy back to their doorways please? You know where they are – they must get there as fast as possible!'

Albert nodded and turned to the two children.

'Alright, follow me!' he said, but they were not quite ready to leave yet. Marcus and Darcy turned to face Clara and for a moment none of them knew what to say, then Clara pulled them both into a tight hug, tears in her eyes.

'I will miss you both dearly,' she murmured. 'I am proud to call you my friends.' Then she whispered something that only the two of them could hear – a private message she did not want to have overheard – to which they both nodded emphatically. They broke apart then, and Marcus and Darcy followed Albert to one of the ring-shaped vehicles waiting nearby. They hopped inside and were driven away to the front gate in a cloud of dust, their eyes never leaving Clara's until they were lost to sight.

'We must clear the city!' Vincent bellowed for all to hear. 'Everyone to the front gate – now!'

As the unmanned machine continued to rush closer and Malone cannoned towards it, there was a stampede of movement as every man, woman and child present began to make their way out of the city. Vincent turned to Lord Algernon and was about to speak when the other man got there first.

'I will see that your children reach safety,' he promised, reading Vincent's mind. 'Go – get Clara home. If we survive this the link still needs to be severed soon.'

Vincent nodded respectfully to his Lord, then turned to Clara.

'Come, Clara,' he said. 'Your world awaits you…'

Together, he and Clara took off running towards the front gate and it was not long before Vincent spotted another of the ring-shaped vehicles down a side street. They had boarded it in moments and were soon speeding across the now lowered drawbridge, surrounded by fleeing people of the Wolf, Bear and Hare.

As they tore across the flats, they both looked up into the sky to see the two distant objects drawing closer and closer to each other.

'Do you think he will…?' Clara began to say, but then – with an impact that they felt even here – the machines collided head-on in mid-air. There was a blinding flash of light as a spherical cloud of smoke and flame erupted like a firework, a boom louder than a thunderclap echoing for miles around.

Clara gasped and clapped her hands to her mouth as she watched shrapnel spiral to the ground leaving fiery trails in their wake. She glanced at Vincent, placing a hand comfortingly on his shoulder.

'I'm… I'm sorry…' she breathed. 'I'm sorry you lost your friend…'

As Vincent stared at the debris still tumbling earthward a sad smile crossed his face.

'I thought I'd lost him a long time ago,' he whispered. 'But it gladdens my heart to know that – in the end – he was still in there, all along…'

The final part of Clara's long, arduous journey seemed to pass in next to no time, and before she knew it, she and Vincent were once more standing beside the shallow pool in the forest clearing – the doorway through which she had first entered Comhlacht. After all that had happened, there was just too much to say; so much that she did not even know where to begin, and so instead she simply hugged him, and he hugged her back fondly.

'I will miss you, Clara Brown,' he said as they drew apart. 'You have a strength in you the like of which I have never seen.' He took her hand. '*Never* let it diminish, for it is a part of who you are, and – if you can – share it; share your strength with others when they have none, and I think you just might find it infectious.'

Clara nodded, determination etched into every fibre of her being.

'I will,' she promised. 'And you – will you be alright…?'

'I would love to tell you that I will be fine,' he replied. 'But I know I will struggle without her… I know it will pain me every day… But that pain will act as a promise – a promise to live as she would have wanted me to live, and, as long as I have my children, I will endure.'

He turned and glanced back; back towards Croí.

'As for the Wolf – like the other Clans we will rebuild and do what we can to help our world rejuvenate,' he continued. 'It will be a long road, but maybe – someday – we will see Comhlacht return to its former strength and glory. As El said, our future – the future of all the Clans – must be about balance: a balance between the technology that advances us, and the tradition and environment that defines us. Striking that balance is never easy, but it is the only path ahead for all of us, for we have seen what happens at the extremes…'

Vincent turned back to her then.

'It is time, Clara,' he said. 'Time for you to return home…'

Clara nodded and faced the pool, staring down at her dull reflection and seeing the resolve on her face looking back at her.

'You know,' she said quietly. 'When I first heard where the Rot came from, I was scared to go back to a place so full of darkness…'

'And now?' Vincent asked.

'If I can do even a little to alleviate that darkness,' she replied. 'Then I will have made a difference…'

Then she fell forward into the pool…

…and sat up in her bed at home…

EPILOGUE
Several Years Later

The stage lights dazzled Clara as she peeked out from behind the curtains, her vision slowly adjusting and the faces she was searching for swimming into focus in the front row – her mother and father, with Jeremy's parents sitting alongside them. For a moment, her gaze locked on her mother's face and just the sight of her beloved, rosy countenance filled her insides with warmth like hot cocoa.

When she had drunk in enough, she let her eyes wander, searching the crowd and finally alighting on the closed door at the rear of the theatre – *where were they…?*

Clara whipped back quickly as Mrs Andrews called the huddled dancers together to whisper words of inspiration. Her eyes found Jeremy's and they shared a look of mutual encouragement, then – without further ado – the curtain was raised, and the recital began.

To most of the audience there, "The Ballad of the Swan Princess" was entirely new, but no one

– not even Clara's parents – had seen this version of it, and everyone there was enraptured by what they witnessed. As the music swelled, Clara, Jeremy and the other dancers flowed around the stage like water, acting out the heartfelt tale of love, loss and hope.

Clara's eyes met Jeremy's again as they twirled together, their bodies touching, and they smiled a secret smile at one another, their hearts soaring to be doing what they loved.

Though there were many other dancers on the stage, there was only one person all eyes were fixed on; one person who the audience all spoke about after. Clara's dancing was transcendent, her body giving silent voice to the music and narrative she had constructed, her movements somehow conveying both great vulnerability, and colossal strength.

As Clara wove from one move to another her gaze kept being drawn to the door at the back of the theatre, and at the end of the recital – as Jeremy raised her above him at the climax of the tale – the door opened wide, and two figures appeared standing side by side.

Clara could not help herself. With a smile on her face she could not contain, she waved at them, and they waved back, beaming with pleasure…